BETTER THAN GOOD

Robin's eyes widened. She searched his face in disbelief. "You honestly think we should give up our home?"

"If you care about keeping everyone here safe," he said grimly, "that's exactly what you should do."

"This is the only home any of us has ever known. This is the only place I can provide for them all."

"You can't provide for any of them if you're dead." Nathaniel knew his words were brutal, but he had to say them anyway. "You could have easily been killed last night if I hadn't been there to help you."

"If you hadn't been there, I could have handled things just fine on my own," she said defiantly. She was sitting upright in her bed now, the covers she had tucked modestly under her arms long ago forgotten in the blaze of her anger. The well-worn fabric clung to the sweet swell of her breasts.

As Nathaniel stared at her, his awareness of her as a woman came rushing back in a dangerous tide. Lord, Robin Matthews was pretty when she was in a temper. He was painfully aware that he was alone with her in her bedroom, and that she was wearing just a nightgown and not much else. He remembered how she'd felt in his arms while he carried her home, and he could still remember clearly the way she'd smelled of roses and lavender.

A part of him wanted to take her into his arms, sink back with her into that featherbed, and make her forget all about her precious ranch. He knew she wasn't indifferent to him. He saw the small looks she slanted his way when she thought he wasn't aware. It would be good between them. He'd help her turn some of that passion she felt for her ranch toward loving, and it would be better than good.

A COWBOY FOR CHRISTMAS

Anna DeForest

ZEBRA BOOKS
KENSINGTON PUBLISHING CORP.
http://www.zebrabooks.com

ZEBRA BOOKS are published by

Kensington Publishing Corp.
850 Third Avenue
New York, NY 10022

All Kensington titles, imprints and distributed lines are available at special quantity discounts for bulk purchases for sales promotion, premiums, fund raising, educational or institutional use.

Special book excerpts or customized printings can also be created to fit specific needs. For details, write or phone the office of the Kensington Special Sales Manager: Kensington Publishing Corp., 850 Third Avenue, New York, NY, Attn. Special Sales Department. Phone: 1-800-221-2647.

Zebra and the Z logo Reg. U.S. Pat. & TM Off.

First Printing: October, 2000
10 9 8 7 6 5 4 3 2 1

Printed in the United States of America

For Meggity-Mo.
Your loving spirit and generous heart have meant so much
to me through the years. Thank you for being such a
terrific sister.

ACKNOWLEDGMENTS

Thanks to Laurie K for sharing your ranching and poultry expertise once again. I'm most grateful to my loyal team of proofreaders. Nana Jane, Dawn, Joyce, Theresa, and Laurie—you ladies are wonderful. Janice T is my new Internet goddess. And special thanks to Rachel, Hesan, and Lyndsey for having kept the wee ones happy while I was writing.

Chapter One

Heavens to Betsy, she hated cows. As far as Robin Matthews was concerned, the Good Lord just wasn't thinking straight the moment He created cattle. He did a mighty fine job on the rest of creation, but somehow He must have lost His concentration when He came to making four-legged critters of the bovine sort. Cows were some of the most fractious, ornery, and just plain stupid animals on the face of the earth.

As much as she disliked cows, she'd give just about anything to see a hoof, horn, or tail of the hundred head that should be grazing in this high mountain meadow right now. Robin stood in her stirrups and searched the terrain carefully for any sign of movement. Normally on a beautiful fall morning like this one, she would have taken time to appreciate the deep blue sky and the way the sunlit aspens on the hillsides all around shimmered and blazed like golden flames. She was in no mood this day, however, to appreciate the pretty view. She had a cold, hard feeling in the pit of her stomach that something had happened to her missing cattle, and she needed every one of those dangblasted cows and the calves they would bear next spring to keep her family clothed and fed.

"Hey, Rob, I think you'd better come take a look at these tracks," her younger brother Jake called out to her.

With a sinking heart, Robin settled back down into the saddle and urged Rusty, her sorrel gelding, into a lope. When she pulled Rusty to a halt beside her brother, Jake gestured at the ground, his young face still and set.

"I reckon that's why we haven't found 'em," he said with a grim nod.

Robin gazed at the horse and cattle prints left in the damp stretch of trail. The story those hoofprints told was plenty easy to read. Her cows hadn't just wandered off. They'd been driven away by cow thieves on horseback.

She let loose with a curse that made Jake glance at her in some surprise. Usually she chided her fourteen-year-old brothers for using rough language, but having a hundred head of cattle rustled off her spread seemed like a good reason to use some profanity. Right now she wanted to hang the worthless skunks who had stolen her cows from the nearest tree.

She made up her mind on the spot. The tracks were fresh, which meant she still might have a chance to catch the rustlers. If she waited to get help, her cattle would be long gone, and with them her last hope of keeping her ranch afloat.

"Jake, I need Pa's old Colt and your cartridge belt. I'm going after them."

Jake looked at her for a long moment before he pulled the Colt and its cartridge belt from where they hung on the horn of his saddle. "We could always ask the sheriff to look into this."

Robin snorted. "By the time Ben Campbell hauls his lazy hide out here, our cows will be halfway to Montana wearing new brands. You know how the outlaw trail works."

Jake was quiet for a long moment, digesting her words. "If you get yourself hurt or killed," he pointed out soberly, "the family's going to be in worse trouble than ever."

"Nothing's going to happen to me. I'll be careful, and I doubt these rustlers are going to have much stomach for trouble. They probably heard about our situation and figured a ranch run by a girl and her younger brothers was easy pickings."

"If you think they'll back down that easy, you should let me go," Jake insisted stubbornly. "I ride as well as you do, and I can shoot almost as well."

Her throat grew tight as she studied Jake. He and his twin Luke had grown and matured so much during the last three years. Although both boys made her proud, she wished with all her heart that they hadn't had to grow up so fast.

"Almost, but not quite, *amigo*," she spoke sternly to hide the softening of her heart. "You ride on back and tell Betsy and Luke what happened. I should be back in three or four days. There's no point worrying or looking for me before then."

They would worry, of course, her sweet young sister Betsy most of all, and the little ones would miss her. Robin was sorry for that, but she had no choice. They needed those cows back. And if word got out that the Rocking M couldn't protect its own, she'd lose the rest of her stock to other rustlers in no time.

"At least come back to the ranch house and let Betsy pack some grub for you," Jake suggested.

"I can't do that. Every hour counts now if I'm going to have a chance of catching these owlhoots. I'll live off the land just like we used to when Papa sent us up into the mountains." She sent him a smile, but Jake was clearly too worried to smile back at her.

"You be careful, Roberta."

Her heart caught at the name he called her. Mama and Papa always insisted on calling her Roberta, even though everyone else seemed to call her by the nicknames Rob or Robin. Times like this she missed Papa so much. She would have looked forward to taking on a dozen rustlers if she had her big, bluff father at her side. Mama and Papa were dead and buried, though, and missing them so much that her heart ached wouldn't bring them back. *It's up to you to do what needs to be done. It's up to you to keep the Rocking M going and to keep your family together.*

"You look after the rest of them for me, Jacob Josiah Matthews."

Resolutely, she turned Rusty about and sent him loping west, the way the rustlers had gone. Before the trail entered a grove of aspen, she glanced back over her shoulder. Jake remained where she had left him, looking more than a little forlorn and scared. He waved when he saw her looking his way, and she waved back.

Feeling more than a little forlorn and scared herself, Robin started after the men who had stolen her cows.

During the next few hours, she came to the sobering conclusion that she was tracking at least four rustlers. She wasn't as good at reading sign as her brother Luke was, but she'd learned a lot from old Three Elks, the Ute Indian who used to work for their father. She'd hoped no more than one or two drifters had decided to run off her head. *Roberta Matthews, taking on four men probably armed with rifles and six-shooters, is a whole lot more than you bargained for.*

Grimly she considered her other option. Going to the sheriff for help wouldn't do her a bit of good. Ben Campbell didn't care a lick about her or her stock. Women didn't vote in Colorado, and Vance Sutherland had backed him in the last election.

Robin gritted her teeth as she considered her nemesis. She wouldn't be the least bit surprised if Sutherland or Rick Dyer, that shifty-eyed, weasel-faced foreman of his, was somehow behind the theft of her cows. Ever since her parents died in a train wreck three years ago, Sutherland had been trying to get his hands on her ranch. The Rocking M had some of the finest grazing in Grand Valley, and Vance Sutherland wanted to add that acreage to the vast spread he already owned.

Sutherland controlled over twenty thousand acres of land and ran thousands of head of cattle on his ranch. Rumors had it that he wanted to be a U.S. senator, and his chances of buying that office for himself were good. Even though she had never understood greed, she was coming to understand how a powerful, unscrupulous man would use any means at his disposal to get what he wanted. Ever since she turned down his offer to buy her out two years ago, the Rocking M had been plagued by a series of mysterious incidents. Cows had been shot or stolen, fences downed, and water holes poisoned.

She had forged on stubbornly, knowing her neighbors thought her misfortunes were due to her inexperience. The Rocking M was all the home she and her siblings had. They had no family to take them in. If she couldn't provide a home for them, the younger ones would be sent to an orphanage. The terrible day she learned of her parents' deaths, she had sworn to herself that she would do anything to keep her family from being split up.

For the moment, Robin reminded herself sternly, *you'd best concentrate on getting your cows back*. Fortunately, Rusty was half mustang, and he was a fine trail horse. She pushed her plucky mount hard until nightfall. Then she stopped for a brief rest, waiting for the moon to rise and letting Rusty drink at a small stream and graze a little. Her toes were going numb, and she could see the breath in front of her face when the moon finally rose over the mountains to the east. Three-quarters full, it shed more than enough light for her to follow the trail the rustlers had left.

Pulling the collar of her sheepskin jacket higher about her neck, Robin tried to ignore the remorseless chill of the mountain night and pushed on. Just before midnight, she spotted the rustlers' fire.

Pulse racing, she rode quietly to within a quarter mile of their camp. There she dismounted and ground-tied Rusty in a small grove of aspen. Her mouth was dry and her stomach tight as she shoved Papa's old Army Colt into the waistband of her Levis. She slung the heavy cartridge belt for her Winchester over her shoulder and pulled her rifle from its scabbard on her saddle. She gave Rusty a final pat and ignored the strong urge to fling herself up on his back and ride away from the confrontation to come. *You can do this, Roberta Matthews, you surely can.*

Using all the stalking skills Three Elks had taught her, she crept up on the rustlers' camp. She found her cattle bedded down in a small meadow beside a stream. A dozen yards from the rustlers' fire, she discovered a small rock outcropping. She circled soundlessly through the spruce and aspen until she could crawl to the top of that outcropping. From there she had a fine view of their camp.

She took her time studying the layout below. What was the best way to make her play? All four of the men lay sleeping in their bedrolls. They must have been certain no one would come after them. That arrogance was going to cost them. They hadn't taken the time to hobble any of their mounts, either. That laziness would cost them, too. She would creep down by the horses, cut their picket lines, and then go back to fetch Rusty. She'd stampede her cattle through the camp, which should shake up the rustlers, spook their horses to hell and gone, and give her a good head start on driving her cows back to their home range.

She'd just started to work her way through the trees toward the rustlers' horses when a big hand covered her mouth and an arm hard as iron clamped about her midsection.

"Boy, don't say a word," a man whispered harshly in her ear. "Come peaceably with me now. I won't hurt you."

Robin froze for a half-second. As the man's grip on her tightened, a deep, instinctive panic almost overwhelmed her. There must have been a fifth rustler on watch. Cursing herself for her carelessness, she fought down her panic and forced herself to think. She wasn't going to scream and bring the rest down on her, but that didn't mean she had to go anywhere with this polecat peaceably.

She shoved an elbow into his gut as hard as she could. The man grunted in surprise, but his grip on her only tightened. Growing more frightened by the moment, she slammed the butt of the Winchester down on the toe of his boot. He swore angrily under his breath and plucked the rifle away from her. That just made her struggle harder than ever. She bit back a scream when she suddenly found herself lifted off her feet. Her assailant carried her swiftly back into the aspens. He stopped and dropped her none too gently on her rump when they were a good hundred yards from the rustlers' camp.

"You damn fool, I'm not one of them. I was just trying to keep you from getting your head blown off," he told her in a low, angry voice.

Robin scrambled to her feet and eyed him warily. Her assailant was a good foot taller than her own five feet and broad through the shoulders. His short-cropped hair beneath his brown plainsman hat looked black as the mountain sky above them. He wore no beard, but she could see the dark stubble on his cheeks in the moonlight. The planes of his face were stark and unrelenting. From the strong line of his cheekbones, she guessed there might be some Indian blood in him. Under the shadow cast by his hat brim, his eyes were cool and watchful. With an odd little shiver, she realized he was a striking man, in a hard, uncompromising sort of way.

"Who the hell are you?" she asked, purposely deepening her voice to make it sound more masculine. She wasn't surprised that he had taken her for a boy. She had tucked her braid up inside her hat, and she had long ago taken to wearing jeans and chaps when she did ranch work. She had a gut feeling it would only complicate this situation if he discovered the boy he was talking to was actually a woman.

"Someone who was minding his own business until those damn owlhoots drove those cows right through my camp. I'd just about settled back down to sleep when you came traipsing along after them. There's only one reason men would be driving cattle after dark. I figure those fellows stole those cows from the outfit you work for. Now you're hankering to be a hero and planning to get those cows back all on your lonesome."

"You only figured part of it right, mister. I don't work for anyone. Those are my cows, and if I don't get them back, no one's going to do the job for me."

"I see," he said after a long moment. "A hundred head of cattle aren't worth dying for, boy," he said in a gentler tone.

"I reckon that's my decision to make, and I'm not plannin' on dying tonight."

"In my experience, folks rarely do," the stranger said shortly.

"I want my Winchester back."

"You'll get it back when I'm certain you're not going to go off and do something foolish. You ride on home and go fetch the law in these parts and have them chase down these cow thieves for you."

"Look here, mister, I appreciate the fact that you're trying to look out for me, but the law in these parts doesn't give a damn about my cows. If I want them back, I'm going to have to take them back. It's that simple. You can go back to your camp now with a clear conscience. You did your best to warn me."

"Hell," he said, a world of disgust and weariness in his tone. "You're not going to give this up, are you?"

"No, sir," she said simply. "I can't. I got too many folk depending on me back home."

He was silent for a long moment, obviously thinking on her words. "Then how did you plan to go about getting your cows back?" he asked in a gruff voice.

As much as she longed to tell him to go back to his camp and mind his own business, her common sense prevented it. She'd be a fool to turn down help against four armed men, and this stranger looked to be a formidable opponent. He wore a tied down six-shooter at his hip, and he carried her Winchester with an ease that spoke of plenty of experience with firearms. With a shiver, she remembered how easily he had stripped the rifle from her and lifted her off her feet. No indeed, if he wanted a part of the action, she'd be happy to deal him in. Quickly she explained her plan to him.

"All right," he said when she had finished, "I'll injun up on that rock overlooking their camp. If any of them wake up while you're setting the horses loose, I'll keep them pinned down from there. Once you stampede the cows, I'll keep these boys occupied for a good while after you vamoose."

"Thanks, mister. I sure appreciate you sticking your neck out for me like this."

"I'm a damn fool to do it," was his abrupt response. Even in the moonlight, she could see his expression was bleak. "Do me a favor, kid. Don't get yourself killed."

The bitterness in his tone made her want to reach out to him. "You ever come through this country again, you're always welcome at the Rocking M. My sister's one of the finest cooks this side of the Mississippi."

He simply nodded in response to her invitation. They walked back quietly through the trees to the place he had surprised her. There he handed back her Winchester and picked up his own rifle, which he had left leaning against a tree. Squaring her shoulders and taking a deep breath, she started off in the direction of the horses.

It was the most peculiar thing. Somehow just knowing that big stranger was going to back her up made all the difference in the world. She was still scared, but she was confident now that she'd get her cows back, and she had a much better chance of coming out of this mess in one piece. Even though she didn't even know his name, somehow she knew in her heart that she could trust him. Who was he, and why had he decided to help her? Somehow he just didn't look like a cowhand. His clothes had been too good, his rifle too fine.

She reached the first horse, and she had no time left to wonder or worry further about the mysterious man who had chosen to come to her aid. Working as silently and quickly as she could, she soon freed all of the rustlers' mounts. Weary from the long day of travel, the horses accepted her presence calmly and remained right where they were when she had finished. She knew, though, that a hundred cows charging through the camp would send the horses galloping on their way in a heartbeat.

She retreated into the trees and gave the camp a wide berth as she worked her way back to Rusty. She was just about to climb up on the gelding's back when she heard riders coming up the trail. Heart pounding, she went to hold Rusty's head. Staying absolutely still, she strained to watch the trail through a clump of small aspen.

Two mounted men appeared shortly. "There's their camp," the first rider declared just as he passed her hiding place. "I told you they were too damn lazy to have pushed much further tonight."

"The boss wanted them out of the county before sunrise," the second commented.

"Well, let's roust out those worthless drifters and get them back on the trail," the first declared, and then they were gone, but not before Robin had gotten a good look at the Rafter S brand on their horses' flanks.

Anger shot through her. She hadn't recognized any of the brands on the rustlers' horses, but these two men clearly worked for Sutherland.

She stared after them, thinking hard and fast. Now she was up against six armed men. She had an ace in the hole in her stranger, but he didn't know there were two more men coming his way. Perhaps it would be wiser at this point simply to ride away, but she didn't know how she was going to make ends meet next year if she lost this hundred head and the calves they carried.

Her only chance lay in getting the cows off their bedding ground and stampeding them through the camp before the rustlers were wide awake and mounted again. If she timed things right, she might even catch the two riders right after they dismounted, and their horses would stampede, too. She waited for a minute, and then sent Rusty trotting through the long grass along the side of the trail. She veered away from the camp when she reached the meadow where her cows were bedded down.

Robin smiled when she spotted the twisty horned cow lying on the edge of the small herd. She'd almost sent that cow off to be slaughtered last year. Twisty-horn was nervous and jumpy as a jackrabbit, but she bore good-sized calves. Right now, Robin meant to put the cow's nervous nature to good use.

Firing her pistol in the air and yelling a wild Ute war cry, Robin sent Rusty running straight at that cow. Twisty-horn was on her feet in a flash, bawling like she was being mauled by a bear. The rest of the cows lunged to their feet. Robin fired her pistol again and waved her hat in the faces of the closest animals. They bolted away from her, lowing in terror and heading straight for the rustlers' camp.

She followed right on their heels, determined to make sure all of the horses stampeded, too. If all six men were left afoot, she wouldn't have to worry about their chasing after her. She pulled Rusty to a halt in the shadows along the edge of the camp and grinned to herself when she saw the chaos her cows had wrought. Six men were shouting and swearing. Four clad only in their union suits had found refuge atop boulders about the camp, and one had managed to climb a tree to keep from being trampled.

A single horse remained, and one of the newly arrived riders was fighting to keep ahold of its reins. Even as she watched, a rifle spat fire from the top of the rock outcropping. The rider cursed and dropped the reins to cradle his shattered hand. The horse took out after the rest.

Robin didn't stay to enjoy the show. She wanted to make sure her cows were headed down the trail toward home. She backed Rusty away from the camp and galloped after her stock. Within a half mile she caught the stragglers. They were heading the right way—east along the trail they had followed just hours ago.

She winced when she heard the sound of several guns firing in the distance. Slowly she reined Rusty to a halt. She just couldn't do it. She just couldn't ride off and let that stranger fight her battles for her. Maybe he could handle four against one, but six against one was a tall order for anyone, especially when it wasn't really his fight.

With a sigh, she turned Rusty about and sent him pounding back up the trail toward trouble.

Chapter Two

You are ten thousand times a fool, ex-Deputy U.S. Marshal Nathaniel Hollister told himself as he squeezed off a shot at the rustler hiding behind the big spruce. *You'd think you'd know better by now than to get yourself involved in a sorry mess like this one.* The men below him were madder than hornets. The hail of bullets flying his way proved just how eager they were to get even. No man takes kindly to being wakened from a sound sleep by stampeding cattle. However, as far as Nathaniel was concerned, anyone low enough to stoop to stealing cows deserved such a rude awakening, and worse.

The rustler skulking behind the big granite boulder by the stream was getting a mite careless. The next time he popped up to take a shot, Nathaniel winged him in the shoulder, just to make the fellow think on the error of his ways. Nathaniel cursed under his breath when return fire from one of the other rustlers sprayed rock chips all over him. If he stayed here much longer, one of those damned idiots might actually get lucky and nail him. He'd move along soon to ensure that didn't happen. He just wanted to hold his position long enough to make certain the boy got away safely.

He smiled grimly when he thought of the stubborn youngster he'd found tracking the rustlers and the cows they had stolen. He didn't think anyone or anything could reach his hardened heart anymore. After fifteen years of hunting down some of the most violent and brutal outlaws in the West and dealing with the carnage and killing they had left in their wake, he thought he had seen everything. Something about that slip of a boy had surprised and touched him. That youngster had the courage, determination, and sense of responsibility of men twice his age.

So here Nathaniel was, getting shot at by a half-dozen men when he could be sound asleep a mile away in his warm bedroll. Shaking his head at his own stupidity, Nathaniel turned to pepper the base of the outcropping with a searching fire. At least one of the rustlers was skulking around down there, figuring to flank him. They were welcome to try, of course, but he was apt to kill a few if they decided to rush him, and he was tired of killing even no-account cow thieves like these.

In the old days he would have relished a fight like this. In the old days he would have taken fierce joy in teaching a hard lesson to men who flaunted the law. Now he was too damned tired of the game. He just wanted to get out of this scrape in one piece. After a lifetime of fighting and hunting outlaws, he simply wished to be left in peace.

He was just about to fade back into the trees and hightail it out of there on Old Blue when he heard a galloping horse fast approaching.

Damn it all to hell, that fool kid is probably coming back to try to help. Nathaniel emptied his rifle in a sweeping arc of fire all about the camp. Swiftly he reloaded and crawled back from the edge of the outcropping. Moments later, the boy burst from the aspen trees and brought his mount to a plunging halt right at the base of the rock. The youngster could ride, he had to grant him that.

Nathaniel snapped off a shot at the last place he'd seen the rustler trying to sneak up on his left flank.

"Come on, mister, let's get out of here," the boy called urgently.

All in all, that seemed like a mighty prudent idea. When the kid shifted his leg forward, Nathaniel made quick use of his empty stirrup. Nathaniel had just gotten a leg over the horse's back when a rifle stabbed fire from the trees. The boy jerked and called out in pain and surprise. He still had the presence of mind to turn his mount and start it galloping back for the cover of the closest aspen.

Swearing viciously, Nathaniel worked the lever on his Winchester as fast as he could, sending a rain of bullets at the rustler who had shot the boy. Savage satisfaction blazed through him when he saw a dark form crumple up and fall flat onto the grass of the moonlit clearing.

"Head more to the right—my horse is over that way," Nathaniel told the kid. Then he stayed silent, watching for any sign of pursuit and hoping like hell the boy wasn't hit too badly. He never should have let the youngster go ahead with that damn-fool plan of his. If this boy died, his blood would be on Nathaniel's hands, and on his conscience. He already had far too much innocent blood on both.

A few minutes later they reached the clearing where he had left his steeldust gelding. Nathaniel slid off the side of the boy's horse.

"Let me take a look at that," Nathaniel said, gesturing to his wounded side.

"I think the bullet just grazed my ribs," the kid said in a strange, choked voice. "I'm sure I'll be fine."

"Well, let's both be sure. You're not going to do anyone back home a favor if you lose so much blood you drop dead."

That argument seemed to persuade him. Slowly the boy unbuttoned his woolen jacket and raised his shirt up just above the gunshot wound, baring white skin and a bony ribcage. He clamped his arm tightly against his body, making it impossible for Nathaniel to raise the shirt any higher. Nathaniel would have been amused over such modesty, but he was too busy wiping away blood with his kerchief and trying to look for bullet holes in the moonlight.

"You're right. The bullet did just graze your ribs," he declared with relief. Swiftly he folded his kerchief into a makeshift dressing. "Hold this in place with your elbow. In a while, I'll strap that gash up for you good and tight. For the moment, your chances of living a long life are probably a hell of lot better if we get a few miles between us and your friends back there. You think you can stay in that saddle without passing out on me?"

"Yes," the boy replied simply, his face white and set in the pale wash of moonlight.

"Good. You got a name, boy?" Nathaniel asked as he went to mount Old Blue.

"Most folks call me Rob. You got a name, mister?"

"Nate will do for now," he said shortly.

"You don't look like a Nate," came the boy's surprising rejoinder. "You look like a Nathaniel to me."

Nathaniel grunted at that one and started back toward his abandoned camp. It was true no one ever dared to call the notorious Deputy Marshal Nathaniel Hollister "Nate," but he was in no mood to tell Rob his real name and endure the spate of questions sure to follow. Of course, he was an ex-marshal now, but the boy wouldn't know that. He would know, as did just about anyone who lived in the West, the legends associated with the name Nathaniel Hollister. Only half of those legends were true, but Nathaniel didn't feel like explaining that fact to a curious kid, either.

Rob followed him quietly. At his camp Nathaniel made quick work of rolling his sugan and picking up his gear. Within minutes they were on the trail again, following the way the boy, his cows, and the rustlers had come earlier that night. Within a half mile, they came across the first of the cows grazing about a moonlit meadow. Rob paused to gather them up and force them back onto the trail. Nathaniel frowned.

"We should be riding straight back to your home and getting you to a doctor," he called out to the boy.

"I'm not riding on without my cows."

"You sure are a stubborn little cuss."

"I've heard that before," Rob said and flashed him a grin.

As they rode down the moonlit trail, Nathaniel found himself hazing cows, much to his amused disbelief. Old Blue, a big, strong horse he'd bought for his speed and stamina, must have worked cattle before, because he went after those tired cows with a verve and an agility that surprised Nathaniel. Considering the fact that the weary cows weren't the least bit interested in hitting the trail again, they still made fairly good time.

"How's that side of yours?" he asked Rob once during the early hours of the morning.

"I think it's stopped bleeding," came the stoic reply.

Nathaniel decided then that the boy would probably be better off if he let his wound alone for the moment. What young Rob really needed was to see a good doctor, and soon. His wound wasn't serious, but Nathaniel had seen less serious injuries go septic and kill men twice Rob's size.

At sunrise, just when Nathaniel was considering calling a halt, Rob suddenly pitched headfirst off his horse. Fortunately for him, the boy's landing was broken by a willow bush beside the trail.

Nathaniel swore aloud and dismounted. As he gently lifted the boy out of the willow bush, Rob's hat fell off. Nathaniel stared in horrified disbelief at the fat braid of blond hair Rob had pinned on top of his head.

Her head. *Goddamn it, the boy you just helped to tackle a half-dozen rustlers is a girl!*

Nathaniel gazed down at her pale face. Anger burned through him. *What the hell is a girl doing in this rough country, tracking down stolen cows and getting shot by rustlers?*

Swiftly he laid her on a patch of grass beside the trail. He unbuttoned her woolen jacket and pulled up her bloodstained shirt. His kerchief was soaked through with blood, but as far as he could tell, the wound didn't seem to be bleeding any longer. He went to his saddlebags and tore up his one clean shirt into strips. Working as quickly and gently as he could, he tied his kerchief in place with bandages wrapped about her midsection. He was careful not to touch her any more than he had to, but he couldn't help noticing how soft and white her skin was beneath his fingers.

From time to time as he worked he glanced at her face. Now that he could see the delicacy of her features in the growing light, of course he could tell she was a girl. She had a dusting of freckles across her nose and cheeks and long golden-brown eyelashes. Her lips were soft and pink and pretty, and the wisps of hair about her face were the rich color of fine whisky. He wrenched his gaze away from her right then.

Old son, you have no business noticing how pretty her mouth and hair are, no business whatsoever. She's probably half your age. After the things you've seen and done, you've no right to even look at a sweet young girl like this one.

Instead he concentrated on feeling angry. Who were her people? Who in their right mind would let a young girl go off on a dangerous escapade like this one? When he got her home, he was going to give someone a piece of his mind. And he was going to get her back home, soon.

When he had finished with her wound, he carefully buttoned up her jacket again. Leaving her lying on the grass, he stripped the bridle and saddle from her tired sorrel gelding. Chances were, the horse would wander back to his home range soon on his own. Nathaniel left the cows grazing along the side of the trail. He'd send someone from her ranch to fetch them later.

Right now his only concern was to get her to a doctor as soon as possible. He lifted her up onto Old Blue's back and mounted behind her. He turned her in his arms so that she lay crosswise on his lap, her head lying on his chest. Following the clear trail the rustlers and stolen cows had left, he set off at a ground-eating lope, grateful that Old Blue had such smooth gaits.

Nathaniel Hollister rode on through the brilliant morning, blind to the beauty of the jagged *Sangre de Cristo* peaks rising above him. All he could think about was the girl he held in his arms, and the fact that if she died, he'd be responsible for the death of another innocent female.

Robin was having the most peculiar dream. In it she was cradled in a man's arms, yet somehow she was also riding a horse. She didn't like being touched by men, but being held in the arms of her mysterious dream man was a wonderful experience. She felt so safe, cherished, and protected. She hadn't felt truly safe since that awful afternoon two years ago, an afternoon her mind refused to dwell on even in her dreams. When she nuzzled closer, enjoying the warmth of him, he smelled like horse, wood smoke, and pine trees.

It would have been an extraordinarily pleasant dream, except for the flashes of pain that kept radiating from her side. Suddenly, the horse they rode leapt over some obstacle in its path, and Robin had to bite her lip to keep from crying out. All at once, she was awake, awake enough to realize somehow her remarkable dream was actually real.

Within moments, fragments of the night before came rushing back to her, the stolen cows, her dogged, desperate search for them, the big stranger with the cool eyes who had so inexplicably offered to help her. She blushed then, blushed so that her face was burning when she realized who was holding her now.

He must have felt her tense, for he reined his horse back to a walk. She could sense he was looking down at her. It would be cowardly to pretend to be asleep when she wasn't, and she refused to be a coward. Robin opened her eyes and blinked when she found herself looking up into a beautiful pair of eyes the deep blue color of a mountain sky on the clearest of days. They were startlingly bright against the sun-browned color of his skin. Clearly he was a man who had spent much of his life out-of-doors.

Now that she could see him, close up in the clear light of day, she had to conclude he was one of the most handsome men she'd ever seen, in a hard and rugged sort of way. His face was definitely dramatic. Thick black brows framed his striking eyes. His jaw was strong, his chin forceful with a hint of a cleft to it. Except for the strands of silver she saw at his temples, his hair was jet-black. His nose was straight and arrogant.

When she glanced at his mouth, she almost shivered. He wouldn't be a man to smile easily, but she still thought his lips were beautiful. A day's worth of stubble darkened his cheeks and made him look rough and dangerous. Yet the concern and worry in his expression were obvious, and they made her feel a little dizzy.

"So, you're awake again," he said, clearly oblivious to the tumultuous effect he was having on her. "How do you feel?"

"My side's felt better, but I expect I'll live. I'm thirsty as all get out, though."

He pulled the horse to a halt and reached for his canteen. She could have tipped the canteen up herself, but she liked the way he held it so carefully to her lips. She drank long and deep, the cool water heaven on her parched tongue and mouth.

When she had finished, he replaced the stopper on the canteen, and then his expression changed. His dark eyebrows drew together, and his blue eyes sparked with anger. "What the hell did you think you were doing? A girl like you had no business tackling those men. You could have gotten us both killed."

So he had discovered the truth. Had he seen her hair, or had he seen something else when he tied the bandage she felt now about her ribs? For the moment, she decided not to dwell on that particular question.

"Getting my cows back is my business, particularly when there's no one else to do it, and I don't remember asking you to help me," she fired back at him, refusing to be browbeaten.

"Where the hell are your parents?"

"Buried in the Grand Valley First Episcopal Cemetery," she replied promptly, "not that their burying place is any of your business."

"Don't you have any brothers or kin to look out for you?"

"I have two fine brothers, but they are both five years younger than I. We don't have any other family that I know of." *Or that will acknowledge our existence,* she thought painfully. She had plenty of kin back Virginia way. After mama up and married her Yankee, though, she and the children she bore him had been dead to the rest of her family.

"Don't you have a foreman to manage your place?"

"We can't afford one. I'm it."

That shut him up for a bit. He looked away from her toward the trail they were following. "A girl's got no business trying to run a ranch," he ground out after a few minutes. "You must be plain loco."

"So I've been told." She closed her eyes wearily. So much for hoping he might actually understand. Surely there had to be an open-minded man out there somewhere that would admit a female could do a good job running a ranch.

When he spoke again, his voice was a little less gruff. "How old are you, anyway?"

"I'll turn twenty in January."

"Christ."

"You shouldn't swear so much. How old are you?" She opened her eyes to study him curiously.

"I'm thirty-four, not that my age is any of your business."

"I don't know. You've been so busy firing questions at me, it only seemed fair that I ask you a few."

His lips twitched at that, and a small rush of pleasure went through her. From the world-weary look in his eyes and the harsh lines about his mouth, she could tell he didn't smile nearly enough. "You sure are cheeky for a little gal."

"I've been told that, too. So what were you doing camped out along Deer Creek?"

"I'm not exactly in the mood for idle chitchat," he declared.

"Well, I am. You should humor me. My side hurts like Hades. Talking will help keep my mind off the pain." She let her voice quiver just a little there toward the end.

He glanced down at her, one eyebrow raised. "And whose fault is it that you are hurting now?"

"Those dangblasted owlhoots who decided to steal my cows."

She had a point there, and they both knew it. He sighed and said after a long moment, "I was just drifting. Six months ago, I quit doing what I've done for the past fifteen years, and I'm looking for something else to turn my hand to."

She longed to ask him what he'd been doing for the last fifteen years, but something about his closed expression warned her that he wouldn't appreciate the question. Besides, folks out West tried to respect other folks' privacy. "We could use a good hand on the Rocking M," she said hopefully.

"I wasn't looking to hire on as a cowhand," he said with such derision in his voice that her hackles rose.

"Well, pardon me. Last I knew, working as a cowhand was good, honest work. I can pay twenty dollars a month and found, and the grub at our place is mighty fine. My little sister Betsy can cook like a dream."

"I'm not looking for that kind of work. I'll see you home and settled safely, and then I'm going on my way. I'm hankering to see some wild country before the West gets any more filled up with people."

She knew she should accept that, but a part of her couldn't help scheming and dreaming. If only she could find a way to make him stay on at the Rocking M. They needed some help on the ranch, needed it badly. Much of the hard, physical work about the place was beyond her and the twins, and she knew already that this man was plenty strong. She'd had a heck of a time hiring and keeping hands. Most men didn't want to work for a female, and the last cowboy she'd hired had been scared off by the Sutherland crew in town.

Now this Nathaniel here, he wouldn't scare easy. Somehow she knew if he took on a job, he'd stick.

"Just how many brothers and sisters do you have, anyway?" he interrupted her contemplating.

"Well, there's just Jake, Luke, Betsy, and me. Little Tommy and Baby Jessie, they aren't blood kin, but they're family just the same. We took them in last year when their mama died of childbirth fever and their pa fell down a mine shaft a month later. Thomas Blednoe had a terrible thirst for liquor, and he wasn't much good anyway."

"So the six of you are living on a ranch with no responsible adult to look after you?"

"I'm looking after everyone just fine."

His lips tightened. "Sure looks like it from where I'm sitting."

She struggled upright, hurt by his comment and determined not to let him see it. "I can ride astride now." She didn't want to loll about in this man's arms a second longer.

"All right." He shifted his arm so that she could swing her leg across the horn and pommel of the saddle. She thought it would feel less intimate riding this way, but now she could feel the length of his thighs pressing against the back of her legs and the warmth of his chest against her shoulder blades. A strange sort of breathlessness came over her. She tried to sit more upright, so that her shoulders weren't brushing his chest, but that made her bottom rest even closer against him.

"Relax and quit squirming. You're not helping that side of yours, and you're going to make Old Blue here skittish," he growled in her ear.

Robin bit her lip and forced herself to relax back against him. It was far more comfortable riding this way, but it still was a peculiar sensation. For some reason she was painfully aware of him and every place their bodies touched. She was very glad they were only a few miles from her ranch house.

"Where are my cows?" she asked when the question suddenly occurred to her.

"They're eating their heads off five miles back. About the time you toppled off your sorrel, I had to choose between rounding up cows and looking after you. I figured you could send someone to go gather them up later."

Robin opened her mouth and closed it again. As much as she wanted to argue with him, her innate sense of fairness stopped her. He had made the right decision, and she was grateful to him for having looked after her so well. As irritating as she found him, she had to admit this Nathaniel, for all his hard, rough appearance, must have a kind streak in him. Few men would have done so much to help a young boy, and a complete stranger at that, against a group of rustlers. He'd been shot at and lost a whole night's sleep as well as ridden miles out of his way this morning just to help her.

After a few minutes, he urged the steeldust back into a lope. Although the big horse had easy gaits, Robin couldn't help drawing in her breath in a hiss when the horse's movement jostled her hurt side against Nathaniel's arm.

"All right, now that you're awake, we'll take this at a walk," he said firmly.

"I'll be all right. I'd rather we got back faster. Everyone is going to be worried sick about me."

"Is that your place?"

She nodded, a lump rising in her throat. She could see the ranch house now, smoke curling from its chimney. Home had never looked so good. Somehow she felt like it had been weeks since she rode off with Jake to check the high pastures, instead of just yesterday.

"We'll take this at a walk, just the same," he declared and reined in his mount. "Why the hell did you come back last night? You wouldn't have gotten hurt if you hadn't come riding into the thick of that mess."

Robin bristled at the anger in his voice. "I couldn't just ride off and leave you to deal with six men. It wasn't your fight."

"That's exactly what you should have done, with all those little ones counting on you."

"If you were me," she said, looking back at him over her shoulder, "you couldn't have ridden off, either," she guessed shrewdly.

"If I were you, I wouldn't have gotten myself into such a fix in the first place," came his crushing rejoinder.

Robin looked away from him and concentrated on counting to ten. He had helped her out of a tough spot, and therefore she was not going to lose her temper with him. Maybe she didn't want him to stick around after all. If he hired on as a hand at the Rocking M, they might end up murdering each other.

They both remained quiet for the rest of the ride. As they came up the lane leading to the ranch house, Robin winced when she thought of how her place must look to him. She loved the Rocking M fiercely, but she knew it was starting to appear run-down. There were holes in the barn roof that needed patching, and several sagging posts in the horse corral needed to be reset. Betsy's precious henhouse was starting to list to the west, thanks to the heavy snows they'd had last winter. No matter how hard she, Betsy, and the twins pushed themselves, they simply couldn't keep up with the work her father and two full-time hands had done about the place.

Ah, well, there wasn't a prettier spread in the whole valley. Despite the pain in her side, Robin couldn't help smiling as she glanced out at the beautiful view over the home pastures, the valley, and the mountains beyond. She was home.

The man she knew only as Nathaniel reined in his horse and dismounted. Before she could slip down from the saddle, he lifted her gently and set her carefully on her feet. Once again, when she felt the hard muscles in his arms, she decided there was nothing for it.

Even if the man infuriated her, she had to find a way to convince him to stay. She and the rest of her family needed Nathaniel's help too badly to let him ride away.

Chapter Three

The moment after Nathaniel let go of Robin, the door to the ranch house flew open. A girl with two long blond braids raced straight to Robin's side in a flurry of skirts and petticoats. She hugged Robin hard. That embrace must have hurt her injured side, but Robin never said a word. Instead, she hugged the girl back and stroked her hair tenderly.

"We were so worried. I was sure you'd go and get yourself killed," he thought he heard the younger girl say between sobs.

"Sh, now Betsy, here I am. You know it would take more than a few dumb, ornery cattle rustlers to do me in."

Two tall, rangy boys followed hard on her heels. They paused side by side and eyed Nathaniel with some suspicion. These must be the twin brothers Robin had talked about, Luke and Jake. They weren't identical. With his blond hair and green eyes, Jake favored Robin. Luke had dark chestnut hair, a face full of freckles, and light blue eyes. With their big hands and feet, they reminded him of yearling hounds who had yet to grow into their full frame and size.

Betsy stepped back from her sister. Her eyes widened when

she spotted the bloodstains on Robin's torn jacket. "You went and got yourself shot. I knew something bad would happen when you went haring off after those cows all on your own. Luke, you go fetch Doc Peterson right this moment."

Nathaniel found himself trying not to smile. Young Betsy sounded exactly like a worried mother. She turned to look for her brother, but Luke had already slipped away, heading for the barn.

"Betsy, I'd like you stop bossing everyone around for a moment and remember your manners," Robin said firmly. "Please say hello to Mister . . ." Her voice trailed off and she looked at Nathaniel helplessly.

"Dawson," he said quickly, using his mother's maiden name. His own name had become as famous as the notorious badmen he had hunted, and for the past six months he'd been on the run from Nathaniel Hollister and everything he stood for.

"Well, Mr. Dawson here," Robin continued steadily, "helped me get our cows back last night, and he brought me home."

"Welcome to the Rocking M, Mr. Dawson. Thank you so much for bringing Robin back to us."

Nathaniel found himself staring down into Betsy's cornflower blue eyes. The light of hero-worship dawning there made him acutely uncomfortable. He was the last person in the world this sweet young girl should respect or honor.

He glanced back at Robin and saw she was starting to sway. He stepped closer in case she toppled over. "We need to get her inside, pronto," he told Betsy and Jake.

Just then Robin's knees buckled. Swearing under his breath, he caught her before she hit the ground.

"Make sure Jake goes to gather up those cows," she said with a sigh as Nathaniel picked her up, and then her eyelids fluttered shut.

"Dammit, those cows are the last thing I'm worried about right now," he growled at her, and then he realized Betsy was staring at him with a shocked expression. He bit back a second oath and headed for the porch steps.

"I'll go fetch them, Rob," Jake said eagerly, obviously glad to do something to help.

Nathaniel climbed the steps swiftly. He stepped through the open door, and then he had to pause. He saw a homey, spotlessly clean parlor on his left, a small study on his right, and a hallway that led toward the back of the house. Betsy bustled past him.

"Bring her this way. Keep your voice down if you please. Tommy and Jessie are both still asleep, and it will be easier for all of us if they stay that way a while longer."

He followed Betsy down the hall past a good-sized kitchen, the delectable smell of fresh-baked biscuits making him realize that it had been a long time since he had eaten a lean jackrabbit for supper last night.

"This was our parent's bedroom, but Robin uses it now," Betsy said quietly. "You can lay her down on the bed, and I'll get her ready for the doctor."

He did as the young girl suggested. He laid Robin down in the middle of the big four-poster bed as gently as he could. He tried to ignore the fear he felt when he saw how pale she was. The wound in her side wasn't that serious. Treated properly, surely Robin would be fine.

On his way out of the room, he paused to glance at the family portrait prominently displayed on the dresser near the door. Done up in their Sunday best, Robin's parents looked vibrant, healthy, and so very proud of their children. He was surprised at the regret he felt when he realized that handsome couple was dead and gone now.

He blinked when he saw a pretty young girl sitting beside her mother. At first he assumed it was Betsy, but when he looked closer, he realized the girl was much older. That must be Robin. She sure looked different in a dress. With her hair all done up in a bun and a fancy hat on her head, she looked lovely enough in that portrait to break hearts. He glanced back over his shoulder and saw Betsy was waiting impatiently for him to leave.

"Please help yourself to some of the biscuits on the stove," she told him. "If Tommy or Jessie wake up, just keep them busy. I'll be out in a few minutes."

Nathaniel stepped through the door, wondering uneasily who the hell Tommy and Jessie were. He thought Robin had said something about taking in their neighbors' small children. Surely Betsy didn't mean he should look after a baby. He'd rather tackle a dozen outlaws with his bare hands than brace an infant or a toddler.

He hesitated in the kitchen. He wanted to go look after his horse, but what if Tommy or Jessie woke up while Betsy was still caring for her sister? While he was trying to make up his mind, he walked over to the stove and helped himself to a golden-brown biscuit warming in the Dutch oven.

Suddenly he heard a whisper of a sound behind him. Nathaniel whirled about, his hand automatically reaching for the pistol at his hip. He froze when he spotted two children standing in the doorway. The older one, a sturdy boy of four or five years with a shock of thick black hair and bright blue eyes, watched him suspiciously. The younger one, clearly a little girl, simply stared at him while she clutched a bedraggled rag doll. She looked like she might be about to cry. Nathaniel wished with all his heart that she wouldn't.

"You're stealing our biscuits," the boy said accusingly. He lifted his hand and pointed his fingers at Nathaniel. "Bang, bang. You're dead."

Here at least was familiar ground. Nathaniel knelt on the floor. "Hey, partner, the first thing you learn when you start pointing guns at people is to be careful that the owlhoot you're bracing isn't stronger and faster than you are."

Nathaniel formed his own fingers into the shape of a gun. "See, my gun is bigger than yours, and I can shoot mine faster. Besides, Betsy said I could have a biscuit."

Mentioning Betsy was clearly the right approach, for the

little boy promptly lowered his pretend gun. "Well, if Betsy said so, I guess you can have a biscuit. Can I see your real gun?"

"I don't think we'll look at it right now, partner." Nathaniel had a feeling strong-willed Betsy wouldn't be too pleased if she walked into the kitchen and saw Tommy inspecting a six-shooter before breakfast. Amused and irritated to realize a slip of a girl had him spooked, he stood up again. "What's your name, partner?"

"I'm Tommy. This is my sister Jessie. She don't say much and she drools a lot."

At the mention of her name, Jessie pulled her fingers from her mouth and finally smiled at him. There was so much joy and friendliness in that beaming smile, he simply had to smile back at her.

Moments later, he realized desperately that smiling at her had been a mistake. Little Jessie let out a delighted squeal and came toddling toward him. She reached out and patted his knee with a decidedly damp little hand. Nathaniel quelled the urge to wipe his jeans and looked longingly at the door to Robin's room. Just how long could it take young Betsy to pile her sister into a nightgown?

The little girl reached her hands up toward him and said clear as anything, "Up." Just then he caught a whiff of a remarkably strong smell. He eyed her suspiciously. Unless he missed his guess, little Jessie was packing a full load in her nappies.

Nathaniel felt himself starting to sweat. Just then, the door to Robin's room swung open. He almost felt like kissing Betsy when she bustled into the room. "Well, look who's up," she said in a sweet, singsong voice.

Relieved, he watched little Jessie turn about at the sound of Betsy's voice and make a beeline for her. He winced when he saw Betsy pick her up. He decided right then that he didn't need to say anything about the state of that baby's diaper. Betsy's nose would discover soon enough the sweet little surprise Jessie had made.

"I need to see to my horse."

"There's hay and feed in the barn. I'll have a good breakfast ready for you in fifteen minutes, Mr. Dawson."

Nathaniel made good his escape. One whiff of that potent diaper had taken much of the edge off of his appetite. As he strode toward Old Blue, he gave some serious thought to mounting up and hightailing it right out of there.

You've done what you could for that little gal, he told himself firmly. *You helped her get her cows back, and you brought her home. No one could expect you to do any more.* Still, he was reluctant to head out until he was certain the doctor was going to come and sew Robin up properly. Besides, Old Blue could use a day's rest after pushing cows half the night, and carrying two riders a fair ways.

He realized he was still holding the biscuit he'd picked up in the kitchen. After he took a bite, he decided Robin's claim that her little sister was a fine cook was right on the mark. It had been a month of Sundays since he'd had a biscuit this light and delicious. Munching contentedly on the rest of the biscuit, he led his horse out to the barn. After watering him and rubbing him down, he turned the gelding loose in a small corral. He brought Old Blue a bucket of oats and several forkfuls of hay. As he worked, he paused from time to time to admire the view out over the *Sangre de Cristo* mountains in the distance.

The Rocking M sure was a handsome spread. The home pastures backed up against some of the prettiest aspen groves he'd ever seen. He glanced at the sturdy log ranch buildings. Robin's parents had built something of value here, something lasting. All he had to his credit after fifteen years of hard work was a decent rifle, a good horse, and a head full of bloody memories.

He planned to change all that soon. For the next year, he

was going to ride all over, searching out the loneliest, wildest country left west of the Mississippi. During the past few months of drifting, he had come to the bitter realization that he had ridden through every territory and state in the West, and long ago he had stopped appreciating the glorious country he rode through. He'd been too busy scheming and planning and hunting, chasing down killers and bringing them to justice.

Now he was going to take in these western lands before the railroaders and the miners and the farmers spoiled it all. When he had finished, maybe all that clean, open country would have pushed the worst of his memories straight out of his mind. Then he'd take the time to figure out what he wanted to do next with his life and start building something that mattered.

Whatever he wanted to try, cattle ranching was just about the last occupation on his list. He despised cows, and after years of drifting, he doubted he could stay in one place for more than a few weeks.

He stepped between the rails of the corral and looked around him. The Rocking M looked to be a good-sized spread. How was Robin managing it? Surely this was too big a place for a nineteen-year-old and a bunch of youngsters to work. If sheer guts and determination counted, though, maybe young Robin could make a go of it. He smiled when he thought of the way she had faced him down last night. She hadn't once complained about her injury, even though he knew from firsthand experience that flesh wounds usually hurt like hell. He had an idea that Robin Matthews might well be the most courageous female he'd ever met.

So the girl's got sand, Hollister, and she's passably pretty when she wears a skirt. Robin Matthews, her family, and her ranch are really none of your business.

He tried to ignore the queer little pull at his heart when Betsy came out on the porch and called to him in her sweet young voice, "Mr. Dawson, your breakfast is ready."

He gave Old Blue a final slap on the rump and went to wash up. There was no doubt about it. He was reacting peculiarly to this whole damn setup. A gut instinct he'd learned to trust long ago was warning him left, right, and center. After he was certain Robin would be all right, he'd be plenty wise to ride straight out of there and not look back.

Chapter Four

Nathaniel spent much of the morning sorting through his gear and cleaning his saddle and rifle in the barn. He knew from Betsy's reports that Robin had awakened, eaten a bowl of broth, and was sleeping soundly now. As far as Betsy could tell, Robin's wound had stopped bleeding. Nathaniel finished up his chores by lunchtime. He was just about to ride into town himself to see what was taking the dangblasted sawbones so long when Luke finally appeared with the doctor in tow.

He was a neat, well-dressed older gentleman. His appearance reassured Nathaniel, for over the years, he'd seen far too many drunken fools masquerading as physicians. He was surprised to find himself pacing back and forth across the front porch while the doctor treated Robin. It didn't make a whole lot of sense, but he still felt responsible for the fact that a young woman with more courage than common sense was lying in her bed now with a bullet wound in her side.

He guessed from the size of the furrow the bullet had plowed that the doc was going to have to stitch her up. Again from firsthand experience, he knew just how unpleasant that could feel. He was waiting for the sawbones when the man stepped out on the front porch.

"How's she doing, Doc?"

"You must be Dawson." The older man nodded in greeting and studied him out of shrewd gray eyes. "My name's Doc Peterson. Roberta told me a little about you. Thanks for getting her out of that dangerous escapade last night. I've known Roberta Matthews and her family since they moved to this valley, and I'm glad to know she's got a fellow looking out for her at last."

Nathaniel started to correct that assumption, but he decided it wasn't worth the effort. He'd be gone in a few days, and then the doc would realize soon enough that he'd been jumping to conclusions.

"That little gal's lost a good bit of blood," Doc Peterson continued. "She needs to stay quiet for the next several days. If you can find some way to persuade her to do that, I'd be obliged to you. I've shown young Betsy how to change her dressing. I expect Roberta should heal up just fine, but I'll be out a few times over the next several days to see how she's doing just the same."

Nathaniel let out a sigh of relief. Despite the fact he'd let her get hurt, now it looked like she'd be right as rain. He'd just tap on her door, say goodbye, and be on his way. After Doc Peterson left, Nathaniel strode down the hallway to Robin's room.

He'd just raised his hand to knock when the door to the bedroom swung open. There stood Robin, fully dressed in male clothing once again. Her hair was still plaited in a long thick braid that fell over one shoulder. Involuntarily his gaze dropped lower. The worn denim outlined her slim legs all too clearly and clung to her shapely posterior. A female wearing pants was apt to give a man ideas. Hell, seeing Robin in those jeans was giving him all sorts of ideas he had no business having about an innocent young woman, especially when he stood in the door to her bedroom. Tearing his gaze from her legs, he focused on her face and the anger building inside him instead.

"What the hell do you think you're doing?"

"I've got to get to work," she said shortly and lifted her chin.

"You're supposed to rest up for a good week or longer. Didn't you hear one word Doc Peterson told you?"

"I heard him all right, but I can't afford to lie about in my bed just now. Winter's coming fast, and we still aren't ready for it. Someone needs to be the ramrod around this place. My brothers can't do all the work here by themselves."

"Those boys are going to end up running this place without you if you manage to rip out your stitches and catch wound fever. You could land in the First Episcopal Cemetery six feet under with your parents, and then where would your family and your precious ranch be?"

Her face paled. He felt a pang of guilt, but damn it, the girl had to see reason.

"That's a low blow. You leave my parents out of this. I can't believe I'm arguing with you in the first place." She swung away from him and stamped to her window. "None of this is your business anyway."

"I agree with you about that right enough, but someone's got to knock some sense into your thick skull." He took a deep breath. He was surprised to realize he was actually shouting at her. He hardly knew Robin Matthews, but she sure managed to get his goat in a hurry. "If you rest up properly now," he managed to say in a more reasonable tone, "you'll be back on your feet and working again a whole hell of a lot sooner."

His words finally seemed to make an impact. Gripping the bedpost, she sat down slowly on the bed. "I know what you say makes sense, but there's just so much to do. The first snowstorm of the season could hit us any time now." She stared at the far wall, her expression tense and worried. He decided with some relief that she didn't look like she was about to cry. He abhorred weepy women. He guessed it would take a heap of trouble to make Robin Matthews cry. The dejected slump to her shoulders got to him just the same.

"Well, if you're that hard up, I expect I could stick around for a few days and help out. Just until you're back on your feet again." He wasn't sure which of them was more surprised to hear him make that offer.

"I thought you said you weren't looking to hire on as a cowhand," she said, eyeing him skeptically.

"I'm not. I'm just offering to lend you a hand for a few days. Now, do you want my help or not?"

She opened her mouth to fire back a retort, but obviously she thought better of it. She straightened her back and met his gaze, her green eyes level.

"Nathaniel Dawson, I'm in absolutely no position to stay up on my high horse right now. I'd be most pleased and relieved if you stayed on for as long as you can."

"All right, then," he said gruffly, suddenly feeling awkward. "Now get back in that bed and stay there. What were you charging off to do, anyway?"

"First I was going to make sure that Jake got back all right, took a proper count of the cows, and settled them in our north pasture. Then I was going to have the boys cut more hay down along the river. We're still light on feed for our stock, and the winters can be mighty cold and long this high up. Then I was going to make sure Jake and Luke finished chopping up that deadfall we hauled in last week. We're still short on firewood, too. Oh, and I had to check the henhouse. Betsy said she lost another hen to a coyote last week, and I hate for her to lose any more chickens."

"Is that all?" he asked dryly.

"Well, that probably would have kept me busy until supper-time or so," she allowed, a sudden smile lighting her face.

He stared back at her, his body starting to tighten. There was no doubt about it. Robin Matthews was a remarkably pretty girl when she smiled. He wasn't sure he'd ever seen a female with eyes the silver-green color of sage before. Hastily he backed out of her bedroom. Swearing at his body under his breath, he stomped off to the barn to saddle up a horse and count some cows.

Robin was still sitting on her bed staring into space when Betsy tapped at her door.

"What were the two of you yelling about, and what on earth are you doing dressed?" Betsy's blue eyes were alight with curiosity as she slipped inside.

"My being dressed is what we were yelling about. Mr. Dawson wasn't too pleased to see me out of bed, either, and he let me know it in no uncertain terms."

"Good for him."

"Whose side are you on, anyway?" Robin asked as she started the slow and painful process of getting undressed again.

"Yours," Betsy replied promptly and came to help Robin pull her jeans off, "which is why I'm glad he talked you into staying in bed."

"I'm not sure he talked me into it—ordered is more like."

"That I would have liked to see," Betsy said with a giggle that made Robin smile despite the fact she still felt ruffled and out of sorts from her recent confrontation with a certain Nathaniel Dawson.

"At any rate, he's offered to stay on for a few days to help out until I'm back on my feet again."

"Well, that was a kind thing for him to offer," Betsy said in a neutral voice.

"Bets, what do you think of Mr. Dawson?" Robin had to ask. Despite the fact that Betsy was only thirteen, she was wise beyond her years and a good judge of character.

Betsy frowned and wrapped the end of one of her braids around her finger. "I think I like him. His face is hard, though, and he speaks so sternly. He did let Tommy sit on his saddle and pretend to ride for a long time this morning, but I don't think he likes babies much. Every time Jessie starts his way, he heads the opposite direction.''

"We'll just do our best to keep Jessie away from him then.''

"That's not going to be easy. She's taken a real shine to him, and you know how stubborn she can be.''

Robin sighed. She did know how stubborn Jessie could be. There were days she thought Jessie caused more mischief around the Rocking M than a hundred land-hungry Sutherlands. Betsy picked up her nightgown, and Robin obediently raised her arms. She couldn't help wincing as the pain burned along her side. Who would have thought a little gash along the ribs could hurt so much?

When Betsy pulled back the covers, Robin meekly climbed into the bed.

"If you need anything, just holler. I'll be working on dinner,'' Betsy said and bustled from the room.

After a few minutes, Robin decided she was too restless to sleep. She got out of bed, drank down a glass of water, and wandered over to the window. She was just in time to see the mysterious Mr. Dawson go riding off to find Jake. She wasn't surprised to discover he had saddled up Thunder, the finest horse they had on the place. Judging by the quality of his own mount, the man knew horses. Something about the set to his shoulders and the way he rode Thunder told her that Nathaniel was still angry.

Why had he offered to stay on to help? Whatever Mr. Dawson might be, she was quite sure he was no common ranch hand. He had been so reluctant to tell her his first name last night, she doubted Dawson was his real surname.

Right now, she was too tired and hurt to care who he was, or why he had decided to stay. For the moment, an able-bodied man was an answer to her prayers. Anything he could do for them over the next few days would be a help.

Robin returned to her bed. She closed her eyes and sank back against the pillows. Instantly, a dark face with thick black brows and striking blue eyes filled her inner vision. Whoever he was, Nathaniel distracted her thoughts and troubled her soul in the most peculiar way. A man that handsome must break hearts wherever he went. A man that good looking would never look twice at a rancher girl who wore jeans and a union suit—which was just as well. Of course, she didn't want him looking twice at her. She knew a rolling stone when she saw one. If she ever tied up with a man, she wanted one who would stay put and build a good life with her.

She could still enjoy looking at Nathaniel, though, until he left. With a little shiver, she remembered what it had felt like to ride with him, his hard arms circling her waist, his warm body pressing close against her own. Angry at herself for dwelling on such an idiotic thing, she tried to think about ranch business, but somehow her unruly mind kept circling back to Nathaniel. How long was he truly going to stay?

She was just starting to wonder if he was married when she drifted off to sleep.

Chapter Five

Nathaniel rested the blade of his hay scythe on the ground. He drew his kerchief from his back pocket and wiped his face. Although the fall day was cool, he'd still managed to work up a sweat. He looked with some satisfaction at the large area of grass he'd cut in the last two hours. He hadn't scythed hay since he left the family farm back in Buford, West Virginia. It was good to know he hadn't lost the knack of it.

Robin's brothers were making good progress on their portion of the field, but they hadn't found the steady, even rhythm to it. That came with years of practice.

Nathaniel stretched his arms and shoulders. He'd used muscles today that he hadn't used in years. He'd probably be sore as an old man tomorrow. Despite the work gloves he wore, he guessed he'd have some blisters, too. He glanced at the ranch house in the distance and shook his head. He still wasn't quite sure why he was out here. Mostly he was making sure Robin stayed put in her bed. Perhaps, too, he was doing penance of a sort. He was trying to atone for having let her risk her life. Last night, he'd almost let another innocent get killed.

Uncomfortable with that train of thought, Nathaniel glanced over at Luke and Jake. The boys had been changing off using the other scythe, and they both were starting to look pretty whipped. Scything was brutal work, and he didn't want one of the boys putting that blade through a foot by accident.

"Don't you think we've cut enough for today?" he called to them.

Both boys brightened visibly at his suggestion

"You got three times as much done as we did," Jake admitted when they walked over to inspect his portion of the field.

"There's a trick to it. My arms are still a good bit longer than yours, too."

"Is that one of those new Smith and Wesson double-action pistols?" Luke asked with great interest when Nathaniel put his shirt back on and buckled his pistol and cartridge belt about his waist.

"That it is," he said shortly. The curtness of his tone discouraged the boy from asking any more questions, just as Nathaniel hoped it would. He knew only too well what fatal fascination pistols could hold for boys, especially with the penny dreadfuls romanticizing gunfighters and gunfighting these days.

When they reached the barn, he set Jake to sharpening the scythes for tomorrow and had Luke show him to the wood pile. He glanced at the cords of wood already neatly split and stacked. Robin was right. Although she and the boys had managed to put up a fair bit of wood, they'd need plenty more to see them through the winter.

Nathaniel had to shake his head at himself as he picked up the ax. Here was another chore he hadn't done since who-flung-the-chunk. He had Luke saw off the smaller branches while he split and stacked several of the sections the boys had cut yesterday. When Jake arrived, the boys went to work on the two-handled saw while he continued to split. They all three traded off jobs over time. Working steadily, they produced a satisfyingly large addition to the woodpile. An hour before sunset, he told the boys they could go for a swim while he went off to do what he could to fix Betsy's henhouse.

Nathaniel was tired clean through by the time he sat down to supper that night, but it was a good kind of tired. Betsy smiled shyly when she served him up a heaping portion of chicken and dumplings. The food smelled like heaven. After he took his first bite, he had to admit his supper tasted every bit as good as it smelled.

"I thought you deserved a special, hot supper since you fixed my henhouse and helped Robin get our cows back," Betsy told him as she sat down at the table.

"How'd you learn to cook like this?"

"I've always liked being in the kitchen ever since I was a little girl. Robin can cook almost as well as I can," she pointed out loyally. "She just doesn't enjoy it as much."

Luke and Jake rolled their eyes at each other. "She'd rather brand a hundred full-grown steers than bake a loaf of bread," Luke said.

"She'd rather clean the whole barn than make a stew," Jake added. Nathaniel was learning the twins often echoed each other's thoughts and even finished each other's sentences.

"Now you boys be fair. If she has to cook, Robin does a fine job of it," Betsy admonished her brothers.

"Her stew ain't half bad," Luke admitted grudgingly.

"Lucas Matthews, her beef stew is just plain delicious, which is why you're always after her to make it. And Jake, you know full well you beg her at least once a week to make an apple pie."

Luke was spared having to make a response to that comment, for Tommy spoke up then, clearly thinking it was time he made a contribution to the conversation. "Rob'n likes to ride horses," Tommy announced with great importance. "And I'm going to marry her some day."

"I wish you both a lifetime of happiness," Nathaniel said gravely after a few moments, since Tommy's comment had clearly been addressed to him.

"Oh, Tommy, she's too old for you," Betsy said, shaking her head. "We've talked about this before. You can marry Lissa Watkins if you want."

"I don't want to marry Lissa. I want to marry Rob'n." From the way Tommy's lip was starting to jut out, Nathaniel could see there was a storm coming.

"Say, Tommy, let's go see if we can find the barn cat and her kittens," Jake suggested quickly. Tommy brightened at that notion and jumped from his chair. When Jake held out a hand, Tommy skipped over to him. At that, Jessie let out a squeal of indignation. Luke quietly rose to his feet, wiped Jessie's face with a damp rag, and lifted the little girl down from her chair. Jessie went toddling after Jake as fast as her plump legs would carry her. After Jake left with the little ones, Luke cleared the table and started to wash the dishes while Betsy fetched Nathaniel a cup of coffee.

Nathaniel leaned back in his chair, impressed with the way these young people worked as a team. The twins handled the young ones well and treated them with constant, good-natured humor, which surprised him. Because his brother Ethan was older and his brother Joshua was only a few years younger than himself, he had never looked after a small child the way these young people looked after Jessie. He strongly doubted he could have been so patient with a toddler when he was fourteen.

"Excuse me, Mr. Dawson, but Robin was hoping she could talk with you before you turned in," Betsy broke in on his thoughts with an apologetic smile. "I cleaned the bunkhouse if you want to take your bedroll out there to sleep tonight."

"Thank you, Betsy, and thanks for a mighty fine meal," he said, meaning every word. He took his coffee and strolled toward the back of the house. It occurred to him as he raised his hand to knock that he was looking forward to another talk with Robin Matthews. She might be too stubborn for her own good, and she could be irritating as the dickens, but she surely wasn't boring.

As soon as he rapped on the door, she called out for him to enter. She was sitting upright in bed, her covers drawn up modestly over her chest. She still looked pale, but he was pleased to see the bruised circles under her eyes had faded a little. Wearing a white, high-necked nightdress with one braid falling over her shoulder, Robin looked even younger than her nineteen years.

"How's that side feel?" he asked as he made his way across the room and settled himself gingerly in the rocker beside her bed.

"Like someone shot a hole in it," she admitted honestly. "I can't believe I slept all afternoon. I've never done that before."

"You've never been shot before. Losing blood like that weakens your whole body. You'll be doing plenty of sleeping over the next few days."

"You sound like you're speaking from experience."

"I've been in a few shooting scrapes in my time," he said shortly.

"I'll just bet you have," he thought he heard her say under her breath, but then she smiled at him brightly. "Jake said you made good progress in the hayfield today."

"That hay should make good feed, even if it is getting cut late in the season. You've got some of the finest natural hayfields I've ever seen."

"That land along the river, along with the view, are the two reasons Mama and Papa chose this place to homestead ten years ago," she said proudly.

"Have you thought about selling out? A fine spread like this ought to fetch some good money from the right buyer, especially while it's still in relatively good shape."

"You think I'm going to let it get run-down," she said, her green eyes turning cool.

He met her gaze steadily. There was no use trying to sugarcoat it. "I can tell you and the boys have been trying, but a place like this takes some real manpower to keep up."

"We'll manage just fine, Mr. Dawson. We have absolutely no interest in selling out." Her expression suddenly turned from cool to downright hostile, as if an idea had suddenly occurred to her. "You can tell that to Vance Sutherland when he asks you."

She spat out that name like a curse. Nathaniel studied her curiously. "I'd be happy to tell that to Vance Sutherland, if and when I meet the gent."

"I'm glad you're not going to pretend you've never heard of the man."

Nathaniel stared at her. Sometimes it was downright impossible to guess how the female mind worked.

"Of course I've heard of Vance Sutherland. He's one of the most famous ranchers in the West. He was one of the first men to drive cattle up the trails from Texas to Colorado. He must own most of this very valley."

"He does, indeed, and he would like to own all of it, including the Rocking M."

Nathaniel pursed his lips in a soundless whistle. "So that's the way the wind is blowing," he said and sat back in the chair.

"Vance Sutherland wants to control every acre of land in Grand Valley, and he will stop at nothing until he's achieved that goal."

"A man like Sutherland respects the law, and he doesn't need to resort to dirty tricks to get his way." Even as he said the words, Nathaniel realized they could be totally false. He had never met Vance Sutherland. Even though the Sutherland name was well respected in the West, Nathaniel had met more than a few well-respected, powerful men in his time who had resorted to murder and worse to get what they wanted.

"If you say so," she said stonily. "I could introduce you to a half-dozen small ranchers who learned firsthand that Vance Sutherland and his men were capable of completely disregarding your precious laws. That is, if those ranchers still lived in the valley. Unfortunately, every single one of them had to sell out. Sutherland's riders harassed them until they finally gave up their homes and dreams here and moved away."

It was a story he'd heard a dozen times before. In the more remote regions of the West, powerful men used, bent, or ignored the law to suit themselves. Still, he was surprised to hear Vance Sutherland might be involved in such a situation.

"I read in a paper just a month ago that he was going to make a try for a senate seat."

Robin sniffed in disgust. "Sutherland's trying to buy himself a seat, all right. He spends so much time in Denver these days, he hardly has time to oversee his own ranch."

"Well, that should be good news for you, then. How much trouble can the man cause you when he's hundreds of miles away from here most of the time?"

"Plenty," Robin said with a mirthless smile. "His foreman Rick Dyer knows exactly how his boss feels about the Rocking M, and Dyer has even fewer scruples than his boss. Remember those two men who joined the other rustlers right before I spooked the herd? They were Sutherland hands. I saw the brands on their horses and heard them talking as they rode up the trail. Dyer sent them to make sure those rustlers kept our cattle moving until they were out of the county. That means Dyer was in league with those men."

As he gazed at her indignant features, Nathaniel's heart twisted for her. He understood now exactly what she was up against and how hopeless her chances were. If Sutherland's men were willing to resort to rustling her cattle, the best thing for the Matthewses to do would be to sell out as soon as possible.

"Tell that to the sheriff, then."

Robin sent him a disgusted look. "I told you before—Sutherland owns the sheriff. He owns all of Grand Valley, for that matter. It would be my word against his. Since the judge and the sheriff know exactly which side their bread is buttered on, you can guess what my chances are of their believing me."

"Young lady, if Sutherland's outfit is already stealing your cows, you're in deep, deep trouble. That's all the more reason for you to sell out. It's not that great a step from stealing to killing, and you don't want your family caught in the crossfire. I've seen what can happen in range wars when the lead starts flying.''

Her eyes widened. She searched his face in disbelief. ''You honestly think we should give up our home to this man?''

''If you care about keeping your brothers and those little ones safe,'' he said grimly, ''that's exactly what you should do.''

''This is the only home any of us has ever known. This is the only place I can provide for them all.''

''You can't provide for any of them if you're dead.'' He knew his words were brutal, but he had to say them anyway. ''You could have easily been killed last night if I hadn't been there to help you.''

''If you hadn't been there, I could have handled things just fine on my own. I probably wouldn't have even been shot,'' she said defiantly. She was sitting upright in her bed now, the covers she had tucked so modestly under her arms long ago forgotten in the blaze of her anger. The well-worn fabric clung to the sweet swell of her breasts.

As he stared at her, his awareness of her as a woman came rushing back in a dangerous tide. Lord, Robin Matthews was pretty when she was in a temper. Her cheeks were flushed with color and her green eyes sparked fire. With that golden braid of hair falling over her shoulder, she looked soft and feminine and far too delectable for his peace of mind. He was painfully aware that he was alone with her in her bedroom, and that she was wearing just a nightgown and not much else. He remembered how she'd felt in his arms while he carried her home, and he could still remember clearly the way she'd smelled of roses and lavender.

A part of him wanted to take her into his arms, sink back with her into that featherbed, and make her forget all about her precious ranch. He knew she wasn't indifferent to him. He saw the small looks she slanted his way when she thought he wasn't aware. It would be good between them. He'd help her turn some of that passion she felt for her ranch toward loving, and it would be better than good.

His long silence must have puzzled her, for the defiance in her gaze faded to uncertainty. Perhaps she sensed the way his thoughts were flowing. Her cheeks flooded with color, and she quickly pulled the blanket back up about her shoulders.

He tore his gaze away from her and stared at the floor. Was there any depth he wouldn't sink to? What was he doing, fantasizing about seducing this girl when she had gotten herself wounded just last night? Clearly, he'd gone too long without having a woman.

He rose to his feet, hoping like hell she wouldn't notice how much he wanted her. He walked quickly to the doorway. There he turned and made one last effort to make her see reason.

"I've lived in the West for fifteen years now. One thing I've learned out here is that powerful, ruthless men usually get their way. If I were you, I'd sell this place for the best price you can get, and try starting out again elsewhere."

He could tell from the mulish set to her chin that she wasn't really listening to a word he said. Biting back a curse, he stepped through the door and closed it firmly behind him. He leaned back against the door for a long moment. Heaven save him from stubborn women. He raised his hands and rubbed his face tiredly. He was more certain than ever that he'd be riding off the moment Robin Matthews got back on her feet. He didn't have the stomach to stay around and watch her destroy herself and her family fighting a battle she couldn't win. With a sigh, he pushed away from the door and went to find the bunkhouse.

Chapter Six

"Rob, there's a rider coming." Jake poked his head in the doorway to Robin's bedroom, his face flushed and breathless. "It looks like Dyer. I thought you'd want to know."

"You're darn right about that." Robin slipped out of bed and started pulling on her clothes as fast as she could. The last thing she wanted was for Rick Dyer to know she'd been laid up. If he knew how weak she was, he and his crew would take full advantage of the situation and dream up all sorts of new mischief to plague her.

"Where are Luke and Nathaniel?" she asked, thinking fast.

"They finished cleaning out the barn, and now they're spreading manure on Betsy's garden."

Rough, tough Nathaniel was spreading cow and horse dung? That was a sight she'd like to see, if Rick Dyer wasn't about to arrive on her doorstep.

"You run and make sure Nathaniel isn't wearing his gun belt when Dyer rides up."

"He wasn't wearing it to spread manure," Jake said puzzledly.

"Fine. Just make sure he doesn't put it on before Dyer gets here."

"I don't know what you're getting so het up about. I think Nathaniel can look after himself."

"I don't doubt that, but my guess is that Dyer has come looking for trouble, and I don't want to give him any excuse to start some. Now go keep an eye on Nathaniel for me."

Jake went at last, much to her relief. Robin winced and tears burned in her eyes as she lifted her right arm and shrugged into one of her father's work shirts. She knew in her bones that Dyer was here because he was furious at her, and he wasn't a good man to cross. She'd thwarted his attempt to run off her cows, and she'd made his men look like fools into the bargain. Nathaniel had definitely shot one Rafter S hand, and possibly more for all she knew. Dyer would want to make her pay for that, even though he was the one who had started the trouble in the first place.

When she finished dressing, she glanced at herself in the mirror on her mother's dresser. She looked far too wan and pale. Relentlessly, she pinched her cheeks until they were bright with color. She strode out on the porch just as Dyer pulled his showy black-and-white pinto to a halt.

"Heard you all had some excitement the other night," he drawled as he leaned one elbow on the pommel of his saddle. She stood upright in the middle of the porch while he studied her.

Robin knew many women in Grand Valley considered him handsome, and Dyer fancied himself quite a ladies' man. She had always thought his sharp, narrow features made him look like a weasel—one of the most vicious killers in all nature. Slim and sleight of build, he always dressed meticulously in dark clothes and white shirts. He wore his light blond hair cropped short, and he sported a thin, carefully trimmed mustache. His pale blue eyes were cold, and she'd rarely seen him smile. Rumor had it in the valley that he might be a bastard son of Vance Sutherland. His only goal in life seemed to be to please his boss, and to build his own reputation with a gun.

Robin repressed a little shudder as she gazed at him. Most anytime visitors came to the Rocking M, she'd ask them inside promptly. Like most western folk, the Matthewses prided themselves on their hospitality. However, Robin had absolutely no intention of asking Rick Dyer to set foot in her house, and they both knew why.

"Some good-for-nothing cattle rustlers decided to run off a hundred cows," she informed him coolly. "It wasn't particularly exciting, but we got our cows back promptly."

"Not exciting, eh? I heard from Doc Peterson that you caught some lead."

"It was just a scratch. As you can see, I'm already back on my feet."

Out of the corner of her eye, she saw Luke and Nathaniel come stand at the corner of the porch. When she glanced over at Nathaniel, she was thankful to see he wasn't wearing his holster belt. He'd borrowed a pair of her father's overalls this morning, and his boots and pants legs were covered with mud and dung. Dressed like a farmer and covered with muck, he still looked like a man to be reckoned with. His blue eyes were cool and watchful, and he never once looked away from Dyer. Just knowing Nathaniel was nearby gave her heart.

"Who's this?" Dyer jerked a head over at Nathaniel. "You hire another chickenhearted hand for yourself?"

"No, this is my first cousin, Nathaniel Dawson. He's been sodbusting in Nebraska for the past few years." She didn't dare look at Nathaniel. She could only pray he'd keep his mouth shut and follow her lead. "He's just come to visit us for a week or two," she continued boldly, "so there's no point in your trying to scare him off."

Dyer spat into the dirt. "Hell, that's just what we need around here is another dumb hayseed."

"I'll thank you to watch your language in front of my family," she said coldly.

"You just don't get it, do you?" he hissed, his eyes warming with anger at last. "You're still carrying on like you're the queen of ranching country. Well, you're going to be the queen of nothing by the time this winter's through."

"We'll just see who's still here come spring, Rick Dyer. Now you get off our land."

"Nobody orders Rick Dyer around," he said angrily and wrenched his pinto about. Betsy cried out when he galloped his horse right over her beloved rose bushes and through the kitchen garden that lay beyond them. Robin clenched her hands helplessly. On the far side, Dyer reined the pinto in and turned him about, clearly intending to trample the garden once again.

Suddenly, Robin noticed a blur of movement out of the corner of her eye. Nathaniel had vanished from the place he had been standing. Moments later she saw him come running around the back of the house, a white sheet from the laundry line bunched in his arms. Dyer had just urged the pinto back into a gallop when Nathaniel reached the edge of the garden. He opened up the white sheet. With the help of the strong morning breeze, the white cloth promptly billowed outward. The high-strung pinto shied violently and came to a dead stop. Rick Dyer went sailing over its head to land face first in a garden freshly spread with manure.

"Luke, go fetch me Papa's shotgun," she told her brother in a low voice.

Reluctantly, Luke tore his gaze away from the fascinating spectacle unfolding in the kitchen garden. "I reckon that's a good idea," he allowed, and he hurried into the house.

In the meantime, Dyer had lunged to his feet, spewing a series of oaths that made Robin want to clap her hands over Betsy's and Tommy's ears. He wiped his face clean with his kerchief. When his eyes were clear, he swung about, and his gaze fastened on Nathaniel. Her heart missed a beat when she saw Dyer reach for his pistol. Nathaniel slowly raised his hands in the air to show he wasn't armed. Dyer drew anyway, and pointed his pistol right at Nathaniel's heart. Robin's mouth went dry.

"You better think twice about pulling that trigger," she heard Nathaniel tell him calmly. "You'd be shooting an unarmed man in front of witnesses."

Luke quietly handed her the shotgun. "You take Tommy and stay on this porch," she ordered her brother. She raced down the porch steps and stopped at the edge of the garden.

"I'd happily spread your guts all over the garden if you did shoot him," Robin called out, trying to get Dyer's attention back on her. She knew what a wild, volcanic temper he had. Right now, Nathaniel stood a hair's breadth away from getting shot. "I'm partial to my cousin, and I'd hate to have to explain to my Aunt Lulabelle why her precious boy got shot visiting me."

Dyer looked away from Nathaniel. His face tightened when he saw the shotgun in her hands.

"Believe me," she said in a quieter voice, "I will pull both triggers on this shotgun if you shoot him. I've been looking for a legal way to kill you for two years now."

After a long moment, Dyer holstered his gun. The anger vanished from his eyes to be replaced by something colder and far more dangerous.

"You'll pay for this. You'll all pay for this before I'm through with you."

With that, he strode to the pinto. After he mounted, he raked it savagely with his spurs. The poor animal lunged into a gallop and went pounding away.

Robin sat down right there on the ground, her legs suddenly gone as weak as water.

Nathaniel came to kneel beside her. "You all right?"

"I'm fine. I'm just feeling a little shaky."

"You had the sand when it counted. I'm proud to call you cousin," he said, a quizzical smile lighting his features. She stared up at him, thinking he looked ten years younger and five times more handsome when he smiled. "But did you have to call my mother 'Lulabelle'?"

"It was the first name that came to me at the time," she laughed helplessly, delighted to discover Nathaniel Dawson possessed a sense of humor.

"I expect you'd better tell me what that was all about later," he said in a more somber voice, and then she was surrounded by her family.

"You both sure showed Dyer," Luke said with a grin.

"Did you see him? He had poop spread all over those fancy clothes of his," Jake crowed with delight.

"I'm glad I don't have to wash his shirt," Betsy said with feeling and went to retrieve the sheet Nathaniel had used to spook the pinto.

"I'm sorry about your garden," he said when she returned with the sheet wadded up in her arms. He gestured to the squash and pumpkin vines that had been trampled. "It might have been better if I'd just let him ride through it a second time."

"It was worth losing a few pumpkin vines," Betsy said firmly, "to have Rick Dyer land facefirst in all that fresh-laid manure."

"It sure was funny to watch that man go flying through the air," Tommy declared in his piping voice.

"That it was, Tommy my boy," Nathaniel grinned at Tommy and ruffled his hair. "That it was. Now that the excitement's over, we all better get back to our chores, and the boss lady here should get back in her bed."

Robin was surprised to see they did exactly as he ordered. Betsy took Tommy and Jessie off for their naps, and the twins went to cut more hay. She found she was the one dragging her heels.

Yet the moment she slipped under the covers, she fell sound asleep. When she awakened hours later, she was surprised to see the sun was almost setting. She spent a lonely suppertime straining to hear the others laugh and talk in the kitchen. This invalid business was getting old in a hurry. No matter what anyone said, tomorrow she was getting dressed and leaving her room.

Nathaniel came to see her after supper. She had been expecting his visit. She hadn't been expecting to look forward to it so much. Holding his coffee cup, he settled himself in the rocker again next to her bed. They talked for a time about the ranch chores he'd completed today working with the twins. She was amazed by how much he had accomplished in just two days. Nathaniel might not want to work as a ranch hand, but when he tackled a job, he clearly did it in a thorough fashion. She found herself enjoying their talk to no end. She took pleasure from simply listening to his deep voice. She wondered where he was from. She thought she heard echoes of the South in his accent from time to time.

At last he drained his coffee cup and placed it on the table beside the rocker. "All right," he said in a no-nonsense tone, "what was that all about this afternoon? Unless I miss my guess, I almost got myself shot today, and I'd like to know why."

"Beside the fact that you helped dump a man wearing a pistol into a garden full of manure?"

"There was a lot more going on there this afternoon, and you know it. The boys told me Dyer is Sutherland's foreman. I gather you've had trouble with him before."

"You could say that," she said coolly. What was between Dyer and herself was truly her own business.

"Do you think he's the one behind your cows disappearing the other night?"

"He's certainly capable of it. Since Dyer started working for Sutherland two years ago, the dirty tricks that outfit plays on us started to get a whole lot dirtier."

"What was that business about your hiring another chicken-hearted hand?"

"Dyer and his boys take great pleasure in scaring off my hands as fast as I can hire them. We could afford to pay a man to work around here, but I can't keep anyone on for more than a week or two before the Sutherland riders chase him off."

"So that's why you came up with the cousin story. You were trying to protect me."

He sat back in the rocking chair looking so stunned, she almost laughed. "Well, you're already doing me a favor. I'd like to keep you from getting beat up the first time you decide to ride into town."

"Is that what happened to your hands?"

"At first, Dyer's boys just used to make threats, and that was enough to send most of my crew packing. The last man I hired had more gumption, and the threats didn't scare him off. He only quit after they broke three of his ribs."

"I see," he said, his black brows drawing together. "I said it before. If it's already gotten this ugly, you should get out."

"And I told you before, this is our home. We're not leaving just because a greedy man who's gotten too big for his britches wants our land."

"I'd say there was something more personal in the grudge between you and Dyer. He came looking for blood this afternoon."

"After what you did today," she reminded him, "it's going to be even more personal."

Nathaniel raked a hand through his hair. "I'm sorry for that. Two-bit badmen like him always get my goat. Besides, I know how much Betsy sets store by that garden of hers." He looked so sheepish, she decided not to tease him about protecting Betsy's rose bushes and vegetables.

"Dyer's killed three men now, two of them in standup gunfights. I think that makes him a little more than two-bit."

"Depends on who he shot," Nathaniel countered, not looking the least bit impressed.

"Well, I can't say that I'm sorry for what you did today, even though Dyer will probably find a way to make us pay down the road. I'll never forget what he looked like with dung and dirt smeared all over his face.'' She couldn't help laughing again, just thinking about it.

"You should do that more often," Nathaniel said, his gaze intent on her face.

"Do what?" she asked.

"Laugh like that," he replied, and then looked uncomfortable. Quickly he rose to his feet and crossed the room.

He paused in the doorway and glanced back at her. "Thanks for backing my play. He was just mad enough, he might have pulled that trigger. You'll do to ride the river with, Robin Matthews."

"So will you, Nathaniel Dawson," she said softly to his retreating back. "So will you." As she plumped the pillows and settled herself down in her bed, she faced a bittersweet truth. His compliment pleased her, but she would much rather he had said more about her laugh. She knew she was being foolish to even start thinking this way. How could he possibly look romantically at a girl who toted shotguns around and dressed in men's clothing?

Roberta Matthews, why do you want him to? a more practical voice inside her asked. Certainly Nathaniel Dawson was easy on the eye in a rough, masculine way she found tremendously appealing, but the more she saw of him, the more she was convinced he was a bitter, restless soul. Something had happened to make him take such a pessimistic view on life, and she wasn't sure she wanted to know what that something was. Nathaniel Dawson was just plain trouble, and she had plenty of that on her plate already.

Chapter Seven

"I still think it's too soon for you to make a trip to town." Nathaniel glowered at her from the doorway to her bedroom. Robin glowered right back at him.

It had been four days now since she'd been shot. Doc Peterson had told Nathaniel she was healing well, but surely the last thing Robin needed to do was get bumped around on a buckboard for an hour on the way to town and an hour on the way back.

"I appreciate your concern, but Doc Peterson said I could handle the ride," she said with a stubborn light in her eyes Nathaniel was coming to know only too well.

"How you talked him into that is beyond me. Look, if you're feeling bored or too cooped up, spend the day out on the porch. Hell, if I'd been lying in bed for four days, I know the walls would have started to close in on me, too."

"You're right about those walls closing in," she admitted, "but I'm not planning to go to town today because I'm suffering from claustrophobia. We're short on supplies."

"All right, write me up a list," he suggested, "and I can drive in with one of the twins and pick up whatever you need.

Someone who got shot four days ago doesn't need to ride two hours on a buckboard.''

"Actually, I think I do. Grand Valley is a small town. Word gets around. I need to show my face and let everyone know my latest run-in with the Sutherlands hasn't gotten us down.''

"It always comes back to that, doesn't it," he said. *Of course it does. You should have that figured out by now, you damn fool.* "You're going to risk opening your stitches just so the townsfolk know you haven't thrown in the towel yet.''

"That's about right. Please tell Luke to have the team harnessed by ten.''

"Yes, ma'am.'' Frustrated by the futility of it all, Nathaniel pivoted on his heel and left her room. He derived some satisfaction from closing the door good and hard after him.

He paused on the front porch. Why did he let her get to him? Why did it matter to him that she was determined to go to town when she should be taking it easy? It was her life, and she was the one who was going to have to live with the choices she made. He looked out toward the *Sangre de Cristos* and drew in a deep breath. Just looking at those mountains made a man feel more peaceful.

Suddenly, he heard the patter of familiar footsteps behind him. "Hey, Nathn'l, what ya doin' this morning?''

Nathaniel let go his breath and turned to face young Tommy. "Well, partner, I thought I'd straighten up a few of those corral posts before they fall over. You want to lend me a hand this morning?''

"You bet," the little boy said, his blue eyes alight with excitement. Whenever Nathaniel worked close to the ranch house now, Tommy was his shadow. At first he thought the boy's ceaseless chattering would drive him crazy. He was surprised to find he was entertained by much of what Tommy said. He was a bright, curious little boy, and he saw the entire world with such wonder. Nathaniel envied him that wonder, and the joy he could take in such simple things.

Just yesterday, Tommy had brought him a cigar box filled

with his rock collection. Proudly, Tommy showed him his favorites.

"Luke told me this one's just fool's gold," he said, holding up a flashy piece of iron pyrite. "I think it's real pretty just the same."

"You know what, partner, I think it's pretty, too. Say, do you know what this one is?"

Tommy had been suitably impressed to learn he had a nice sample of copper ore. Nathaniel had gotten a big kick out of seeing his eyes go all big and round.

Yep, Tommy was a fine boy. They were all good kids, but they were clinging to a sinking ship, and he didn't want to be around when it went down.

Before ten o'clock rolled around, Nathaniel quit his post hole digging and washed up. He'd had his fill of ranch work over the past few days, and a ride to town sounded like a good break. As he went to saddle Old Blue, he told himself he wasn't going in to keep an eye on a certain mule-headed lady rancher. If she got herself into trouble today, he meant to let her find a way out of it all on her own.

Right at ten, he rode over to the ranch house. When he glanced up toward the porch, he felt like he'd been kicked in the stomach. Robin stood there straight and slim and looking prettier than just about any woman he'd ever seen. She was wearing a simple green calico dress, a straw bonnet, and a shawl about her shoulders. She'd caught her hair up in a bun like the one she'd worn in the family portrait.

He wanted to walk right up on that porch, sweep that bonnet off her head, and kiss the living daylights out of her. It made no sense at all. She was fourteen years younger than he. She made him so angry half the time he wanted to dunk her in the closest horse trough. But when he saw her smile at Tommy, her spirit and love shining through, a part of him started to warm inside—a part he thought had been frozen forever.

Nathaniel's thoughts snapped to the present when Tommy ran out in front of the team and startled the animals. Nathaniel strode after him and gave him a stern lecture about running around horses.

It took a little time to get everyone including Jessie, her nappies, and her blanket loaded up in the buckboard. Robin directed the proceedings like an army general, though, and soon they were off. During the ride to town, Nathaniel had a lot to think about. Why did Robin Matthews have such a strong effect on him? He'd had a dozen women far more beautiful in his bed. Females from all walks of life seemed drawn by the badge and the guns he wore and the reputation he carried. He had enjoyed what those women offered, treated them as decently as he could, and walked away when the next assignment came his way.

Robin Matthews's nose was too pert, her jaw too strong for her to be truly beautiful. She even had freckles and tanned skin from working outside so much. Nathaniel glanced at her sideways. She was leading everyone in a spirited rendition of "I've Been Working on the Railroad," while she drove the buckboard. There was a spark in her, though, a kind of blazing vitality that drew a man's eye and held his attention.

She surely looked different today in female dress. Although she was on the slim side, that dress made it clear that she had curves in all the right places. Why she wasn't married and raising a brood of children was a mystery. Then again, he concluded ruefully, maybe that strong will of hers had scared off most the eligible young men in Grand Valley.

Tommy was literally jumping up and down by the time they drove onto the main street of Grand Valley. Betsy was beaming, and even Robin was smiling and waving to folks she knew. Nathaniel felt bemused by their excitement. He'd seen and forgotten a hundred small towns like this one. As he looked about at the false-fronted stores lining the street, and the rows of neat cabins and houses on lots behind them, he had to admit to himself that Grand Valley looked to be a tidy and prosperous sort of place.

Robin drove the buckboard straight up to the hitching rail

in front of Johnson's General Store and Dry Goods. A short, slim old woman with snow-white hair and warm brown eyes came bustling up the boardwalk. Her lined face lit up with a wide smile.

"Goodness Robin, this is an unexpected pleasure. I'm glad to see you looking so well. Doctor Peterson told me all about your run-in with those scoundrels. I was planning to drive out tomorrow to see how you were feeling."

Nathaniel had dismounted and was standing by the buckboard, hoping to be excluded from their conversation rather than included. Unfortunately, Robin's manners were too good for that.

"Well, I've saved you the trip. I'm feeling right as rain now. Nathaniel, this is Mrs. Agnes Beacham. She was my teacher in school, and she taught Luke and Jake. She'll be teaching Tommy his letters in another year. Don't let her size or her age fool you. Mrs. Beacham is a woman to be reckoned with, and she's just about an institution in this valley."

Mrs. Beacham stuck out a hand and shook his own heartily. "Doc told me all about you. I'm so glad Robin here has a strong fellow looking out for her interests at last."

Nathaniel sighed inwardly. The way folks around here kept making the wrong assumption, it was probably time for him to set the record straight. "Ma'am it's a pleasure to meet you, too, but the fact is, I'll be moving along just as soon as I'm sure Miss Matthews is all healed up again. I'm a footloose, fiddle-footed sort of fellow, and I've lots of traveling to do before I even think about hanging my hat someplace."

"Really? Now isn't that a shame." The way she cocked her head to the side and eyed him out of curious brown eyes, the old lady reminded him of an inquisitive chickadee. "A likely looking man like you ought to be settled and raising a family of your own by now. You're not married, are you?"

Nathaniel had to give the shrewd old lady credit. She'd worked that question right into the conversation within the first minute of meeting him. Robin still hadn't gotten around to asking him if he was hitched. Then again, he wasn't exactly sure whether or not she cared about the answer.

"No ma'am, I'm not," he got out.

The old woman shot Robin a delighted look. His only consolation was that Robin looked even more exasperated at this overt effort at matchmaking than he felt. "Well, then," Mrs. Beacham said, "we'll just have to do our best to convince you while you're here that Grand Valley is just about the finest place in the whole West to put down roots."

"Mrs. Beacham," Robin said hastily, "I think we'd best get on with our shopping. Tommy is going to wriggle right out of his overalls if we don't let him go take a look at Mr. Johnson's striped candy."

"Of course, my dear. You stop by my house on your way out of town if you have time. Bring your nice young man along with you."

Dumbfounded, Nathaniel looked after the old lady as she sailed down the boardwalk. Surely she needed spectacles. No one had called ex-deputy U.S. Marshal Nathaniel Hollister a nice young man in at least a decade.

Robin patted his arm consolingly. "I know. She leaves you feeling kind of breathless and topsy-turvy. She's a dear woman, though. I don't know what I would have done without her support after my parents died."

Robin took Tommy's hand, who was indeed dancing with impatience by now. Betsy carried little Jessie, and Luke and Jake slipped away to talk with their friends in town. Nathaniel followed Robin into the store, intending to make a few purchases of his own. Within minutes, however, he found himself keeping Tommy out of mischief. Betsy was too entranced with ribbons and bolts of fabric to keep a close rein on him, and Robin was busy picking out little trinkets for everyone in the family.

Nathaniel was quite certain the fishing hooks she selected were for Jake and Luke. The length of blue ribbon had to be for Betsy, because he already knew that blue was her favorite color. If there was anything in that little pile for Robin, he couldn't guess what it would be.

When the storekeeper finished filling the previous customer's order, Robin stepped to the counter and handed him her list.

"I'm sorry, Miss Matthews," Nathaniel overheard the storekeeper say, "but I can't extend you any more credit. You're going to have to start making your purchases elsewhere."

Standing near the corner of the counter where he was trying to keep Tommy from touching every shiny thing in sight, Nathaniel could see Robin's profile. She looked stunned.

"You know we always pay up after we ship some cows in the fall. What's different about this year?" she asked in a faltering voice.

"Right now you owe me more than you've ever owed before, and I've got good reason to believe you won't be able to pay the whole sum."

"If you are referring to my parents' deaths, they've been gone for three years now, and last October and the October before that, I was able to make good our debt to you."

"What happened last year doesn't matter this year," the storekeeper blustered.

"Vance Sutherland's behind this, isn't he?"

"Mr. Sutherland has nothing to do with this. Nobody tells me how to run my business—and it is a business. I can't afford to run it like a charity, and you folks are just too far behind."

That did it. Robin's chin went up, and her green eyes grew frosty. "The Matthewses have never accepted charity from anyone. We will pay our debt to you after we've shipped our cows, and after that, we will take our custom elsewhere. Mr. Johnson, my family helped start this valley, and they've loyally supported every business in this town. You know my parents kept buying from you instead of ordering from Sears, Roebuck whenever they could. This is a sad day for all of us."

By the end of her little speech, Nathaniel almost felt sorry for the storekeeper. His cheeks had grown bright red. Robin turned about on her heel and looked around the store. "Come along, Betsy, we're not staying where we aren't wanted."

With one last wistful glance at the bolt of blue calico she'd been eyeing, Betsy obediently followed her older sister from the store. Nathaniel went, too, practically dragging a reluctant Tommy along with him.

"But I wanted some striped candy." The little boy's eyes filled with tears, and his lower lip trembled. "Robin always buys me some candy when we come to town."

"I know, partner." Nathaniel knelt down beside Tommy once they reached the boardwalk outside the store. "This wasn't Robin's fault. She wanted to buy you the candy, but the storekeeper wouldn't let her."

"Rob'n promised. I want my candy."

Nathaniel looked up at Robin helplessly. She held out her arms, and Tommy flew into them. He buried his face in her skirts, his small shoulders shaking with sobs.

"We don't come to town very often," she said, her green eyes looking suspiciously bright, "and that candy is the high point of Tommy's whole month. I'd like to wring Ray Johnson's neck. I'm sure Sutherland threatened to take his business elsewhere if Johnson continued to give us credit."

Nathaniel nodded and cleared his throat. "I do have some things I need to purchase in there," he said apologetically.

"I know," she said with a sigh, "and it's the only dry goods in town. We'll be over at the feed store. I know we'll still have credit there. Papa helped to save most of Mr. Tuckett's stock when his first livery burned down eight years ago."

Feeling like a Benedict Arnold, Nathaniel went back into the store. He bought a ready-made shirt to replace the one he'd used to bandage Robin's side, pistol and rifle cartridges, coffee for his saddlebags, and some soap. The few times Johnson tried to make conversation, Nathaniel scowled at him, and soon the storekeeper quit his efforts at friendly conversation. As Nathaniel stood at the counter, the candy case drew his eye.

Curtly he told Johnson to add a dozen peppermint sticks to his order.

When he stepped outside the store again, he spotted Robin immediately. Her rig was down by the livery, but she was looking at a saddle in the window of the saddlemaker's shop. Just as he started to stroll toward her, he saw two cowhands swagger up to her. One was tall and thin with a wide handlebar mustache. The shorter one was stocky with a scar on his cheek. They must have said something that offended her, for she quickly turned away from them both. The taller of the two stepped around her so that they both blocked her way up and down the boardwalk.

Robin's chin lifted a fraction higher, and she picked up her skirts to step off the boardwalk into the street. When the short one reached out and grabbed her arm, Nathaniel found himself breaking into a run.

Chapter Eight

Just as Nathaniel reached the place where Robin stood trapped between the two cowboys, he heard the short, stocky one say to Robin, "Why are you in such a hurry, little lady? Why would you want to ride a stock saddle when you could ride me instead?"

The shocked, sick look in Robin's eyes made Nathaniel see red. He grabbed the short one by the shoulder and swung him around. "Take your hands off my boss," he gritted, and then he punched the cowboy in the mouth hard enough to loosen some teeth. The stocky one reeled back, and Nathaniel pivoted just in time to block a wicked roundhouse from the tall one.

He derived a great deal of satisfaction from burying his fist deep in the man's gut. When the cowboy doubled over gasping for air, Nathaniel smashed his mouth with his knee. By then, Shorty wanted back in, and Nathaniel was glad to oblige him. He wanted to make them pay for saying such filthy things to Robin. He wanted to make them hurt for daring to lay a hand on her.

He drove his fists into Shorty's face and body. Within

moments, Shorty was backing away, reluctant to take any more punishment. Nathaniel grabbed him by the collar and landed a final blow on his jaw, which sent Shorty flying off the boardwalk into the dirt. Nathaniel turned around, looking for the tall cowboy. He found him leaning over a nearby water trough, washing his bloody mouth with his kerchief.

"We've had enough," the tall one said sullenly. "Goddamn it, I think you broke two of my teeth. The boss is goin' to hear about this, and he ain't gonna be happy."

"You can tell his sons all about it right now," Robin spoke up, her voice clear and firm.

Rubbing his sore knuckles, Nathaniel glanced away from the whipped cowboys just in time to see two young men come riding down the street. One was well-dressed in a dark gray broadcloth suit. He was slim and slight with mouse-brown hair and intelligent features. The other was much bigger. His eyes were dull and vacant until they focused on Robin. Then a beatific smile lit his face, and he started to wave at her excitedly.

"Hello, Robin," the first one hailed her. "How are you today?" He looked almost as happy and eager to see Robin as the big fellow beside him. Nathaniel leaned back against a hitching rail and watched their interchange with great interest.

"I've been better, Alan," she declared, her hands on her hips and her green eyes snapping with anger. "Two of your father's men just accosted me. If my cousin hadn't stepped in and taught them some manners, I'm not sure how far they would have gone."

Alan's eyes narrowed and he glanced at the two cowboys who were still nursing their wounds. "Shorty, Pete, what happened here?"

"We was just havin' a little fun with her. We didn't mean no harm by it."

"Shorty held my arm, and they both said filthy things to me." Robin jabbed an accusing finger at both men in turn.

Alan's cheeks colored. "I am so sorry. You know, if you'd

just sell out to Pa, this sort of unpleasantness would come to a stop.''

"If you had any backbone, you'd tell your father to make it stop.''

Alan's cheeks grew even redder. "I promise you I'll speak with him, but you know how Pa is.''

"Oh, I know, all right,'' Robin said, a world of bitterness in her tone.

"Hello, Miss Robin,'' the larger young man bobbed his head at her.

"Hello, Buck. How are you today?'' Robin sent him a smile full of such sweetness and warmth, Nathaniel felt himself start to bristle. He'd been shot at, ripped up his shirt to bandage her side, and just risked a beating to help her out, and she'd never smiled at him that way.

"Just fine, I reckon. Pa gave me a new whistle last week.''

"That's just prime, Buck. Maybe you can come by and show it to me sometime.''

"Pa says he don't want me riding out to your place no more,'' Buck said sadly.

"I'm sorry to hear that, Buck. Tommy, Betsy, and little Jessie enjoy your visits.''

"I sure miss them. You say hello to Miss Betsy for me.''

"I will do that.'' After a final smile to Buck, Robin pointedly turned away from Alan and strode toward the livery. Alan sent furious glances at the two cowboys. Nathaniel watched him ride off down the street. He was certain that Sutherland's hands were about to get a talking-to from the boss's son. From the conversation he'd just overheard, he doubted it would do Robin much good.

He followed Robin to the livery stable where Luke and Jake were just starting to load the feed she'd ordered into the back of the buckboard. When she finished talking with a tall, bald smiling man who must be Zachary Tuckett, she came straight over to Nathaniel.

"Thank you for what you did back there. It was nice to see

someone give those Sutherland hands a sound thrashing for a change."

He shrugged off her thanks. "This town must have one sorry excuse for a sheriff if he lets cowboys be so rude to decent womenfolk."

"You've got that just about right," she said dryly. "Ben Campbell doesn't do much of anything except corral drunks and collect fines from them when they've sobered up again. Let me see your hands."

Unwillingly, he held them out. The backs of his hands were skinned, and his knuckles were starting to swell. If he'd known he was about to get into a brawl, he would have had the sense to wear his work gloves. She skimmed the skinned places on his hands with her fingertips, her touch feather-light. He was none too pleased to find that touch had his heart beating faster.

"I'm sorry," she said sincerely. "We can soak them when we get back home tonight. That should keep them from being quite so sore tomorrow."

"Thanks, but my hands will be just fine," he said gruffly. Being the focus of her wide green eyes had a most unsettling effect on him. He dropped his hands and stepped back from her. "I think Alan Sutherland's sweet on you," he said, to change the subject and to test her reaction.

"I know," she said with a sigh and looked away from him. "I suppose it would have been easier for everyone if I could have had the good sense to fall in love with Alan. Then Vance would have had the land he wanted, and my family could have had the protection of the Sutherland name. But as Mama always said, I never do seem to find the easy way to do anything. How could I love a man who will always stand in his father's shadow? I don't think Alan's stood up to his father once in his entire life."

"Plenty of womenfolk get married out West without loving the man who proposed to them."

"That's true enough, but I've always hoped to marry for love. My parents eloped because they were head over heels for each other, and they were one of the happiest couples I've ever seen. At the very least, I'd want to respect the man I married, and I could never respect Alan.''

It figured she had a head full of romantic notions about love and marriage. Nathaniel almost groaned aloud. He had to admit, however, Robin had a point about Alan Sutherland. A decent marriage did have to be based on respect. His own parents hadn't loved each other after their first flash of passion bound them together, but they had respected each other's strengths, which is how they managed to survive being married to each other. Robin was probably right not to encourage Alan Sutherland.

Nathaniel frowned when he saw Robin rub her injured side as if it pained her. Then again, her life certainly would be a great deal easier, and safer, if she did make a play for Sutherland's son. Yet somehow the notion of Robin Matthews hitched to that lily-livered milquetoast he'd just seen didn't set well with him, either. He wondered what had happened to Sutherland's other son, the one Robin had called Buck. Had he been born slow-witted, or had some accident happened to make him that way?

Before Nathaniel could ask Robin that, Tuckett called out a question about her order, and she turned away. When they finished loading up the feed, Robin and the rest headed out to Mrs. Beacham's house for tea. Nathaniel stayed behind at the livery because Old Blue had a loose shoe. There, he enjoyed talking with the blacksmith, Lionel Brigham. A big, quiet man with a way with animals, Lionel was an ex-slave who worked for Tuckett. An hour later, Nathaniel rode out to Mrs. Beacham's house where he found Robin and her family just taking their leave.

Mrs. Beacham beamed at him as he rode up. ''Here, Mr. Dawson, I made up this parcel of gingersnaps and sugar cookies for you. Betsy told me she suspects you have a sweet tooth, and this might make up for the fact that you couldn't join us.''

Nathaniel stared down at the parcel, amazed that the old

lady had made such an effort just for him. "Why, thank you, ma'am," he said at last. "I have to say I'm particularly partial to gingersnaps."

"I'm so glad." She lowered her voice when she saw Robin was helping Tommy up on the buckboard. "Robin told me what you just did in town. It's about time someone took those Rafter S riders down a peg or two. Those boys are getting entirely too big for their britches. I'd like to take a paddle to them myself."

He could well believe it, looking down at the old school-teacher with the martial glint in her brown eyes. He was quite certain this formidable lady kept firm control of her students when school was in. Soon, the Matthews clan was loaded on the buckboard, and they headed back toward the Rocking M.

When the road was wide enough for Nathaniel to ride beside the buckboard, Robin said little to him. Her expression was distant and pensive. He guessed she was wrestling with the problem of where she was going to purchase her supplies and how she was going to pay for them.

Tommy and Jessie quickly fell fast asleep. When he saw they had nodded off lying on an old quilt, Nathaniel told Robin in a quiet voice, "I bought them some candy back at the dry goods."

He wasn't quite sure how she'd take that news after her recent run-in with Ray Johnson. Instead of being upset, her face lit up. She smiled that lethally sweet smile of hers. "You did? That's wonderful. I'm so grateful. I have so few ways I can spoil them. Tommy will be beside himself."

He found he couldn't take his gaze away from her. He'd have to remember this from now on. One sure way to trick a smile out of her was to give a gift to those kids she cared about so much. Nathaniel straightened up and looked away from her, appalled by the track his thoughts had just taken. Why the hell did he care whether or not a nineteen-year-old girl who preferred wearing jeans to petticoats smiled at him? If he didn't watch it, he was going to develop a real case on her.

The idea was so foreign to him that it almost sent shivers down his spine. Nathaniel Hollister didn't take a shine to women. They always took a shine to him, and that's the way he wanted it.

Caught up in their own thoughts, Nathaniel and Robin said little for the remainder of the drive home. Back at the house, Robin and Betsy rustled up a cold supper of bread, cheese, and ham while Jake, Luke, and Nathaniel went out to do their last chores of the day. After everyone ate, Nathaniel quietly handed Tommy the bag of peppermint sticks he'd bought in town. He got a big kick out of the way the boy's eyes grew large as saucers.

"These are all for me?"

"Well, I thought it might be nice if you shared a stick or two with your little sister."

"I can do that," Tommy said, looking heroic. He reached down into the bag and handed one to Jessie. He handed a second stick solemnly to Nathaniel. "Nathn'l, you gotta have one, too."

"Okay, partner," Nathaniel said, trying to keep a straight face. "Let's go out on the porch and eat some before you have to get ready for bed." They went out on the porch and had a long talk about the best kinds of candy in the world.

The young folk went to bed early, tired out by their exciting day in town. Nathaniel went to the bunkhouse intending to do the same, but he soon discovered he was too restless to sleep. He decided to take a walk along the river. When he left the bunkhouse, he was surprised to see there was still a light burning in the study. Surely Robin had gone to bed with the rest. She had to be more tired than anyone.

When he prowled closer to the house, however, he discovered Robin indeed was still up. She sat at the oak rolltop desk in the study, staring at a ledger book.

Nathaniel swore softly under his breath as he watched her through the window, familiar frustration rising inside him. Why didn't she have the sense to look after herself properly? After making a trip to town she never should have taken in the first place, she should have headed straight to bed. Instead, here she was, wrestling with ranch accounts. She was probably trying to figure out some way to pay for those supplies they needed for the winter—something she could have easily tackled tomorrow morning when she was better rested.

He headed for the front door. He was hardly surprised to find it unlocked. With all the trouble she'd had with Dyer and Sutherland, she ought to be more careful. He walked quietly into the front hall and stood there watching her. Perhaps she had tried to sleep, for she wore an old blue dressing gown, and she'd taken her hair down and left it in a thick braid hanging down her back.

All at once, she must have sensed his presence, for she twisted about in her chair and her hand went to her throat. "Oh, it's you. I think you just scared ten years off my life. Why are you still up?"

"That's a question I was planning to ask you. You should be sound asleep."

"I tried to go to bed," she admitted, "but I couldn't sleep until I figured out how to feed my family. We're almost out of flour, beans, sugar, and just about everything else."

He'd been right about her worrying about their supplies. "You mentioned to Johnson that you usually sell some cows off in the fall."

"That's right. Normally, I'd be heading to Kansas by now with one of the twins and forty or fifty head. Thanks to Dyer's little stunt, I had to put that trip back. We'll probably head out next week."

That's just what she needed. After getting shot in the side, ten days of hard riding through all sorts of weather was apt to give her pneumonia or worse. "What if one of the boys and I drove some cows up to Colorado Springs?" he found himself saying. "I rode through there just a few weeks ago, and they had some stock buyers happy to purchase anything that had four feet and horns. Beef is selling better than ever up in the mountains with the silver boom on. With the money we get, we can buy the supplies you need and haul them back here.''

''I thought you said you hated cows,'' she said, looking as if she were trying to figure him out.

''I do,'' he replied shortly. ''Spending two or three days driving those stupid, stinking animals along a trail is just about my idea of hell. I can't ride out of here, though, knowing I left a house full of children short on grub. I'll do this last thing for you folks, and then I'll light a shuck.''

''Agreed,'' she said suddenly. ''Now, I want you to come to the kitchen with me, and we'll do something about those hands of yours. If you let me soak them, I'll even give you a slice of that apple pie Betsy baked yesterday.''

He looked down at his hands. Unconsciously, he'd been rubbing his sore knuckles. ''My hands will be fine.''

Already she'd gotten to her feet and walked toward the kitchen, obviously assuming he'd follow her. Unwillingly, he did exactly that. *If you know what's good for you, Hollister, you'll head right back out to that bunkhouse. You shouldn't be spending any more time with her than you absolutely have to. And you sure as hell shouldn't be spending any time with her when the two of you are alone.*

Telling himself it was the pie he wanted, not more of her company, he went into the kitchen and sat down in the chair she pulled out. First she brought a nice big slice of that pie she had promised him.

''I'm trusting you to be a gentleman about this,'' she said teasingly before she handed him a fork.

He forced himself to look up from her pretty pink lips to meet her gaze. He wasn't exactly feeling gentlemanly right now. It was the damnedest thing. Every time she stood close to him, his body went haywire.

''If you eat this pie, you have to let your hands soak for a good twenty minutes. You can keep track by our steeple clock.''

''All right,'' he said, wondering where she got the gumption to tease him the way she did. Usually he scared the hell out of proper young ladies.

"What a man will do for a piece of pie," she said, laughingly shaking her head, and went to the pantry to fix her remedy. The moment he finished the last bite of pie, she swept the plate away and plonked a ceramic bowl full of a frothy white liquid down in front of him.

"Do I want to know what's in here?" He eyed her concoction skeptically.

"Probably not, but it works," she told him with a serene smile. "I've made it plenty of times for Jake. Because he inherited our father's quick temper, he's gotten into more than his fair share of fights at school. He actually asks me to make it for him now after he's been in a scuffle."

If it was good enough for a fourteen-year-old hothead, he supposed it might do something for him. Besides, he couldn't just get up and walk away when she was watching him so earnestly. Gingerly, he placed his hands in the bowl. After a few moments, he had to admit the warm liquid did feel good on his sore hands. She sat across the table from him and started to mend one of the boy's shirts.

He thought she'd plague him with chatter, but instead, she sat quietly and concentrated on her sewing. After a time, he leaned back in his chair and relaxed, enjoying the comfortable silence. A part of him took surprising pleasure from the entire scene—the house hushed and dark around them, the fire settling in the warm stove, light from the lamp casting a golden halo about the cozy room. He admired the arrangement the girls had made for the table from golden aspen and late-blooming lavender asters.

He supposed this was the part of life he'd missed during the past fifteen years of hunting down outlaws while his friends back home got hitched one after the other. He'd always congratulated himself on being clever enough to escape the marriage noose. Now, after all he'd been through this past year, he was beginning to wonder if his friends back in Buford weren't the clever ones. They had families and homes and good, satisfying work—accomplishments they could point to for their years of consistent endeavor.

He had absolutely nothing to show for the last fifteen years of his life. For a long time he thought in his own way he was making the West a more lawful, peaceful place for families like the Matthewses. Now he knew an individual man couldn't make a bit of difference, and he'd been damned foolish to think otherwise.

The familiar bitterness rose inside him in a choking wave. He looked at Robin's calm face, and somehow the bitterness began to ebb. A small frown creased her forehead as she concentrated. He was tempted to reach across the table and try to smooth that frown away. Knowing such an action would probably startle her and land them both in trouble, he kept his hands right in that bowl.

For a time he simply watched Robin sew in quick, mesmerizingly efficient movements. Her hands were small, well formed, and so very capable. As he stared at them, he began to wonder what it would feel like if she touched him, really touched him in the way a woman touched her man.

The moment the idea occurred to him, he couldn't seem to think about anything else. His body grew heated and full. He stared at her, drinking in the little details of her appearance. He liked the way small tendrils of hair always escaped her braids and buns and wisped about her temples. He admired the way she filled out that soft dressing gown she wore. He'd been with women on the row who wore flashy scarlet dressing gowns and sexy striped tights. Robin Matthews, in a faded old wrapper and worn slippers, seemed a hundred times more appealing.

Hollister, you are one sorry excuse for a human being. What are you doin', comparing this little gal to whores on the row? Just because you want her doesn't mean you can have her, or that you have any right to think about her this way.

"You don't need to stay up," he got out gruffly. "I promise I'll soak my hands for the full time without you keeping watch."

"I know I don't, but I will until you've finished your twenty minutes just the same."

The last five minutes seemed to drag by forever. He made himself look at the clock, the stove, the floor, the aspen leaves on the table, anywhere but her. At last the long hand slid to six on the old steeple clock, and she smiled at him approvingly.

"There, that wasn't so bad, was it?"

The soaking part wasn't so bad. It was keeping my hands in this damned bowl and off of you these past five minutes which was the hard part. He pulled his hands out of the bowl. Still smiling, Robin bustled over to a drawer and brought him a clean rag to dry them.

Wiping his hands, he stood up quickly. To hell with his good intentions. He couldn't resist her a moment longer. He simply had to taste those lips he'd been looking at for days now. Before she could step away, he reached out and placed both hands on her shoulders.

She glanced up at him, her sea-green eyes wide and startled. Ignoring the hundred and one damn good reasons why he shouldn't do it, he bent his head and kissed her.

Chapter Nine

Robin was so stunned at first, she didn't know what to think. She could only react and feel. His hands on her shoulders were warm and pleasantly heavy. His lips were surprisingly soft. The feel of them against her own was just heavenly. She thought standing this close to him, having him touch her like this might make her panic, but he did nothing to frighten her. For such a hard man, she was amazed he could be so gentle. He coaxed and smoothed his lips over hers, cajoling a response from her.

He tasted like apple pie. He smelled like the world out-of-doors—fresh, clean, and wild. Hesitantly, she kissed him back. She wondered if her relative inexperience showed. Somehow she had a feeling Nathaniel Dawson had kissed plenty of women in his time. Deciding she ought to do something bold, she reached her hands up and placed them on the top of his shoulders. She discovered instantly that they were hard and broad, the material of his worn shirt soft beneath her fingers. He was so big and male and vital, he made her head swim.

His lips left hers. She stood absolutely still as he kissed her cheekbones, her eyebrows, the line of her jaw. It was the most wonderful sensation. When he kissed the skin beneath the base of her ear, he sent little shivers racing down her spine. She could feel the roughness of the stubble on his cheek against her own, and she gloried in the sensation.

When she was fourteen, she had let Joey Parkins kiss her behind the outhouse at school, and it had been a thoroughly disappointing experience. His lips had been wet and the wispy excuse of a mustache he'd been trying to grow had made her sneeze. Nathaniel was a mature man, the kind of man women noticed and set their caps for, and he kissed in a sure, exciting way which made her body respond to him down to her toes.

One of his hands slipped to the small of her back and urged her closer. She found herself breathing harder as their bodies touched. When her breasts brushed against his chest, she tingled all over. A strange, intense curl of pleasure began someplace below her stomach when she felt the hardness of his legs pressing against hers. Dreamily, she realized how dark and quiet the house was. They could be the only two people awake in the world right now.

His lips returned to claim her own, and she kissed him back boldly. He must have liked the enthusiasm of her response, for he groaned deep in his throat. His arms tightened about her and his kiss became more forceful.

All of a sudden, she didn't feel dreamy or comfortable any more. She felt trapped within the hard prison of his arms. She stepped back from him abruptly. After an infinitely long moment, he let her go.

She was shocked to discover her breath was coming in ragged gasps. She drew some consolation from the fact he seemed to be breathing hard, too. His eyes were dark, and his black brows were drawn together in a scowl. They stared at each other, struggling to come to terms with the startling thing that had just happened between them.

"I reckon you were right to cut that off. This was a damn stupid thing for us to do." With that singularly romantic comment, he turned on his heel and left the kitchen. She heard him open the front door and close it behind him a moment later.

She stood there for a long time, wondering if she would ever be able to move again. Her body felt so strange. Her limbs felt heavy, and her nerves still hummed. She reached a hand up and traced her lips wonderingly.

So this is what it feels like to be kissed. I'm glad my first real kiss came from someone who's good at it. I'm glad it came from him.

Eventually she realized how long she'd been standing there. She'd be totally mortified if Nathaniel looked in the window and saw her mooning over his kiss. Quickly, she picked up the lamp and fled to her room. She shut the door and leaned against it. When her heart returned to somewhere near its usual pace, she walked over to the mirror on her mother's dresser and peered at her reflection.

She didn't look like herself at all. Her eyes were big and dreamy, her cheeks flushed. For a moment, she almost convinced herself that she looked pretty. Then she spotted the freckles on her nose, the way the sun had tanned her skin a most uncomplimentary shade of brown, and the thinness of her cheeks.

For the life of her, she couldn't see why Nathaniel Dawson would want to kiss her. What could he possibly find appealing about a young woman who wore jeans and worked a ranch like a man? She didn't mind the notion that Nathaniel wanted to kiss her. At least, she didn't think she minded. Over the past few days when she'd been resting in her room, she'd had far too much time to reflect. During some of that time, she couldn't help wondering what it would be like to be his woman. To be the one he cared about would be amazing and frightening and wonderful. Glumly Robin turned away from the mirror. She had as much chance of getting a man like him to care about her as she did getting Vance Sutherland to leave her ranch alone.

For her first real grown-up kiss, though, that had been mighty fine. It had been better than fine. *You best keep your head about this, Robin Matthews. A kiss that was just plain spectacular for you probably didn't mean much of anything to him. Maybe he was just trying to express his gratitude for making his hands feel better.*

Deciding that had to be the reason for his inexplicable behavior, Robin finally got ready for bed. It took her a long time to fall asleep that night. She kept remembering the feel of his lips on hers, and the heady sensation of being held by him. Before she'd panicked, being kissed by Nathaniel was just about the nicest thing that had happened to her in a long, long time.

The next morning when Robin went to the kitchen for breakfast, Nathaniel greeted her politely as always. It was as if the wonderful kiss they'd shared the night before had never happened. She searched his face carefully as they all sat down to a fine batch of flapjacks that Betsy had cooked up. Nathaniel's cool, controlled expression convinced her that she'd been right last night. What had moved heaven and earth for her really didn't mean much at all to him.

Although that conclusion made her feel wistful, Robin couldn't stay glum for long. It was a beautiful, sunny fall day. Her side hurt less, and she was feeling a great deal stronger. Best of all, Nathaniel had lifted her most immediate and pressing burden from her shoulders. With his help, soon her family would have supplies to see them through the fall and winter.

Throughout breakfast they talked about the drive to Colorado Springs. Jake and Luke were cock-a-whoop over the prospect of a trip to a big town. Robin still couldn't quite get used to seeing large, formidable Nathaniel at her kitchen table. She was amused to see Tommy had insisted on sitting next to him. Every time Tommy spoke to him, which was frequently, Nathaniel listened politely. Jessie constantly smiled and waved at Nathaniel, trying to catch his attention. Once, she could have sworn she caught Nathaniel making a funny face back at her.

"I thought I'd take one of the boys with me today and cull some steers for the trip," Nathaniel told Robin toward the end of the meal. "The other one can stay here and start putting together the gear and food we'll need."

"All right," Robin nodded. "I'll ride out with you and look them over. I want to send along a dozen cows who were barren this spring."

He sent her a glacial frown she guessed probably froze most folk in their tracks. She was starting to look beyond his cool, tough exterior. She realized his glower mostly came from his concern for her.

"I promise I'll just ride out and take a quick look at the cattle. Then I'll ride right back here and laze around the rest of the day."

"Somehow I doubt you'll do that," he said with a resigned shake of his head, "but at least I can make sure you don't spend the day hazing cows."

She had to give the man credit. When Nathaniel Dawson made up his mind to do something, he went out and got it done—even if it meant working cows. By late afternoon, he'd cut out a hundred head and left them grazing in the home pasture. After supper, she walked out to the barn with him to look over the food and equipment Jake and Betsy had spent the day laying out.

"It looks like they did a good job," he announced after looking through the gear and sacks of food stacked neatly on a large oilcloth.

"I've noticed you like your coffee, so I'm sending the last we have along with you. We're light on flour and cornmeal, though," Robin told him apologetically. "In fact, we're light on just about everything."

"That's all right. We won't go hungry. We'll probably have a chance to take a shot at something, or do some fishing along the way." He turned away from the food, crossed his arms, and looked at her. Once again, she caught herself admiring his eyes. They were the most remarkable color of blue. It was the same rich royal blue of her grandmother's willowware platter. *There should be a law against a man having eyes that devastating a color,* she thought ruefully.

"You know, I need to take both boys," he said slowly. "I need one to drive the buckboard to carry the supplies home, and one to drive the cows with me—unless you want me to try hiring a man in town."

"I know," she admitted. "I've been thinking the same thing. Unfortunately, you won't be able to get anyone to hire on, even for just a few days. Rick Dyer's done too good a job of roughing up men who try to work for me. I know we'll do just fine without the boys. I figure you'll probably be gone six days at the most. We should be able to handle things here just fine. Betsy's a good little rider, and I shoot better than most men."

He uncrossed his arms and placed his hands on his hips. "I don't want you riding anywhere while I'm gone, much less shooting a gun. If you run into any trouble with Sutherland or that Dyer, I want you to promise me that you'll take the little ones straight into town and stay with your friend Mrs. Beacham."

She returned his level stare. "I appreciate all you've done for us, but I don't know where you got the idea that you can order me around. I'm the boss of this outfit, and I'll do as I see fit."

"Hell." He threw up his hands and stalked away from her. "You don't have the sense God gave a flea, do you?" he asked.

Robin squared her shoulders and told herself she wasn't intimidated by the anger radiating from him. Surely all this fury wasn't really directed at her. Nathaniel Dawson was an angry man. She doubted that she would ever get to know him well enough to know what trouble rode him so hard.

"I've been holding off the Sutherlands for three years and doing a pretty good job of it," she told him firmly. "I'm hardly going to turn tail and run at the first sign of trouble because you tell me to."

"You owe it to the little ones to take them out of harm's way."

"Of course I do," she replied indignantly. "At the same time, I'm not leaving my home unless I have to. It's their home, too. If we leave it, we're apt to find it burned to the ground just the way the Abbotts did when they left their place overnight. I don't know how I can keep my family together if I don't have a place for them to live."

"At least they would be alive. They won't be if they catch a bullet, or Dyer's men decide to burn this place down around your ears. You think on that." He stamped out of the barn and headed toward the bunkhouse.

She looked after him sadly. Why did their talks have to escalate into arguments quite so often? For a time they had been talking together peacefully, like most folk managed to do. She had enjoyed that. With a sigh, Robin went to work packing up the gear and food spread out before her.

Vance Sutherland strode down to the horse barn. He had to ride to town to talk with Floyd Haskins at the bank and to send two telegrams to Denver. He curbed the old feelings of frustration, impatience, and guilt when he realized Buck had fallen behind him. He looked back over his shoulder. Buck had stopped to stare at a blue jay perched on a nearby fence post.

"Come on, boy, we don't have all day."

"Pretty," Buck told him with a wide smile. "Pretty bird."

Vance's breath caught. When Buck smiled like that, unusual animation lighting his dark brown eyes, he looked so much like his mother. Jenna used to smile that way, too, before Buck's accident, and before she lost five babies in childbirth. If only he'd stayed away from her. Trying to bring that sixth doomed baby into the world had been too much for Jenna. How he missed that woman. They'd made a good team back in the old days.

Wondering at his sudden sentimental mood, Vance continued

on toward the barn. "Catch up my sorrel for me, would you, Pete? And catch Blackie for Buck," he called out to the tall cowboy loitering by the horse corral.

"Sure thing, boss," Pete replied and quickly turned away. A few minutes later when Pete led up the sorrel, Vance noticed his swollen lips. Dammit, he didn't like the men brawling amongst themselves. It wasn't good for morale. He'd have to speak to Rick about this. Since he'd let his bastard whelp start working as his foreman, the boy'd been running a pretty tight ship.

He sure as hell did a better job running the ranch than Alan ever had. Vance sighed when he thought of his spineless younger son. Just last night, Alan had been after him again to ease up on the Rocking M. Alan just didn't have the vision or the ambition to understand what was at stake here.

"What the hell happened to you?" Vance asked Pete as he checked over his saddle and cinch.

"I got into a little scrape in town."

Rick Dyer walked up. "Fact is, Robin Matthews has a cousin staying with her now, and he had a run in with both Pete and Shorty in town yesterday."

"He better have ended up looking worse than Pete here."

"Supposedly he just walked away without a scratch on him."

Vance let go a string of oaths and turned on Rick. "I thought you were pushing the Rocking M hard these days. You said Robin Matthews didn't have any hands working for her anymore."

"We've made damn sure no one will work for her. This fellow's her kin."

"Who is he, anyway?"

"Robin claims he's just some sodbuster from Nebraska."

"And he whipped both Shorty and Pete? Hell, the last thing we need is a stubborn farmer out on the Rocking M who thinks he knows how to fight." Vance was quiet for a moment while he considered the situation. Given time, he knew Rick could handle a farmer, and Robin Matthews for that matter. The boy knew how to play rough when the game called for it.

"All right, Rick. For the moment, I'm going to leave this mess for you to handle. I told you before—I want Robin Matthews and all her kin off that ranch by next spring. It's up to you how to make that happen."

"Yes, sir. I already have a couple of plans in mind. I reckon we'll be paying her a visit sometime in the next few days," Rick said coolly, but he couldn't quite hide the eager look in his eyes. Vance looked away, trying to ignore the sudden feelings of unease and repugnance that often assailed him in Rick's presence. It was one thing to play rough, and another thing entirely for a man to enjoy doing it.

"Can I go see Robin, too?" Buck asked eagerly.

"No, son," Vance said with a sigh. "We've talked about this before. I don't want you riding out to see those girls anymore."

"I miss Robin. She's my friend."

"She's not your friend, and you're to stay away from her." Ignoring Buck's crestfallen expression, Vance swung into the saddle. After Pete helped Buck get settled on Blackie, Vance headed for town. He glanced back over his shoulder. He couldn't help smiling when he looked at his imposing ranch house and outbuildings. Yes sir, Jenna would have been proud of him. He'd built the foundation to an empire here, one that would last, one that was destined to keep growing. The Sutherland name would go down as a great one in American history.

Grand Valley was the cornerstone to his empire. Owning it all was the crucial first step. A stubborn young woman foolish enough to think she could run a ranch wasn't going to stand in his way.

Chapter Ten

BOOM! went the second barrel of the old Parker shotgun. Nathaniel looked on with approval as the grouse fell to the ground. Jake had led the bird well with his gun and downed it with his second shell.

"That will make for some good eating." He grinned at his tired young trail partners. All three of them were dusty and bone weary from the trip to Colorado Springs. They'd gotten a good price for their cows, and the buckboard was loaded down with all the supplies Robin had asked him to buy—plus a few surprises thrown in.

"I'll say. Just wait till you see the way Betsy cooks this up," Jake said in the reverent way only a teenage boy can talk about food.

Just then a second grouse broke cover from almost under Old Blue's feet. The steeldust tossed his head and snorted, but he was too tired from six days of constant riding to put up much of a fuss. All that talk about roasted grouse had gotten Nathaniel's stomach juices flowing. Without thinking, he slipped the leather thong from his pistol and palmed it. He brought the bird down with a single shot.

Luke and Jake exchanged surprised glances.

"No, I don't usually shoot game with my pistol," he told them irritably. "That bird was so close, he was almost under my feet."

"You sure got that gun out fast," Luke said, his eyes still wide.

"Hunger has a way of sharpening a man's reflexes," Nathaniel said abruptly and dismounted to fetch the grouse. He tied the bird to the back of the wagon.

When he climbed back into the saddle, he glanced toward the mountains. Surely they only had another hour to go before they reached the Rocking M. A part of him itched to ride off and leave the slow-moving buckboard behind.

He wanted to make sure Robin and the little ones were all right. He'd worried about them every day of the trip, which had made him irritable, because Robin Matthews and the children she had collected were really none of his business. Once he brought these supplies to the ranch, he figured whatever debt he owed for letting her get shot was well and truly paid.

Fortunately for Nathaniel's limited patience, Ned and Nod, Robin's team of draft horses, sensed they were finally nearing home and picked up the pace.

At last the weary travelers reached the dirt track that led to the house. As they started up it, Nathaniel spotted Robin waiting for them on the porch. That gold hair of hers gleamed in the late afternoon sun, brighter than any aspen tree. Tommy stood beside her, waving for all he was worth. Betsy was standing next to Robin, holding little Jessie in her arms. As he looked at the solid ranch house, Nathaniel sighed. He couldn't remember the last time anyone had waited or watched for him to come back from a trip. Hell, he hadn't really had a home in fifteen years.

You watch it, boy. You're getting just plain sentimental in your old age. You don't have anyone watching for you, or cooking for you, but you also don't have anyone nagging at you or expecting you to do things her way. You can come and go as you please, and that's the way you like it.

As they drew closer, Tommy obviously couldn't contain himself any longer. He leaped from the porch and came racing down the lane toward them. "Hey, Nathn'l, you're back! Hey, Jake! Hey, Luke!"

Without really thinking about it, Nathaniel reached down to the beaming boy and gave him a hand up. Tommy's wide smile grew even wider as he settled himself in front of Nathaniel and looked around from his new perch on the pommel of Old Blue's saddle.

"So how'd you all do while we were gone?" Nathaniel asked him.

Tommy turned about in the saddle and looked at him solemnly while he recited his news. "Well, Jessie tried to catch the rooster by the tail and he pecked her and she cried. A bird came down the chimney. He flewed all over the house and Robin had to catch him in a coat. And two of her bulls got shot dead."

Nathaniel stiffened and glanced around the ranch outbuildings. If Sutherland's hands had done any other damage to her place, he couldn't see it.

Robin came down from the porch as he dismounted. She smiled at him, but her eyes looked strained.

"Tell me what happened to the bulls."

She glanced at Tommy ruefully. "I should have known he'd tell you. I was hoping we could wait until we'd all had a good supper. Someone came on to our range last night and shot my two best breeding bulls. We heard the shots, but by the time I could get out to investigate, the men were gone."

"You mean to tell me you went riding out after Sutherland's men in the dark by yourself?" He felt the same helpless rage build in him again. When would he ever be able to get her to take more care?

"Indeed I did, since Jessie doesn't ride, and Tommy's a wee

bit small to be carrying a rifle," she smiled at him brightly. "If you're going to give me another lecture, maybe you could do it after supper. Betsy's got a fine meal on. By the way, it's nice to see you, too, and how was your trip?"

"If you don't beat all, girl," he said, charmed by the spirit in her smile even though he damn well didn't want to be. In fact, as he looked at her, a part of him was tempted to sweep her into his arms and steal a good long kiss. Even though she was wearing her male work clothes again, she looked pretty and fresh. The fact he wore a good deal of trail dirt and smelled like sweat, cow, and horse kept him from giving into temptation.

"My father often told me the very same thing," Robin laughed at him. "Now, let's get these supplies unloaded and you dusty fellows washed up, and then you can tell us all about your adventures while we eat."

As he stared at her smiling face, he decided he was too tired to have a row with her now. He was just happy she was all right. They all pitched in, including Jessie and Tommy. Despite the little ones getting in the way, soon the supplies were unloaded and put away. Nathaniel went off to the bunkhouse to wash. There he was pleased to find that all the clothes he'd left behind had been laundered. Wearing a shirt that smelled suspiciously like lavender, he walked down to the ranch house carrying the parcel of odds and ends he'd bought for the various members of the Matthews clan. Remembering what a commotion Tommy had raised over the candy, he slipped his parcel behind a table in the parlor and decided to tell Robin about it later.

Supper that night was truly a feast. Betsy had really pulled out all the stops. She'd fixed a roast with potatoes and carrots from her garden. Each bite was a treat for Nathaniel after getting by on trail fare for almost a week. He was surprised to learn the roast had come from one of the recently departed bulls.

"I couldn't let all that fresh beef go to waste," Betsy admitted, "but we weren't strong enough by ourselves to hang the meat properly. We just took some of the best cuts and left the rest to the coyotes.''

Nathaniel stared at Robin and Betsy. He'd slaughtered enough deer and elk in his time to know how hard the girls must have worked. Was there nothing these Matthews females wouldn't do on their own?

Betsy looked proud of their accomplishment, but Robin appeared to be embarrassed by it and soon changed the topic. ''Tell us more about your trip. I've read in the papers that Colorado Springs is becoming a very posh sort of town, with lots of Europeans coming to take the cure.''

''It's definitely grown a great deal since the first time I rode through there ten years ago.''

''Did you see any of those fancy hotels or the fancy people who stay there?'' Robin asked dreamily.

He looked at her in some surprise. Did she long for a different way of life? She seemed so fiercely determined to hold on to the Rocking M, he had assumed the ranching life was all she wanted for herself.

''We rode down a street right past several of them.''

''Did you see any of the ladies staying there? How were they dressed?'' Betsy asked eagerly.

He looked helplessly at the twins. They just shrugged their shoulders and shook their heads.

''Don't expect them to help you. Luke and Jake wouldn't notice what a lady was wearing unless she had a horse on her head,'' Robin said with chuckle.

''Well, I guess they were wearing big hats with lots of feathers, birds, flowers, fruit, and such.'' The enraptured look on the girls' faces encouraged him to continue. ''Those bustle contraptions women wear these days looked bigger than ever. There were lots of gents in dark suits with those fancy top hats walking about, too.''

''It sounds wonderful. How I'd like to see it.'' Robin sighed.

''Haven't you ever been to Colorado Springs?'' he asked her curiously.

"We went once when I was younger, but I haven't been away from Grand Valley for almost four years now. Don't get me wrong. I like it fine here, and I'd be happy to live out my days here on the Rocking M. I would just like a chance to get away and see city sights and city lights from time to time."

She'd have that chance if she'd give up her foolish notion of running this ranch on her own, but Nathaniel kept that thought to himself for the moment. It had been a pleasant meal, and he was in no mood to spoil it by provoking Robin right now.

After stuffing himself with two slices of rhubarb cobbler, Nathaniel wandered down to the bunkhouse. Yes sir, that meal had been something, and tomorrow night, he could look forward to Betsy's roasted grouse. Based on Jake's description, he gathered that meal promised to be another treat.

Except that you were planning to leave tomorrow. That realization brought him up short. Of course he meant to ride on soon, but did he really have to ride on tomorrow? It'd be rough on Old Blue after the long trip they'd just made. Besides, he needed a day to reorganize his gear and get some good travel grub packed up. Certainly the day after tomorrow would be soon enough. He'd a hankering to ride over toward Ouray and Telluride and take a look at the San Juans, which were some of the wildest, most sheer mountains in the state.

He wanted to turn in, but he was too full from the supper he'd just eaten to rest well. He decided to take a walk along the river to let his supper settle a little more. When he walked outside, he glanced toward the ranch house and spotted Robin sitting in a rocker on the front porch. Before he took his walk, this was a good chance to tell her about the things he'd bought in Colorado Springs for her family. *Of course, you aren't walking up to the house just because you want to talk with her.*

Still, as he drew closer, he had to appreciate the picture she made. She'd wrapped herself up in a big woolen blanket, for the night was frosty. Her braid fell over her right shoulder. She was looking off dreamily toward the mountains. He wondered if she was imagining herself walking down the streets of Colorado Springs, exchanging nods with countesses and earls.

He hated to break in on her dreaming, but he didn't want to stand there all night, and she looked like she might be building castles in the air for a good while longer.

"Robin—"

She started visibly at the sound of his voice and twisted about in her chair to face him. The frightened look in her eyes pained him. A girl her age should be able to sit on her porch without being scared.

"You do walk quietly," she said, smiling in a gallant effort to hide her fright. "You'd think I'd be used to that by now."

"I'm sorry I startled you. I just wanted to tell you that I picked up a few things for everyone in the Springs. I left the package in the parlor."

"You bought us all presents?"

"I wouldn't call them presents, exactly. I just picked up a few things I thought you and the others might like . . ."

She was already out of her chair and heading for the parlor. She came back moments later clutching the parcel he had hidden. She turned up the lantern she had hung on a nearby nail. After she sat down in the rocking chair, she swiftly opened the package. She exclaimed as she started to explore its contents.

"You don't need to go through it all now," he said, wishing he had never bought a single thing in Colorado Springs. He hated giving or getting presents. His mother had stolen all the joy from such simple rituals long ago.

Nathaniel, dearest, I bought you that penknife you've been wanting. Don't you like it? Nathaniel, I spent weeks making that jacket for you, and you never wear it. Old feelings of guilt and claustrophobia started to rise in him like a choking wave. He slammed shut the door on his memories of a needy mother he had constantly disappointed. Instead, he looked at the innocent young woman smiling delightedly over the trinkets he'd bought on a whim, and some of the tension inside him eased.

"But if I don't go through these, how will I know whom to give them to?" she asked him reasonably.

"I think it's pretty obvious."

"Let me be sure," she said blithely, "and then I'll put them away. Oh, this must be for Betsy," she said, holding up a length of ribbon the same color as Betsy's eyes. "It will go perfectly with her best dress. I'm guessing these fishhooks must be for Luke, and this penknife for Jake, our ardent whittler. Tommy will go wild when he sees this top, and this pretty ball must be for Jessie. If it keeps her out of mischief for an hour or two tomorrow, you'll have all our gratitude."

She put the ball back into the parcel and looked at him curiously. "You certainly figured out my family in a short period of time. You must be a good observer."

She was right about that. In his old line of work, that trait had been essential. Uncomfortable with her praise, he decided to change the subject. "There's one more there in the bottom someplace," he said unwillingly. "I got something for you, too."

"You did?" She glanced up at him, looking both surprised and pleased. "Goodness, you certainly didn't need to do that," she declared, but she began rummaging eagerly through the pile again.

"Here," she said triumphantly and held up two hair combs to the light so that she could see them better. "Why, they're lovely." She stroked the tortoiseshell hair combs with her fingertips. "Look at the mother of pearl inlay on these." After she had examined them for several moments, she shook her head sadly. "They are much too fine for me. I'm not sure when I'd ever wear them, and I'd be most apt to lose them if I did."

"I'm not riding all the way back to Colorado Springs to return them," he said with some exasperation.

"You should give them to your sweetheart someday," she said firmly and held them out to him.

He stared down at the combs. He'd never had a sweetheart.

Men like him didn't have sweethearts. Her simple assumption brought home to him again what a huge gulf lay between them. Instead of courting sweet, decent young women, he'd spent the past fifteen years consorting with whores and worldly widows. Afraid that if he opened his mouth now, he'd say something sarcastic or scathing that would hurt her feelings, he took the combs silently and shoved them back in his pocket.

"Thank you so much for the rest," she told him with a sunny smile. "I'm not sure why you bought us presents. We should be buying you gifts to thank you for all the hard work you've done around here."

"I guess I had the impression that times have been tough for you for a long time now," he said evenly enough. "You all deserve some spoiling."

He wasn't quite sure why he'd bought these things, either. Once he got started picking the presents out, though, he'd enjoyed shopping for each and every one of the Matthewses over in the Springs. Thanks to the money he had inherited from his father, the salary he received as a marshal, and the occasional bounty he picked up, he had a fair bit of money stashed away, and he'd never really had anyone to spend it on.

"We'll wait until morning, and then you can give your presents to everyone yourself."

"That's all right," he said, looking away from her. "I'd rather you gave them out."

"Half the fun of giving presents is seeing people's faces light up when they see what you bought them."

"These aren't presents," he growled. "They're just some things I picked up on a whim."

Something in his tone got through to her at last.

"All right," she said quietly. "If that's what you want, I'll slip them into everyone's rooms tonight." She folded up the parcel again, much to his relief, and set it carefully on the porch beside her.

Now, you best head off for that walk you were planning to take earlier. Disregarding that wise voice inside his head completely, he sat down on the porch steps and leaned back against the wide pillar.

"Tell me about what happened to your bulls."

She sighed. Wrapping her arms around her legs, she rested her chin on her knees. "Everything had been quiet and easy as anything while you were gone. I should have known it was too good to last. Last night around midnight I heard four shots. After I woke Betsy up to look after the little ones, I slipped out with Papa's Winchester to take a look around.

"Just when I reached the barn, I heard riders galloping away from the home pasture where we keep the bulls. Despite what you seem to think about my common sense, I was relieved to hear the riders go. I wasn't so relieved when I discovered what they had done."

"Losing the bulls was a blow, wasn't it?"

"We'd made pets of them. We called them Pappy and Lord Hugo. They were both Herefords, and my father spent a small fortune buying them four years ago. Our longhorn cows have been bearing much bigger calves with more meat on them since we introduced the Hereford strain into our herd. It's a blow, all right. I can't afford to replace them. What hurts most, though, is that those bulls were a fundamental part of my father's dreams for this place."

"I'm sorry." He realized when he said it that he really meant it. He'd forgotten what it was like to have dreams, but he regretted that another bit of her family's dream had been wrenched away from her. He was afraid she'd be losing her whole dream shortly, but she didn't seem to realize that she was fighting a losing battle.

"I appreciate your sympathy. If we get a little ahead, I'll try to buy another Hereford bull down the road. In the meantime, we still have almost four hundred white-faced cows those bulls sired."

"They must be worth some money. If you sold them and this place, you could move to Colorado Springs and see those hotels and fancy folk you were asking me about."

"I don't want to live in Colorado Springs." She rose to her feet in some perturbation and left the blanket lying on the rocker. "I just want to visit a place like it from time to time. I'd go crazy if I tried to live in a real city. Grand Valley is exactly where I want to be, and the Rocking M"—she gestured toward the hayfields stretched out below them—"is all I want. Please, let's not argue about this again. Not tonight."

He got to his feet and stood staring down at her. When she looked at him that way, her green eyes wide and pleading, it was hard to argue with her. He couldn't remember ever having this problem with a female before. All he could think about was how appealing she looked in that old blue wrapper she wore, and the way the light from the lantern shone off that golden braid of hers. "All right," he said at last.

"Thank you so much for getting my family those things you just picked up on a whim," she said with a twinkle back in her eye. "I know they'll all be so happy and pleased tomorrow."

She leaned up on her tiptoes and planted a quick kiss on his cheek.

He reached out and caught hold of her shoulders before she could slip away.

"If you want to thank me, I think you should give me a proper kiss on my lips," he said hoarsely. A part of him was sickened to hear himself asking for something in return for the presents he had given her family. He'd been given far too many gifts with strings attached. Yet another part of him wanted to take full advantage of this opportunity. His body had gone tight again, and all he could think about was holding her.

She blushed furiously and bit her lip. He watched her with fascination. When was the last time he'd spent time with a female who could blush?

He reached up and gently touched her lower lip with his thumb.

"You shouldn't do that," he told her.

"Do what?" she asked, her green eyes wide and uncertain.

"You shouldn't do anything to hurt these pretty lips of

yours." He traced the outline of her lips with the pad of his index finger, relishing their softness. She trembled. More blood pooled in his loins, and yet he'd hardly touched her. The way things were heating up between them, they were both in a world of trouble. He'd never been a man to fear trouble, but something about this situation, something about Robin Matthews scared him in a way he'd never been frightened before.

Shoving such irrational thoughts to the back of his mind, he concentrated on cajoling what he wanted from her at this particular moment.

"I'm still waiting for that kiss," he reminded her.

"You mean a real, full-on-the-mouth kind of kiss?"

He nodded, not quite trusting his voice, or his own self-control. He was about a half second away from grabbing her and stealing that kiss.

"Well, all right," she said slowly. She rose up on her toes again and brushed her lips against his. He caught a tantalizing whiff of lavender. Her mouth was butterfly soft against his own, and then it was gone. Lord, he wanted more from her. He wanted everything. Yet he had absolutely no right to touch her, much less be thinking of ten different ways he'd like to make love to her at this very moment.

"I don't call that a kiss," he managed to get out. "Don't you Colorado gals know any better than that?"

Her green eyes shot daggers at him. "I'll show you how Colorado girls kiss, all right," she said. Just as he had hoped, her anger helped her forget much of her shyness. She reached up this time and wrapped both of her arms around his neck. She tugged his head down and plastered her lips against his.

He had to give her points for enthusiasm, if not for finesse. He almost grinned. This kiss convinced him once and for all that Robin Matthews had spent very little time sparking or spooning. Somehow that realization made him feel protective, happy, and more scared than ever. Enjoying the feel of her warm, soft body pressed against his, Nathaniel let his hands slip down to her waist. She was a little bit of a thing, but she sure had curves where he wanted them to be.

When she eased up a bit, he tugged gently at her chin. She opened her mouth, and he kissed her more deeply, the way he'd been thinking about kissing her for two weeks now. She looked startled at first, but she caught on fast. Soon they were tasting and exploring each other's mouths, and he was rock-hard.

He slipped his hands lower, cupping her sweet round buttocks and pulled her tighter against him. Someone groaned. He was stunned to realize it must be him, but it felt so good, holding her like this. She was soft, and sweet, and yielding . . .

Suddenly, it occurred to him that she wasn't exactly yielding anymore. In fact, for some reason she'd gone stiff as a board.

"Please," she said in a low voice, "let go of me."

It took a few moments for her words to penetrate the cloud of desire fogging his brain. A part of him wanted to pull her down right there on the porch and show her how good it could be between them. How could he have possibly gotten so hot in such a short time for a girl almost young enough to be his daughter?

Appalled, frustrated, and confused, he forced himself to let go and step back from her. He was still breathing hard, much to his chagrin. The self-hatred and anger that seemed so much a part of him now rose in a dark, choking wave.

"If I ever try to talk you into kissing me again, you ought to run as hard and as fast as you can in the opposite direction."

"Why?" she asked, her own voice hardly steady.

"Because the next time I start kissing you, I might not be able to stop." Before he pulled her back into his arms, he turned on his heel and stalked down the steps into the welcome chill of the mountain night.

Chapter Eleven

When Nathaniel awoke the next morning, he was in a foul mood. Last night he'd ended up walking up and down the river for an hour before he'd headed back to the bunkhouse. Once he'd climbed into his bunk, sleep had eluded him. While he tossed and turned, he'd done his level best to forget what it felt like to hold Robin Matthews in his arms and feel her lips against his. She'd made it plenty clear she wanted no part of him, and he could only applaud her decision. Robin did have some common sense, after all—at least where he was concerned.

He scowled through breakfast. Since he usually didn't say much in the morning anyway, no one seemed to notice his black mood. They all thanked him warmly for their presents. Tommy was particularly taken with his top and could hardly wait until breakfast was over so that he could play with his new toy. Robin looked bright, cheerful, and well rested, which somehow made him feel even more disgruntled. After breakfast, he stomped away from the table while Robin and the twins were still discussing their chores for the day.

What was he still doing here on the Rocking M? he asked himself as he strode to the barn. He'd brought the Matthewses the supplies they needed. Robin was up and around and doing light chores now. They didn't need him. He surely didn't need to get any more tangled up with a stubborn young woman with moss-green eyes to haunt his dreams and a full set of lips to turn a man upside down.

He was staring at his saddle, seriously contemplating saddling up Old Blue and riding straight out of there when the twins walked into the barn. Quietly, they set to work harnessing the team.

"Where are you two headed?" he asked, his curiosity getting the better of him.

"Robin wants us to drag those bull carcasses farther away from the house and the river. Knowing how you feel about cows, she thought you wouldn't want any part of this job," Luke told him with a wry face.

"She did, eh?" Right then and there he decided he wanted to help. "Your sister doesn't know nearly as much about other folks as she thinks she does."

"That'd be news to her," Jake replied with a grin. "You sure you want to help us? Pappy and Lord Hugo must be smelling to high heaven by now."

"They'll be worse by tomorrow," he pointed out grimly. "You boys best find some chains. It'll be easier to wash the stink off them than that old rope you just set out."

He walked out with the boys and the team to the place the bulls had been killed. His blood turned cold in his veins when he realized the animals had been shot less than a quarter of a mile from the house. He could imagine only too well what might have happened if Robin had come before the men left. Sutherland's riders were growing dangerously bold.

With his help, the boys and the team made quick work of dragging the first bull to a little hollow at the far end of the hay meadow where the scavengers could pick the carcass clean. Walking back to fetch the second carcass, Nathaniel wondered if there might be some way to help Robin in her struggle against Sutherland before he left. She was planning to ride into town that afternoon and use the money he brought her from the Springs to settle her debt at Johnson's Dry Goods. Maybe he'd invite himself along. Robin had mentioned the fact that Sutherland's hands had harassed and forced other small ranchers off their places. If he could talk two or three of them into making sworn statements, that might give Vance Sutherland pause, especially now that he was considering making a run for public office.

It was a long shot, but it might help. If Robin's problems with Sutherland kept escalating at their current pace, someone on the Rocking M was apt to get seriously hurt. Of course, what happened to Robin and her motley collection of small fry really wasn't his problem. But hell, he'd think about them all and wonder how they were doing once he went on with his travels.

After noonday dinner, Nathaniel and Robin got ready to go to town. When she bustled out of the ranch house, Robin was wearing a dress again—a more formal one now. This time Nathaniel was prepared for the change in her appearance, but he still couldn't help admiring the way she looked. She was wearing a dark plaid maroon dress with a lace collar. She'd pulled her hair back in a neat bun, and she wore a jaunty little hat with a feather in it that made her look as feminine as all get out.

Before she climbed up on the buckboard, Robin handed Nathaniel ten dollars. "This is your pay for the past two weeks," she flummoxed him by saying.

"I'm not working for you."

"I know you aren't officially one of my ranch hands," she said carefully, "but you've worked hard over the past two weeks and done a great deal for us. I can't go on pretending that just feeding you Betsy's fine cooking is reward enough."

He looked down at those ten dollars she held in her hand. He knew exactly how much money she'd had left after he bought supplies for her. He didn't know how big her debt was at the store, but he guessed she wouldn't have much left to tide her family through this fall and winter.

"I've more saved away," she said, obviously guessing the trend to his thoughts. "We'll be fine. I insist on paying you a decent wage. Now all the debts between us are well and truly paid. I think you've stayed on here because you believed that my getting shot was somehow your fault. It wasn't in the least, but you helped us tremendously by driving our cattle to Colorado Springs and buying our supplies for the winter."

Understanding dawned at last. "You're trying to get rid of me."

Her cheeks bloomed pink, but she didn't look away from him. "No, I'm not. I'm trying to get rid of any sense of obligation we might feel toward each other. If you want to stay on, I'll be grateful for any work you do, and I'll continue to pay you what we've always paid our hands. I just don't want you thinking that what happened last night is going to happen again."

She had that one damn straight. Swearing to himself, he took her money and stuffed it into his vest pocket. He walked over to Thunder and swung aboard. So, she was trying to put distance between them by reminding him that she was the boss lady of this place. After what happened last night, she was probably smart to do exactly that. The gesture still steamed him.

He stared toward the Sangre de Cristos. *Robin Matthews, you'll be rid of me soon enough—but Nathaniel Hollister doesn't leave a place until he's good and ready.*

Their trip to town that afternoon was a quiet one. Nathaniel rode beside her buckboard, but his distant expression discouraged Robin from trying to make conversation with him. Nathaniel Dawson had her well and truly confused. Just when she thought she was starting to figure him out, he did something that baffled her completely.

She wondered at the obvious inconsistencies in him. The

fact that he thought to buy everyone in her family presents touched her deeply. Yet the man didn't seem to know how to give gifts, or how to enjoy giving them. The anger she sensed in him frightened her. It was always there, just simmering below the surface. She'd seen how hard he worked to control it, and she was grateful that he'd never once let his temper show in front of Jessie and Tommy.

Did he care about them? It was difficult to tell with that poker face he wore much of the time. His blue eyes were usually so cool and unreadable. Yet for some reason he continued to stay on at the Rocking M. Every morning when she heard his deep voice in the kitchen, she said a quick prayer of thanks. Every mealtime as she watched him tease Betsy and talk easily with her quiet brothers, she smiled to herself. Of course, she didn't want him to stay on because each day he fascinated her more and more. She hoped she'd find him sitting down to the kitchen table for breakfast one more day because of the valuable work he did about her ranch.

Why on earth had he asked her to kiss him last night? She'd asked herself that question a hundred times since he'd stalked off into the dark. She was beginning to think he actually wanted her. When he'd pressed himself against her last night, his arousal had been all too evident. The very notion flattered, confused, and alarmed her all at once. She was coming to like Nathaniel very much. A part of her feared she could all too easily fall in love with him. She was quite positive, however, that the reverse wasn't true. She was bound and determined that she wouldn't give her heart, or her body, to a man who would move on when the fancy struck him.

When they reached town, they headed straight to the blacksmith shop.

"Howdy there, Lionel," Nathaniel hailed the big quiet, blacksmith with a warm smile.

"Howdy yourself," Lionel said, grinning back at him.

"You got some time to look at Miss Matthews' right wheel on this rig? The rim's fixin' to work itself loose any time now."

"I kin look at it just as soon as I finish up with Mr. Jessup's mare."

"That'd be just fine." Nathaniel settled himself on a bench against the wall, and the two men began to talk as if they were old friends. Puzzled, Robin went to pay off her bill at the dry goods. She'd hardly heard Lionel Brigham say more than two words to anyone in the entire time he'd lived in Grand Valley. Nathaniel certainly had a way with people. After coolly giving Ray Johnson the money she owed him, she deposited the remaining fifteen dollars at the bank. Afterwards, she went to the Wells Fargo office to see if there was any mail for her.

"Good morning, Mr. Peabody," Robin greeted Grand Valley's Wells Fargo agent with a cheerful smile. Besides working for Wells Fargo, Mr. Horace Peabody served as the town surveyor and ran an assay business on the side. Another one of her father's good friends, Mr. Peabody always seemed particularly pleased when she came to check for mail. Because Horace Peabody was an incurable gossip, Papa had always maintained he kept working for Wells Fargo so that he could know everyone's news before they knew it themselves.

"Well, hello, Miss Matthews. I've been hoping you'd come to town soon. We've got a letter for you, and it's come all the way from Virginia. That's where your mama was from, wasn't it?"

"That's right," Robin said faintly, her heart thudding in her chest. To the best of her knowledge, her mother had never received a letter from her parents after she eloped with her Yankee against their will. For years she had watched her mother come to this very office, always asking if there was mail for her from Virginia. Sometimes her old friends had written, but the one letter she had always hoped to receive from her parents had never come.

After Mr. Peabody handed her the letter, Robin stared at the graceful handwriting addressing the letter to her. Was it from one of her mother's old friends, or could it possibly be from a member of her own family at last? *There's only one way to find out, you ninny. Standing here staring at it isn't doing you a bit of good.*

With trembling hands, she carefully opened the letter. It read:

August 14, 1880

My dearest granddaughter,

My husband Benjamin Elijah Lee, your grandfather, passed away three months ago. At last I am free to write to you. You have been in my thoughts every day since I first learned of your birth. I still grieve for your mother's death and hope you have come to terms with her passing. She was the sweetest, most loving of daughters, and I know she is happy dwelling with the Good Lord's angels now.

Although times have been difficult since the war, the land here at Tarrington is rich, and we get by well enough. I hope you will consider coming to live with us. I read your letter after your parents' deaths with both amazement and dismay. I respect your determination to keep your parents' ranch, but it seems a formidable task for one so young and alone in such rough country. Please, come home to live with your family. At Tarrington, you would be surrounded by aunts, uncles, and cousins. I promise that we will make you, Jake, Luke, and Betsy feel most welcome.

Your loving grandmother,
Amelia Lee

Robin folded up the letter and stared blindly out the door of the office. The offer of reconciliation had come too late to ease the ache in her mother's heart. *Oh, Mama, I'm so sorry.*

"I hope it's not bad news," Mr. Peabody asked kindly, his eyes gleaming with curiosity.

"I suppose it's good news. It just came three years too late," she said bitterly and left the Wells Fargo office. Her thoughts were still awhirl by the time she returned to the blacksmith shop.

There she discovered a drummer had arrived with a gaudily painted wagon from which he obviously sold a variety of patent medicines. Tiberius J. Fortnum claimed to make elixirs that strengthened one's blood, eased catarrh, and helped female nervous disorders. Since she had never believed much in female nervous disorders or suffered from weak blood, Robin was inclined to think Tiberius J. Fortnum was a first-class charlatan.

As she drew closer, she was surprised to hear Nathaniel's voice raised in anger. "This rig is too heavy for this old horse to pull. No wonder he's skin and bones."

Robin winced when she saw the condition of the old gray draft horse harnessed to the wagon. The animal's head was hanging in exhaustion, and she could literally count its ribs.

"I don't see how the condition of my horse is any of your business," a man with a high, nasal voice replied. "Now, if you would like to sample some of my elixir, I'd be happy to fetch you some. If I might suggest it, sir, you look as if your digestive system might very well be dyspeptic."

"I'd like to take one of your medicines and cram it down your throat and see if you don't develop dyspepsia right now." The threat in Nathaniel's voice made Robin break into a run. He sounded furious enough to do violence.

Sure enough, when she rounded the wagon, she found Nathaniel had picked up a small, round, pompous-looking drummer and held him pinned against the side of his wagon.

"I demand you unhand me at once, or I shall make a complaint to the sheriff," Tiberius J. Fortnum blustered.

"The sheriff don't give a damn about what happens around here, my friend," Nathaniel said with such menace, shivers went down Robin's spine.

"Nathaniel, put that man down at once," she cried, striding forward.

He glanced over his shoulder at her, his blue eyes cold as ice. "Look at his horse's back," he countered.

She bit her lip and walked close enough to see. She had to stand on her tiptoes, for the old horse was at least eighteen hands high. She winced when she saw the welts and open cuts crisscrossing his back. Some of the older ones were infected and oozing with pus. Robin clenched her fists and stepped back.

"On second thought, you have my permission to skin Mr. Fortnum alive."

A glimmer of humor stole into Nathaniel's gaze. "Why, Miss Matthews, my Cherokee grandmother would be proud of you." He looked away from her to glare at the drummer.

"Either I do as Miss Matthews suggests, or I'll buy this old bag of bones from you for ten dollars." He let Fortnum down. Hastily the man straightened his coat and collar.

"Why, ten dollars, th-that's highway robbery," the drummer sputtered. "I paid twenty for him back in Nebraska City."

Idly, Nathaniel drew a long, wicked-looking knife from behind his head. Robin stared at him in fascination. Had he been carrying a knife in a sheath down his neck all this time, and she'd never noticed? *Just exactly who was Nathaniel Dawson?*

"If you paid too much for an old draft horse, that's your problem. He's not even worth ten now the way you've worn him down." Nathaniel drew a whetting stone from his pocket and began to sharpen his knife with great deliberation. Fortnum watched him out of frightened eyes.

"I used to run with a renegade band of Injuns back when I was a kid," Nathaniel continued on in a conversational tone. "We caught a drummer once who sold us a tonic that poisoned us."

"W-what did you do to him?" Tiberius J. Fortnum asked in a quavering voice.

"We tied him to a tree, and then we scalped him," Nathaniel replied with a wolfish smile.

The drummer stretched out a trembling hand. Nathaniel drew the ten dollars Robin had given him from his vest pocket and handed it to him. Wordlessly, the man took the money and walked away.

Looking very pleased with himself, Nathaniel pocketed his whetting stone and slipped his knife back into its sheath. Robin let out a peal of laughter. "I think I just watched one confidence man out con another."

"I'm sure I don't know what you mean, Miss Matthews," Nathaniel replied as he gave the old horse a pat and began to unharness him.

"Well, for one thing, I have a hard time believing you ever scalped anyone, and I have my doubts about your Cherokee grandmother."

"My grandmother's name was Running Bird, and she was a full-blooded Cherokee," he replied promptly. "My friends and I did tie a drummer to a tree once. The tonic he sold to my best friend killed his little brother."

"Did you scalp him?"

"No, but it was January and none of us ever went back to see if he'd managed to work himself free before he froze," Nathaniel said so coolly that another set of shivers went down her back. When he said things like that in his harsh way, she wondered if he was trying to scare her.

"Well, now you are the proud owner of one well-past-middle-age draft horse," she forced herself to say cheerfully to Nathaniel. "What are you going to do with him?"

"I don't rightly know. Maybe he could help pull your hay wagon this winter."

He looked so hopeful, she refrained from pointing out that she already had a strong, healthy team of horses.

"Did you finish all your business in town?" he asked.

"I've done my errands for today, but I was hoping to stop by Mrs. Beacham's place for a quick chat before we head home," she said apologetically. She doubted Nathaniel was going to be thrilled at the notion of spending the next hour in Mrs. Beacham's parlor. "She'd have my hide if I didn't stop by and say hello to her."

"You don't suppose she might have some more of those gingersnaps, do you?"

"If she doesn't have a fresh batch of gingersnaps, I can promise she'll have something equally tasty to serve up."

"I expect I'll tag along then," he surprised her by saying.

"You can leave that ole horse here for now," Lionel suggested. "I'll see he's fed and watered properly and do somethin' about his back."

"Thank you, Lionel, I'd appreciate that," Nathaniel nodded to him. "I'll be back to fetch him in an hour or two. I'll settle up with you then."

Mrs. Beacham was thrilled to see them both. She promptly ushered them into her parlor and insisted they sit side by side on a narrow loveseat. There was so little room on it that Robin couldn't help but be acutely aware of Nathaniel. Their shoulders brushed from time to time, and she could feel the warmth radiating from his body. Sometimes she forgot what a big man he was, but sitting this close to him, she felt positively dwarfed.

Soon Mrs. Beacham served them tea and a heaping plate of gingersnaps, much to Nathaniel's obvious relish. After he leaned forward to help himself to another cookie, he shifted until his leg rested against Robin's. Even through her petticoats and skirts, she could feel the hardness of it. She kept hoping he'd shift again, but he never did, which left her having to cope with the odd sort of breathlessness that always stole over her when she was close to him.

When she wasn't being distracted by Nathaniel, Robin was amused to see that he could act the part of a perfect gentleman when he wanted. He flirted gently with Mrs. Beacham and dodged her sly queries about his background with great politeness. As she watched him sip his tea, she couldn't quite believe this was the same man who had threatened to scalp Tiberius J. Fortnum behind the livery just an hour ago.

"I received a letter today from my grandmother in Virginia," Robin told them when a lull finally came in their conversation.

"Isn't that exciting," Mrs. Beacham said to her with a pleased smile. "Why did she finally write to you?"

"My grandfather passed away a few months ago. Out of respect for his wishes, she hadn't contacted me before. I gather he never could find it in his heart to forgive Mama for running off with Papa. She invited me to come live with her, along with Betsy and the twins."

"You should take her up on that invitation," Nathaniel said abruptly. "You could sell out to Sutherland and with the proceeds arrive in Virginia in style. You could probably catch yourself a husband and be all settled down and raising babies in no time."

"Thank you for arranging my future for me so nicely. It just so happens that particular future isn't what I want for myself." Robin was aware of the fact that Mrs. Beacham was watching their interchange with great interest.

"You need a strong husband to keep you from getting into trouble." Nathaniel crossed his arms and frowned at her.

"I take it you're not volunteering for the job," Mrs. Beacham interjected dryly.

"Me? Hell no." Nathaniel looked so horrified, Robin wanted to kick him in the shins. "I'd never be a fit husband for a young woman like her."

"And why would that be, exactly?" the old woman asked with great interest.

"I'm fifteen years too old to start with, and I've lived the kind of life that hardens a man. I don't have the nature to be a good husband. Besides, I have plenty of trails to ride yet before I settle down."

"Ah, yes, you mentioned that you wanted to do some traveling before," Mrs. Beacham said serenely. "Well, my dear," she said, turning back to Robin, "your grandmother's letter certainly has given you a great deal to think about."

"It has indeed." Robin looked at the tea leaves in the bottom of her saucer and wished she could read her future there. "I hate to disappoint her, but leaving the West and moving to

Virginia is just about the last thing I want to do. I'd love to go visit her sometime, though."

"In the meantime, you should write and tell her that. Think of the joy you both could take from a regular correspondence now."

"Since Robin's obviously going to be obstinate and refuse to do the sensible thing," Nathaniel said soberly to Mrs. Beacham, "there's a question I want to ask you before we go. Have you kept in touch with any of the small ranchers Sutherland forced out?"

"Well, let me see. The Williamses moved to Fresno. I received a letter from them just a few months ago. I heard the Schmidts ended up in Eugene, Oregon, and the Jeffersons were in Holdrege, Nebraska last I knew."

Robin was puzzled to see Nathaniel looked disappointed at this news. "So none of those families actually stayed in Colorado."

"Is that bad?" Mrs. Beacham looked just as puzzled as Robin felt.

"I was hoping I could talk them into making sworn statements against Sutherland. If he owns the judge along with the sheriff in Grand Valley, I probably couldn't make any headway in the local courts, but I might be able to make a reporter up in Denver take notice. Usually big men in a land grab like this one get away with it because they don't care what people think of them. Sutherland's made himself vulnerable by wanting that senate seat so much."

"I suppose it wouldn't look very good if people found out what he and his men have been doing here in Grand Valley," Mrs. Beacham said slowly.

"It's a good idea," Robin said, "but we'll never be able to track those families down now, and besides, Vance Sutherland is probably good friends with all the editors up in Denver."

"If he declares as a Democrat," Nathaniel said with ironic emphasis, "the Republican editors will be plenty interested to dig up dirt on him, and if he declares as a Republican, the

Democrats' editor won't be his good pal anymore. Just you wait and see.''

"Well, I don't have time to wait until the next election," Robin said firmly. "Sutherland's riders are a big problem I have to deal with in the here and now. Speaking of time, we promised Betsy we'd be home in time for supper. I'm afraid we need to be on our way."

She rose to her feet. After thanking Mrs. Beacham for the lovely tea, Robin led the way to the door. Mrs. Beacham disappeared back into her kitchen and returned shortly with another parcel of her cookies done up for Nathaniel. When she handed it to him, he leaned over and kissed her cheek.

"If I was just ten years older ma'am," he declared with one of his heartbreaking smiles, "I'd come courting you myself."

"Oh, go on with you," the older woman waved him off, her eyes twinkling.

After saying their farewells to Mrs. Beacham, Robin and Nathaniel climbed up on the buckboard and drove back through town. They stopped at the livery and tied the old draft horse behind the buckboard. They were halfway down Main Street when Robin noticed a stranger staring at Nathaniel. After a long moment, the stranger jogged his mount across the street directly toward them.

"Well, if it isn't Deputy Marshal Nathaniel Hollister, large as life," the stranger greeted Nathaniel with a wide grin. "What the hell are you doing in Grand Valley?"

Chapter Twelve

Robin turned and stared at the man sitting beside her on the buckboard. Surely the stranger was mistaken. Nathaniel couldn't be Marshal Hollister. Nathaniel couldn't possibly be the legendary lawman who had tracked down some of the most famous and infamous outlaws in the West.

As she searched his face, it occurred to her she knew almost nothing about the man who had been working for the Rocking M for two weeks now. She'd been trying to respect his privacy, but now she wished she had pushed harder to find out who he really was.

"Do I know you?" Nathaniel's voice sounded as cold and hard as she'd ever heard it.

"Well, you may not remember me," the stranger said, "but I sure as hell remember you. My name is Ben Ames, and you tracked down the robbers who hit our bank back in Sage Creek, North Dakota. Miss, I swear, he and his posse worked so fast, those owlhoots didn't have a chance to spend a dime of that money they took. His men shot three of those robbers to dollrags and the rest went to jail. We got every penny back. Yes sir, Nathaniel Hollister is one popular man in our town.''

"Is he right?'' Robin desperately tried to keep a quaver from her voice. What did it matter to her who Nathaniel was, anyway? Somehow it did matter, and it hurt her deeply that he hadn't shared the truth with her. ''Are you Nathaniel Hollister?''

"He's right,'' Nathaniel said grimly, ''except that I'm not a marshal anymore. I quit six months ago.''

Here then was the source of the bitterness she had sensed in him. What had gone wrong six months ago? Why had he abandoned the job that had made him famous? As much as she longed to ask him those questions, this obviously wasn't the place to do it.

"You quit?'' Ben Ames looked honestly aghast. ''Well, that's a damn shame, pardon my strong language, miss. The West was a safer place for folks with men like Marshal Hollister catching outlaws and making them pay for their crimes. You staying in Grand Valley, Marshal, or just passin' through?''

"Just passing through, and I'm not a marshal anymore,'' Nathaniel replied impatiently. She could tell from the tense set to his jaw that he wanted to end this conversation as soon as possible.

"I'm sorry, we need to get back to my ranch before it gets dark. Good day to you, Mr. Ames,'' Robin nodded to him politely and then said, ''Geeuup,'' to her team and slapped the reins across their backs.

"My Gawd, who'd of thought I'd run into Nathaniel Hollister here in Grand Valley? I'm going to write the missus this very night and tell her,'' Ben Ames called after them, so loudly that a half-dozen people on the street heard him. Robin saw them turn and stare at Nathaniel much the way she had.

"I bet he hits a saloon in the next hour or two,'' Nathaniel said bleakly, ''and he'll tell every fool who'll listen that I'm in town.''

"Is that bad?'' Robin asked him curiously.

"It is when a man just wants to be left in peace.''

"I see."

"I doubt that you do," he said shortly and said not a word after that, which left Robin far too much time during the long drive home to stew.

Why hadn't he told them who he was? Did he think she would have pestered him? Did he think she somehow would have importuned him because he was the great Nathaniel Hollister? Not once had she really pushed to find out more about him, even though they had all been dying to learn more about his background.

The more she thought about the fact he'd purposely hidden his name from her and her family, the angrier she became. By the time they started up the lane leading to the ranch house, she could hardly bring herself to speak to him in a civil fashion.

"I want you to tell the rest who you really are over supper." She was pleased to hear her voice sounded polite and detached. "The news will be all over town in the next day or two, and they'll look foolish when their friends tell them who you actually are."

"All right." He was quiet for a long moment, and then he turned to look at her. "For what it's worth, I'm sorry I didn't tell you earlier."

She refused to meet his gaze. "You don't need to apologize. I don't know you well enough for you to hurt my feelings," she said coolly.

"If I didn't hurt or offend you, then why are you mad as a wet hen right now?" he asked in a dry tone that made her long to kick him where it really counted.

Fortunately, she was saved from having to answer that question when her family spilled out onto the porch, and Tommy came running up to greet them. Everyone was intrigued and excited by the old draft horse tied to the buckboard. Robin had no choice but to tell them the story right then and there of how Nathaniel had acquired him. Much impressed, they all made a fuss over the old fellow who looked surprised but pleased by his abrupt change in circumstances. Betsy promptly christened him Hercules. Jake and Luke offered to see to the team, Thunder, and Hercules, while Robin and Nathaniel went their separate ways to wash up for supper.

Supper that night was an excruciating experience for Robin. The twins thought the news that Nathaniel Hollister had been sleeping in their bunkhouse and eating at their table was just about the most exciting, remarkable thing that had ever happened on the Rocking M.

"But you helped us drag those stinking bull carcasses halfway across the ranch," Jake said dazedly.

"You helped drive our cows to Colorado Springs," Luke said, shaking his head.

"Worst of all, you helped dig our new privy," Betsy looked horrified by the notion.

"Maybe we'll post a sign on it, 'Dug by the Most Famous Lawman in the West,' and charge admission," Robin said tartly.

Nathaniel sent her a speaking glance across the table.

"Would people really pay to use our outhouse just 'cause Nathn'l dug it?" Tommy's eyes were wide. Robin could tell the whole conversation was beyond him. Nathaniel already was a hero in his eyes.

"No, sweetheart, I was just teasing Mr. Hollister, and reminding everyone else at this table that he's still the same kind gentleman who's been helping us out since I got hurt."

How she wished she could believe her own words. As Robin looked at him across the table, she wondered how she hadn't guessed that he was someone larger than life. She had always known he was a dangerous man capable of violence. She supposed she should feel reassured that he had been a lawman. Still, the fact remained he had killed—several men, in fact— if the stories about him were true, and it was going to take her a good, long time to come to terms with that notion.

Between their excitement over Hercules and learning they had a famous lawman staying with them, it took Robin a long time to get her family to bed that night. Before she turned in herself, she thought of Hercules and the cuts and welts upon his back. She went to the kitchen and fetched a salve her mother made to doctor their livestock.

When she stepped out onto the porch, she was surprised to discover the barn door was open and someone had obviously taken a lantern inside. After her first surge of panic, she remembered Sutherland's hands always did their dirty work in the dark. Nathaniel must still be up. When she peeked in the barn, she discovered him talking to Hercules in a deep, singsong voice she found mesmerizing. He was rubbing the old horse down thoroughly with a wisp of hay. Hercules, Robin saw with some amusement, had his eyes closed in an equine expression of bliss.

As she watched Nathaniel care so tenderly for the old horse, much of the anger she had been harboring all night evaporated into thin air. How could she stay angry at a man capable of such kindness? She watched his strong, sure hands grooming the old horse, and a strange shiver stole down her back.

Feeling baffled and unbalanced, she hesitated in the doorway. *You always seem to be off kilter around him. Perhaps you should just slip away and come back later.* Nathaniel must have sensed her presence, for he asked her in a dry voice, "You plannin' to stand in that doorway watching me all night long?"

"No, I brought this salve for those welts on his back." *Blast and tarnation. Roberta Matthews, you are not going to blush.* Her cheeks heated anyway as she walked over and handed him the jar. "My mother used to make this. My father swore it made cuts on his livestock heal up twice as fast."

"Thanks," Nathaniel said, his expression unreadable.

Aware that he was watching her steadily, she went to stand by Hercules's head. The old horse shoved his muzzle against her, begging to be petted. "You are a sweet fellow, aren't you?" She looked away from Hercules and offered Nathaniel a tentative smile. "He has a mighty handsome set of eyelashes."

Nathaniel snorted at that comment and went back to his grooming. "More importantly," he countered, "he's a strong old cuss. He's got some good years left in him. Feed him well, and he'll be back pulling wagons again in no time."

In the face of such enthusiasm, she still couldn't point out that she could barely afford to feed her own team through the winter much less this sweet old hulk of a horse.

"Why didn't you tell us who you were?" she asked him instead.

"Besides the fact it really wasn't any of your business?" Nathaniel shot her one of his glowering looks. Robin refused to be intimidated.

"You've eaten at my table and lived with my family for two weeks now. My brothers and my little sister have become very fond of you. Tommy worships the ground you walk on. I think you could have done us the courtesy of telling us who you really were."

He sighed and tossed the wisp he had been using to the ground. "I expect I don't take much pleasure from telling folks who I am anymore," came his unexpected answer.

"Why? I should think you could take great pride in what you've been and what you've done. Look at that man today. He said you were a hero in his town."

"Well, you think wrong." He looked at her at last, and the bitterness in his gaze made her want to cry for him. "There are more than a few towns whose citizens would just as soon string me up or tar and feather me if they had the chance."

"Why?"

"Does it really matter to you?" he asked impatiently. "It's a long, boring story and we both have a long day ahead of us tomorrow."

"It matters plenty," she replied, and to prove it she promptly sat down on an old wooden milking stool.

"I should have known you'd be just as stubborn about this as you are about everything else," he said shaking his head.

"You betcha. Now are you going to start telling me this story before I fall asleep on this stool?"

"Stubborn, and cheeky to boot," he said, a glimmer of

humor back in his eyes. The glimmer soon faded, though. In an offhand, almost careless voice, he started to tell his story.

"I began working as a town marshal almost fifteen years ago. My father was a judge, a damn good one in fact, and he taught me to respect the law. He used to read Blackstone to my brothers and me before we went to sleep at night, and he used to talk to us by the hour about the cases he judged and the basic principles of jurisprudence. He was killed trying to stop a gang of men robbing our bank. When our town marshal wouldn't organize a posse to go after them, my brothers and I did it instead. We caught the robbers, brought them all back for trial, and got most of the money back.

"It was a real blow losing Pa, but in time, we all felt a little better knowing the men who had killed him paid for their crime. The folks in Buford appointed me town marshal, and I found I liked the work. Eventually, that job led to another in a larger town, and then the U.S. Marshal's Office contacted me. I'd always wanted to travel and see some of the West, so I signed on with them.''

He paused and was silent for so long she was afraid he wouldn't go on with his story.

"You built quite a reputation for yourself," she said, trying to encourage him to keep going with his narrative. "I remember when I was just a little girl hearing the story about the time you tracked down One-Eyed Dixon and the Findley gang."

"Hell, you couldn't have been that little." Nathaniel looked positively irate. "I only caught up with Dixon back in '74."

So the man was sensitive about his age. Robin filed that fact away in the back of her mind and hid a smile. "I guess I wasn't so little after all, now that I think about it," she said soothingly. "At any rate, you were good at what you did. You caught lots of outlaws and built quite a reputation for yourself. And then something bad must have happened to make you resign."

"Yeah, something bad happened, all right." He ran a hand through his hair and stared at the dirt floor of the barn. As he talked, she knew he wasn't seeing her at all, but the events he began to relate in a harsh voice.

"The boys and I were on the trail of a gang hitting banks all over southwestern Kansas. Jack Carson and his brothers were slick and clever, and my boss wanted them stopped. We were feeling pretty full of ourselves, for we'd been successful in bringing in a string of badmen, and folks were talking about us from Texas to Montana. We got a tip that the Carson gang had been seen casing a bank in Cameron, so we staked the place out.

"The plan went bad on us. We found out later that Jack Carson knew we were watching the bank, but Carson liked his own reputation for pulling off spectacular heists, and he was determined to hit it anyway. The fourth day after we arrived in Cameron, one of my boys who was supposed to be watching the bank decided to mosey down to the row and visit one of the hurdy-gurdy girls he'd grown real friendly with. The moment my man left his post, Carson and his men came a-running, and they proceeded to rob the bank in broad daylight. I just happened to walk by the bank and noticed that there were a lot of fine-looking horses tied to its hitching rail.

"I looked in through the window, and they spotted me about the time I spotted them. They started pouring lead through that window at me, and if there hadn't been a good, thick water trough right in front of the bank, they'd have filled me full of holes. Well, it turned into as rough a shootout as I've ever seen. Carson and his men came into town loaded for bear, and my boys were itching for a fight."

Nathaniel paused for a long moment, and when he spoke again his voice was strained. "A young woman by the name of Mary McAllister came running up right after the shooting started. She thought that her husband was inside the bank. Before any of us could stop her, she stepped into the thick of things and caught two bullets. She died right there on the street before we could get a doctor to her."

Nathaniel looked at her then, and his eyes were full of

anguish. "She was only twenty, and she had two small children—a boy just turned three and a girl just a little older than your Jessie. Eventually Carson tried to make a break for it, and we shot him and his brother. With those two dead, the rest of the gang surrendered.

"We all wanted to go to Mary McAllister's funeral, but the minister at her church made it plenty clear that we weren't welcome. Next the mayor came to our rooms at the hotel where we were staying and told us we'd better leave before the townsfolk turned vigilante and decided to string us up themselves."

"Why were they so angry?" Robin asked in surprise. "I don't understand. What happened to that poor young woman was terrible, but it was hardly your fault. You'd think they'd be grateful that you protected their savings in that bank."

"That's not quite the way they saw it. We hadn't told the folks of Cameron that their bank might be hit. Because Carson and his gang always seemed to have inside information on the banks they robbed, we didn't want their friends warning them that we had that bank staked out."

Nathaniel folded his arms and looked out the door of the barn into the darkness. "The mayor was a shrewd, sharp old gent who reminded me in many ways of my own father. That night he made me realize that we'd actually done Mary McAllister's family unforgivable harm. We should have given the people of Cameron some warning that the bank could be a dangerous place to visit. We got so caught up in trying to catch the Carson gang that we forgot the main reason why we became marshals. Our first job was to protect people like Mary McAllister—not get her killed.

"The next morning we left Cameron, and I resigned from the U.S. marshal service a week later." Nathaniel glanced at her once and then stared at the ground as if he were waiting for her to pass judgment.

She let go a long, trembling breath as she considered the tragic story he'd just told her. "I still don't think that Mary

McAllister's death was your fault." Robin rose to her feet and went to stand before Nathaniel. "If those men had kept robbing banks, other innocent people would have gotten killed eventually."

When Nathaniel met her gaze, his blue eyes were haunted. "You don't know that. I don't know that. I just know Mary McAllister is dead and her children don't have a mother now."

He swung away from her and began pacing up and down the barn. "Don't you see? That old man was right. I cared more about being Nathaniel Hollister than preserving innocent lives. I forgot about basic right and wrong and what my work was all about. I liked my name and the look that used to come into people's eyes when they learned who I was."

He came to a stop before her, his expression filled with self-loathing. "Now I don't much like my name at all, and that's why I don't care to use it."

"I think you are dead wrong about Nathaniel Hollister." Greatly daring, she reached up and cupped his face in her hands and forced him to look at her. "A man who goes out of his way to help a boy confront a half-dozen cattle rustlers cares about right and wrong. You could have gotten yourself killed that night trying to help me. Whatever you may say about yourself, I know human life matters to you."

"Sweet, sweet Robin-girl," he sighed. He looked down at her, his gaze searching. "I didn't think anything or anyone could matter to me again, but you do," he said slowly, "and that scares the hell out of me."

Chapter Thirteen

Before Robin could say anything in response to this amazing pronouncement, Nathaniel gathered her gently into his arms and kissed her. Any words she had meant to say vanished from her mind. Instead, she simply felt, dazed by the pleasure and joy it gave her to be in his embrace again.

He kissed her with a tenderness that made her knees weak. The way he smoothed his hands across her hair and cheek made her feel cherished. The reverence in his touch made her feel feminine and precious in a way she never had before. This gruff, hard man had so much gentleness and caring hidden inside him. He was terribly wrong about himself. Someday, somehow she'd find a way to prove it to him.

She nestled closer, relishing the warmth of his body. The way he was holding her now, not too tightly, was just right. She breathed in the sweet scent of hay mingled with horse and a musky male odor that was all Nathaniel's own.

Of her own volition, she opened her mouth and invited him to kiss her the way he had kissed her once before. He made a sound of male satisfaction deep in his throat and promptly made the most of her invitation. They nipped, sampled, and explored, learning the texture and taste of each other. She realized her own heart was beating faster, and that delicious pang of longing was starting again somewhere deep in her belly.

He broke off the kiss. She looked into his eyes and saw that they were burning with a blue fire that made her skin go all shivery. His face looked as hard and harsh as she'd ever seen it. Slowly, he raised his hand and cupped her breast. She closed her eyes, for the intensity of his look became too much for her. She felt the tips of her breasts harden, and her cheeks started to burn.

With her eyes closed, she became even more acutely aware of his touch. He stroked her gently with his fingertips. Waves of pleasure radiated outward from the peak of her breast. She was wearing just a camisole and an old cotton dress. Through those two thin layers of fabric she could feel the warmth of his hand. She gasped when he rolled and plucked her nipple between his fingertips. An answering pang of pleasure pulsed deep inside her.

He moved his hand to her waist. He leaned forward and kissed the line of her jaw. His breath was warm on her cheek. He traced the curve of her ear with his tongue, sending exquisite, sensuous shivers down her back.

Eager for more contact, she pressed against him. This time it didn't frighten her to feel his hardness. A part of her gloried in the notion that he wanted her so much.

His grip on her waist tightened for a long moment. Then he let go and stepped away from her. Startled and bereft, she opened her eyes. The fire in his gaze scorched her now, and his chest was rising and falling as swiftly as her own.

"I'm about a heartbeat away from pulling you down in that hay over there and doing something we both might regret later."

Slowly, his words penetrated the sensual daze in her mind.

"Right about now, a roll in the hay sounds mighty prime to me," he said harshly, "but I'm not sure it's what you really want."

Don't make me think. Don't make me make a choice, a part of her wanted to cry out to him. She didn't want to make a responsible decision now. She just wanted to feel and let him sweep her away. She wanted to find joy sharing her body with a man, for she had good reason to fear that possibility could never happen for her.

But he was a principled man, despite the fact that he didn't see himself that way. The haze in her mind began to evaporate, and the cold, hard reality of her life returned to her in a choking wave. She was responsible for herself. She'd been responsible since the day she found out her parents had been killed, and taking care of her family had become her number one priority. She couldn't afford to make love to him. She couldn't afford to risk his riding away, leaving her pregnant and heartbroken.

She gazed up at the handsome planes and lines of his face, features that had become so familiar and dear to her in such a short time. She loved his thick, black brows, and his strong cheekbones. She liked the smile she enjoyed teasing from him, and his eyes that could make her heart do flip-flops. With a queer wrench deep inside her, she realized the heartbroken part of that scenario she had just imagined was only too likely. She couldn't afford a broken heart with so many others depending on her. She needed to be strong to continue her fight to keep her ranch and her family together.

"You're right, of course," she managed to say huskily. "This isn't what I want." Gathering what was left of her dignity together, she turned about and left the barn.

Her legs felt heavy, and her face was flushed. As she walked back to the house, she faced a troubling question. If she had just made the right decision, why did her heart feel heavier than a rock inside her?

Nathaniel straightened up from the hole he was digging and wiped his damp face with his kerchief. The boys he used to work with sure would laugh if they could see him now. Whoever would have guessed Nathaniel Hollister would spend whole days digging privies and fence post holes?

He never would have guessed he could gain such simple pleasure from this kind of hard, physical work. Yet as he glanced around him, he had to admit the corral was really starting to look shipshape. Knowing he had wrought such a change brought him a deep, abiding sense of satisfaction. Next, he had his eye on Betsy's henhouse. Most likely the roof on it wasn't going to make it through another winter. Considering what incredible meals that little gal could cook up with the eggs her beloved hens produced, he figured it was in his best interests to keep her cluckies happy and warm.

He frowned at the fence post he was resetting. He was actually considering staying on through the winter. Something had changed between him and Robin last night—before he'd gotten carried away and started pawing at her. He'd meant it when he'd said she mattered to him now. He'd respected her courage from the start, even though the obstinate side of her nature just about drove him crazy. Her dry sense of humor matched his own. He liked talking with her, when they weren't arguing, for she was quick and clever. He looked forward to meals when he could watch her sitting at the end of the table, listening to her little brood and looking pretty as all get out with her gold hair and sea-green eyes.

He knew where her fight with Sutherland was going to lead, but he didn't know what would be worse—staying and watching her break her heart over losing this place, or moving on and wondering what had happened to her. Last night he had decided that if he stuck around a while longer, at the very least he could keep her from doing something truly reckless like trying to tackle a half-dozen rustlers on her own.

Luke appeared by his side and smiled at him quizzically. "You going to set that post or just stare at it all day?"

"I thought I'd wait until a strong, young whippersnapper like you came along and could do it with me."

"Well, I don't mind helping you, but we might want to hold

off for a few minutes. There's a rider coming. Jake spotted him.''

Moments later, Nathaniel heard the hoofbeats himself. He went to stand by the rifle he had left leaning against the fence. He looked down the lane and saw a big man on a large buckskin approaching at a jog. As he stared at the rider, something about the way he sat his horse seemed familiar. Could it possibly be Joshua? Last time he heard, Joshua was up in Montana someplace hunting down Horsetooth Johnson.

By the time the dusty rider dismounted, Nathaniel was shaking his head in amazement. With a wide grin, Joshua strode over to Nathaniel and wrung his hand.

"I hate to admit it, but it's damn good to see you, big brother."

"What the hell are you doing in Grand Valley?" Nathaniel said by way of greeting.

"I might ask you the same question." Joshua jerked a thumb at the post hole Nathaniel had just dug. "You give up the marshal business to become a rancher?"

"Not exactly. It's a long story. Did some owlhoot lead you down this way?"

"Nope. It just occurred to me that it had been a good three years since I saw you last, and I thought it was time we caught up. Of course, that notion had to strike me when I was in Port Townsend—about a thousand miles from here."

"How'd you track me down?"

"Nathaniel Hollister is a name folks tend to remember," Joshua said wryly. " 'Course, you made finding you a little more of a challenge when you stopped using your name a few months back. Still, it didn't take me all that long when I put my mind to it. Hunting men is what I'm good at. I still think I'm even better than you."

It was an old issue and an old rivalry between them. Joshua had been waging his own private war against lawbreakers for years now. Long ago, he'd grown tired of the restraints working as a peace officer had placed upon him. Instead, he'd gone into bounty hunting and become damn good at it.

"Excuse me, sir. You wouldn't happen to be Joshua Hollister, the bounty hunter?" Luke couldn't keep quiet any longer. His eyes had gone big and round, and he kept looking back and forth at the two of them.

"He's one and the same," Nathaniel said, happy to have the focus of the twins' admiration switch to someone else for a change. "Joshua, I'd like you to meet Luke Matthews. Luke, this puny little feller here is my baby brother."

"Pleased to meet you," Joshua nodded to him. "Pretty place you have here."

"Thank you, sir. I'll see to your horse, if you'd like."

"All right, I'd appreciate that. He could use a good rubdown, water, and some feed. Be careful not to give him too many oats. He'll eat like a hog if you let him."

Nathaniel looked after Luke with some amusement. To the best of his knowledge, Luke had never called him sir.

"Come on in, and I'll ask Betsy to rustle up some grub for you. The eating here is mighty fine."

"You're digging post holes here because the grub's so good?"

"Not hardly," Nathaniel said. How was he going to explain to Joshua what he was doing here when he didn't really know the answer to that question himself?

Just then, Robin came out on the porch. She must have changed into that green calico dress he liked so much when she saw she had company coming. An hour ago she'd been wearing her work clothes. She'd even taken the time to put her hair up. She stood where the afternoon sun shone on her hair, turning the tendrils beside her temples bright gold. She smiled warmly at them both, such welcome and friendliness in her expression that something inside Nathaniel twisted. Robin Matthews was going to make some decent man mighty happy some day. Yet the very prospect of another man having her brought a hot, fierce anger to a boil inside him.

Joshua stopped dead in his tracks when he spotted her. "That's a fine-looking little lady," he said quietly. "Now I see why you're digging holes like a gopher around here."

"As usual, you see nothing and understand less."

"I see just fine, brother. In fact, I can see well enough to tell already that she's not your usual cup of tea. I think your taste in women is finally improving."

Nathaniel's response to that comment was a muttered profanity he never would have uttered where Robin or her family could hear. Joshua laughed and strode forward to meet her.

"Welcome to the Rocking M. You two have to be related," Robin said to Joshua and extended her hand in greeting.

"You sure know how to hurt a man's feelings, miss," Joshua took her hand and bowed low over it with great ceremony. "I'd hate to think I resemble this ugly cuss in any way, even if he is my big brother."

"Though your coloring is fair, you surely have the same eyes and features." Robin looked at Nathaniel, obviously expecting him to do the honors. Nathaniel sighed inwardly. "Robin, this is my brother Joshua. Joshua, this is Miss Robin Matthews, owner of the Rocking M. By the way, you could give her hand back now."

"Why would I want to do that, when it's such a pretty little hand?" Joshua said, beaming down at Robin. Nathaniel gritted his teeth when he realized Robin was beaming right back at him. Joshua had always had a knack for charming women.

"What I want to know," Joshua said, his gaze never leaving Robin's face, "is how you had the misfortune to meet my brother."

"I stumbled across him while I was trailing a bunch of cow thieves who had rustled a hundred of our head."

"I knew you were my kind of gal. This is a story I have to hear from start to finish," Joshua declared with relish.

"Come on inside," Robin invited him. "I'll introduce you to the rest of my family and tell you that story. We were just about to sit down to supper. I do hope you will join us. You can wash up on the back porch.''

"Now that's an invitation I can't turn down.''

Without a backward glance at Nathaniel, the two walked into the house. Nathaniel had no choice but to follow them. The thought occurred to him as he stalked up the steps—if he wasn't so glad to see his baby brother again, he'd be tempted to murder him.

Supper that evening was a festive affair. Robin's green eyes sparkled, and Betsy was positively giddy with excitement over the unexpected visitor. Tommy was so wild that he ran circles about the table until Luke forced him to sit down, and Baby Jessie giggled and grinned at Joshua while smearing her supper of mashed yams all over her face.

Joshua regaled them with stories of his travels and some of his most exciting captures. From his own experiences tracking down violent outlaws, Nathaniel could guess at some of the more grim details his brother left out. After they ate, they all moved to the parlor where they held an impromptu concert. Joshua fetched his guitar, and Robin settled herself beside him on the piano bench. Nathaniel was intrigued to hear she played well, with remarkable emotion and skill. She could even play a variety of selections, from popular songs to hymns, all from memory.

She must have sensed his surprise, for she looked his way while they took a little break and confessed, ''I always liked Mama's music lessons better than her cooking or her sewing lessons. I'm afraid piano playing isn't the most practical accomplishment a woman can possess, but it makes me popular at our town dances.''

"What man would care about your sewing when you can tickle the ivories like that?''

"Well, thank you, sir,'' she said with a self-deprecating

smile, "but I'm not sure all fellows hoping for well-mended clothes would feel the same way."

Nathaniel knew his voice sounded like a bullfrog's. When their sing-along resumed, for the most part he kept quiet. He liked music, though, and he enjoyed listening to Robin's clear soprano accompanied by Joshua's rich baritone. They made quite a picture, their two blond heads bent close together while the rest of the Matthews clan gathered around them and sang along enthusiastically. At last Jessie fell sound asleep on Betsy's shoulder, and Tommy, who had crawled into Nathaniel's lap midconcert, dozed off with his head resting on Nathaniel's arm.

"I think we should call it a night," Robin declared regretfully when she realized the little ones had fallen asleep. "It's time to get Jessie and Tommy to bed."

"I'm bushed, too. It's off to the bunkhouse for me," Joshua declared. He looked at Betsy and Robin, and his gaze softened. "Thank you for sharing your table and your music with me. I haven't had an evening I've enjoyed this much in a long while."

"The pleasure was all ours. Any kin to Nathaniel Hollister will always be welcome here," Robin declared with one of her sweet smiles. She walked over to Nathaniel, and she smiled again when she saw Tommy sprawled across his lap.

"That looks plenty comfortable for him, and not so comfortable for you," she commented softly. "If I'd noticed, I'd have taken him off your hands earlier."

"That's all right. He doesn't weigh more than a feather just yet."

She leaned over to pick the little boy up, but Nathaniel forestalled her by saying, "Let me carry him for you. Seems like we're less apt to wake him that way."

He was aware that Joshua was watching him with a bemused expression as he lifted Tommy into his arms. He followed Robin back to the twins' room where Tommy slept on a trundle bed. It seemed the most natural thing in the world to help Robin quietly strip off the little boy's shirt and trousers and help him into his flannel nightshirt. Tommy hardly moved throughout the entire process. He slept on, his cheeks flushed with sleep.

"Did I ever sleep that soundly?" Nathaniel wondered aloud.

"It's amazing, isn't it?" Robin shook her head. "He just goes until he drops in his tracks. Tomorrow morning, he'll pop up fresh as a daisy and full of mischief to start all over again." She leaned over and pressed a quick kiss on Tommy's cheek. Nathaniel couldn't resist reaching out and tousling his black curls gently.

Together they left the room so that the twins could get ready for bed. Of one accord, Robin and Nathaniel headed for the kitchen. Nathaniel poured himself a cup of coffee, and Robin made herself a cup of tea. They sat down at the kitchen table, enjoying a last bit of quiet before heading off to bed.

"I like your brother," she offered after a time.

"He likes you, too, but don't let his charm fool you into taking him seriously. Joshua has always had a way with women."

"I won't. I could tell he's one of those fellows who flirts as naturally as he breathes." She propped her chin on her fist and looked at him thoughtfully. "There's a distance in him despite all that charm and gaiety. He's been hurt—worse than you, I think."

He glanced at her, surprised by her perceptiveness. Robin might be young, but she understood people plenty well.

"He was hurt, all right. Joshua married his childhood sweetheart when he turned eighteen. They had three of the sweetest little girls you ever saw. Your Jessie reminds me of Annie, their youngest. One night when Joshua was off buying livestock for the farm, some Confederate guerrillas who were determined to keep fighting the Civil War raided his place. They killed his wife and the girls and burnt his house to the ground. That was over ten years ago."

Robin sat bolt upright, her green eyes filling with tears. "That's awful. How did Joshua ever manage to cope afterwards?"

Nathaniel cleared his throat. "Actually, he went kind of crazy for a time. He spent the next five years hunting those guerrillas down, one by one."

Robin rubbed her arms. "He-he didn't murder them, did he?" she asked in a small voice.

"He gave them all a chance to face him in a fair, standup fight, which was more than any of those varmints deserved. After he found and dealt with the last man in that guerrilla band, he started chasing down other killers."

Nathaniel stared down at the checkered tablecloth. "I think I went to work as a sheriff in large part to honor my father's memory. For Joshua, hunting down killers was personal. It's still personal. It's his whole purpose in life."

"I hope he finds another purpose someday besides bounty hunting. That has to be a lonely sort of life."

"Being a marshal wasn't much better." He couldn't help feeling a little aggrieved that Joshua was getting so much of Robin's attention and sympathy tonight.

"No, I suppose it wasn't," she admitted. "You worked with other men, though, didn't you? Joshua said he always works alone."

"I worked with different groups at different times."

"Did any of them become your friends?"

Nathaniel paused, surprised to find that was a hard question for him to answer. Some of them could have been, he supposed. There were men he'd ridden with whom he'd both liked and respected. He'd been so focused on the job, though, he hadn't gotten to know any of those men particularly well. He'd liked the boys he'd worked with in Kansas best of all. He'd worked with them the longest, but that was the crew who'd been with him that fateful day in Cameron. He'd never seen any of them after he'd resigned.

"I guess not," he had to admit at last.

"Well, whatever occupation you choose next for yourself, I think you should find one where you can stay put and make some friends. A man needs human ties of some sort. What's the point, otherwise?''

What was the point, indeed? It was ironic to hear her sum up in one brief question what it had taken him the last fifteen years to understand. ''A sage word of advice from a young lady who's seen so much of the world and done so much,'' he commented dryly.

''I may be young, but I'm entitled to my opinions,'' she said, obviously nettled.

''And you have plenty of them,'' he said, unable to resist teasing her further.

''That goes without saying,'' she relaxed and admitted with a chuckle. ''Here's another one, for what it's worth. You worked hard today fixing up that corral. I'm most grateful to you. My corral might actually keep some livestock in it now. You deserve a good night's rest, so I'm not going to keep you up talking any longer.''

Before she could rise to her feet, he reached out and took her hand in his own. ''You could give me a kiss to show me how grateful you are,'' he suggested and tried to look as wistful as he could.

''I believe you already gave me some good advice on the topic of turning down invitations to kiss you,'' she said with such dignity he felt ashamed of himself.

''Then I hope you will accept my thanks for making my brother feel so welcome here,'' he said in a more serious voice.

She looked down at their joined hands. He couldn't see her expression, but he could see her color had risen. ''I meant what I said,'' she said, her voice strangely taut. ''You and your kin will always be welcome on the Rocking M.'' With that, she rose to her feet and pulled her hand from his grip. Without meeting his gaze, she slipped away and retreated to the safety of her own room.

Nathaniel sat at the kitchen table for a long time. It scared him, how much he wished she hadn't listened to his advice.

Chapter Fourteen

When Nathaniel walked out to the bunkhouse, he found Joshua was reading by the light of an oil lamp beside his bunk.

Joshua nodded to the vase of flowers Betsy must have put on the table beside him. "Cozy setup you have here," he said with a grin. "Those little gals sure take good care of you."

"They're damn hard workers. The boys pull their weight, too."

"This is too big a spread for a bunch of young folks to work," Joshua said in a more somber tone and closed his book.

"I know. I've tried to tell them that, but they won't listen to me. They're headed for some serious trouble, too." He proceeded to tell him about their problems with Sutherland. It didn't take Joshua long to grasp the lay of the land. He, too, had seen this kind of situation too many times.

"It's a damn shame," he said when Nathaniel had finished. "I'd like to help them out. I'm between jobs right now. Maybe I could track down a couple of those families you mentioned and see if they'd make statements against Sutherland."

"That could be a big help. Now that he's got his sights set

on politics, I don't think Sutherland would like folks knowing how he became such a big rancher. So, how's the scalp-hunting business treating you?'' he asked Joshua, keeping his tone deliberately casual.

"Pretty well, all and all. I make a good living with all the bounties I collect. I could end up a rich man if I don't watch out. Plus I get to see some really fine country while I'm at it.''

"You given any thought to settling down and trying a safer line of work?''

"Nope. This life suits me fine for the moment. By the way, there're times you sound and look so much like Pa it's spooky,'' Joshua commented. "That's just the sort of question I expect he'd be asking me if he were still alive. It's also kind of an interesting question coming from my brother, the famous lawman who brought in One-Eyed Dixon and Black Jack McDougal.''

"The famous *ex*-lawman,'' Nathaniel corrected him automatically.

"I heard you'd resigned, which is why I hightailed it down here. What made you up and quit like that?''

"Would you believe I just got tired of chasing down killers and rapists and scum so low they'd steal from their own mothers?''

"I would, if I hadn't heard from Ben Landry what happened in Cameron. I don't think it's coincidence that you quit a week after Mary McAllister was killed.''

Nathaniel swore. Ben Landry had been his boss for ten of the past fifteen years. "Where the hell did you see Ben?''

"He tracked me down up in Idaho. I got a notion he went out of his way to find me because he was worried about you. Ben told me all about what happened in Kansas. You know, that woman's dying wasn't your fault. The Carson gang would have gone on shooting and robbing and killing more folk if your boys hadn't stopped them that day.''

"That's just what Robin says.''

"Well, that little gal is sharp as a tack, and spunky, too. I like her."

"She likes you as well, which just goes to show what poor taste women can have."

"She could be the best thing that's happened to you."

Nathaniel looked away. He'd almost rather go back to talking about Cameron. "I don't reckon I could ever be the best thing that happened to her," he said shortly.

"I bet you're thinking you're too old and hard for her," Joshua guessed shrewdly.

"Something like that." Nathaniel got to his feet and began getting ready for bed. Maybe if he jumped into his bunk, Joshua would get the hint and stop palavering.

"Seems to me only a gent who's lived on the wild side can appreciate a place like this and a sweet little gal like her."

"Can you honestly see me as a rancher? I hate cows, and I haven't stayed put in the same town for more than a month in fifteen years. I like rambling. I might winter here, but come next spring I'm off to see some country, without having to worry about bringing some murdering polecat to justice."

"Guess I can see your point, after all. So sweet Robin and her ranch aren't for you." Nathaniel felt a little deflated when Joshua agreed with him so easily. "You gonna stick around and help her when Sutherland makes his final push?"

"I don't know. People I try to help just seem to get hurt."

"It's going to be hard to stay on the fence if the lead starts flying," Joshua pointed out soberly.

"I know. I just hope when things get rough, I can talk her into selling out."

"Well, you seem to know what you're about, big brother. You usually do." Joshua yawned and slipped down under his covers. "Guess I didn't need to come haring down here to make sure you were all right."

"I appreciate the thought just the same." Nathaniel blew out the oil lamp and slipped into his own bunk. Within moments, Joshua's steady breathing told him his brother was already asleep. Nathaniel had a feeling he wasn't going to be so lucky. Their talk had stirred up too many worries inside him.

As he stared up into the darkness, he wondered if Joshua was right. Usually he knew what he was about. Usually he knew exactly what he wanted. Now that he thought about it, that morning beside the trail when Robin's hat fell off had been a symbolic moment. His world had gone topsy-turvy on him and he hadn't really righted it yet.

It was the damnedest thing. He'd seen a hundred girls just as pretty as Robin Matthews in his day. More than a few had tried to set their caps for him. Nary a one had the effect on him that this one did. He was pretty darn sure Robin wasn't even trying. She was just plain skittish around him, even though he was almost certain that she wanted him as much as he wanted her.

He fell asleep thinking how right and natural Robin and Joshua had looked playing their music together, almost as if they were family.

They were all up bright and early the next morning. Betsy cooked up a big breakfast of bacon, flapjacks, and scrambled eggs. Jessie, Nathaniel was amused to see, would have nothing to do with her high chair. She climbed right into Joshua's lap and insisted on eating her breakfast there. Joshua just smiled and laughed at Robin's and Betsy's efforts to relieve him of his little companion.

After they ate, the Matthewses all gathered around to see Joshua off.

"I wish we could talk you into staying a little longer," Robin told him.

"I sure appreciate the offer, Miss Matthews, but there are some people I need to see before the winter weather sets in." Joshua sent Nathaniel a meaningful look. Nathaniel stepped closer while Joshua was tightening his cinch.

"I'll send you a telegraph if I make any progress," Joshua promised in an undertone.

"Thanks, and thanks for coming to find me," Nathaniel said.

Joshua nodded to the Matthews clustered around. "I think you're in mighty good hands for the moment."

His gaze softened when it fell on little Jessie. He opened up one of his saddlebags and took out a small rag doll. Nathaniel's throat went tight. He was almost certain that doll had belonged to Annie, Joshua's youngest daughter.

"Here, Jessie-girl," Joshua said, kneeling before her, "I've got a present for you."

"Babee!" Jessie shrieked with pleasure and plucked the doll from his hands. She held it to her shoulder and began to pat its back.

"That's right, sweetheart. That's a baby for you to care for." Joshua kissed her forehead and straightened up.

"You keep that little angel safe, big brother. You keep them all safe, you hear?" There was a distant look in Joshua's eyes, and Nathaniel guessed he was thinking of another family—the one he had failed to keep safe years ago.

"I'll do my best," Nathaniel pledged. As he waved to his brother riding off down the lane, he wondered if he would possibly be able to keep that pledge.

After Joshua left, Nathaniel's days on the Rocking M soon fell into a pattern. He rose before dawn and ate breakfast with Robin, Betsy, Luke, and Jake. Between them, they divided the chores for the day and went to work. There was plenty of it to go around, for winter was fast approaching.

The last of the leaves fell from the aspen trees, and the days grew shorter and cooler. One morning they woke up to find two inches of snow on the ground. Tommy was wild with excitement and went out right after breakfast to make snowballs. Robin just looked worried and drove herself even harder.

He found her that day chopping wood behind the house.

"Let me do that," he said and almost plucked the ax from her hand. "There're lighter chores you can do." They'd had this fight a half-dozen times before. As long as he was around, there was no reason for her to chop wood, or set fence posts, or tackle the rest of the other heavy jobs she kept trying to do when his back was turned.

"I can chop wood as well as any man," she said fiercely and tried to take the ax back from him. "I've been chopping wood for my family for three years now."

"All right," he said, suddenly tired of wrangling with her. He took out his pocket watch. "Let's see how much you can split in five minutes. And don't go putting an ax through your foot while you're at it."

After sending him a speaking glance, she took the ax from him. As he watched her work, he had to give her credit. She had a smooth, neat way of splitting wood that was surprisingly efficient. At the end of five minutes, though, her chest was heaving and her cheeks were bright from exertion. Without a word, he helped her stack the pile she had split.

"All right. Now you take the watch," he said.

"I don't see the point of this. I-I know you'll be able to split more than I did."

"Just take it," he bit out. Her eyes narrowed at that. She snatched the watch from him and stood well away from the splitting stump.

He put much of the pent-up frustration he'd been feeling for weeks into the next five minutes. CRACK! He brought the sledge down with such force on the wedge that he split the round with one hit. Why the hell did she have to push herself so hard? CRACK! Why the hell didn't she have the sense to see there were some jobs men were more fit for? CRACK! Why did she have to fight him when he was just trying to help her?

By the time his five minutes were up, he was breathing hard, too, but the ground around the stump was littered with wood ready for her stove. Wordlessly, she picked up the lengths and stacked them. His contribution to the pile was clearly twice as big as hers had been.

When she had finished, she sat down on the splitting stump and drew in a deep breath. "I know I was stupid to claim I could split as much wood as you," she met his gaze levelly. "All of us still need to keep putting up wood when we can. You don't know what the winters can be like up this high. The winter after my folks died, I didn't realize how much wood Papa usually cut. There were always stacks and stacks of it near the house, but I'd never paid much attention. That first winter was a hard one. April came, and we were already running low on wood, and then a blizzard hit. That storm raged for five days straight. It was just Betsy, the twins, and me then, and the four of us almost froze. I'm not sure I've ever been that scared, or that cold. We've got to put up more wood."

So that's what this was all about. He tried to picture what it had been like. She had been sixteen then, the boys eleven and Betsy only nine. They must have been terrified.

"I've wintered in the high country before," he told her gently. "I do know what it can be like. We've put up plenty of wood, and the boys and I can always cut more later in the season."

"You could, if you're here. I've been trying not to ask, but in a dozen different ways your going or your staying affects my planning. I guess I've got to ask you straight out now. Are you planning to winter with us?"

It was a fair question. He was surprised she'd managed to wait this long to ask it. Looking at her sitting on that stump, her back straight, her chin raised in that indomitable way she had, he knew he couldn't walk away from her—not yet. She infuriated him constantly. She confused him in a dozen different ways, but still she drew him in a way no other woman ever had.

"I reckon I'll stay until spring."

He thought he saw some of the tension drain out of her. "I'd like to tell everyone tonight. They've all been wondering, but

I wouldn't let them ask you. Betsy will be so pleased. They'll all be happy that you'll be here through the winter, and for Christmas as well. We always make a big celebration out of Christmas.''

"I can imagine you do." He couldn't remember the last time he'd truly enjoyed Christmas. "And you? How do you feel about my staying on?"

She was quiet for a moment while she considered his question. "Part of me feels happy and relieved that you'll be staying on, but another part of me is scared to death," she replied frankly. She rose to her feet and walked away, leaving him to his thoughts. Trust Robin to give him an honest answer, even if it wasn't the easy one he wanted.

To ease Robin's worries about firewood, Nathaniel spent the next three days using the team to drag in a dozen more deadfalls he and the boys could cut up later in the winter if their wood ran low. Robin never mentioned what he'd done, but one day he found a heaping plate of gingersnaps in the bunkhouse.

After that morning when he'd made up his mind to winter at the Rocking M, he promised himself he'd do his best to keep his hands off Robin. She was right to be scared of him. The way he saw it, he could only bring her grief in the long run. He was careful to keep his distance and managed rarely to be alone with her. Somehow, though, his overall plan was backfiring on him. The more he tried to avoid Robin, the more aware of her he became.

He found himself dreaming about her at night—the kind of sweaty, visceral dreaming that left his body aching and impassioned when he awoke. The third time he had one of those dreams, he gave some serious thought to riding into town and visiting a gal on the row. Yet night after night, he found himself too weary from a long day of hard physical labor to fancy making the long ride to town. Somehow, too, after spending the day in the company of Betsy and Robin, the whole notion of paying for sex in a whorehouse seemed particularly unclean and sordid to him. Therefore, he kept a tight rein on his desire and went straight out to the bunkhouse right after supper was over.

One day around noon in early November, Nathaniel arrived in the back hall just in time to listen to Robin and Betsy having a heated discussion. The two sisters so rarely disagreed, he was startled into eavesdropping.

"I think we should go," Betsy was saying in a tight voice very unlike her usual tone. "It would be good for us to get away. Luke's sweet on Kathy Ferguson, and this way he might have a chance to dance with her."

"I know he is. I know you all want to go. I'm just scared to leave this place right now. I think we're overdue for some more trouble. I promise we'll go to some dances this spring."

"That's months from now. You don't really want to go to a dance. Just because you don't like to get gussied up in dresses doesn't mean I feel the same way. I'm tired of worrying what Mr. Sutherland might do next. We never have fun anymore. We haven't had any fun since Mama and Papa died." He heard the tears in her voice as Betsy went running from the kitchen.

He waited for a long moment and then stepped into the kitchen. Robin leaned against the Dutch sink, her face stricken.

"I suppose you heard all that," she said wearily.

"It was hard not to. What was that all about?"

"Betsy wants us to go to the Harvest Dance. It's kind of a harvest festival and Thanksgiving celebration all rolled into one. Our church puts it on."

"Sounds like a good idea to me. You all could use some time in town."

"I don't want to leave the house overnight. The Abbotts got burned out one evening when they stayed over in town. I don't know what I'd do if we lost our home."

"Then go to this shindig early, and don't stay in town. If you leave the dance by nine, you could still be back here by eleven to check on things, and Betsy and the boys could still have their fun.''

"I'm just not sure it's a good idea right now." Robin looked away from him. "It's been so long since we've had trouble with Sutherland's boys, I know they must be cooking up something.''

"Maybe Betsy's right about something else," he guessed. "Maybe you don't want to go to this dance in the first place.''

"She's right about that," Robin admitted, meeting his gaze again. "I don't much care for getting gussied up or going to dances, but I'd do it for the rest in a heartbeat. I feel so bad for my sister and my brothers. Jake, Luke, and Betsy have missed a great deal of school to help me out here and to look after Tommy and Jessie, which means they rarely get to see their friends.''

"All the more reason to let them go to this shebang, and you as well. How are you ever going to meet a likely young fellow to marry and help you run this spread if you don't go to dances and such?''

It seemed a perfectly logical question to him, but as soon as he asked it, he could see he'd made a strategic error. She stood bolt upright and looked at him disdainfully.

"Since I have absolutely no interest in marrying a man to help me run the Rocking M, that's exactly why I don't much care for dances. Now, if you'll excuse me, even if you don't think I'm doing a particularly good job of it, I have a ranch to run.''

"Ah, hell, Robin-girl, that's not what I meant," he called after her, but his only answer was the front door slamming.

Chapter Fifteen

Robin didn't come to dinner that day. Nathaniel stared at the bowl of slumgullion Betsy dished up for him, and wondered why he didn't have more of an appetite. Before he could start worrying about Robin in earnest, Luke explained where she was.

"She rode up into the forest to do some hunting. She usually does that when she's sore about something and wants to think."

"I shouldn't have pestered her like that about the dance in town," Betsy said contritely. "She has so much on her mind these days."

"You've got a right to tell her how you feel," Nathaniel smiled consolingly at her. "I think your going to this dance sounds like a fine idea."

"You do?"

"Sure. You young folks spend too much time out here alone. You should go to town more often."

"I'd love to," Betsy said with a sigh. "Don't get me wrong. I love the ranch. We all do. It just used to be so different. We used to ride into town all the time when Mama and Papa were alive. Robin doesn't seem to like town anymore. She's changed from the way she used to be. I remember when she laughed and smiled all the time. Papa used to call her his little ray of sunshine.''

"It's a big responsibility looking after you all and this place," Nathaniel had to point out.

"I know. That's why we all work so hard to help her."

"Well, maybe she'll come around."

"Maybe," Betsy said, but she didn't look hopeful.

They were a quiet bunch when they sat down to supper that night. Everyone but Nathaniel avoided looking at Robin. Her face was pale and set. After they said grace, she cleared her throat.

"I want you all to know that I did some hard thinking this afternoon about what Betsy said to me this morning. I think she made a good point. We all spend so much time worrying about what Vance Sutherland might do to us next, we aren't living much of a life in the here and now. I'm all for us going to the Harvest Dance.''

The twins grinned at each other and let out Indian war whoops. Tommy did a little jig beside the table, and Baby Jessie clapped her hands and giggled.

Robin watched them all carrying on, a wistful smile tugging at her lips. She really wasn't happy about going to the dance, Nathaniel realized, and that puzzled him. Most womenfolk seemed to like dances and social occasions. Maybe she didn't want folks to think she was looking for a husband, but he guessed there was more to her reluctance than that.

Betsy was in seventh heaven. "I'm going to wear my blue velvet. Luke and Jake will wear their suits. Nathaniel, do you have something nice tucked away in your saddlebags? Otherwise, we could lend you one of Papa's suits."

"I expect I've got something that will do." He couldn't help smiling at her enthusiasm.

"Tommy's got a good shirt and trousers, and we have two

or three pretty things we could dress Jessie up in." Betsy's gaze fell on Robin last.

"I figured I'd just wear my good old, reliable Sunday-go-to-meeting dress," she said before Betsy could ask.

"You can't wear that," Betsy almost wailed. "This is a special occasion. Right after supper, we're going to look at Mama's clothes to see if there isn't something of hers that we can make over for you."

Clearly Robin wanted to say no, but her gaze softened when she looked at Betsy's eager face. "All right, Bets," she said quietly. "We'll do just that."

When they finished eating, Betsy was out of her seat like a shot. "Just leave the dishes. I'll wash up later."

"I expect I can rinse a dish or two if the twins will ride herd on the young'uns," Nathaniel offered.

Once she got over her surprise, Betsy grinned at him and bounced about the table. "Under that scowl you wear, you may just be the sweetest man in the whole world." After making that remarkable pronouncement, she kissed him on the cheek and skipped away to Robin's bedroom. Her older sister followed in her tracks, considerably more slowly.

As he rose to his feet, Nathaniel fingered his cheek. Betsy Matthews was a pistol, no doubt about it. If he wasn't careful, she'd have him wrapped around her little finger before the winter was through.

He'd just finished with the plates when he heard a commotion out in the hall.

"Nathaniel, we need you," Betsy called out. "We need a second opinion on which dress she should wear."

"No, we don't," he heard Robin hiss. Clearly Robin's willingness to cooperate with her sister had just reached its limit.

"Luke and Jake will be no help at all, and Tommy would think you were pretty if you wore a flour sack over your head. Nathaniel's the only one around here besides me that knows a thing about women's fashion."

Nathaniel had to smile at that. This was certainly the first time anyone had claimed he knew something about women's dress. He stepped into the hallway just in time to witness Betsy doing her very best to drag Robin down the hallway and into the parlor.

"Looks like she's balking on you." Nathaniel leaned against the wall and crossed his arms, prepared to enjoy the show.

"I am not balking," Robin ground out and let Betsy lead her the rest of the way into the parlor. "Mules balk. I just don't see the point in this."

"The point is," Betsy explained patiently, "that Nathaniel is the best one around here to judge which of Mama's dresses suits you."

"I doubt he spent much time chasing down female outlaws over the past fifteen years. I don't know why you think he's such an expert on fashion."

"Actually, you're right about that," he sent Robin a wicked grin. "Mostly females chased me."

"The poor, misguided things," Robin replied tartly. "I pity the ones who caught you."

He opened his mouth to assure her that in fact, he'd made most of them plenty happy, but she raised a hand to forestall him.

"All right. Let's get this over with. I for one would like to get to sleep sometime soon."

"Turn around so I can take a look at you," he ordered. Looking pained, Robin turned about once, less than gracefully. "You look pretty in that," he had to allow. Now that he was paying attention, he realized Robin did look well. Her color was high from their bantering and her eyes were still bright with repressed annoyance. He was so used to seeing her in large flannel shirts and jeans, he was always surprised by how shapely she looked in traditional female clothing. Somehow, though, he didn't think the beige shade of the dress did much for her coloring.

"Just wait until you see her in the next one," Betsy promised. She hustled Robin back into the bedroom. Nathaniel made himself comfortable on the big horsehair sofa and looked around him. He liked this parlor. Unlike the one in his own home where he grew up, this was a cozy and welcoming room. There was a knitted throw over the back of the sofa and crocheted doilies on the table and chair backs. The upright piano had a well-used look to it, and the girls had draped its top with a brightly colored scarf. This was a room people lived in.

The parlor in his childhood home was so formal, he never had dared set foot in it. That room had purely been for show. His mother had kept it spotlessly clean for the terribly important times she had ladies over for tea. He frowned, remembering how she had worked and slaved, preparing for the brightest moments in her life when she could entertain, even though the cream of Buford society was such a disappointment to her. She had always hoped that her husband would take her away to a bigger town, or even a city where she could associate with other women as refined as she.

"All right. Here we come," Betsy sung out.

When he looked up, his bitter memories of his mother quickly fled. Robin stood in the doorway, dressed in a silver-green gown that shimmered in the lamplight. The color was just right to bring out the unique shade of her eyes. The square neckline was lined with lace but plunged too low for his peace of mind. He could see far too much pretty white skin and the tantalizing start to the cleft between her breasts. The full skirt and bustle helped to emphasize her slim waist.

He had to clear his throat once before he could speak. "I reckon that's the right one." He gestured for her to turn around, just so that he could enjoy the view a little while longer.

"The style's old-fashioned," Betsy said doubtfully, "but that green silk is pretty."

"I expect the whole point of a dress's style is to make a woman look good, and this one does the trick." Hell, he'd have to fight the young men off with a stick if she went to a dance wearing this rig. *It's what you want for her, isn't it? You were the one saying just this morning that she needs to find a*

good husband to look after her and this place. You should be
happy Betsy found something Robin can shine in.

"We'd have to shorten the skirt, too, and I know the bustle
is all out of date," Betsy was frowning as she walked around
Robin. "Maybe this isn't the right one after all."

"You asked me, and I'm telling you," he spoke so grimly,
they both looked at him in some surprise. "If you want your
sister to turn heads, that's the dress." With that he got up and
stalked from the room.

The next two weeks seemed to fly by. The first real snow
of the season fell, but the Rocking M was ready, thanks to the
long hours everyone had put in. As hard as they all had labored,
Robin knew Nathaniel had worked harder than any of them,
and she was deeply grateful. By the time the first real storm
hit, leaving them a foot and a half of snow, they had plenty of
hay, feed, and wood.

When the day of the Harvest Dance arrived, the Matthews
decided to take the day off from all but the most essential
chores like feeding livestock. They took turns heating up water
on the stove and taking baths. Robin washed her hair and then
spent a good hour in front of a crackling fire in the parlor with
a brush drying it. She was startled when some sixth sense
warned her that she wasn't alone any longer.

She looked up to find Nathaniel in the doorway. He stood
there, a kind of concentrated stillness in him that caught her
attention at once. He was staring, seemingly mesmerized by
the simple act of her brushing her hair. How long had he been
standing in the doorway? She couldn't be certain.

"I'm sorry," he said abruptly when he realized she was
looking at him. His voice seemed more gruff than usual. "I'll
come back later."

"That's all right," she said, scrambling to her feet. Loose
and freshly washed like this, her hair was such a nuisance. It
seemed to take on a life of its own, clinging to her hands and

arms. She shoved the mass of it back over her shoulders as she walked toward Nathaniel. She'd considered cutting it a hundred times, but it was her one vanity. Her mother had always told her it was one of her greatest assets. Robin had let it grow, so when it was loose like this, it fell to her waist.

"What did you want to ask me?"

He seemed to have trouble looking away from her hair.

"I just wanted to check and see what time you wanted us to harness up the team this afternoon," he said, a muscle ticking in his jaw.

"I think we can all be ready by three. We'll stop by Miss Beacham's to warm up, and then we'll go on to the church."

"All right," he said shortly and walked away.

As she stared after him, a little shiver went down her spine. She was almost certain that look had been back in his eyes again, the look she'd seen there right after he'd kissed her. Seeing her hair down had aroused him, and knowing she could have that effect on him was arousing her.

As much as you need his help this winter, you may be making a huge mistake to let Nathaniel stay on. Trying to ignore that sobering thought and the sudden restlessness in her body, she returned to the fireplace to finish drying her hair.

When she returned to her bedroom, she found Betsy had laid out a set of linen undergarments she had never seen before. The linen was so fine it was almost sheer. Robin leaned over the bed and touched the embroidered camisole, drawers, and petticoats reverently. Tiny silk ribbons threaded through the delicate lace edging every piece.

"Where on earth did you find these?" she asked Betsy when her sister bustled into her room.

"They were Mama's. She told me once that she was married in them. Her grandmother made them for her as part of her trousseau. She couldn't take most of her hope chest with her when she eloped, but she did wear these. I found them the other day when I was going through her trunk. It seems a shame they never see the light of day. Tonight is such a special event, I think you should wear them.''

"I'm not sure I think a dance qualifies as a special event.''

"Well, I do.''

Betsy looked so excited, Robin gave in. Besides, a very feminine side of her longed to try them on. As she carefully lifted up the camisole to slip it over her head, the scent of sandalwood and roses enveloped her.

"They even smell like Mama,'' she said, a catch in her throat.

"I know,'' Betsy agreed. They were quiet for a long moment, thinking of the wonderful mother they both still missed fiercely.

The fine old linen felt soft and smooth against her skin. With Betsy's help, Robin soon managed to don three layers of petticoats. With a good-natured groan, she even let Betsy lace her into a corset, a contraption she hated almost as much as she hated walking boots with heels.

After she put a warm shawl about her shoulders, she sat down at her mother's dressing table and let Betsy do her hair. Over the past few years, Betsy had become very adept with a curling iron and hairpins.

After a few minutes, Robin started to fidget. "Ouch,'' she yelped, the first time she turned her head into the tip of the hot iron Betsy was using to curl her bangs.

"That will teach you to sit still,'' Betsy said less than sympathetically. "I think you're worse than Tommy sometimes.''

"Speaking of Tommy, I hope that Luke and Jake are keeping a close eye on him.''

"I told them I wouldn't bake them pie or cookies for a month if they let Tommy spill anything on his trousers. I think he'll still be presentable by the time we're done.''

"The dance may be over by the time you're done,'' Robin grumbled.

"Who's forever telling Tommy he needs to learn patience?'' Betsy rolled her eyes at her.

At last Betsy was finished. Robin had to admire the end

results. Betsy had swept her hair back into a chignon and pinned an ivory silk rose over her right ear. She had fluffed and curled her bangs becomingly, and allowed small ringlets to dangle softly beside her ears. The style emphasized her high cheekbones and made her look older and quite elegant.

"Bets, this looks wonderful," Robin shook her head in amazement. Then her gaze fell on her mother's jeweled watch lying on the dressing table, and she remembered the time. "Come on, now, we'd better both get dressed."

First, she helped button Betsy into her best dress, a pretty party gown made from pale blue velvet. Betsy already wore a blue satin ribbon in her hair, the one Nathaniel had purchased for her over in Colorado Springs.

Next, Betsy helped Robin into the voluminous folds of her mother's green silk. The gown fit perfectly now, thanks to a few tucks Betsy had taken in at its waist. As she gazed at herself in the mirror, Robin was almost glad she had spent a whole evening with Betsy hemming up the skirt. The dress did miraculous things for her figure and her coloring. In fact, tonight she almost believed that she could pass for pretty. She didn't have to pinch her cheeks to make them rosy. They were already flushed with excitement and anticipation. Betsy insisted on spraying a little of their Mama's precious rose water on her wrists.

"Only if you use some, too," Robin said firmly.

"Well, all right. I'm not sure Reverend Case would approve of a girl my age wearing perfume . . ."

"That's his problem. Oh, Bets, thank you for turning me out so well." Robin gave her sister a hug. "I never could have managed this on my own."

"It was my pleasure. Nathaniel was right. You are going to turn heads tonight."

Robin strongly doubted that, but it gave her confidence knowing she looked the best she could. As she moved about the room, her mother's silk dress swished so elegantly.

"Are you ladies just about done in there?" Nathaniel called

from outside the door. "There are some young gents out here who are gettin' mighty impatient."

"Tell Luke and Jake they can just hold their horses," Robin called back. "We're almost done."

As a finishing touch, Betsy handed her Mama's fine black Madeira lace shawl, a green silk reticule, and a pair of white gloves. She started to reach for a green silk fan that matched the dress, but Robin shook her head vehemently.

"I can't manage a fan, too. I'm going to be lucky to keep track of this dang reticule and the shawl and the gloves as it is."

Feeling almost like a woman about town, Robin rustled to the door. "You go first," she told Betsy, her stomach suddenly all a-flutter. She shouldn't care what Nathaniel thought of her in this getup, but she did, just the same.

Nathaniel was waiting for them in the parlor, his expression grim. Robin's heart did a somersault when she took in his appearance. He was dressed in a white shirt, black jacket, black trousers, and a very dashing blue satin waistcoat. He'd combed his hair back from his face, which accented the dramatic lines of his features, and he'd trimmed his sideburns. Sophisticated and polished, he should have looked like any well-to-do western gentleman. Yet there still was a hardness to his expression and an aura of restlessness and danger that his fancy clothes did little to dispel. He certainly was going to set the hearts of all the unmarried ladies in town aflutter.

His grim expression vanished, and his eyes lit up when he saw Betsy. "Well, don't you look pretty. I predict the boys in Grand Valley are going to lose their hearts to you tonight."

"Why, thank you, sir," Betsy curtsied gracefully before him, and he bowed gallantly in return. Laughing in delight, she skipped to the side, obviously wanting him to have a clear view of Robin. When he straightened up again, he glanced at her briefly and his bleak expression returned.

"I guess we better get going," he declared curtly and went to fetch his jacket from the hallway.

"What about Robin? Doesn't she look pretty, too?" Betsy demanded impatiently.

"She looks mighty fine," was all he said.

For one tempting instant, Robin considered throwing her reticule at his head. So much for hoping she might see that look in his eyes again. Steaming inwardly, she went to find her own wool jacket. She was so furious that her eyes prickled with tears, but she refused to shed a single one.

Tommy came to her and tugged at her hand. "I think you're the most beautifullest girl in the whole world."

"Thank you, sweetheart." She bent over and pressed a kiss on his forehead. "I think you're going to be the most handsome young fellow at the dance tonight, and I'm pleased to have you as my escort."

After making sure her young swain was properly bundled up in his winter clothes, Robin swept out of the house. She'd show Nathaniel Hollister. Clearly she wasn't pretty or polished enough for him. That was just too bad. She was still going to have a good time at the dance tonight, come hell or high water.

Chapter Sixteen

It was a beautiful, clear, frosty November afternoon. In the distance, the Sangre de Cristos rose majestically white and jagged against a brilliant blue sky. Because the team was feeling frisky, Nathaniel let Ned and Nod set off at a spanking trot down the snow-packed lane. He'd been relieved when Robin had chosen to sit in the back of the sleigh with Betsy, Jake, and the little ones all burrowed deep in woolen blankets and buffalo robes. Instead, quiet Luke sat beside him, which was fine by Nathaniel. He wasn't in the mood to talk with anyone right now.

He stilled an urge to look back over his shoulder at the ranch house. After convincing Robin to go to this dance, he sure as hell hoped nothing happened to her place while they were gone. The cold weather this afternoon was good news in one respect. Sutherland's hands were much less apt to have an appetite for making trouble when it was this chilly. Mindful of the cold and worried about Tommy and Jessie staying warm, he kept the team moving at a good clip.

When they reached her house, Mrs. Beacham made a big

fuss over their party clothes. Jake and Luke blushed, and Betsy positively beamed at her praise. The old lady's eyes filled with tears as she gazed at Robin.

"My dear, you look so much like your mother, you take my breath away. She would be very proud if she could see you now."

"Thank you," Robin said and kissed the old schoolteacher's cheek. "That's the nicest compliment you could have possibly given me."

"Goodness me, here I am prattling away when you should all be warming up by my fire." She ushered them into her parlor and promptly served them hot chocolate and cider. Nathaniel and Jake slipped outside to settle the team in Mrs. Beacham's stock shed. After the Matthewses were warmed through and through, they ventured back out into the cold and headed for the First Episcopal Church.

The moment they walked into the dance, Robin and her family were thronged by friends. Robin insisted on introducing Nathaniel to everyone who came up to talk to her. Because the townsfolk cared about her, they seemed willing to like him as well, and surprisingly few brought up his career as a marshal. Although he liked these friendly people well enough, the crowd began to wear on him.

At last he managed to slip away. Standing against the wall, he sipped some punch and watched Robin mingle.

He knew he'd angered her by not making more of a fuss over her appearance. Seeing her rigged out in that green gown, though, had been like a punch in the belly. He knew Robin Matthews could be pretty, but that afternoon in the parlor was the first time he'd realized she could be downright, gut-wrenchingly beautiful, and he didn't know how to handle it. He'd seen plenty of beautiful women in his time, but none had ever had the stunning impact on him that Robin had in that moment.

The last thing he had wanted to do was take her to a dance where she'd be fair game for every randy single fellow in the county. He'd driven her into town just the same, and now he had to stand here on the edges of the hall and watch her be mobbed and salivated over. Just as he had predicted to himself, once the music started up, a half-dozen young men converged on her from several directions at once. Robin looked surprised but pleased, and accepted an invitation from a tall, scholarly-looking young man Nathaniel thought might be the son of Floyd Haskins, the town banker.

It turned into a long evening for Nathaniel after that. He'd meant to keep an eye out for a likely husband candidate for Robin, but each male that asked her to dance either seemed too young, too old, or too interested in gazing at the creamy white skin of her bosom. There were a few who were so obvious about trying to look down her bodice that he almost stalked over and forcibly pulled them away from her. He relaxed a little when he saw her stomp on the foot of one of the fellows, and simply walk away from the other. He should have known Robin could look after herself.

He watched with some satisfaction as she turned down an invitation to dance with Alan Sutherland. Instead, she spent that dance talking quietly with Buck in a corner well back from the dancing. He spotted Rick Dyer out on the dance floor several times. He seemed to be a great source of interest to the young unmarried ladies in town. Once he actually caught Dyer's eye. The Rafter S foreman shot him a look full of venom. Nathaniel tipped his hat and grinned in return, delighted that Dyer was still furious with him.

Just when he was considering slipping out of the dance and trying to find a quick drink of something stronger than punch, Mrs. Beacham marched up to him. "Are you going to prop up this wall all night long, my boy?" the old schoolteacher asked him with a challenge in her merry brown eyes. "You hardly strike me as the wallflower type."

"No ma'am," he replied with a smile. "I've been waiting for just the right lady to come along. Would you do me the honor of being my partner for this next dance?"

"I'd be delighted," she said with a chuckle. "I believe there are a dozen young ladies right now who would kill to be in my shoes. You're causing quite a stir tonight."

That old lady sure was light on her feet. She whirled around the room with the energy of a twenty-year-old. She didn't even look winded when the music to the lively polka ended.

"Goodness, that was fun. Now, there are a few folks here I want you to meet. I know you plan to move on soon, but I'm hoping you'll see that there are some men in these parts you would enjoy as friends if you did decide to settle here." Holding his arm so firmly he couldn't slip away, she maneuvered him back into the crowd.

To his surprise, he did enjoy talking to Fred Dreyer, owner of the *Grand Valley Record* and Jim Halpert, proprietor of the only hotel in town. They were both down-to-earth sorts with dry senses of humor common to most western men. Throughout his conversation with them, Nathaniel found himself still keeping an eye on Robin and Betsy.

Robin, he saw with some irritation, was dancing for a second time with a pretty-faced blond young sprig of a cowpoke with a black-and-white calfskin vest who held her far too closely for Nathaniel's peace of mind. The young cowboy was plenty intrigued with her bodice and what was beneath it, too. He was just better at hiding his interest than the others. He only peeked down her dress front when Robin glanced away to smile at friends.

Nathaniel was startled to find himself heading their way the moment the music ended. The young cowboy was still holding her hand, clearly intending to steal the next dance with Robin as well.

"She promised this next dance to me," Nathaniel informed the young man bluntly and sent him such a murderous look that the protest the cowboy was about to make died on his lips.

"Why, sure, Marshal Hollister. Guess I'll just mosey along then." The young cowpoke flashed Robin an apologetic smile and beat a hasty retreat.

"I never promised you this dance," Robin told Nathaniel, her eyes snapping with irritation. "You never asked me for one."

"I'm asking you now," he said abruptly and swung her into his arms just as the band began playing a waltz. "That young fellow was holding you way too tightly, and his hands were starting to head places they had no right to roam."

"He was fun to talk to, and he was a good dancer," Robin countered indignantly. "Besides, whom I dance with and how they hold me is absolutely none of your business."

"Someone has to look out for you since you obviously don't have the sense to do it yourself."

"I believe we've had this discussion a hundred times before," she said with a sigh. "Could we be quiet for once and enjoy this dance? I love waltzing."

The wistful look in her eyes disarmed him completely. "All right," he agreed. "Let's do exactly that."

They waltzed well together, despite the differences in their height. She was graceful and light on her feet. As he gazed down at her face, he decided she looked like she ought to be a debutante at some society ball back east with her fine, delicate features. Her mother must have been quality. Betsy had told him once that their Virginia relations could trace their ancestry back to the nobility in England. On his father's side, Nathaniel came from a long line of self-made men. He was proud of those humble origins, and he took secret pleasure in his Indian blood.

The differences in their background, though, brought home to him once again how impossible it was to think of their having anything together. *Hell, you of all people should know how useless it is to worry about what you can't have. Just enjoy what you do have this very moment.*

He tightened his grip and pulled her closer. He concentrated on how good it felt to have her in his arms. He liked the rose scent she wore. Remembering how lovely she looked before the fire this afternoon, he fantasized about pulling out her hairpins and bringing the elaborate coiffure Betsy had styled tumbling down about Robin's pretty white shoulders. That kind of thinking got him hard with longing in no time.

She looked just as dazed as he felt when the music finally ended. He glanced up from her and saw the young cowpoke was looking hopefully in Robin's direction. Nathaniel glared at him, seeing red all over again.

"If you dance with that pretty boy in the calfskin vest again, I may have to take him outside and pound some manners into him."

He ignored her gasp of outrage and went to find himself something stronger to drink. After throwing on his coat, he stepped outside and headed for the closest saloon. He didn't bother to button his coat against the cold November wind. His body needed to cool off. As he stomped down the street, he was too frustrated to appreciate the glorious winter sunset turning the western skies vivid orange and scarlet.

At the Golden Spike, he promptly downed two good belts of whisky. He didn't dare stay for long. Lord only knew what sort of trouble Robin might stumble into while he was gone. He was mildly relieved when he returned to the church to find she was taking a turn at the piano. At least for the next hour or so she wouldn't be dancing with any partners with roving hands.

Shortly after Nathaniel returned to his spot along the wall, a tall, distinguished-looking man with gray hair and a gray handlebar mustache approached him.

"Nathaniel Hollister, we haven't met," the older man said genially, "but I believe it's in both our best interests that we do so. My name is Vance Sutherland."

As they shook hands, Nathaniel studied Sutherland with interest. So this was the famous cattleman he'd heard so much about. Vance Sutherland was a big man with plenty of strength in his grip, even though he had to be in his sixties. He was dressed like a prosperous rancher, in a dark suit that had been tailored well. His face was tanned and lined from years spent out-of-doors, and his pale blue eyes were cool and shrewd.

"So, how do you like Grand Valley?"

"Seems like a pleasant enough place," Nathaniel replied. His gut instinct told him Sutherland wanted something from him.

"I understand that you recently retired from law enforcement."

"That's right."

"I might just have a job for a man of your talents."

"Just what did you have in mind?" Nathaniel said, playing along for the moment. It couldn't hurt to listen to the rancher, although he had absolutely no interest in working for the man who had caused Robin so much trouble.

"You've a reputation for getting the job done. A big outfit like mine faces constant challenges from upstarts and Johnny-come-latelies who believe they're entitled to their share. They have no idea of the kind of effort, guts, and gumption it took to build the Rafter S into what it is today."

"The Matthewses are hardly latecomers," Nathaniel pointed out dryly.

Sutherland's genial expression turned cold. "No, but the idea of a bunch of children running that place is ludicrous."

"I suppose some folks might think that."

"That foolish young woman is managing her range and her herds poorly, and her spread is falling apart. It's appalling that she doesn't have the sense to sell out."

Even though some of Robin's outbuildings might be falling apart, she was doing a fine job of managing her cattle and her range. Nathaniel decided then and there that Vance Sutherland was an arrogant son of a bitch. He had guessed that he wouldn't like the famous rancher, based on the hard time his cowboys had been giving Robin. From his experience as a law officer, though, Nathaniel had wanted to reserve judgment until he'd met the man in person.

"From what I can see, she and her brothers are doing a pretty good job with their place."

"I had hoped I might be able to count on you to talk some sense into her."

"Miss Matthews is one headstrong young woman."

"Her headstrong nature is going to lead that young woman straight into disaster."

Nathaniel stood up a little straighter. "Exactly what sort of disaster do you mean?"

Sutherland shrugged his shoulders and looked away. "Lots of things could happen to her and her family. Ranching can be a risky business. She's going to run that ranch right into the ground, and when she gets around to trying to sell it, the Rocking M will be worth a fraction of what it's worth now. However, I didn't really come over here to discuss Miss Matthews or her misguided effort to run her own ranch."

Like hell you didn't, Nathaniel thought savagely.

"Let's go back to that job I had in mind for you. I'll pay you a hundred dollars a month if you come to work for me. You'd be second only to my foreman, Rick Dyer."

Nathaniel hid a grin over that notion. Dyer would be thrilled to be working alongside the fellow who helped dump him face first into a garden full of manure.

"What exactly would I be doing for your outfit?"

"You'd be in charge of taking care of problems. You have certain skills that could come in handy for us."

"You mean, my being fast with a gun and all," Nathaniel drawled.

"That, along with a certain mindset you possess. I've heard that you're the sort of man who doesn't flinch from doing what needs to be done."

Nathaniel's stomach twisted. Clearly Sutherland thought he was no better than a hired killer. He barely managed to hold on to his rising temper.

"Thanks for the offer, but I got a job I like pretty well right now. I think I'll stay on at the Rocking M for a while longer."

There was no sense telling the man he planned to ride on come spring. He wanted to let Robin profit from whatever protection his name gave her for as long as possible.

"Let's put this another way," Sutherland said grimly. "I'll make it worth your while to ride right out of Grand Valley tomorrow. I'll pay you five hundred dollars to stop working for the Rocking M."

Five hundred dollars? That old bastard really did want to get his hands on the Rocking M. "And if I don't?"

Vance Sutherland's eyes turned cold as ice. "Then you'd be a fool, and you don't strike me as a fool, Mr. Hollister. Working for Robin Matthews has proven to be a dangerous occupation recently."

"Are you threatening me?"

"Just making an observation."

"Here's an observation for you. The last man who threatened me is buried six feet under back in Kansas. You tell your boys to lay off the Rocking M, or they'll be answering to me."

Nathaniel drew a great deal of satisfaction from walking away from one of the most famous and powerful ranchers in the West.

Vance Sutherland stared after Hollister, so enraged he wanted to smash his fist into the marshal's face. Unfortunately, he'd worked too hard to build his standing in the community to destroy it all by brawling at a dance. The moment he'd heard Robin Matthews's sodbusting cousin was actually Nathaniel Hollister, he'd been furious. No wonder the man had managed to whip Shorty and Pete so easily. Hollister had a well-deserved reputation as a ruthless fighter.

It was a bad stroke of luck that he seemed to have staked his claim on Robin Matthews and the Rocking M. Still, he was only one man, and the boys working at the Rafter S had always been a salty bunch.

Rick Dyer, who'd come to read the old man's moods well,

sensed an opportunity. Purposely, he strolled over to Vance's side.

"Arrogant son of a gun, ain't he?"

"Boy, if you can find a way to get rid of Hollister for me, I swear you'll always have a place for yourself at the Rafter S." Sutherland strode off, obviously still fuming.

Rick Dyer smiled. What a piece of luck. He'd been thinking about bracing Hollister anyway. He owed him for landing him in a garden full of shit and making him look like a fool. To be the man who fetched Nathaniel Hollister would be a way to make a real reputation for himself overnight. It only made matters sweeter that Hollister had made it possible for him to finally get a piece of the Rafter S.

Dyer leaned back against the wall and watched Hollister work his way across the room. For a living legend, Hollister didn't look too tough. Hell, he was getting gray. Dyer ignored the girls trying to catch his eye and indulged himself in imagining the fame and fortune that would come his way after he shot the most famous ex-lawman in the West full of holes.

Chapter Seventeen

After talking with Sutherland, Nathaniel went to find Robin. It was past nine o'clock, and this dance business had suddenly gotten mighty old. He found her sitting along the far wall with Tommy slumped tiredly against her.

"Did you have a nice chat with Vance Sutherland?" she asked him sweetly.

"Don't start with me now. I'll tell you about it later. You just about ready to quit this shebang?"

"I think so. Jessie's fast asleep under the table, and Tommy's apt to nod off any moment now."

"I'll round up the rest so you don't have to move him. That little man's had a big day."

He found the twins deep in a pack of boys about their age in one corner of the church, and he discovered Betsy in a group of giggling girls in another. Soon he had everyone gathered up and headed toward the door. He was surprised by how many folks called out goodbyes to him as he left. He couldn't remember half of their names, so he just smiled, nodded, and wished Robin would hurry up saying her farewells.

All in all, he was glad when he finally had everyone loaded up in the sleigh at Mrs. Beacham's and they headed back toward the ranch. The night was cold and clear. The moon, three-quarters full, shone off the snow and turned the mountain world around them almost as bright as day. The wind whistling down from the high peaks was icy cold.

Nathaniel welcomed the glacial wind, for it helped to score away some of his shame and fury. He shouldn't care what a greedy, land-hungry man like Sutherland thought of him. Somehow it still stuck in his craw that the rancher clearly believed Nathaniel Hollister was a ruthless, conscienceless man, willing to sell his gun and himself for the right price. Is that what his reputation had become?

The closer he drove to the Rocking M, the more another worry began to plague him. What if something had happened while they were gone? When they drove up to the ranch house and found everything was fine, he was deeply relieved. Sutherland had probably told his riders to back off the Rocking M until he'd had a chance to make his job offer.

Now, though, things were apt to get dicey. Nathaniel knew he had angered Sutherland tonight. The rancher was a man used to people fearing him, and he was used to getting his own way. Trouble from the Rafter S was likely to start up again. That news Nathaniel dreaded having to share with Robin.

After unloading everyone at the house, Nathaniel went to the barn to put up the team. When he finished, he went to the kitchen to thaw out, drink some coffee, and talk with Robin if she was still awake.

He'd only been sitting at the table for a few minutes when she came downstairs from helping to put Tommy and Jessie to bed. Still done up in her mother's fancy dress, she fetched hot water from the stove and made herself some tea. Tendrils of hair had escaped from her hairpins. She appeared slightly mussed, soft, and very feminine. Just looking at her in that get up made him ache. She sat across the kitchen table from him and sent him an earnest smile.

"I wanted to thank you for talking me into having us all go to the dance tonight. I think it was wonderful for everyone, particularly the twins and Betsy. You were right. They do need to get into town more often and spend more time with their friends. I've been so caught up in our problems out here that I've lost sight of what's best for my family."

"I think that's putting it a little harshly."

"I'm not so sure it is. This whole dance business has made me do some hard thinking about our situation here. You can tell me it's none of my business, but I'd really like to know what Sutherland had to say to you."

"He offered me a job at the Rafter S, working as segundo to Rick Dyer, for damn good money."

"Are you thinking about taking it?"

"I don't think I'd like working for Sutherland much, and I know Dyer and I'd probably end up shooting each other within a week. I told him I wasn't interested."

She leaned back in her chair, unable to hide her relief.

"Then he offered me five hundred dollars to leave the Rocking M and go elsewhere."

She blinked at that. "That's a pile of money," she said slowly. "That's enough for you to start your own spread, or your own business, or just about anything you might want to do."

"Maybe so, but I didn't take him up on that offer, either. I told him I'll leave Grand Valley when I'm good and ready."

"I bet he didn't like that much. No one says no to Vance Sutherland."

"Except you."

She had to smile at that. "Except me. I guess you're in excellent company."

"Damn fool company, more like. I made him plenty angry. I'm guessing you'll start seeing trouble out here again, and for that, I'm sorry. He told me to tell you to sell out. I didn't tell him I'd only advised you to do that a hundred times already."

"Thanks. Maybe I should sell out and go live with my

grandmother. If I wrote to her and explained the situation, perhaps she would take in Jessie and Tommy as well.''

Restlessly, she stood up from the table and began to pace back and forth across the room. ''I love this place, but tonight made me see I might be trying to hold on to a dream that only I believe in. Maybe the Rocking M isn't the best future for Jake, Luke, and Betsy.''

''Maybe you should ask them. They all have good heads on their shoulders. I'd say they're plenty grown-up and deserve a say in this decision.''

Robin paused in her pacing, obviously struck by his suggestion. ''I might just do that. I hope they won't vote to stay for my sake. I could always come back out here after they're married and settled in good lives in Virginia.''

''What about you getting married and settled?''

She wrinkled her nose at that. ''I don't think I could be a traditional wife after living the way I have these past few years. Besides, ranching's in my blood.''

''You really love it all that much?''

''I can't say I care much for cows, but I love working outside all day. The days I stay in with Betsy and help her do the laundry and clean the house just about drive me crazy.''

She had a point there. He wouldn't much care for doing chores like that inside all day himself. ''Go catch yourself some rich Virginia planter, and then you won't have to clean your house or do your own laundry.''

She looked at him for a moment and then burst out laughing. ''It's a good plan, but what rich man would possibly want to marry me? Look at me. I'm tanned darker than a turtle, and I've more freckles than a spotted hog.''

''What's wrong with a few freckles? You look a sight more healthy than those pale girls who stay indoors all day.''

Her smile faded. ''Look at my hands, then,'' she said quietly. ''I've never been good about wearing work gloves.'' She walked around to his side of the table and held her hands out for him to inspect.

Since it seemed so important to her, he looked. By the light from the table lamp, he could see small white scars scattered across the backs of her hands. Most had probably come from working with barbed wire, he guessed. She turned them over, and he could see the calluses on her palms.

"These aren't the hands of a gentleman's wife," she said bitterly.

"If that's all a man cares about, he doesn't deserve you as a wife."

She looked so unconvinced, he rose to his feet and took her hands in his own.

"A man would have to be blind not to want you." The desire he had been fighting for weeks now leapt to life. "The more time I spend around you, the more fetching you seem to me. Tonight, in this rig, I bet you'd outshine the finest belles in Virginia."

She looked at him, a world of hurt in her mist-green eyes. "Don't tease me so. I know I've never been pretty."

"I don't know how you ever got such an addlepated notion in your noggin."

"I was homely as a stick when I was Betsy's age. I was always scrawny as a wet hen, and my eyes were too big for my face. The boys at school used to call me frog eyes."

"I'll have to take your word for it. Sometime since you were twelve, your looks changed considerably. I thought you were pretty from the first moment I saw you passed out cold beside the trail. As soon as I saw you with your hat off, I knew you were a young woman, and a fine-looking one at that."

"I'm still not sure I believe you, but you're mighty kind to say such a thing to me anyway."

"Kindness has absolutely nothing to do with it. I'm not a kind man." He raised her hand to his mouth and kissed the backs of her knuckles. She drew in a breath and her eyes darkened. He turned her hands over and pressed a kiss to the sensitive skin at her wrist. In that moment, he wanted to make sure that she desired him as much as he desired her. He pulled her into his arms. Although he longed to devour her, he remembered how skittish she had been before and forced himself to take it slow.

Rather than home in on her lips, he kissed the line of her jaw, and then detoured lower to taste the creamy flesh at the base of her neck. With a small laugh, she flung her arms around his neck and nestled closer to him of her own accord.

"How can you do this to me with just a few kisses?" she admitted breathlessly. "My knees feel like water, and there's the oddest feeling deep in my stomach."

Lord, she was so innocent. He eased back so that he could look at her. "You shouldn't admit such things to a gent. He's liable to take advantage."

"I'm beginning to wonder if I would mind that so much, with you," she said, her eyes wide and candid.

"Christ, you shouldn't be admitting that, either," he said roughly and pulled her full against him. This time he couldn't hold back. He plundered her lips, loving their softness and the generous response she gave him. He smoothed his hands over her shoulders, enjoying the sinful texture of the silk in her dress. He found that he liked the smoothness of the skin of her neck and arms even better. Drinking in the delicate rose scent she wore, he kissed her cheeks, her eyelids, her nose, and returned to sample her lips once again. He wanted everything from her, and he wanted it now.

Shocked by that thought, he forced himself to ease back from her. *Hell, boy, if you don't watch it, you'll spook her again.* As he gazed down at her, he had to admit she didn't look spooked. Her cheeks were flushed, and her eyes were dark with a passion that matched his own. Most of her hair had come loose from its pins, making her look disheveled and more appealing than ever. Remembering when she had brushed that gold fall of hair before the fire this afternoon, he almost groaned.

Purposefully, he reached out and began searching for her remaining hairpins and removing them. He wanted to see that remarkable hair of hers down again, loose about her shoulders. She stared at him, her eyes questioning.

"Sh," he said, unconsciously employing the voice he used to calm wild things. "I just want to see your hair again, like it was today."

"All right," she said after a long moment. "Let me do it. You'll never find all the pins."

She raised her arms up to reach the hairpins she mentioned and began removing them with quick, deft movements. Nathaniel swallowed hard. In that position, he could see the graceful line of her neck and the way the bodice of her dress tightened across her breasts.

She removed the last two pins, and the heavy mass of hair at her nape fell free. Neatly, she placed the pins on top of the others on the table, and then she looked at him, that unsure, questioning light in her eyes again. Wordlessly, he reached out and gently pulled a large section of her hair forward over her shoulder.

He held her hair to the light. The different colors in it fascinated him. The top layers had been bleached by the sun to the shade of palest flax. Beneath that, her hair darkened into shades of gold and amber. He pulled more of her hair over her other shoulder, and then he stepped back to admire his handiwork. She reminded him of an illustration he'd loved as a boy in one of his childhood books. It was a picture of a princess with a river of hair like Robin's, and the same look in her eyes— grave and shy. Now, the adult in him found her as seductive as hell.

"Don't you ever, ever think of yourself as homely again," he said, his voice gone thick with desire. He picked her up and set her on the kitchen table. He lifted her chin and kissed her deeply. Lord, he wanted her, but he couldn't forget all the reasons why he couldn't take her. He stepped closer, using his hands to urge her legs apart beneath her skirts. He couldn't bear to stop just yet. He just wanted to touch a little more. Then he would stop.

He reached down and lifted her skirt and petticoats. He found her calf, deliciously soft and warm through the thin fabric of her drawers. He smoothed and massaged up and down her legs and stepped even closer, until the part of him that ached to be buried inside her touched the warmth of her center. Surely he could just explore a little further—and then he would stop.

Her hands clenched on his shoulders. Afraid she might be about to voice a protest, he kissed her deeply and began to rock gently against her. She squirmed against him, clearly enjoying the sensation. She raised one leg and urged him tighter against her.

Her passionate response was too much for his self-control. He slipped his hands upward under her skirts until he cupped her buttocks. He thrust and thrust again, mimicking the act of love, so tight and hot he thought he would explode then and there.

Trapped so deep in his own passion, it took him a moment to realize there was suddenly something different in her movements. She was still squirming, but now she was pulling away from him, and she was actually hitting at his chest and shoulders. He let go of her at once and stepped away. She'd gone white as a sheet, and she was trembling.

Desperately, he tried to fight down his desire and think. What was wrong with her? He could have sworn she was just as aroused as he was moments ago.

She wrapped her arms around herself and stared at the floor, her body wracked with tremors. Slowly, it dawned on him. He'd seen this kind of behavior before, in the victims of violence who had survived the worst kind of shock. He finally realized what must have happened to her, and a black rage boiled up inside him. Why hadn't he guessed it before? The signs had been there, but she was so plucky and cheerful, she'd done a damn good job of hiding it.

"I'm s-so sorry," she got out between trembling breaths. "I don't mean to be a tease. Really I d-don't."

"You don't have a thing to be sorry for, but I'm guessing

someone else does,'' he said bleakly. "Did someone rape you?''
The words were brutal, but he'd also come to realize that getting
women to talk frankly and matter-of-factly often seemed to
help them cope better with the terrible experience of being
violated.

"No,'' she said, not meeting his eyes, "but he tried.''

"Who was it?'' As he asked the question, he thought of all
the men he had met in Grand Valley, and then he knew. "It
was Rick Dyer, wasn't it?''

She nodded.

He was stunned by the force of the fury sweeping through
him. If Dyer had been within arm's reach right then, he would
have killed him. He would have drawn his gun and shot him
in the heart. It was simple as that. He had never really understood crimes of passion—the kind of intensity of feeling that
led husbands to shoot unfaithful wives or their lovers—until
now.

Dimly, he realized she had begun to speak in a low, strained
voice. "I was out checking the range one day when Dyer and
two of his friends, Shorty Wilcox and Pete Johnson rode up.
Vance had hired Dyer just a few months earlier, and I didn't
know then what he was like. I let them get close, and they got
the drop on me and forced me to get off my horse.''

She paused and drew in a deep, shuddering breath. When
she spoke again, her voice was stronger and more bitter. "Dyer
told me he was going to rape me, and then his friends were
going to have me, too. They'd do it again, any time they had
a chance, until I came to my senses and sold out to their boss.
They would have raped me that day, except for Buck. He had
been visiting out at our place, and he'd come to say goodbye
to me. I don't think he understood what Dyer meant to do, but
he could see he was hurting me, and so Buck just tore into
him. He's tremendously strong, and he broke Dyer's arm pulling
him off me. Shorty Wilcox and Pete Johnson didn't dare shoot
Buck because he was the boss's son.''

"Thank heavens Buck came looking for you.''

"Buck got me home, and I never told the twins or Betsy what happened that day. Ever since then, I just about freeze up when a man touches me or even looks my way. I stopped going to town unless I absolutely had to, and I felt so much safer wearing Papa's clothes. For a time I think I went a little crazy. I almost cut my hair off, too, but I remembered how much Mama and Papa had liked it. I just didn't want any man to think that I wanted, that I . . ." Her voice caught, and she stared down at her lap.

Gently, Nathaniel reached out and tipped her chin up so that she had to look at him. "Of course you didn't want a man to use you that way. Nothing you did encouraged or enticed Dyer. He's a cruel, brutal animal, and he was looking for a way to shame and intimidate you into giving up your ranch."

"I've told myself that a thousand times, but it's still hard to believe it. I am so sorry. I had hoped it might be different with you, but I can't seem to get past what almost happened to me."

"Robin Matthews, you have absolutely nothing to apologize for."

He could tell she wasn't really listening to him. "I just keep remembering what it felt like," she said, her voice gone high and tight, "his pawing at me, the ugly things he said he was going to do to me while he pulled at my clothes." A deep, wracking sob escaped her, and she buried her face in her hands.

"Shh, now, it's all right. It's going to be all right." He wasn't quite sure how to handle a sobbing female, so he acted on gut instinct. Taking her hand, he led her to a chair. He sat down first and gently pulled her into his lap. She buried her face in his shirt front and cried her eyes out. He patted her back, tried to say reassuring things from time to time, and let her tears run their course. With all that pent up inside her, she was entitled to take her time letting it out. When she finally seemed to be slowing down, he handed her his handkerchief.

She accepted it with a grateful sniff. "I've gotten your best shirt and jacket all wet," she said woefully.

"They'll dry out just fine."

"I don't know what came over me. I hardly ever cry. I hate women who start weeping at the first bit of trouble."

"Guess I don't much care for weepy women myself, but you, Robin Matthews, are not a weepy female. The woman who took on six rustlers and rode uncomplainingly through the night with a hole in her side is not the type to start leaking tears easily."

She let go a watery chuckle at that. "Thank you. You do come up with the most original compliments."

"I aim to please. Now, I'm going to give you some less than original advice. You've had quite a day, and it's past time you got some sleep." He urged her to her feet. Obedient as a child, she followed him down the hallway to her room. On the threshold, she stopped dead, color rising in her cheeks.

"I need to go fetch Betsy. She said she'd wait up for me. I can't get out of this rig on my own," she gestured toward her dress.

"I'll go get her for you," he offered and slipped upstairs. When he reached Betsy's room, he discovered she had already fallen sound sleep in her dressing gown on top of her counterpane, her lamp still turned up. Little Jessie slept soundly beside her in her trundle.

He smiled as he looked down at them. They both sure had enjoyed that dance tonight. Betsy had laughed and smiled her way through it, and Jessie had run about beaming at everyone. Quietly he pulled a heavy quilt up over Betsy's shoulders and blew out her lamp.

"She's dead to the world," he explained when he returned to Robin's room. "I can wake her if you want, or I can undo those dress hooks for you. I expect you're wearing so many layers under that thing, I won't see anything the least bit interesting."

"All right," she said simply. Either she was too spent to argue, or too practical, or too trusting. She turned to present her back to him and lifted her hair out of his way. Even though he had no intention of taking advantage of Robin, he still discovered that unfastening her hooks was a very intimate experience. A jolt of desire shot through his body when his hand brushed the soft hair at her nape. Another jolt surged through him when his fingers touched the smooth skin above the camisole she wore. Ruthlessly he ignored the growing heat in his own body and concentrated on undoing those hooks as quickly as he could.

He couldn't escape the irony of the situation. He'd imagined himself undoing her dress in this very room more than a few times, but the circumstances were considerably different in his fantasies. Tonight she was played out from all that crying she'd just done and the long day she'd put in. He glanced at her reflection in the dressing table mirror. Her eyes were still red, and there were purple shadows under them. He still found her more desirable than any female he'd ever seen, and that notion still puzzled and alarmed him no end.

He cleared his throat when he realized he had finished with the last of the hooks. "That's it," he said gruffly.

Quickly she turned around, holding her dress up with her hands. That remarkable hair of hers rippled about her shoulders like a golden curtain. She looked like a young, innocent girl caught playing dress-up in her mother's clothes. Yet she wasn't an innocent. Not after what Rick Dyer had tried to take from her. The very thought sent Nathaniel's temper soaring once again.

"Thank you again for convincing me to go," she offered him a shy smile. "I did have a good time tonight, and I know Betsy and the twins loved every minute of it."

"You're welcome. I enjoyed it, too," he lied through his teeth. Watching her dance with every single buck at that dance tonight hadn't been his idea of a good time, nor had he much enjoyed his little chat with Vance Sutherland. Right now, keeping himself from touching her wasn't something he was enjoying, either. *You'd best walk out of here, Hollister, before you do something you both might regret later.*

Once he closed her door behind him, he headed for the kitchen. He poured himself a cup of coffee, but he found he didn't want to drink it. All he could think about was what Robin had just told him in this room. The more he thought about Rick Dyer, the angrier he became. The idea of that skunk putting his hands on his sweet Robin-girl made him want to tear the man apart.

He tossed the coffee into the stove, where it evaporated instantly with an angry hiss. Right then and there he knew what he had to do. He was going to ride into town and teach Rick Dyer a lesson.

Chapter Eighteen

Old Blue was none too pleased at the prospect of being saddled up and leaving his warm stall. Once they started on the road to town, though, the steeldust seemed to reconsider the matter and moved along, his breath creating small frosty clouds in the moonlight.

The long ride through the frozen night only honed and tempered Nathaniel's resolve. His need to call Dyer to account for his actions didn't have anything to do with Robin's struggle with Sutherland. This was strictly personal. As the snowy road slipped away beneath Old Blue's hooves, Nathaniel realized that he cared for Robin Matthews in a way he hadn't felt about anyone in years. Her pluck, her courage, her humor, her endless optimism all touched him. Dyer had tried to destroy that, sully her innocence, and quench that buoyant spirit that made Robin so unique, and that very notion made Nathaniel burn with rage.

An hour later, he was still coldly furious when he stalked up the steps into the church. He found a dozen folks still there, cleaning up after the night's festivities. He was hardly surprised to find the energetic Mrs. Beacham among them.

"Have you seen Rick Dyer?" he asked her curtly.

"Not recently. I would guess he and his friends headed to one of the saloons. Most of the young cowboys tend to do that after dances, I believe. Why do you ask?"

"I have a score to settle with him," he said simply and walked away.

"Oh, dear me. They say he's very fast with a gun, you know," she called after him.

"I don't aim to kill him, and I don't aim to let him shoot me," he called back, just to allay her fears.

When he stepped outside, he remembered there were only three real saloons in all of Grand Valley. He found Dyer at the Silver Dollar. Dyer was in the midst of a poker game with three Rafter S hands. Nathaniel recognized two of them as the men who had accosted Robin on Main Street. His anger rose again until it was an acrid taste in his mouth. He strode straight up to Dyer's table.

"I don't intend to waste a bullet on you. I plan to beat you within an inch of your life," Nathaniel declared.

"Like hell you will," Rick Dyer said and threw his cards on the table. He started to reach for the gun at his hip, but Nathaniel shoved the table into him so hard, he knocked Dyer's chair right over.

His friends rose to their feet, shouting and swearing angrily.

"You boys stay out of this. This is between the two of us."

He didn't know if they'd hold by it, but for the moment they looked like they were willing to back off. He spared a moment to wonder if anyone truly liked Rick Dyer in this town. He walked around the table to where Dyer lay on the floor struggling to get his breath back. The moment he spotted Nathaniel, he reached for his gun again. This time Nathaniel let him get his weapon out of its holster. As soon as Dyer cleared leather, Nathaniel kicked the pistol away.

"I'm going to take you apart with my bare hands."

"You're about twice my size," Dyer said sullenly as he got to his feet. "This don't seem like a real fair matchup."

"You should have thought of that before you started picking on folks younger and weaker than yourself." He didn't want to say anymore. He didn't want anyone in town to know what Dyer had almost done to Robin. She didn't need that sort of gossip, yet he did want the Rafter S foreman to know why he was about to get his pretty face rearranged.

He saw the flash of understanding in Dyer's eyes. Then Nathaniel hit him full in the face and felt the cartilage of his nose give under his knuckles. He followed up with a fist in Dyer's belly. The slight foreman doubled over clutching his stomach. Nathaniel stepped back, suddenly disgusted with the whole business. Dyer needed to be taught a lesson, but he was right. This whole match up wasn't really fair. The Rafter S foreman was small and slight and obviously not used to fighting with his hands.

Dyer finally managed to straighten up. His lower face was a mask of blood and his nose looked crooked. Nathaniel was surprised to see Dyer start toward him. At the last moment, Nathaniel saw the flicker of the blade Dyer held in his hand. *Hell, you should have known a snake like him would pull a knife.*

Nathaniel leapt back from his first lunge just in time. Dyer swiped at him again, amazingly quick and agile. This time his knife ripped across Nathaniel's arm, slicing through his thick jacket and first layers of flesh.

Nathaniel swore under his breath. If he pulled his own knife, he'd end up sticking Dyer. He'd do it if he had to, but he was sick of killing. The next time Dyer came after him, he spun away and got hold of Dyer's wrist. He twisted it until the foreman cried out, fell to his knees, and dropped the knife.

"This is for her," he said so quietly in Dyer's ears that the others couldn't hear him. "You ever touch her again, I'll shoot you down like the dog you are."

He lifted Dyer up and slugged him in the belly again. When Dyer staggered upright once more, his face was green. Nathaniel wound up and landed one so hard on his jaw that Dyer's head snapped back. He crumpled to the ground and lay still.

Nathaniel looked at Dyer's companions, who were eyeing their foreman with some shock. "Which one of you is Shorty Wilcox and which one is Pete Johnson?" he asked them grimly.

The tall one exchanged an uneasy glance with the short, stocky cowboy who was obviously Shorty Wilcox. "Ah, hell, we don't want to tangle with you again, Marshal," Shorty said.

"I'm not giving you boys any choice."

"Hollister, you break up my place, you're gonna pay for it," the barkeep interrupted them anxiously.

"That's fair enough," Nathaniel nodded to the man before he went in swinging.

This was more like it. The third cowboy had decided to join in, too, just for the hell of it. As he took on all three of them, Nathaniel finally found a vent for the anger that had been riding him since he had learned what had happened to Robin. Every punch he threw also helped him vent the frustration that had been growing in him ever since he came to the Rocking M— and found himself unable to ride away again.

He was holding his own and giving just about as good as he got when from out of nowhere, someone hit him hard alongside the head. He saw stars and fell to his knees, fighting to stay conscious. He glanced up and saw Shorty Wilcox held a chair leg in his hand, and he was grinning with a mean light in his eye. "It's a real pleasure to give you back a little of what you gave us, Marshal."

He saw Shorty raise the chair leg. Nathaniel tried to lift his arm to block the blow he knew was coming, but somehow he couldn't pull his hand up in time, and then the world went dark.

The next time he awoke, he was lying on his back, gazing up at a black sky full of ice-white stars. *Boy, you've gone and done it this time*. His body ached in a million places, and his head throbbed. Maybe he'd died and gone to heaven, or maybe he was in some sort of purgatory where he'd just have to look at heaven from a distance for the rest of eternity. Maybe that wouldn't be so bad. He'd always liked looking at stars. Just one thing puzzled him. If Shorty Wilcox had stove his head in, and he was dead, why did he hurt so much? Still vaguely contemplating that question, he passed out again.

Next time he awoke, Robin was peering down at him. Instantly, he saw the tears swimming in her beautiful green eyes. *Hell, someone had made her cry again.*

"You mustn't cry, Robin-girl," he said. It hurt like the devil, but he managed to raise a hand up and smooth away one of those tears. She took his hand and held it against her cheek. The sorrowful way she looked at his face made Nathaniel realize the truth. She was crying over him.

"You shouldn't shed a single tear over me. I'm not worth it."

"I'll cry over you if I see fit," she said tartly and lowered his hand to the bed.

He would have smiled at that if his face hadn't hurt so much. His girl still had her spunk. Worried that he seemed to have so little spunk left in himself, he glanced around. He spotted the bedposts and the pretty white curtains in the windows, and he realized at once that he was lying in Robin's bed.

Damn, Hollister, how come these things never quite come about the way you want them to? He was amused to see someone had dressed him in a large nightshirt. He hoped like hell the twins had done it instead of Robin and Betsy.

From the way the sunlight slanted through those curtains, he guessed it was morning now.

"How'd I get here, anyway? Last thing I remember, Shorty Wilcox was about to crack open my skull with a chair leg." His mouth felt curiously thick and heavy as he spoke. He reached up and discovered that he had a good-sized knot on his lower lip.

"I gather he gave it a pretty good try, but your skull was just too tough for him. After he knocked you out, the Rafter S riders were roughing you up pretty badly when Mrs. Beacham walked in with Lionel Brigham and Zachary Tuckett. She made them stop, and Lionel and Mr. Tuckett helped her load you into one of Mr. Tuckett's wagons and bring you here. She would have kept you at her place, but she was afraid the Rafter S boys might come looking for you there.''

He tried to picture the old schoolteacher facing down a half-dozen rough, tough Rafter S cowhands. It must have been quite a scene. ''That old lady sure has guts. I'm beholden to her.''

''You'll have a chance to tell her yourself. She said she'd be out in the next few days to look in on you. Between the two of us, I think she's developing a real soft spot for you.''

''I think I'm getting sweet on her as well.''

''Speaking of people being sweet on other people, the girls in town may not be so sweet on Rick Dyer anymore. I don't think he's going to look nearly so pretty now that you've broken his nose. I wish you hadn't done it, but I'm grateful just the same.'' She leaned over and kissed his forehead. The sweetness of it caught him by surprise.

''I'm going to fetch you some breakfast. I'll be back in a bit.''

He smiled up at the ceiling after she left, even though it made his mouth hurt. Lord, he was coming to like the scent of roses and lavender. Despite his best efforts to stay awake, he drifted off to sleep before Robin came back with his breakfast.

When next Nathaniel awoke, it was late afternoon. Almost at once he sensed that something was wrong. Despite the pounding in his head, he pushed himself up on his elbows and listened. He heard voices. Luke and Jake were talking urgently beneath his window.

''You go out to the barn. I'll cover the house from the horse trough. Robin said she didn't think it would come to shooting, but you never know with these boys.''

It took just a few moments for the implications of those words to sink in. Damn, the Rafter S hands had come after him. He should have considered this possibility and prepared for it, but he hadn't really been thinking straight this morning.

They'd ridden to the Rocking M, probably not out of any fondness for Dyer himself. They had come to exact retribution, either because of their loyalty to the brand they rode for, or because they feared what Sutherland would do when he found out his foreman had been beaten.

He winced as he pushed himself upright. Every muscle and nerve in his abused body screamed in protest. From his point of view, getting pounded to within an inch of his life was certainly retribution enough for taking Dyer apart, but he doubted the Rafter S boys saw it that way.

As quickly as he could, he pulled on his clean clothes he found sitting on a trunk at the foot of the bed. Ignoring his splitting head, he pulled on his socks and stomped into his boots in record time. When he stood up, the room started to spin away from him. He staggered to the doorway and held onto the doorframe until the room steadied again.

He had to find his guns, and he had to find them quickly. There was a chance Robin had stashed them out in the bunkhouse, but he was hoping she'd placed them on the gun rack in her father's study. As he strode toward the front of the house, he started working and stretching his stiff hands. He had to have them limber enough to pull a trigger shortly, despite the pounding he had given them last night.

He looked into the darkened study. Sure enough, she'd hung them up high on the rack, where Tommy and Jessie couldn't reach them.

Swearing at his stiff, swollen hands, he buckled on his cartridge belt as fast as he could. He peered through the shutters at the drive in front of the house. A half-dozen riders were clustered there. Robin stood alone on the porch facing them, her father's big twelve-bore slung under one arm. Nathaniel took his Winchester from the rack, checked its load, and headed for the hallway. Robin had left the door partially open, and through it he could clearly hear what the Rafter S riders were saying to her.

"We want you to hand him over, and then we'll go peaceably," a burly cowboy with a gray ten-gallon hat demanded.

"Mr. Hollister works for me. I'm not handing him over to anyone. You'll go peaceably, and you'll go right now."

"He jumped our foreman for no reason and beat him pretty bad, and we mean to make him pay. Then we're going to put him on the first train out of here," the burly one said with relish.

"I'd think you boys would think twice before you tried to run a man like Mr. Hollister out of town."

"He wasn't so tough the other night," sneered Shorty Wilcox, standing in the front of the group.

"And exactly how many of you boys did he take on at once? I heard he was pretty much holding his own until you snuck up from behind and knocked him out with a chair leg, Shorty."

"Hell, we aren't getting anywhere with all this palaver," the burly man said impatiently. "You hand him over, girlie, or we'll take him ourselves." All six of the riders dismounted and started for the front porch.

"The first man who sets foot on those stairs is going to get a belly full of buckshot," Robin told them coolly, and she cocked both barrels on the shotgun.

"You don't have the guts to pull that trigger," Shorty snarled at her.

"Oh, don't I? Who wants to risk his life to find out?"

Nathaniel could tell she was getting riled now. He decided he'd better show himself before she lost her temper and actually shot one of these fools. They also probably thought he was too laid up to be a threat. He winced as he reached for the door handle. He almost was too banged up to be of much good to anyone, but he sure as hell wasn't going to let them see that.

"Howdy, boys. Mind if I join this party?" He stepped through the doorway and raised the muzzle of his rifle until it was trained at the burly cowpoke's midsection. He shifted several steps to the right, away from Robin. If shooting started, he wanted them aiming at him instead of her. Facing two guns at such close range sobered them some—just as he thought it might.

"By the way, Miss Matthews's brothers have you boys in their sights as well," Nathaniel pointed out in a cordial tone. "Say, Jake, who do you think you could hit from where you're sitting?"

"I reckon I can plug the one with the red muffler real easy," Jake sang out. The cowboy with the red muffler blanched and looked around wildly, trying to spot Jake.

"How about you, Luke?"

"I've got Shorty dead to rights. I suppose I could miss at this range, but I'd probably wing someone else while I was at it."

Nathaniel hid a smile. Those boys made him so damn proud.

"Mr. Hollister, I'm up here, too, and I'm quite sure I can drop the gentleman with the ten-gallon hat if I put my mind to it," Betsy said in her sweet, ladylike voice from her upstairs window. Nathaniel smiled openly this time. These Matthews females were surely something else.

"There you have it, boys. You're bucking a stacked deck. What happened between Dyer and me was strictly personal, but believe me, he had a whipping coming."

The silence stretched. The Rafter S hands wanted his blood, and they hated to back down. He'd seen groups of men work themselves into this kind of killing frenzy before. As much as they longed to nail his hide, none of those riders was prepared to die today. He could see it in Shorty Wilcox's eyes—that cowboy wanted to take him worse than anyone, but he was the biggest coward in the lot.

"All right, Hollister," Shorty said angrily. "It looks like you're holding all the aces this time, but we ain't through with you, not by a long shot. Mark my words, you yellow son of a bitch. You step off this ranch where you don't have a bunch of kids to protect you, and we'll be looking for you."

Nathaniel's blood raged at the insult. In another life, he would have called their bluff and reached for his guns. A cold, rational voice in the back of his mind warned him—there were too many of them, his hands were too stiff, and Robin stood too close to risk an all-out gun battle.

"The next time I come to town, I'll be looking for the two of you." He nodded to the big cowboy and Shorty. "Now get off the Rocking M before my boss gets trigger happy."

They went, their expressions sullen. Nathaniel didn't relax his guard until they had ridden out of sight.

When he glanced over at Robin, she was studying him curiously. "You almost took on all six of them, didn't you?" she asked.

"The thought crossed my mind," he had to admit.

"You'd think someone in your line of work would know better," she said with a sniff.

"Well, I didn't do it in the end. I didn't want those boys shooting out all these nice glass windows of yours or getting blood on your stairs," he replied mildly. He kind of liked the way she got all huffy when she was worried about him.

"Thanks for caring so much about my windows," she said with a wry smile.

"Thank you for refusing to turn me over to them."

"The Rocking M protects its own." She held his gaze defiantly, daring him to contradict her claim that he was a part of her ranch. He didn't say a word. The way he felt right now, one standoff was about all he could handle. Besides, he almost liked the notion of being a part of a place, even if it was only on a temporary basis.

After a long moment, she turned on her heel and walked inside. Nathaniel followed and hung his guns carefully on the rack in the study. Later, he meant to take them back to Robin's bedroom. There was always a chance the Rafter S hands might change their minds and come raiding in the night.

"I've got some soup here for you," Robin called to him. Ignoring his pounding headache, he went to the kitchen and downed two large bowls of chicken soup and a cup of coffee. After telling the twins to keep watch through the night, he got his guns, went back to Robin's room, and put his aching body straight to bed. When he pushed his feet down under the covers, he almost jumped out again. There was something hard and warm wrapped in cloth at the bottom of the bed. Gingerly, he reached down and fished it out.

Son of a gun. After holding their own during a real Mexican standoff, Robin and Betsy had thought to put a hot brick in the bottom of his bed. Grinning to himself, he shoved the brick back down to the bottom of the bed. Enjoying the unaccustomed warmth by his feet, he soon fell fast asleep.

Chapter Nineteen

Over the next few days, Nathaniel stayed in bed and slept a great deal. Every time Robin went into her room to tend him, she had to bite her lip to keep from crying. Nathaniel's face had swollen from the terrible beating he had taken until she hardly recognized him. She could tell he hurt from his slow, stiff movements. Doc Peterson came out to examine him.

"He's got a concussion and a cracked rib," Doc told her after he finished with his exam. "He's damn lucky he's got such a thick skull. He's got two good-sized knots on his head and bruises all over the rest of him. It was a darn good thing Agnes Beacham got him out of the Silver Dollar when she did. Those Rafter S boys might have beaten him to death."

The very thought of it made Robin's throat go tight. She felt so guilty. She knew Nathaniel had gone to find Dyer that night just because of what she'd told him. How she wished now that she had managed to keep her secret to herself. Still, it was as if a tremendous weight had been lifted from her shoulders. Until four days ago, she had never realized how that awful afternoon with Rick Dyer had haunted her. Somehow simply sharing the truth of what had happened had lightened a burden that had been bearing down on her for two years.

Two days after the Rafter S hands had tried to take him from the ranch, Mrs. Beacham came to call on Nathaniel. He was awake and trying to ignore the way his head pounded when the old lady came bustling into the room.

"Well, don't you look a sight," she hailed him cheerfully.

"I take some comfort from the fact that Rick Dyer probably looks worse."

She chuckled at that and settled herself in the rocker beside the bed. "I expect your head hurts like the devil, and Robin tells me you're being stubborn about taking laudanum."

Nathaniel made a noncommittal noise. He didn't want to be all drugged up if the Rafter S boys decided to come calling again.

"I expect you don't want to be feeling foggy if some of Sutherland's riders show up, but I thought if you took a nip of this from time to time, you might be able to take the edge off your headache."

To his amazement, she handed him a neat little whisky flask. He unscrewed the top and caught a whiff of its contents. Grand Valley's schoolmistress had indeed just brought him some mighty strong whisky.

"In general I don't approve of drinking spirits, but there's no question in my mind that whisky can have medicinal value. Go ahead and have a sip."

"Mrs. Beacham, you are something," he said admiringly and did as she urged. The neat whisky burned its way down his throat.

"Well, I think you're something special, too," she said with a prim smile, "so we're even." She rose to her feet and shut the door.

"Now, tell me why you took it into your head to go after Rick Dyer like that," she ordered once she returned to the rocker.

Nathaniel considered her request. That incident with Rick

Dyer was really Robin's business, but if he left the valley, he wanted someone to know the threat Dyer posed to her. And so he told the old woman what Dyer and his friends had tried to do.

Mrs. Beacham was livid by the time Nathaniel finished. "I was afraid something like that must have happened. Robin changed so much, and I didn't think it was all because her parents had died, but I never could get that girl to confide in me. Something must be done. Vance Sutherland is ruining this town. I've tried to get people to see it, but most of the shopkeepers don't want to lose his custom. He's become a lawless bully. Dear Jenna would have been so ashamed."

"Who was Jenna?"

"Vance's wife. She was a gentle soul and far too good for him. She seemed to think the sun rose and set on Vance, though, until Buck's accident."

"I've been meaning to ask someone if Buck was born slow or if something happened to him."

"There was an accident, all right. Buck was kicked in the head by a horse when he was only five years old. He was unconscious for several days, and when he woke up, he was never again the same bright boy he had been before. Jenna was devastated, but she and Vance never told anyone how the accident happened. After that, Jenna bore a series of stillborn babies, and she died bearing the last one. When she was still alive, Vance seemed content with his lot. After she died, he became more greedy and ambitious as the years wore on."

Nathaniel shook his head. He'd seen men change like this before. "Sometimes men who have the most try to grab more and more, but they can't grab enough to make themselves happy."

"That's the sad trap Vance has caught himself in now," she agreed with a mournful shake of her head, and then her expression changed.

"Now, I've one more question to ask you. I don't expect

you'll want to answer it, but I think you'll agree that you owe me after I got you out of that saloon the other night."

Nathaniel didn't like the steel glint in her eyes in the least. "What's the question?"

"Why are you so convinced that you'd make a poor husband?"

He closed his eyes, and his head began to pound worse than ever. She was right. He didn't want to answer her question, but he could hardly shout her out of the room.

He opened his eyes and glared at her. "You know what kind of man I am. I've killed a half-dozen men in my time. I've paid whores in just about every town I've ever passed through. I've spent so much time with hard cases and outlaws, I'm hardly fit to talk with civilized folks, much less live with them."

The old lady didn't look the least bit intimidated. "Those are merely habits." She dismissed his claims with an airy wave of her hand. "You know better, and you could change them if you really wanted to."

He was silent while he counted to ten. He really didn't want to swear at a sweet, interfering old lady who probably had saved his life. "I don't think I have the right nature to be good to a woman," he growled.

"Why is that?"

"I'm too cold and self-absorbed."

"Who told you that, I wonder?" Mrs. Beacham studied him curiously.

"My own mother and just about every woman I've ever spent any time with."

"I see." The old woman looked at him sympathetically. He braced himself for a question about his mother, but instead she surprised him with a different comment. "Betsy and Robin don't seem to think you're cold or selfish."

"Those little gals are hardly fit judges of human character. They see the best in everyone."

"They are shrewder than you give them credit, and they've good cause to be wary of people these days. Yet they've taken you in and made you a part of their family. Would a cold, selfish man go riding into town to avenge the honor of a sweet young woman he cares for deeply? You think on that while you're healing up.''

Before Nathaniel could think of a convincing counterargument, the old woman swept from his room, leaving him to his headache and his bitter thoughts.

The next morning Robin found Nathaniel sitting up in bed reading *Kennilworth.*

''Hope you don't mind my borrowing this,'' he gestured to the book. ''I got restless in the middle of the night and fetched this from your father's office.''

''I mind that you got out of bed, but I don't mind your borrowing a book in the least.''

He liked to read Sir Walter Scott? Nathaniel Hollister never ceased to surprise her.

He must have sensed her reaction, for he smiled at her sheepishly and said, ''My father used to read *Ivanhoe* to us by the hour when he wasn't reading law texts to us. Maybe, if you have some time later, you could read a little to me. It hurts my head if I read for too long.''

''I'd be most pleased to read to you, right after I finish with my morning chores.'' If anyone had told her three months ago that she would have ended up reading Sir Walter Scott to the legendary lawman Nathaniel Hollister in her own bedroom, she never would have believed it in a hundred years.

An hour later she settled herself in the rocker beside his bed and began reading. From time to time, she caught him looking at her with a wistful kind of expression that made her wonder if he was concentrating on the story at all. It felt so right to have him here, in her house, almost a part of her family. Yet she knew full well that one day in the spring, he was going to saddle up Old Blue and ride right out of their lives to go see that wild country that meant so much to him. The very thought made her voice begin to quaver.

This wasn't going to do at all. When she came to the end of the chapter, she closed the book firmly.

"Have you thought much about Christmas?" she asked him.

"I don't suppose I have," he replied, a quizzical look in his eyes. "Am I supposed to?"

"Well, it's only five weeks away now. I believe I told you before that we put a lot into celebrating the holiday. We've a few traditions I thought you ought to know about."

"Such as?" he looked at her dubiously.

"At the start of Advent, we all make Christmas wishes, and then we do our level best to find out what those wishes are and make them come true for each other. It's just a silly game that keeps us all occupied, and we keep the wishes simple. Even though Betsy and the rest don't know what your wishes might be, I figured you ought to know they're all planning to give you presents. Since we don't have much money, we always make gifts for each other.

"They don't expect you to give them anything back," she added hastily, for he was looking more cool and distant by the moment. "I just didn't want you to laugh or be surprised on Christmas Day when you see what they've made for you. Sometimes our gifts can be a little homely."

"I promise I won't laugh. It's been a long time since anyone thought to give me a Christmas present, much less make me one."

"Don't you ever spend Christmas with your brothers?"

"Joshua is always on the move, and it's tough to catch up with him. I saw my older brother Ethan back in Buford at Christmas about eleven years ago. He was still so bitter and angry about losing his leg in the war, it wasn't much of a holiday."

"But it's not Christmas without family," she countered. "We always drive into town for church on Christmas Eve.

That night, we put up a tree and trim it. Christmas morning we open up our presents and have the best feast we can manage.''

He tugged at his sideburn and looked worried. ''I don't know if I'd be much of a hand at making presents or figuring out anyone's wishes. I expect I could help chop down a tree, and I wouldn't mind picking up a thing or two in town for the little ones.''

She was disappointed, but she didn't want him to see it. She supposed it was too much to expect him to enter wholeheartedly into the simple traditions that had given her family so much pleasure and joy over the years. ''That would be prime. Now, I best get back to the kitchen. It's laundry day, and I promised Betsy I'd lend a hand.''

Robin shook her head after she shut the door and started down the hallway toward the kitchen. Nathaniel Hollister hadn't celebrated Christmas with a family member in ten years. What a sad business that was. One thing was certain. *You and your family are going to do your very best to give Nathaniel Hollister a Christmas to remember.*

That night before she went to bed in Betsy's room, Robin stopped by to see if Nathaniel needed anything. Because his lamp was still on, she assumed he was awake. She tapped on his door lightly, but he didn't answer. She opened it quietly and slipped inside. He'd obviously dozed off while reading, for *Kennilworth* lay open against his chest. She had to smile. She had seen her father, who was an ardent reader, fall asleep in just this position many a time.

Quietly she stole over to the rocker and eased down in it. She rarely had a chance to look at Nathaniel this way. Of course, right now a woman who had never seen him before would hardly think Nathaniel was a handsome man. His lower lip was puffed out, he had a ding-dong dilly of a shiner, and the cut along his right cheekbone gave the whole right side of his face a swollen and misshapen appearance. Yet to her he still seemed handsome, particularly since he had won those bruises punishing the man who had tried to harm her.

He stirred, shifting his legs under the covers, and then he groaned, a sound she was sure he never would have made had he known he had company. His glorious blue eyes opened, and instantly he came alert. She wondered if his wariness had anything to do with the dangerous life he had led. What would it be like to be worried someone might be trying to kill you as you slept? He glanced around the room and spotted her at once.

"I didn't realize you were here," he said with a frown.

"Do you want me to fetch you some laudanum? Doc Peterson said there was no reason for you to be uncomfortable."

"No thanks."

She couldn't help sighing. He'd stubbornly refused to take anything to help against the pain his battered body must be feeling.

"I wouldn't say no to some whisky, if you have some," he said after a few moments. "Mrs. Beacham smuggled me some that I've already finished off, and it seemed to help."

He really must be hurting tonight. All thoughts of her protesting his drinking strong spirits under her roof promptly fled. "All right. We still have a few bottles that Papa kept to entertain his men friends when they came to visit. I'll go fetch you some."

When she returned from the root cellar, she held the dusty bottle out for Nathaniel to inspect.

His expression became reverent after he read the label. "This isn't rotgut, saloon-type whisky. This is the really fine stuff."

"Papa had a friend from Scotland who used to bring him a few bottles of whisky every time he came to visit. Will it help, do you think?"

"A glass of this will definitely help take the edge off, and it will taste damn good on the way down."

"I wish you wouldn't swear so much," she said as she poured him a glass.

"I've been trying. It's damn hard to change the habits of a lifetime."

She glanced up to see he wasn't looking particularly repentant.

"You seem to manage not swearing in front of Tommy, but you still slip up in front of the twins. I'm afraid the boys will start saying some of your profanities any day. They look up to you in so many ways. I swear Jake walks the way you do now, and Luke has taken to wearing a kerchief just because you wear one."

"I said I'll keep working on it," he said shortly, and she knew she would have to leave it at that.

"Do you want me to read to you again?"

"No."

She stood up from the rocker, feeling just a bit miffed.

"I would like it if you stayed and just talked to me until this whisky takes hold. Tell me about your father."

She sat down in the rocker again, remembering the time she had been laid up and Nathaniel had stayed to entertain her. Even though she was weary to the marrow of her bones, she leaned her head back and thought about her father.

"He was a kind, hardworking man. He had a real gift for telling tales and for finding the good in any given situation. His mother was a Scot, and his father was a poor English cabinetmaker who emigrated to Philadelphia. Papa didn't like city life or the furniture trade much, and as soon as he turned sixteen he headed West. He signed on with some military surveyors and rambled all over this region. When the war broke out, he joined up to fight for the Union. As soon as the fighting ended, he headed West again and bought the land for this ranch from the Utes. He met Mama while he was back East looking for cattle to improve his herds. Her folks wanted her to have nothing to do with him because he was poor, and he was a Yankee. She decided to elope with him, and I don't think either of them ever regretted that decision."

When she closed her eyes, she could see his face so clearly.

''My father was a cheerful, optimistic man. He loved music, and he was always singing or humming as he worked. He loved this ranch, and he loved us, but he loved Mama most of all. I can still remember the way he looked at her sometimes, as if he couldn't believe she was really his wife.''

Robin's throat grew tight. Would anyone ever gaze at her the way her father had gazed at her mother? Somehow she doubted it. How could any man treasure a young woman who wore union suits and jeans and could outride and outrope most cowhands?

She opened her eyes again to find that Nathaniel was watching her curiously. Feeling her cheeks warm, she hurriedly continued with her account. ''I know some of Papa's happiest times were when he sat in the parlor and listened and watched Mama play the piano.''

''What was your mother like?''

''She was the stubborn one. Once she took a stand on something, she wouldn't budge. She had to be strong-willed. She was only sixteen when she decided to run away from her family and all that she knew to come out West to live with my father. For all her ladylike ways, she had a temper, too. She and Papa had some jim-dandy fights. One time I remember she upended a pail of milk over his head because she was so furious with him. Another time, she wouldn't speak to him directly for over a month. Instead, she spoke through us, which just about drove us all crazy before they finally decided to make up.''

''Hm, seems to me there's at least two traits you inherited from your mother,'' Nathaniel declared, a teasing light in his eyes.

Robin could only sigh in agreement. ''Folks always say I look like Mama, but those who knew her well say I have her temperament, too.''

''You must miss them both very much.''

''Our family will never be the same without them. They were good people and good parents. If I ever have a marriage half as caring as theirs was, I'll consider myself lucky.''

Out of the corner of her eye, she caught Nathaniel yawning. "That's enough about me and my parents for one night," she said briskly and rose to her feet. "Do you want me to blow out your lamp?"

"Yep. That whisky did its job. I feel like I could sleep until Gabriel blows his horn," he admitted and yawned again.

She leaned over to blow out the lamp beside his bed. When she finished, the room was lit only by the light of the lamp she had brought with her. As she looked down at Nathaniel, she couldn't help wincing once again at the sight of his swollen, bruised face.

"It looks that bad, eh?" Nathaniel asked in a droll tone.

She couldn't resist reaching out and stroking a lock of his hair away from his forehead. "You've looked better," she smiled down at him. "Doc Peterson told me you'll heal up and look just fine a month from now. I'm so sorry this happened. I never should have told you about Rick Dyer."

"I didn't do it just for you," his voice was drowsy now and his eyelids were starting to flutter shut. "Man like that had to be taught a lesson before he hurt someone else."

"I know." For all Nathaniel said he was done with his career as a marshal, she knew he still had a deep-seated sense of right and wrong.

"Problem is, a beating probably wasn't enough to teach a cur like that to change his ways. Someone may have to kill him, and I don't want to be the one to do it. I've too much blood on my hands as it is."

She wanted to lean down and kiss away the bitterness in his expression. Yet she had absolutely no business kissing him, much less being alone with him in her bedroom this time of night. He'd said to her once that being in her bedroom was apt to give a man ideas. The ideas she was having about him now made her blush from head to toe. Before he could notice, she ducked down and pressed a quick kiss on his forehead. Then she picked up her lamp and beat a hasty retreat.

Her body still felt flushed when she slipped into bed beside

Betsy. Despite her weariness, Robin found she couldn't fall asleep. She kept thinking of the way Nathaniel's broad shoulders filled out her father's nightshirt, and the contrast between his brown skin and the snowy white color of the linen. When she remembered the shadow of dark hair at the neck of the nightshirt and the way his large body seemed to dwarf her parents' bed, a shiver went through her.

Most of all, she couldn't forget the sad way he spoke of holidays and the yearning way he looked at her. She simply was not going to fall in love with him. Some of that strength of will she inherited from her mother had to stand her in good stead now. A person couldn't fall in love if she absolutely refused to do it, could she?

That question kept her awake for a long time that night.

Chapter Twenty

Before the inhabitants of the Rocking M could concentrate on their serious Christmas preparations, they had Thanksgiving to celebrate, and they did that with traditional Matthews enthusiasm. Luke and Jake spent two days hunting up in the mountains on snowshoes, and came back with a deer, two spruce grouse, and a stray Canadian honker that had been fatally late in heading south for the winter.

Robin had planned on serving Nathaniel his portion of their traditional feast in bed, but that day he insisted on being up and around. She sighed and accepted the inevitable. She had a feeling it was quite an achievement to keep him in bed for three days in the first place.

Her heart beat faster in her chest when he sat down at the foot of the table opposite her that night, wearing his fancy suit and shirt. The bruises on his face had bloomed into a variety of shades of purple, and yet he still managed to look debonair and dangerous in his broadcloth suit. That night it was hard for her to keep her eyes off him as they all dug into the mountains of grouse, venison, goose, squash, yams, corn, and beans she and Betsy had spent the day preparing. In honor of the holiday, Robin opened a bottle of her mother's special chokecherry wine. Although Robin and the rest drank sparingly, just a little of the spirits at this altitude had a real impact. They all laughed more than usual. Robin thought the whole room took on a special kind of golden haze before the meal was over.

They were polishing off the pies when Jessie decided she did not want to stay in her high chair a moment longer. She toddled over to Nathaniel and imperiously demanded, "Up."

Busy recounting a hunting story to the twins, Nathaniel automatically reached over and lifted her into his lap. Robin and Betsy exchanged incredulous looks. The man who had just about run from Jessie on countless occasions was holding her at last. Jessie looked immensely pleased with herself and proceeded to help herself to the last two bites of his pie.

Nathaniel glanced across the table at Robin a few minutes later, his expression so bland that she knew he was completely aware of their reaction and amused by it. "If she has an accident on these trousers, I'm not washing them," was all he said, and then he returned to his hunting discussion with the twins.

That night after the little ones went to sleep, Robin talked Nathaniel into playing cards with them, even though she feared he might be bored by such simple entertainment. Surely he was the sort to play poker for high stakes. He surprised her by entering the spirit of old maid, seven-up, and flinch wholeheartedly. At one point he threatened to shoot Luke, and at another, he told Jake he was going to toss him down the well. The twins just grinned, Betsy giggled, and Robin found herself smiling and shaking her head.

She was going to miss Nathaniel if and when he decided to return to the bunkhouse. Somehow he seemed so much more a part of the family when he stayed in the house. She brought up that very subject later that night, after Betsy and the twins retired, leaving Nathaniel and Robin sitting alone before a crackling fire in the parlor. Between them, they were working on finishing off the last of her mother's wine. Robin knew from past experience that she might have a little headache on the morrow, but she thought she deserved a rare evening of indulgence.

"I've been thinking," she said after a time. "It works just fine, my sleeping in Betsy's room. There's really no need for you to return to the bunkhouse. It's much warmer for you here in the house, and we'll save more wood if we don't try to keep both places heated."

"I doubt that's a wise idea, but I'll think on it," he said and stared into the fire. "Thanks for that meal. I haven't sat down to a real Thanksgiving dinner in a long time."

"Betsy did all the hard parts."

"Seems to me you both were in the kitchen most of the day, hustling about."

"Well, despite my help, the meal did seem to turn out pretty well," she had to allow. As the silence lengthened between them, she couldn't help stealing a glance at him. Perhaps it was the effect of the wine, but in that moment, she longed to touch him so badly she almost cried. *It's been so long since he's kissed me. At the rate he's holding to those darn principles of his, he may never kiss me again.* Her glance fell on the playing cards, and then a daring idea occurred to her.

"I want you to play poker with me," she said before she could talk herself out of making such a bold proposal.

He glanced at her, a skeptical gleam in those shrewd blue eyes of his.

"One of our hired men taught me how, but I haven't found anyone willing to play since. Most males have some old-fashioned, half-baked notion in their heads that a woman shouldn't play such a game."

"That's a notion most God-fearing, Christian folk share, I do believe."

"Please, if you don't play with me, who will?"

"There are probably a half-dozen good reasons why I

shouldn't do this,'' he said, but she let go a breath when she realized he was reaching for the cards.

"We need something to use for chips."

"Would matches work?" she asked eagerly.

"They'll do. The real question is, what stakes are we playing for?"

"Since I don't have much money, I don't fancy playing for that." She rose to her feet and fetched the tin of matches from the kitchen. When she returned, she kept her voice deliberately light and casual. "What if we played forfeits? If I win more matchsticks by the end of the night, you have to do something I want you to do. If you win, I have to do something you want me to do."

"Those conditions are a little open-ended, aren't they?" There was a wary, speculative look in his eye now.

"We can't ask the other one to break the law, or do anything life-threatening," she replied jauntily. "Come on, this will be fun."

"Why do I have a feeling I may regret this?" he said rhetorically.

"Because I'm probably about to thrash you. I always win at cards."

"Is that so? A Hollister never turns down a challenge. Here's a fair warning for you. If I hadn't decided to be a marshal, I was going to be a gambler instead."

Thus they started off their poker game in a light, teasing manner. Robin was highly aware, though, that the atmosphere began to change as the contents in the wine bottle lowered and the night wore on. While she studied her cards, she knew that Nathaniel was studying her. She thanked her lucky stars that she had let Betsy do her hair nicely, and that she had worn her blue winter wool, her second best dress. She looked as good as she could look.

She was surprised to see the piles of matches before them remained fairly even. For all her bravado, she had expected Nathaniel to clean her out fairly quickly. Luck was with her, though, and the cards ran her way. At last, the clock on the mantle chimed midnight, and she realized guiltily that she shouldn't keep him up much longer.

"I say we should go winner-take-all on this last hand."

"Why, Robin Matthews, until tonight, I never realized what a reckless gambler you could be." He sent her a smile with such wicked fun in it, she had to grin back at him.

"Just goes to show how little you know about me."

"Hmm," he said noncommittally, and deftly dealt their two hands.

They were playing five-card stud, and she proceeded to draw two aces to match the ace she held in her hand. He raised, she met and called. She laid her cards down with a little crow of delight. Her three aces beat his pair of kings cold.

"I propose a toast to the winning poker player," she said gaily and raised her glass.

"I think you've done enough toasting for one evening," he said firmly and removed the glass from her hand. "You, Miss Matthews, are three sheets to the wind."

"I am not. For your edification, I'm just a little under the influence," she said with great dignity. She felt warm and happy and very alive, but she could still think and speak clearly. Surely that wasn't the same as being intoxicated.

"If this is you a little under the influence, I'd hate to see you pie-eyed, knee-walking drunk."

"Ladies never get pie-eyed," she countered indignantly.

"I don't think I'm going to touch that one right now," he said with a sigh. "What exactly do you want for your forfeit?"

"I want you to kiss me," she blurted the words out before she turned too chickenhearted to say them.

"So that's what this was all about." He crossed his arms and leaned back in his chair. "Robin Matthews, you could try the self-control of a saint, and Lord knows, I'm hardly that."

"Does that mean you are going to kiss me?" she asked hopefully.

"That means I'm definitely going to kiss you, even though I shouldn't lay a hand on you in your current state."

"I know exactly what I'm doing."

"Hmm. I'd like to believe that. Well, come on over here, and we'll start on that kiss you asked for."

Despite his lazy, teasing tone, there was a light burning in his eyes that made her heart beat faster. Robin made her way around the table. It occurred to her to wonder a bit hazily if she somehow hadn't played right into his hands. Could he possibly have dealt her that winning hand, guessing exactly what she had in mind? When she reached his side, he pulled her down into his lap, and then her suspicions suddenly seemed irrelevant. Finally, she was where she had wanted to be for weeks now.

She wrapped her arms around his neck and buried her face in his shoulder. He smelled wonderfully male and musky combined with the sweet scent of chokecherry wine. His arms closed around her and for a long moment they simply sat. She relished the feel of his legs beneath hers, hard and warm. The fine wool of his suit jacket was slightly scratchy against her cheek. The room was dark and quiet. The only sound came from the hiss of the flames and the sigh of the logs settling in the hearth. Nathaniel sat as still as she. Could he possibly be treasuring this moment as much as she was?

"Seems to me I owe you a kiss," he said at last. His voice sounded like thunder in his chest.

"You don't really have to kiss me if you don't want to."

"The things you say, Robin-girl." He laughed, a wonderful rumbling sound. "I want to kiss you, all right. We'll have to see if I can manage to keep it at that despite all the liquor I have in me. That wine your mother made packs quite a wallop."

He tilted her face up, his hand gentle beneath her chin. He took her hand and slipped it under his jacket until it lay over his heart. His blue eyes almost looked angry. "This is what you do to me. It's the damnedest thing, and I still can't figure it. I've ridden some hard trails in my time and dealt with some mighty rough characters. I've had more than my fair share of women, and not a one made my heart beat faster the way you do.''

"I'm glad," she said fiercely, for she couldn't begin to describe the effect he had on her. Suddenly impatient, she tugged his head down and kissed him. He tried to go gentle and slow, but she wouldn't let him. Intoxicated by the taste of him, boldly she threaded her fingers through his hair and stroked his tongue with her own. Just when he began to kiss her back, she retreated. Stealing a page from his own book, she kissed his face, relishing the feel of his rough stubble beneath her lips. She kissed his nose, his eyes, those thick dark eyebrows of his, the skin above his collar, allowing herself to explore some of the places she'd dreamed about touching him.

At last he grew impatient. He framed her face with his hands and guided her mouth back to his. He kissed her back, and her toes curled with pleasure. Lord, this man was good at kissing. He took his time and focused that amazing concentration of his on a single kiss. She did likewise, until all the world narrowed down to their sensitive mouths and the places their bodies touched.

Longing to get closer to him, she wriggled about his lap. Suddenly, he went completely still, and his hands tightened on her arms.

"Whoah, now, you're going to get us both into a world of trouble.''

"I don't care," she said rashly.

"That's your mother's chokecherry wine talking.''

"No, it isn't." She drew in a breath and decided to tell him the truth. It wasn't in her to be coy about something so important. She leaned back so that she could look him in the eye. "I've wanted for ages to be with you like this.''

At first he looked angry. "I told you not to say things like that, particularly to a gent who's half drunk." She refused to be intimidated by his bluster, and he was the one to look away first. "Hell, you wouldn't be you if you weren't so honest.''

He was silent for a long moment. She was encouraged by the fact he couldn't seem to let go of her.

"Turn around."

Somehow there was a world of promise in those two words.

Her heart thudding in her chest, she did as he told her. He shifted in the chair until she was sitting between his legs. They were warm and hard against her own. Deftly, he unbuttoned her dress until the bodice fell halfway to her waist. She drew in a breath when he leaned forward and kissed the nape of her neck. Somehow he kept finding these places she had no idea were so sensitive. As his lips kissed a leisurely path down her backbone, kissing her through the thin layer of her camisole, wonderful shivers spilled across her skin, and pleasure pulsed deep inside her once again. Now she was glad she hadn't worn a corset. She was shockingly happy that she didn't have another layer of clothing between her and his clever hands. He slid the fabric of her gown down her arms, kissing the skin he bared until he reached her wrists and pulled her sleeves free.

He placed his hands on her shoulders and firmly turned her about until she was lying across his lap, her back leaning against the padded arm of the chair. She felt so exposed, with only her camisole between her and his smoldering blue gaze. Drawing on all the self-control she possessed, she managed to keep from raising her arms to cover herself. She wanted to find out what happened next. Judging from that intense look on his face, she was about to.

Slowly, he undid the ribbon that gathered the top to her camisole and then, one by one, the mother-of-pearl buttons beneath it. He pushed the thin cotton fabric back, his fingertips brushing her lightly and leaving burning trails across her skin.

He was silent for a long moment while he gazed down at her. Robin stared at the ceiling, barely daring to breathe. How she wished there was more for him to see. She'd filled out considerably since those days boys used to call her frog eyes, but she would never be voluptuous.

"Robin Matthews, you are the prettiest thing I've ever seen."

Somehow she doubted those words could be true, but in that moment, he made her feel as if they were, and she wanted to throw her arms around his neck. She didn't move, though, for a strange lassitude had seized her. In her everyday life she always had to be the boss, and there was something tremendously arousing about turning the reins over to his control for a change.

He reached out and gently traced the tip of her breast. She felt herself harden and that pulse between her legs came again. As if from a long distance, she heard herself moan. He played and touched and skimmed, until her entire body was on fire and she longed for him to touch her everywhere.

Just when she thought the sensations couldn't possibly grow more intense or pleasurable, he bent his head and kissed her. She closed her eyes and concentrated on the remarkable new feelings assailing her. She loved the cool softness of his hair brushing the underside of her breast. She reveled in the feel of his clever mouth and tongue caressing her.

Suddenly, he made an impatient sound deep in his throat and gathered her into his arms. After he stood, he headed toward the sofa, his intentions obvious. Robin swallowed hard. A treacherous part of her so hoped he was about to make love to her. Abruptly he stopped in the middle of the room. She looked at him. His face was taut, a muscle ticking in his jaw.

"As much as I want this, I'm not going to do it. It's not right."

He set her on her feet and stepped away. Cheeks burning, she dove for the bodice of her dress and slipped it back over her shoulders. She had to ask, even though she wasn't sure she wanted to hear his answer. "If I was pretty and feminine, would you want to make love to me?"

"Robin-girl, your looks have nothing to do with it." He glanced down at his aroused body and grimaced. "Actually, I expect they do, but not in the way you mean. Believe me, I want you so much I can't sleep. I've been lying in that bed of yours night after night, thinking of all the different ways I want to make love to you.''

Robin shivered at the very thought. "But I'm not going to do it," he continued on, his voice hard and gruff. "I'm not going to let you give yourself to a used-up, fiddle-footed fellow like myself. You should go to a decent man the night of your wedding as sweet and innocent as you are this very moment. Now I'm going to head out to the bunkhouse, and we're both going to forget this ever happened between us.''

A wave of warmth washed over her. She still couldn't believe that he'd been thinking about her in much the same way she'd been thinking about him night after night. "I'm not going to forget this happened," she said in a low voice.

He looked away from her. "Tomorrow, when your head's sore from all that chokecherry wine you drank tonight, you'll be glad I managed to make the sensible choice for both of us.''

"You can think that if you want, but it won't be true." Gathering her dignity as best she could, she walked to the door of the parlor. "I'm still going to sleep in Betsy's room tonight. It's too cold out in the bunkhouse. You could move out there tomorrow.''

"I think it's a much wiser idea if I move out there tonight," he said with such bleakness in his tone that she shivered again. He started for the other door of the parlor that led to the front hallway.

"There are some extra blankets in that old wooden chest out there." What on earth had she just said? She just couldn't seem to help herself. Five minutes ago, they had been embracing each other passionately, and now she was worrying over him like a mother hen. Nathaniel Hollister hardly needed a keeper.

He stopped and his lips twitched, as if the same thought had occurred to him. He crossed the room to her and pressed a quick kiss on her forehead. "Robin-girl, I don't deserve this kind of caring, but I appreciate it just the same. I promise you that I'll fire up the wood stove out there, and I'll have it all warmed up in no time.''

He walked to the door of the parlor and turned to look back at her. "Thank you again for today," he said, and then he was gone.

Robin started for the stairs, but she realized she couldn't go to sleep yet. Her body still felt so strange and restless. She sat down on the couch and stared into the embers of the dying fire.

Nathaniel Hollister wanted her. He wanted her the way she wanted him.

Well, I'll be just plain hornswoggled. It had been clear enough he'd been interested in her upon occasion, but she'd written much of it off to simple proximity. Mama had explained to her once that all healthy men, even the best ones, had strong urges, and they needed to have those urges satisfied from time to time.

Nathaniel Hollister had been living at the ranch now for over two months, and to the best of her knowledge, he hadn't had a chance to satisfy that sort of urge, unless he'd found a prostitute before he'd beaten the stuffing out of Rick Dyer. Somehow she doubted Nathaniel had gone straight from the Rocking M to a brothel, and then on to the Silver Dollar.

No matter what the reason, it still seemed like the sweetest sort of miracle that a man like Nathaniel Hollister wanted to be her lover. Although he didn't see himself in that light, he was such a good man. Only a good man would have stayed on at the Rocking M because he knew how much she and her family needed him. Only a good man would have turned down what she had offered him so freely just now.

As she stared at the fire, she faced a sobering truth. Nathaniel Hollister made her so mad at times that she couldn't see straight. He made her so sad some days, she wanted to cry her heart out for what they could never have together. When he was in one of his charming moods, no one could make her laugh harder. He had her all twisted up inside with such strong emotions because she loved him—loved him with all her heart.

She'd told herself she could keep from loving him if she only put her mind to it. What a fool she had been. She'd never had a chance. Nathaniel Hollister was a man who was larger than life. She could see why legends had grown up about him. That first night he had helped her against the rustlers, the afternoon he had beaten the Rafter S hands who had harassed her on Main Street, the day he had coolly faced a furious, manure-covered Rick Dyer, and the night he had helped them stand off those raiders—each of those times she had seen first-hand the way he could handle dangerous situations. He was a warrior, a man meant to fight battles and win them.

A little voice spoke in the back of her mind: *He can be violent in a way that terrifies you, but you know he would never harm anyone he cared for.*

Yet there was so much more to him. He was the man who bought an old draft horse rather than let it be mistreated. He was the man who put up with a five-year-old constantly tagging at his heels. He was the man who had quietly gone out with her team and spent three days hauling up deadfalls so she wouldn't worry about running out of firewood this winter. He was the man who dumped Rick Dyer in the manure to save Betsy's roses—this was the real Nathaniel Hollister, the one who had stolen her heart.

Robin rose to her feet. He was the only man with whom she would ever feel safe. He was the only man who could make her feel true passion. After what had happened with Rick Dyer, she didn't think she could ever desire a man. She never thought she could bear to let a man kiss her much less touch her in intimate ways. Nathaniel had taught her otherwise.

She wanted a husband someday. She wanted children, and she longed to have a happy marriage like her parents. Yet she couldn't imagine lying with a man and letting him touch her in any sort of intimate fashion. The very thought made bile rise in her throat and her innards clench. Instead of imagining herself with that good, decent man Nathaniel wanted her to marry, all she could picture was Rick Dyer's face twisted with lust and cruelty. For the past two years she'd tried to get past her fear with no success, until Nathaniel came.

Nathaniel could make it right for her. Nathaniel could take away her fear and make her feel clean again. Nathaniel could teach her how it was supposed to be between a man and a woman. She knew he wouldn't stay. She knew they had no future, but he could give her this.

Before she went to him, she decided to wait long enough to be certain it wasn't the influence of the chokecherry wine that had made her come up with such a bold and reckless plan. She had just finished with her menses. Her mother had told her that she believed women were much more apt to conceive in the middle of their cycle. It was worth the risk. To be rid of this fear that had been weighing her down for two years, it was more than worth the risk.

She sat in the quiet, darkened parlor searching her heart. Two hours later, she felt cold sober again, and she was only more set in her resolution. She loved Nathaniel, and she wanted him. Unless she could find a way to convince him to make love to her, she was afraid she would never be able to have a natural relationship with another man.

Taking a deep breath, she stood and went to find her wool jacket. Somehow she would find the strength and courage to convince one stubborn, worldly, principled ex-marshal to make love to her tonight.

Chapter Twenty-one

When Robin stepped outside the house, a light snow was drifting down, hushing the night to silence. Usually she loved snow. Usually, she would have stopped to admire the way the flakes swirled and danced about the lantern she carried to see her way. Tonight, however, she was too nervous to do anything but walk quickly toward the bunkhouse.

She wasn't hurrying because she was afraid that she was going to lose her nerve or change her mind. Her stomach was tied up in knots because she was afraid that Nathaniel would refuse her. For a variety of reasons, she knew he'd object strenuously to what she had in mind. Somehow, she would find a way to convince him.

The moment she stepped inside the bunkhouse, she heard the unmistakable click of a pistol hammer being cocked. She looked toward the far end of the bunkhouse where she could see Nathaniel lying on a bottom bunk. Resolutely, she forced her numb legs to carry her closer.

"What the hell are you doing here? I could have blown your

head off.'' Nathaniel eased the hammer back and shoved his pistol into a holster hanging on a chair beside his bed.

Although she had been rehearsing a speech she wanted to say to him for the past two hours, the words froze in her throat. She stopped at the base of his bunk. As she gazed at him leaning on one elbow, his black hair tousled, his blue eyes wary, the enormity of what she was asking came to her all at once. How could she expect this amazing, beautiful, masculine man to love her?

Yet tonight he had told her he wanted her while that fire in his eyes melted her bones, and she had believed him. She clung to those words he had spoken to her in the parlor as if they were a lifeline.

He was growing impatient waiting for her answer. She wasn't a coward. She didn't want to live with her fear another night.

"I want you to make love to me." She abandoned the elaborate speech she had made up and forced out these simple words instead. As soon as she had said them, they seemed so stark and forward and unromantic, she wished she could catch them back.

"Like hell you do."

"Please don't swear at me."

"I'll do that and worse if you don't rattle your pretty little hocks back to your safe little ranch house where you belong."

"I'm sorry. I don't think I can do that."

"All right then, I'll just carry you there." He threw back his covers and sat up in his bed. She was relieved to see he was wearing a union suit.

"Please, I just want you to hear what I have to say. Then, if you still feel the same way, I'll go."

"No dice, lady. I want you out of this bunkhouse this instant. This isn't a game we're playing."

He got out of bed and stalked over to where he'd left his boots by the door. Her nervousness started to give way to hot and glorious anger. How dare he ignore her and what she wanted to tell him? Robin's gaze fell on the pistol by his bed, and suddenly, she knew what she had to do.

While he grumbled and swore under his breath, pulling on his socks and stomping into his boots, she walked quietly over to the holster by his bed. He'd just gotten his second boot on when she pulled the pistol from the holster and turned to face him. It took him a moment before he realized that she was pointing his pistol right at his midsection.

"Have you lost your mind? No one touches my guns but me."

"I just have, and I'm getting mad enough to put a hole in you if you don't stop and listen to what I have to say."

He eased back in his chair, his eyes smoldering.

"All right. I'll listen, and then you're going to pay for pulling a gun on me."

Robin swallowed hard. She didn't want to be intimidated by Nathaniel Hollister, but when two hundred pounds of solid, muscular male looked this livid, it was difficult to hold her ground. Remembering what was at stake, she lifted her chin.

"It comes down to this. I want you to make love to me because I don't want to be scared anymore about being with a man. Since that afternoon with Rick Dyer, I've had nightmares about my wedding night. I don't understand why, but it's different with you. I don't freeze up when you touch me." *The Good Lord knows—just the opposite happens to me. When you touch me, I almost burst into flames on the spot.*

"If it's different with me," he said tightly, "it could be different with another man."

"I don't think so. I certainly don't want to take that risk, and I sure don't want to keep running away from marriage and men just because I can't face what's going to happen in my marriage bed."

He sighed and ran a hand through his hair. "This is just about the most loco notion I've ever heard."

"It doesn't seem the least bit crazy to me. I think it makes a world of sense."

He rose to his feet, his gaze going back to his gun. The sight of it in her hands seemed to bring his anger back full force. "Put that damn thing down."

"I'm sorry. I can't." He was so much bigger than she was. This was the only way she could keep him from hauling her straight back to the house.

His eyes narrowed at her flat refusal, and he started toward her.

"Don't you come any closer." She couldn't quite keep a quaver from her voice. Desperately, she cocked the hammer on his pistol.

"I'm coming closer, all right, by your own invitation."

He closed the distance between them in three strides. She was tempted to pull the trigger and fire over his shoulder just to make a point, but she couldn't take the risk of actually hurting him. None too gently, he pulled the gun from her grasp, his fingers hard as iron. Wordlessly, he eased back the hammer and slammed the pistol back in his holster.

He spun around to face her, his face set. In that moment, she realized she had never seen him so furious. Involuntarily, she stepped backward. He came after her until she bumped into the cold, hard logs of the bunkhouse wall. She had nowhere else to retreat. He grabbed her shoulders and covered her lips with his own. His kiss was hard and punishing. Robin forced herself to stay absolutely still while tears burned in her eyes.

She'd asked for this. She hadn't wanted it to be this way between them, but she couldn't back down now. Her stupid, reckless behavior had provoked this response from him, and now she had to take the consequences. His hands slipped to her hips and he pulled her full against him. She gasped when she realized he was fully aroused. He ground himself against her and plundered her mouth. She waited for the familiar panic to strike, for he was holding her so tightly she almost felt crushed.

The panic didn't come. Perhaps she should fear him, but she didn't. He could overpower her in a heartbeat if he wanted to, yet this was Nathaniel. She knew in her heart he couldn't truly hurt her.

Moments later, he let go of her and stepped back, his chest heaving. He gazed down at her out of tormented eyes.

"I can't do this in anger. Not with you. Not ever with you, sweet Robin-girl. I'm so sorry."

"Sh, I'm the one who's sorry." She stepped forward and laid a finger across his lips. He caught her hand and held it between his own. "I shouldn't have used your gun," she admitted in a choked voice. "But I had to get you to hear me out. This means too much to me."

"Are you absolutely sure this is what you want? You're handing me heaven on a plate, and I'm not going to be able to hold out much longer."

"That's good news, because I'm like to catch pneumonia if this standoff goes on much longer."

Her prosaic comment made his lips twitch, just as she hoped it would. "Robin Matthews, you do beat all."

"Is that a compliment or an insult?"

"I'm not sure. I think it means you have me so confused half the time I don't know if I'm a-coming or a-going."

"That makes two of us."

"I do know this. I want you so much right now you've got my heart pounding again."

"I'm glad," she said fiercely, and she was glad, with all her own pounding heart. "Please, show me now how it's supposed to be between a man and a woman." Knowing he wouldn't make the first move now, she stepped forward and wrapped her arms around his waist. Reaching up on tiptoe, she pressed her lips to the base of his throat.

"All right," he agreed at last, his voice husky.

She breathed a silent sigh of relief when his arms curved around her. "You're probably going to want to take my pistol and shoot me with it tomorrow, but I can't say no to you another time."

He gave her a long, sweet kiss that had her heart racing

twice as fast by the time he raised his head again. Despite the warmth from his body, her back was chilled. She couldn't help shivering.

"Come on. Let's get you under the covers before you truly do catch pneumonia." He took her hand and led her to the bed. They sat side by side on his bunk to take their boots off. He wrenched his own off with quick, practiced twists. Because she was still busy unlacing her left boot, he knelt before her and helped unfasten her right.

Her breath caught as she watched him. While he knelt before her like this, his shoulders seemed a mile wide. The lamplight shone on the stubble of his cheeks and the strands of silver hair at his temples. His lashes were so long and thick—they would have looked feminine if the rest of his face wasn't so completely male. She could see the curls of dark hair on his chest where the first button of his union suit had come undone. His lips were well-formed, not too thin and not too full. Just looking at Nathaniel took her breath away and made her ache with longing.

When he finished with her right boot, he pulled it off gently and set it aside and then did the same for her left. Unable to resist temptation a moment longer, she set her hands on his shoulders. They felt warm and hard beneath her fingers. She tilted her head and kissed his lips. They were smooth and soft and tasted faintly of the coffee and the chokecherry wine they'd drunk together. His eyes closed in appreciation.

"Umm, I surely like that, Miss Matthews," he declared, opening his eyes again, "but we aren't getting you warmed up yet."

He urged her gently to her feet. After he helped her slip off her jacket, he tossed it on the upper bunk. He held her shoulders and turned her so that her back was facing him. He made quick work of her buttons, his fingers surprisingly nimble with the fastenings. When the bodice fell to her waist, he kissed her neck, the warmth of his mouth a sensual contrast to the cool air of the bunkhouse. He skimmed the sleeves down her arms, and helped her step out of the skirt. Neat as any lady's maid, he draped her dress across the upper bunk.

Robin couldn't help smiling at the incongruous thought. Somehow she couldn't see Nathaniel serving anyone. Suddenly, she remembered she was standing before him clad in only her underclothes, and her cheeks started to burn.

Perhaps he noticed her embarrassment, for he turned away. "Why don't you lie down in my bed and start warming yourself up while I add another load of wood to the stove," he suggested practically.

After shedding her petticoats, she did as he suggested, and then lay there, stiff and scared, her mind awhirl. His bed was warm, and his scent clung to the pillow beneath her cheek. She heard the thud of the logs he pushed into the stove, the clang of the metal door closing, the crackle of the wood as it caught fire, and the creak of the floor boards as he crossed the room quickly.

When she looked toward the end of the bed, she realized he was stripping off his union suit. She drew in a deep breath to steady herself. *He has to undress to make love to you, idiot.* After he shoved the union suit down around his hips, she stared at his naked back. She never realized a man's back could be so beautiful. She was mesmerized by the ridges of his vertebrae, the play of his shoulder blades, the way his torso tapered from broad shoulders down to such lean hips. Nathaniel's body in its maleness was so foreign to her, and yet so compelling.

She hadn't begun to look her fill when he turned toward her. She gulped and glanced away before she could see all of him. With some chagrin, she realized her cheeks were on fire.

Coward, she scolded herself. Yet she still couldn't make herself look at him when he came to stand beside the bunk. Then another fit if panic seized her. How could they both possibly fit in such a narrow space? She shifted over as far as she could, until her shoulder touched the cold log wall.

He lifted the blankets and lay down beside her. After he turned on his side, she found there was enough room for them both, barely. She was extremely aware of his nakedness and every place their bodies touched. His legs were hard and long. She knew he was watching her intently, but she couldn't meet his gaze. She stared hard at his chest and wondered miserably where all that conviction and determination she'd possessed just minutes ago had fled.

He drew the covers up over them both, and almost at once the bed grew warmer. *Why, he was better than a hot water bottle.* She must have spoken that thought aloud, for when she ventured to look at his face, she found he was grinning at her.

"Glad to know I can be of some use to a lady," he said, a glint of mischief in his blue eyes. She was glad of his teasing. Now that she was actually lying here in his bed, the enormity of what she had asked threatened to overwhelm her.

"We'll just take this nice and slow," he said, obviously reading her mind. He reached out and tucked a lock of her hair behind her ear.

He brushed a soft kiss across her temple. His lips ranged lower, along her jaw to the sensitive skin at the base of her neck, calling a delicious, shivery response from her nerves. He moved even lower, and kissed his slow, tantalizing way across her chest just above the upper edge to her camisole. She felt the peaks of her breasts harden. When would this wretchedly clever man caress her there?

At last, he undid the tie to her camisole again. This time as he unfastened the buttons, he kissed the flesh he exposed step by step, but still he ignored the tips of her breasts until she almost ached with frustration.

She gasped when he touched them at last, gently grazing her nipples with his palms until they became even more sensitized. He gently circled them with his fingers, building an unbearable tautness inside her. Finally, he lowered his head. As his lips and tongue began to her caress her, she moaned aloud. Restlessly she ran her hands up and down his back, relishing the feel of his ribs and muscles and smooth male skin beneath her hands.

Somehow his leg had become wedged between her own

where it felt wonderfully hard and heavy. She found herself pressing against it, trying to ease the tension building deep within her. With every stroke of his tongue, the pleasure coiled tighter and tighter until she felt as if her nerves were on fire.

"Please, Nathaniel, I want . . ." she gasped, but she didn't know what she wanted.

"Shh, now," he said in his deep voice, "I'll show you the way."

He moved his leg, and swiftly undid the tie to her drawers. His warm hand slipped across her belly. He touched her gently in that very place her body felt as if it were burning. At once the tension became more intense. The pads of his fingers rubbed against her in just the right place, and she thought she was about to fly apart into a thousand pieces.

Shamelessly, she found herself pressing up against his hand. There was somewhere she needed to reach, some safe haven in this storm of incredible feeling. It was too much, too new, too intense. She started to panic, and then his voice reached out to her.

"Just relax and go with it, sweet Robin-girl."

She gazed into his beautiful blue eyes, full of his concern for her. Nathaniel wouldn't hurt her. Nathaniel would only give her something wonderful. Her fear receded. He kissed her lips and caressed her a final time. Her body tightened around his hand, and suddenly the pleasure burst outward from where he touched her in dizzying waves. All she could do was hold tight to his shoulders while the amazing sensations raced through her. They seemed to go on forever, but at last they faded, leaving her panting and enervated.

"My heavens," she managed to say when she had gotten her breath back. "Am I still alive?"

"Sure looks like it to me. Now you know why the Frenchies call it 'the little death.' " He managed to smile at her, but she saw the tension in his features.

"But you haven't gone yet, I mean you haven't had your . . ."

If only she could talk about these intimate matters with more aplomb. She must seem so naïve to him.

"No, I haven't," he said gravely, only a hint of a smile lurking in his eyes, "and I'm surely looking forward to it. First, I wanted you to catch your breath, and I wanted to make sure you understand this may hurt some, it being your first time and all."

"I know." Thank heavens her mother had explained what she should expect in her marriage bed in plain and sensible terms. She understood that it probably would hurt the first time Nathaniel entered her, but with time and practice, it could become very pleasant. Since he had already given her an experience far beyond pleasant, she figured she was due for the hard part of lying with a man.

She spread her legs and closed her eyes. "I'm ready," she told him valiantly.

Nathaniel couldn't help smiling this time. As much as he longed to bury himself inside her, he was determined to go slow and make it good for her. It was a novel sensation for him, to say the least. He was more used to taking rather than giving. Until a few minutes ago, he'd forgotten what a sensuous experience it could be to give pleasure. He'd almost lost his control when he'd watched her go over the top.

There would have to be pain for his sweet Robin-girl, but if he possibly could, he would help her find her own release again.

Determinedly, he set about arousing her once more, exploring some of those sensitive places he'd just discovered and finding others, enjoying the small, breathless sounds she made, and loving her sweet efforts to caress and arouse him in return. She was pink and white and gold and so lovely she made his head swim.

By the time he was sure she was ready for him, he was so tight and hard he didn't know how he could wait a moment a longer. As he knelt between her knees, the trusting look in her eyes steadied him. Slowly, he entered her until he reached her barrier. It took every ounce of self-control he possessed to stay completely still and find the coherence to ask her, "Are you ready, sweet Robin?"

She nodded. He kissed her forehead and stroked her feminine place just as he pushed past her maidenhead. Her eyes widened, and her body tensed. After he was completely sheathed inside her, he remained still once again while her body grew accustomed to him.

"Is it better now?" he managed to ask.

"It's fine," she said bravely.

Slowly, so slowly, he moved just a little and watched her eyes. She looked surprised. "That really didn't hurt," she said wonderingly. He moved again, and her eyes fluttered shut. "Mm, that's starting to feel awfully nice." Her eyes flew open a moment later. "Does this feel nice for you?" she asked with such concern he had to smile through his passion.

"Nice doesn't even come close," he assured her.

"I'm glad," she smiled at him shyly. He rotated his pelvis gently, and she gasped with pleasure. Soon they were both beyond speech. Instinctively, she rose to meet his thrusts, her agile body twisting beneath him, urging him on. After he showed her how to wrap her legs around him, he discovered a whole new heaven as he plunged more fully inside her.

When he knew he couldn't wait any longer, he reached down and stroked her a final time. He dove deep, and her body closed around him as she crested. Her pleasure only helped to intensify his own. He let go a wordless shout and buried his face in her glorious hair as the waves rushed through him. Perhaps because he had denied himself for so long, his climax seemed to go on forever.

When it ended, he drew in a deep breath and kissed her forehead. He loved the feeling of her cuddled beneath him, their bodies still joined. He would have liked to stay linked with her longer, but he was afraid he might be crushing her with his weight. After he withdrew from her, he went to the washbasin in the corner of the bunkhouse and wet a clean rag.

Returning to the bunk, he started to clean Robin gently over her sleepy protests.

"Sh, now, you take care of everyone else around here. Let me do this for you," he told her sternly, and she subsided with surprising meekness. He grinned at the notion. Perhaps he'd finally found a way to quell the argumentative side to Robin Matthews—he just had to love her senseless.

When he slipped under the covers again, she settled back into his arms as if they'd lain together a thousand times. Within moments, her even breathing told him she was asleep.

Nathaniel propped himself up on one elbow so that he could watch her. Careful not to disturb her, he reached out and took a lock of that pretty hair of hers and smoothed it between his fingers. The more time he spent around her, the more he thought everything about Robin was pretty—except maybe her temper and her stubborn nature. Yet he had to admire those parts of her personality, too, since he possessed those same flaws in abundance. Her skin was so smooth and soft. He liked the way her brown eyelashes curled against her cheek when she slept. From the start, he had loved her mouth, and now he knew what heaven it could be to kiss it, and to feel her lips kiss him.

Watching her like this was a bittersweet pleasure. He was coming to think that Robin Matthews was everything he had ever wanted in a woman. She was spunky and caring, feisty and sweet. Now he knew she was a passionate and generous lover as well.

If you care this much about her, and she suits you so well, why don't you give more thought to staying on? You could always slip away for a few weeks here and there to see that wild country you've been hankering to explore. Hell, you could take Robin with you. She'd probably love it just as much as you.

Several ugly answers to that question stared him in the face—the same ones, in part, that he'd given to Mrs. Beacham just a few days ago. He didn't deserve a sweet young woman like her. He couldn't give her the love and tenderness she deserved, either. Over time, if they tried to make a go of things, she'd rightfully expect more from him than he could give her, and she could end up as bitter and disillusioned as his mother had been. That thought chilled him to the core. He cared for Robin too much to stay and let that happen to her.

Because he cared about her, this was the very first and last time he was going to make love to her. A better man would have found some way to convince her that she needn't be afraid after what that skunk Dyer had tried to do to her. Instead, he'd taken everything she'd offered, but he didn't want to take advantage of her that way again. *There's far too good a chance you'll plant a baby in her belly, and the last thing you want to do is shame her in the eyes of her family and friends.*

He finally dozed a little. An internal clock he'd always been able to depend upon woke him around four. He didn't dare let her stay any longer. What if Betsy missed her? He looked down at the gentle swell of Robin's breast, and his body tightened. He longed to make love to her again. Instead, he pressed a feather-light kiss on her shoulder and forced himself to get up and dress.

She stirred when he loaded more wood in the stove. She stretched, one pretty white arm raised above her head, affording him a delectable view of her shoulders and pink-tipped breasts. He clenched his jaw and looked away.

"What time is it?" she asked sleepily.

"Time for you to head back to the house. It's almost four-thirty. There'll be hell to pay if Betsy notices you've been gone all night."

His harsh tone seemed to get through to her. She slipped from the bed and dressed quickly. As much as he wanted to help her, he stayed away because he didn't trust himself. Only when she pulled her dress back on, and obviously needed his aid with the fastenings did he go to her. He didn't say a word as he buttoned up the back of her dress and helped her into her coat.

She offered him a smile, her green eyes dreamy.

He ached to take her into his arms. Instead, he hardened his heart and voice, for her sake. "I hope you got what you wanted. I already think this was a mistake."

Her smile faded. "I'm sorry you feel that way," she told him with grave dignity. "This was the most wonderful night of my life."

Desperate to make sure she didn't come to him again, he said the most hurtful thing he could think of. "It was pretty fair, considering your lack of experience and all."

"I see." Her eyes darkened with pain. He longed to tell her he was lying through his teeth, but he had to find some way to drive her off. If she gave him the slightest opportunity, he knew he'd make the most of it, and they'd end up in his bunk again. That road could only lead to shame and heartbreak for her.

After a moment, her chin went up. "Well, I suppose I should thank you for tonight. You certainly gave me everything I asked for. You needn't worry about my troubling you again." With that, she opened the door and strode from the bunkhouse, her carriage erect and proud. Nathaniel watched her until she was safely inside her home. Only the telltale quaver in her voice at the end of her little speech had given her away. He'd just wounded her feelings terribly.

He closed the door and stared at it for a long moment. Then he slammed his fist against the wall.

Chapter Twenty-two

Nathaniel studied the piece of harness strap he was trying to repair. The last three stitches he'd made were crooked as hell.

He thrust the strap away from him and stood up from the workbench. Restlessly, he went to pace before the doorway of the barn. He couldn't concentrate on anything today, not after what had happened last night, and his right hand hurt like fire.

What on earth was he going to do about Robin Matthews?

Making love to a woman had never been like that for him before. Somehow, in the process of trying to please her, the entire experience had become much more intense and pleasurable for himself. Robin had been remarkable, too. She had been just as generous and giving as he'd dreamed she'd be. In the end, he'd taken and enjoyed everything she'd come to the bunkhouse to give him.

How can you blame yourself when she asked you to make love to her—at gunpoint no less? That was hardly surprising, considering the fact he'd all but seduced her two hours earlier.

Damn your weak, conniving soul. Why couldn't you have kept your hands to yourself?

Nathaniel sighed and tried to shut out the arguments he'd been having with himself all morning. The only thing that mattered was sweet Robin, and he guessed she was hurting right now. She'd been distant and polite to him this morning, the shadows under her eyes the only sign she'd had little sleep last night. He longed to go and apologize to her, but a cold, realistic side of him was certain that she would be much better off if he stayed as far away from her as possible from now on.

Just when Nathaniel was contemplating working on the harness again, Tommy wandered into the barn, his expression woeful.

"What's the matter, partner?"

"Jake and Luke and Betsy gots good things to give Robin for Christmas, and I cain't think of nothin'. I love her mostest of all. How's she gonna know that if I don't give her a good present?"

"She knows that already, pard, but I can understand you're wanting to give her a present she'll like. I've been giving that question some consideration myself."

"What do you think I should give Robin for Christmas?"

"Well, now, let's think on that for a bit." He'd considered buying her some things, but somehow he couldn't see her getting excited about a new dress or a piece of jewelry. He wanted to give her something she'd actually use, and something that might make her think of him once he was gone.

He looked down at the harness he'd been trying to repair. He used to do some fancy leather work back on the farm. He'd even briefly considered opening a saddle shop of his own. He'd been keen to see the world, though, and being tied down to any business had sounded like hell.

"What if you and me worked on making her something special together?"

Tommy's face lit up. "I'd like that. I'd like that just fine."

"We've got to keep what we're working on a secret."

"Cross my heart, I promise I won't tell no one what we're making."

"All right, then, this was what I had in mind," Nathaniel said, and he went to fetch a piece of hide he'd been soaking in a vat. They'd had to put a yearling down two days ago, after it broke its leg in a gopher hole. He'd saved most of its hide, thinking it might turn out to be useful.

Over the next few days, he was surprised when Luke and Jake came to him, too, asking him for advice on presents and how to make them. People were sneaking off all the time to work on their Christmas projects in secret. Betsy chased him out of the parlor one afternoon when he obviously had interrupted her working on some sort of gift. She looked more fierce than he'd ever seen her.

Damned if he didn't find himself starting to get into the spirit of things himself. Once he'd come up with the idea of doing leather work, he thought of good presents he could make for Jake and Luke as well. Betsy was a bit more tricky.

As time wore on, Nathaniel found he was glad to have something to occupy his mind and give him a good excuse to stay clear of Robin. Memories of making love to her came back to haunt him at the oddest times. He'd see her kneading bread in the kitchen, and he'd remember the way her hands had felt on his body. He'd see her laugh at Jessie, and he'd remember the way she'd laughed that night when they'd played poker and drunk chokecherry wine together.

He told himself it was just as well that she'd never trust or come to him again. He told himself keeping her at arm's length was the only way to play this hand. Despite the distraction of Christmas, he was miserable. He'd hurt Robin badly, and that was the last thing on earth he'd wanted to do.

A hundred times he considered saddling up Old Blue and riding out. It wasn't the winter weather that stopped him. It was the fear that Sutherland's riders might make a move on the ranch at any time. They'd already managed to shoot Robin once. He didn't want to give them a chance to finish the job.

* * *

Three weeks before Christmas, Rick Dyer waited at the Grand Valley train depot for Vance Sutherland's train to arrive. The old man had just spent several days in Denver, doing more informal campaigning and holiday celebrating with his new cronies at the capital.

Rick didn't mind the old bastard's new fixation with politics. He liked the notion of his father being a U.S. senator. It sounded grand and powerful. More importantly, the job would take Vance away from Grand Valley, which meant Rick could run the Rafter S the way he wanted—particularly if he could find a way to get rid of Alan

Rick looked at his two legitimate half brothers with loathing. He still meant to get even with Buck someday. He'd never forgotten the afternoon when he'd been about to teach Robin Matthews a lesson, and that slobbering half-wit had broken his arm. Rick hated Alan's guts even worse. That weak-willed milksop had everything that should be his.

Rick spat his chew into the snow. If his stupid slut of a mother had been smart enough to insist Sutherland marry her before she spread her legs for him, he'd be standing first in line to inherit the Rafter S. Instead here he was, working like a slave and having to settle for whatever scraps the old man decided to toss him.

Alan Sutherland stood in his way, but Rick was going to make sure something happened to Alan soon, some kind of fatal, tragic accident. Rick had killed that way before. It wasn't as exciting as shooting someone in a standup gunfight, but a man did what was necessary to get ahead in the world.

Right now Alan continued to have a say in the way the ranch was run, but the men looked to Rick more and more these days. They feared him, and they sensed the old man was coming to rely on him to get things done. That's why he had to deal with the situation at the Rocking M, and deal with it soon. Vance wanted that ranch, and Rick was determined to be the one to give it to him before springtime. Besides, now he had a score to settle with Robin Matthews and Hollister.

Vance stepped off the train, carrying a portmanteau. Rick hurried forward to take the old man's bag. Sutherland took one look at Rick's swollen nose and shook his head in disgust. Without saying a word, Vance handed him the luggage and turned away to greet Alan and Buck.

The old man knew what had happened that night at the Silver Dollar, and he'd been furious. After the dance, he'd made it plenty clear once again that he wanted Nathaniel Hollister out of the way. Rick still planned to put the bastard six feet under. He was just waiting for the right chance to make his play.

Rick watched the old man wring Alan's hand and clap Buck on the back. The three of them walked to the waiting sleigh, never once looking back to see if he was with them. Feeling like a damn servant, he hoisted the heavy bag up on his shoulder and stalked after them.

Rick fumed as he drove the team back to the ranch. Someday they would all treat him with more respect. He craved respect. He liked the way people treated his father. He liked the way people treated him since he discovered he was quick with a gun and had the guts to kill with it. No one had respected him when he was a boy in the gutters of St. Louis where he'd grown up. He'd learned the hard way what happened to a whore's son who couldn't look out for himself.

People in Grand Valley respected him now, ever since he'd killed three men. He'd begun to earn the old man's respect, too, until Hollister had come along. Just thinking about that two-bit, worn-out, poor excuse for a lawman made Rick see red.

Rick's mood hadn't improved by the time he sat down at the table with his half-brothers and the man who had yet to acknowledge him as his son. His mother had sworn Vance Sutherland was the first man she ever gave herself to, and he believed her. Hell, he looked more like the old man than Alan or Buck, for all the good it did him.

He knew he was sitting at this table tonight not because he was Sutherland's bastard, but because Vance needed him. The old man was using him to look after his interests while he chased his political dream. Rick was using the old man, too. Someday he aimed to own all of the Rafter S and have folks look up to him the way they did to Vance.

"All right, boys. Tell me what's happening over at the Rocking M," Vance declared when he had finished his plate of sirloin and potatoes. "Have you gotten that Matthews girl to see reason yet?"

"I want to go see Robin and Betsy," Buck said, his face lighting up at the idea.

"I don't want to hear any more about you visiting those girls. We've been through all this before," Vance said sternly. "Juanita, please see Buck to his room now." Crestfallen at his father's obvious displeasure, Buck shuffled from the room, following the Sutherlands' housekeeper.

"We've been trying to buy Robin Matthews out for three years now. I think it's time you boys took more direct action."

Alan set down his fork. "Exactly what sort of action did you have in mind?" he asked.

Vance didn't answer. Instead, he looked at Rick. Rick sat up straighter, having a good idea of what the old man wanted him to say. "Sure would be hard for the Matthews to get through the winter if something happened to their barn, or even their house," he drawled.

Alan shoved his chair back from the table and stood up. "I'm not going to go along with this. You two are going to leave the Rocking M alone from now on."

"That little gal has no right to that ranch," Vance replied, his face starting to flush with anger. "She's going to run it into the ground."

"I've told you a hundred times—it's her place to run whatever way she wants. She has every right to the Rocking M. Her folks came to this valley before you did and worked just as hard as you to build their ranch. I've looked the other way for years now while you've forced good people from their land. It comes down to this, Pa. If you let Rick burn out the Matthewses, I'm going to leave Grand Valley, and I'll never come back.''

"Don't you dare threaten me, boy," Vance roared in anger.

"I'm not threatening you. I'm just trying to make you see reason." Alan paled before his father's fury, but he held his ground. Rick watched the two of them with cool interest.

"No son of mine speaks to me this way." Vance slammed his fist on the table, hard enough to make the cutlery rattle and jump.

"Then I guess I just won't be your son anymore." Alan turned away and walked to the door of the dining room. He paused in the threshold and looked back over his shoulder at Vance. "You know, I used to be proud to have you as a father. But since you decided you had to own every acre in this valley, you've made me ashamed to be a Sutherland."

"Go on. Get out. Get the hell out of here," the old man bellowed at Alan's retreating back. Despite Vance's bluster, Rick could see the stunned expression in his eyes when Alan kept going. Vance hadn't thought Alan could walk away. Tonight's scene surprised Rick as well. He'd known for sometime that Alan was sweet on Robin Matthews, but he never thought Alan had the gumption to stand up for her this way.

Rick stared down at his plate, trying to hide his fierce elation. This could be the chance he'd been looking for. Maybe he wouldn't have to get rid of Alan after all. The damn fool was shooting himself in the foot by bracing the old man this way.

After he gave Vance a minute to get himself together, Rick looked over at him. "What do you want me to do, boss?"

"I want you to do whatever it takes to get that stubborn little bitch off that place, and do it now," Vance gritted, obviously finding a new outlet for his anger.

"All right, boss. I'll see to it."

Rick rose to his feet. He paused for a long moment, but Vance didn't even look at him. Instead, the old man continued to stare morosely into his wineglass. Rick spun about on his feet and headed for the door. Tomorrow night, he'd head out with all the boys who had the stomach for a raid like this one. Surely after he handed the Rocking M to the old man on a silver platter, things would be different around here. Whistling cheerfully, Rick went off to make plans with Shorty and Pete. Soon they would make certain Robin Matthews's place went up in flames.

Robin was working on her accounts in the parlor when she spotted Alan Sutherland riding up. It was midmorning, and bright sunshine sparkled on the crystalline surface of the snow that had fallen last night. After she walked out on the porch to greet him, she eyed the heavy saddlebags behind his saddle curiously. Alan looked like he was about to go on a trip, but unless they had to, folks rarely traveled in the mountains of Colorado during the winter.

"Light and set," she told him with a smile. "It's nice to have some company. Betsy just took some corn muffins out of the oven a few minutes ago."

"They sound mighty tasty." Alan sent her one of his serious smiles and tied his mount to the hitching rail.

She showed him into the kitchen where Betsy was minding Jessie. Tommy was out in the barn with the twins and Nathaniel, working on various secret Christmas projects. Despite the strained state of their relationship right now, Robin tried to be happy that Nathaniel was getting into the Christmas spirit.

Every time she thought about Nathaniel, she felt as if someone was twisting a knife in her heart. That he could consider what they had shared that night a mistake still crushed her. It wasn't just his words that had hurt—it was the casual way he had dismissed their being together that convinced her once and for all she'd been terribly mistaken about his feelings toward her. While he made love to her, she'd thought the entire experience had meant as much to him as it had to her. He'd been so tender and careful and giving. His callous, abrupt leave-taking afterward had been so unexpected that it had hurt her even more.

Just because you love a man doesn't mean he's going to love you back. You fooled yourself into seeing something in him that night that just wasn't there because you wanted to see it and believe in it so badly.

Happy to have a distraction from brooding over Nathaniel, Robin sat down at the kitchen table across from Alan. Betsy served the muffins along with a crock of fresh butter and poured them coffee. For a time, they all talked easily about happenings in town. As she watched Alan smile and laugh at Jessie's clowning, Robin felt a wave of sadness wash over her. If only she could feel something more for Alan. She did care for him, the way she cared for any dear friend. That was why she felt so betrayed and disappointed that he hadn't helped her against his father.

At last, Betsy slipped away to put Jessie down for her nap.

A long silence stretched between them after she left. Alan looked across the table at her, the expression in his toffee-brown eyes melancholy.

"We used to have some good times together, didn't we?"

"We did," Robin had to admit. Sometimes she thought she'd been happiest back in school when Alan had been one of her best friends—back in the days before her parents died and the heavy burden of running the Rocking M had fallen upon her shoulders.

"We used to be good friends."

"We still are," she said softly.

"I know that what my father's done has come between us. I'm sorry I haven't been more of a help to you. I have tried to make him see reason, but he's gotten so he doesn't listen to anyone anymore."

"I know it must have been hard for you," Robin said.

His mouth twisted. "Don't try to make excuses for me. I

know I've been a complete coward. I finally stood up to him last night, but I guessed it would come down to this. I'm leaving Grand Valley on the afternoon train, and I'm never coming back.''

Robin stared at him in dismay. ''Surely you don't have to leave here forever.''

''I don't think my father will ever forgive me. My leaving is for the best, really. I haven't been happy here for a long time. I'm looking forward to starting a life of my own, someplace where no one cares that my last name is Sutherland.''

As she looked into his earnest face, she felt a new respect for Alan dawning inside her. ''I think you are making a very good decision.''

''Before I left town, I had to warn you. Father ordered Rick to drive you off soon, and they mean to fire your place. That's what we fought about last night. The men might even come tonight.''

''Thank you for the warning. It might make all the difference.''

''Dyer's been hiring some real rough types recently. There could be some shooting.'' Alan's eyes were full of worry as he gazed at her. ''I don't want you to get hurt.''

Robin thought about her recent confrontation with the Rafter S riders over Nathaniel, and her shootout with those cattle rustlers. Thanks to his stubborn, greedy father, her life had already gotten plenty dangerous. ''We'll keep a sharp lookout for trouble during the next few nights,'' she said simply.

''There's something else I had to ask you before I leave. I think I know what your answer will be, but I have to ask it just the same.'' He got to his feet and began to pace back and forth across the kitchen.

Robin felt a lead weight settle in her stomach. She wished she could think of some way to keep him from asking the question she would have to say no to, but he was already speaking rapidly, his brown gaze fixed on hers.

"I figure that when I leave here, I'm going to head for California. I've got some money I inherited from my mother's family. I thought I'd use that to start up a business of some sort. I'm a hard worker and I think I can make a real go of it. I should be able to look after my wife and children well. I could even provide for her family, if she had some brothers and sisters she had to look out for." He stopped right before her and drew in a deep breath. "What I'm trying to say is, Robin Matthews, would you marry me?"

Robin shook her head, her throat suddenly gone tight and full. "You honor me by asking, but no, Alan, I can't. I care for you very much, but I don't love you the way a wife should love her husband."

"Mightn't your feelings change with time?"

"No, I truly don't think so. I'm so sorry."

The naked pain she saw in his eyes at that moment humbled her. She had never meant to hurt him so. She had never guessed Alan felt that deeply about her. She rose to her feet and went to him. Gently she reached out and touched his arm.

"I wish I felt differently. You are a good man."

He turned to face her and placed both of his hands on her shoulders. "How I wish your answer could have been different." He leaned forward and pressed a kiss on her forehead. "I know you're carrying a torch for Hollister. I saw the way you looked at him that night at the dance. I hope you'll be careful. He's a hard man, and I wouldn't put it past him to take advantage of your innocence. There's already been some talk about the two of you in town."

Robin swallowed a bitter laugh. Nathaniel had hardly taken advantage of her. She was the one who had thrown herself at Nathaniel's head.

Alan was still holding her when Nathaniel suddenly walked into the kitchen, carrying a branding iron. "Luke and I just fired up that old forge in the corner of the barn and fixed this. Do you want me to try reworking that cracked ring on the double tree?" he asked, and then he looked up. He went completely still, and his black brows drew together. Hastily Robin stepped back from Alan, her cheeks burning.

''Well, well, well, isn't this a touching scene,'' Nathaniel said in a hard, hateful tone. Robin wished the earth would open up and swallow her on the spot.

Chapter Twenty-three

"Alan was just saying goodbye. He's going to be leaving Grand Valley," Robin said, angry that her voice sounded so breathless. After the way Nathaniel had almost tossed her out of the bunkhouse the other night, it was absolutely none of his business whom she let kiss her.

"Good. That means there will be one less Sutherland around here for us to worry about," Nathaniel declared.

Alan's cheeks turned dull red, but he met Nathaniel's gaze steadily. "I know you probably don't have much respect for me—"

"You got that one damn right. If your pa has his way, this little lady and her family are going to be out in the cold. They shot her once, and there's far too good a chance they'll do it again."

"Then you'll just have to make sure she stays safe."

Nathaniel's face tightened. In that moment, Robin thought of the woman he hadn't been able to keep safe, and she wished with all her heart that Alan had phrased his words a little differently.

"When the lead starts flying, it can be hard to keep anyone safe," Nathaniel said harshly. "It would be a whole sight better if you could talk your old man into calling off his dogs."

"I did my best. He won't listen to me. Brute force, strength, and power are all he respects. Those are qualities that you possess, and I don't. Use those to fight him, and you might be able to keep Robin from harm. I'll pray that you can."

Alan turned back to her, and his expression softened. "If you change your mind, or if you need help leaving Grand Valley and settling some place else, write to my uncle in Denver. He'll know where I'm staying."

He walked to the front door, and Robin followed behind him. To her intense irritation, Nathaniel lingered in the parlor, where he could hear and see them both.

After Alan shrugged into his coat, she opened the door for him. He hesitated on the threshold. "Goodbye and good luck to you, Robin Matthews. You'll always hold a special place in my heart."

"Good luck to you, too," Robin said, past the large lump still tightening her throat. Alan Sutherland was about to walk away from his home and his family because of her. She leaned up on tiptoes and kissed his cheek, and then he turned away from her and strode for his horse. She stepped out onto the porch, deliberately closing the door behind her, and watched him ride off. She waited for a long time, even though it was chilly, for she was hoping that Nathaniel would be gone when she went back into the house.

When she finally opened the door and stepped inside, her heart fell. Nathaniel was waiting for her. He was leaning in the doorway to the parlor, his arms crossed, obviously raring for a fight. "You shouldn't have let him walk out the door. I still say marrying Alan Sutherland would solve all your problems."

"We've been over this ground before," she said, suddenly feeling worn out.

"Are those tears I see in your eyes—tears from the young woman who never cries? Maybe now you've let Alan Sutherland go, you're figuring out that you care for him more than you realize.''

"In a way, you're right. I've always valued Alan as a friend, and I'm sorry the conflict with his father almost destroyed that friendship. I'm also sorry that because of me, he's about to give up his life in Grand Valley.'' *And I'm sorry most of all that I can't love a kind, gentle man like him, because I love you instead, for all the good it will do me.*

"It will probably be the best damn thing that ever happened to him. Sutherland casts a long shadow.''

Even though she agreed with Nathaniel, she wasn't about to admit it. "I don't want to talk about this anymore.'' She felt too raw and wounded today to enjoy a fight with Nathaniel.

"I think you're running off to have a good cry all on your own. That weak little worm isn't worth your tears.''

"He's not a worm, and I'm not going to cry, and even if I did, it wouldn't be any of your business. Why are you hounding me like this? What do you want from me?''

"Just this,'' he said in a rough voice, and he left the doorway so quickly she didn't have a chance to react.

Moments later, his arms closed around her, and he was kissing her the way she'd dreamed about in her most private moments. His lips claimed hers with a fierce kind of possessiveness that made her blood warm. He tugged on her chin, forcing her to open to him, and then he plundered the insides of her mouth. His hands began to range up and down her sides, across the small of her back, branding and caressing her, urging her treacherous senses to life.

He was angry, she realized dimly. He was angry that he'd seen her with Alan, and yet he didn't want to claim her in any sort of permanent way for himself. The injustice of it kept her from being swept away completely. He must have sensed she held some part of herself back, for he promptly set about trying to demolish the last of her defenses.

He gentled his onslaught, his lips clever and teasing, coaxing a response from her despite her best efforts to keep her guard up. He kissed her cheeks and eyes and nose, and lavished attention on the sensitive spots beneath her ears and the hollow at the base of her throat. Soon she forgot she was standing in the doorway to the parlor, forgot it was daytime, forgot anything but the glory of being in his arms and being kissed as if he could never bear to let her go.

He slipped his hands to her hips. Need curled deep in her belly as his big hands cupped her hipbones and his fingers splayed across the small of her back. He brought her against him close enough that their lower bodies touched, just close enough for her to feel how much he wanted her.

The wildness in his blue eyes almost scared her. In that moment, she realized the fight he was having with himself. He wanted to take her, and God help her, she was an instant away from letting him.

He stepped away from her, his own chest heaving. She staggered back against the doorway, her knees weak. How could he do this to her with just a few kisses? She felt as if her body was on fire, and her nerves seemed to be humming and tingling all over. She wanted him to keep touching her, wanted it so badly she almost hated herself in that moment.

"I'm sorry," he said hoarsely. "It made me crazy, seeing you in his arms just now."

"Leave me alone," she said, a sob catching in her throat. "Please, just stay away from me." Even though she knew it was cowardly, she turned away and fled to the privacy of her bedroom. There she indulged herself in a good long cry— mourning the loss of her childhood friend and the pain she had caused him, but most of all, she cried for herself, trapped by her love for a man who could never love her in return.

As much as Robin longed to stay in her room for hours, she needed to warn her family about the sobering news Alan had brought. What was happening between her and Nathaniel didn't

really matter. Betsy, Luke, Jake, Tommy, and Jessie mattered—
and her ranch mattered. They would still be with her long after
Nathaniel had gone.

After bathing her face and eyes, she left her bedroom and
went in search of Nathaniel. She knocked once on the door to
the bunkhouse and marched right in. She found him sitting on
his bed. She noticed he shoved something out of sight under
his pillow, but she didn't have time or energy now to wonder
what he might be making.

"Alan said his father ordered Dyer yesterday to fire our
buildings, and to do it soon," she told him bluntly.

She was relieved when he didn't ask why she hadn't told
him such important news an hour ago. "They probably won't
come until tonight. You and your family have some time to
decide if you want to leave, or stay and fight. You best have
that talk with them I mentioned to you a week ago."

Was it only a week? It already seemed a lifetime ago that
he had advised her to ask her brothers and sister if they wanted
to stay or move to Virginia to live with their kin there.

"All right," she said after a long moment. "I'll go ask them
now, and then we can plan accordingly."

Briskly, she went to round up Luke, Jake, and Betsy. Soon
they were all settled at the kitchen table for a family powwow.
They watched her out of worried, serious faces. How grown-
up they had become over the past few years. With some chagrin,
she realized this was a talk she should have had with her siblings
some time ago. She had no right to risk their lives holding onto
a dream they didn't believe in.

After clearing her throat, she plunged straight to the heart
of the matter. "Alan said the Rafter S hands are going to hit
the Rocking M soon to try to fire our buildings just the way
they burned out the Abbotts and the Jeffersons. We can stay
and fight, or we can pack up and leave before they come.
Grandmother Lee has already asked us to come live with her,
and we might be able to talk her into giving a home to Jessie
and Tommy as well."

She drew in a deep breath and met their glances one by one. "For a long time now, I've just assumed you all wanted to stay on here as much as I do. Nathaniel helped me realize that you could feel very differently from me, and that I should ask you what you want. When the riders from the Rafter S come, I don't think we'll be able to bluff them the way we did last time. We're going to have to fight if we want to keep this place."

Betsy, Luke, and Jake exchanged glances. "We've already talked this over amongst ourselves," Betsy admitted, "right after you got that letter from Grandmother Lee. We decided then that we didn't really want to go to live in Virginia, not unless we absolutely had to. I love Grand Valley, and I couldn't imagine living anywhere else."

"Ranching's all I've ever wanted to do," Jake joined in, "but I know Luke feels differently."

Robin looked at the most quiet and serious of her siblings.

"Down the road aways, I want to get more schooling," Luke admitted, "and maybe even try to start a business and live in a city. Wherever I go, though, I need to know the Rocking M is still ours, and that you are all happy and safe living here. If a home's not worth fighting for, what is?"

Robin felt her eyes mist with tears. Mama and Papa would be so proud of the fine, articulate young people their children had become. "You're all sure about this? I could always move to Virginia and come back here and buy another ranch after you've made lives for yourselves in the East."

"There will never be another ranch like this one," Betsy said firmly. "The Rocking M is our home. I'd like to go visit Grandmother Lee and our Virginia relations, if I can save up the rail fare someday, but for now I want to stay here."

"All right, then." Robin struggled not to show them how relieved she felt. "I'll go fetch Nathaniel from the bunkhouse and we'll turn this family conference into a real council of war. He hasn't said so directly, but I think he's willing to help us." *Lord, please let me be right.* She could face just about any threat if she knew cool, calm, capable Nathaniel was fighting at her side.

While he waited to hear the outcome of the Matthewses' family talk, Nathaniel was not feeling particularly cool or calm. He was trying, unsuccessfully, to concentrate on stitching a knife sheath he was making for Luke. At last he grew too restless and shoved the project aside. He got to his feet and began to pace up and down the bunkhouse.

Somehow he'd known it would come down to this. Somehow he'd known he'd face this impossible choice in the end. The Matthewses were going to choose to stay. Now he had to decide whether or not he was going to help a bunch of kids try to fight the saltiest, roughest men Sutherland had working for him. The only way to stop the Rafter S hands if they came with torches was to shoot. If those men were shot at, they were going to shoot back. Robin, Betsy, Luke, or Jake, or even the little ones could get badly hurt or killed.

He couldn't take responsibility for that. He couldn't take part in a fight with such risks involved. Staring blindly at the log wall before him, he saw Mary McAllister instead, sprawled in the dusty street, her life ebbing away into a scarlet puddle in the dirt. He couldn't let more innocent people get killed. His only chance was to ride on and hope his desertion would convince Robin and the rest to abandon the ranch and their hopeless confrontation with Vance Sutherland and his men. Surely the Matthewses were much more apt to fight because they thought they could count on his help.

Besides, it was past time he left, for Robin's sake as well as his own. All he could think about was the night they'd shared in this very bunkhouse. He couldn't remember the last time he'd made love to a woman instead of having sex. This was the first time the most intimate of acts had been intimate for him. That night had meant so much, in fact, that he still felt shaken by it. Robin Matthews kept breaching his defenses and warming frozen places inside him he thought no one could ever warm again.

He glanced at his bed where she had lain, so eager and generous and sweet in her loving, and his body hardened. He was fast losing his judgment and his control around her. An hour ago, he'd almost taken Robin right there in the parlor of her home, in front of God and everyone.

He simply had to go. Now if Robin could just come to her senses before she got herself or anyone else in her family killed.

He was still pacing about the bunkhouse when a firm knock came on the door. He called for her to come in. One look at her determined face told him what the outcome of her family powwow had been. *Damn it all to hell. What would it take to make these naïve young fools see reason?*

"They decided they want to stay and fight," she announced. "And no, I didn't talk them into it."

"Well, I'm sure as hell going to try to talk them out of it." He grabbed his coat and stalked past her toward the house. Betsy, Luke, and Jake were all still sitting around the table when he strode into the kitchen.

"Are you three absolutely sure a piece of land is worth dying for? Because if you try to take on those Rafter S riders, the bullets are going to fly and one or more of you could get killed. Are you willing to pay that price?"

They looked shocked by the vehemence of his bitter words, but Betsy was the first to rally. "It's not just a piece of land to us. It's a dream our parents built for us. It's our home, and our future."

"You think your parents would have agreed with your risking your lives to hold onto this place?"

"I think they would have understood why we have to do this better than anyone," Robin replied for the rest.

For a moment, he couldn't speak past the anger and frustration clogging this throat. "I think you're all loco, and I won't be a party to it. You can face those Sutherland riders, but I'm not going to be here to see it. I'm riding out as soon as I get packed up."

He watched Robin as he spoke. He could tell his words had surprised her. What did she expect? He'd told her from the start he thought she was foolish and misguided to try to hold on to her ranch.

"Very well. I can understand your decision." She lifted her chin in that proud, stubborn way she had. "It's not your fight. I'm grateful for everything you've done for us. Perhaps you could help us one last time and tell us what we should do to prepare to defend the Rocking M."

"Fetch every weapon you've got on this place and get 'em loaded up. Have plenty of buckets of water and blankets ready. Keep the little ones in the interior of the house where stray bullets won't hit em, but don't put them in the cellar in case the Rafter S riders do fire the house. Take up defensive positions behind walls or objects that are solid enough to stop bullets. Get plenty of clean bandages ready in case someone does get shot."

He paused for a long moment to give emphasis to his final comment. "There's one last thing you could do to keep your family safe."

"What's that?" she had to ask when he didn't immediately volunteer his final suggestion.

"Give up this crazy idea and head for town before it's too late." With that parting salvo, he turned on his heel and left them.

Nathaniel went straight to the bunkhouse and packed up his gear. It didn't take him long. After fifteen years of rambling, he didn't have much to stow away in his saddlebags. *Not too many possessions to weigh you down, no strings to bind you to a place, that's the way you like it, old son*, he told himself, and went to saddle up his horse.

When he led Old Blue from the barn, the view of the Sangre de Cristos had never looked prettier. All of the range except the black crests of the peaks were blanketed with brilliant white snow, and the sky above them was the deepest of blues. The ranch outbuildings looked a great deal better kept, thanks to his efforts this fall. The corral was sturdy, the henhouse stood upright, and the barn roof would hold off rain and snow much better this winter than it had in years.

He'd spent hours shaving shingles for that roof. As he mounted Old Blue, he tried not to think about the fact that the whole barn might go up in flames soon. It was impossible not to think about it, and about every one of the young people he was leaving behind, Robin most of all.

He'd been square with her from the start. He'd never led her to believe he'd help her commit suicide. He still felt unaccountably guilty as he started his mount down the road leading away from the ranch.

"Wait, Nathaniel, please wait," Betsy called after him.

Cursing under his breath, he pulled Old Blue to a halt and glanced back over his shoulder. Somehow he wasn't surprised to see they were all standing there on the porch to see him off, even Robin. Luke and Jake looked grim, Tommy was crying, and Robin's face was pale and set. Betsy came running up to him, carrying a burlap bag.

"Here's some trail food for you. I didn't have time to put much together for you, but there's some bread, cheese, and ham to tide you over."

"Thanks," he said, his voice gruff. "You didn't need to do that."

"You didn't need to help us the way you did. We'll miss you. We'll all miss you very much," Betsy said earnestly as she handed him the bag. He wondered if he had imagined the special emphasis she had put on the word "all."

Suddenly, Tommy wriggled out of Jake's hold and came flying down the steps. "You just cain't leave us, Nathn'l," he cried, his face twisted with tears. Betsy drew him to her and put a comforting arm about his shoulders, but the little boy still shook with sobs.

Swearing silently, Nathaniel slipped from Old Blue's back. He couldn't leave Tommy like this. He knelt in the snow in front of him.

"Hey, partner, what's all this fuss about?"

"I thought we was going to play outlaws tomorrow, and we haven't finished making Robin's present yet."

"I know, partner, and I'm real sorry about that. I need to head on down the trail now. Jake and Luke can help you finish up our project now we got such a good start on it."

"It won't be as fun making it with them."

"Well, I think it will be, and I'm counting on you to get it done."

"I'll try, I guess," Tommy let out a big sniff and rubbed his eyes on his coat sleeve. "You ever gonna come back and see us?"

"I just might. It will probably be a while, though. You'll probably be a real big fellow by then."

Tommy sent him a watery smile. "Maybe I'll even be taller than Jake."

"Wouldn't that be a sight? You take good care of everyone, you hear, especially your little sister. That's what big brothers do."

Tommy nodded earnestly, looking so much like a little man in that moment that Nathaniel's heart twisted. He leaned forward and gave the boy a big hug. How had this little fellow come to mean so much to him in a few short months? Nathaniel stood and glanced at the rest of the Matthewses and Jessie up on the porch. How had they all come to matter so much to him?

Lastly, he looked at Robin. She held little Jessie cradled in her arms as if she wanted to shield her from all the harm in the world. Robin wore that stubborn, proud look he knew only too well. As their gazes met, the coolness in her green eyes melted away. "You take good care of yourself, Nathaniel Hollister," she said sternly, and then she even managed a smile.

His heart was heavier than a boulder in his chest when he swung up into the saddle again. He urged Old Blue into a jog and refused to look back over his shoulder at the little family he was leaving behind.

Chapter Twenty-four

Every step Old Blue took away from the Rocking M, the more miserable and worried Nathaniel became. He tried to distract himself by thinking of where he wanted to head next. Maybe he'd take a train to San Francisco and spend the winter there. Or he could head east and hit the gambling parlors in St. Louis. With his skill at cards, he probably wouldn't have to touch his savings.

Yet things he'd wished he'd thought to tell Robin and the rest kept intruding on his planning. Hell, he should have told them to lead the stock out of the barn. While he was picturing himself in the midst of a card game at some fancy saloon in St. Louis, he remembered he hadn't told Jake and Luke to clean their guns.

Damn it, this wasn't going the way he'd planned. He'd always thought he could just ride away from Robin and her family when the time came. He had to close the book on this whole Rocking M adventure—close it now, and for good. *You're doing them all a favor by leaving. They'll only cling to*

their foolish dream longer if you stay and help them. They're
better off without you. She's better off without you.

The farther he rode, the more chilled he grew. He wrestled
with his fear for Robin and her family, and fought an unreason-
able, instinctive urge to turn back.

He'd made it most of the way to town, and the sun was just
setting in the west when he reined Old Blue to a halt. He kept
seeing Robin, her young face so determined and resolute, and
the way she had held Jessie in her arms as if she wanted to
protect her from hurt. If he wanted to get a decent night's
sleep, he was going to have to go back and make certain the
Matthewses had left their ranch. If they hadn't, he'd find some
way to force them to go.

The moment he made up his mind, he turned Old Blue about.
He gave the gelding his head, and the steeldust forged into a
ground-eating lope. It was dark by the time they reached the
ranch, but a half-moon in the clear night sky shed plenty of
light for Nathaniel to see his way. He rode Old Blue into a
grove of aspen to the east of the ranch buildings.

He couldn't see any signs of the Matthewses packing up to
leave. Instead, he spotted the twins carrying buckets of water
to the various outbuildings. All the stock they usually kept in
the barn were penned in corrals. Clearly the Matthewses were
getting ready to do their best to stand off the Rafter S riders
when they came. So much for hoping Robin and her family
had come to their senses after he left.

He was just about to ride down to the ranch house intending
to carry Robin off to town by force if necessary when Old Blue
pricked his ears and looked to the south. Moments later, the
gelding neighed loudly.

Nathaniel's stomach tightened. Damn it all to hell, it was
too late for the Matthewses to leave now. The Rafter S riders
were coming.

Nathaniel swore bitterly. He finally had to face the terrible
choice he'd been hoping to avoid ever since he decided to stay

on at the Rocking M. He couldn't ride away and let Robin and the rest face Sutherland's ruthless, violent men on their own.

The last time you tried to help Robin, she got shot, a cold, remorseless voice reminded him. *The last time you tried to help a whole town, you were too arrogant and careless, and Mary McAllister ended up bleeding her life away into the street.*

Tonight, he simply wouldn't get careless—he couldn't afford to. Too many lives he cared about were on the line.

Grimly, he spurred Old Blue into a run. He pulled him to a plunging stop in front of the barn. Jake and Luke hurried up to him, both carrying rifles.

"The Rafter S boys are coming from the south," he told them swiftly. "They could be here any moment. Where are Betsy and Robin?"

"They're inside."

"Jake, I want you to stand behind those big old timbers framing the door to the barn and fire from there. Luke, I want you to cover the ranch yard from behind that horse trough. You boys keep your heads down as much as you can. You understand?"

The twins nodded. They looked scared, but he had a feeling they both would stick. "I'm going to cover the house from behind that big boulder in the front ranch yard—and then I'll probably move about. Do me a favor and don't shoot me by mistake. I'm going inside to check on the girls."

When he stepped into the back hallway, he saw Betsy was at the kitchen table calmly loading up her father's twelve-bore. She looked up at him, and a wide smile lit her face. After placing the shotgun back on the table, she launched herself at him and hugged him hard.

"I knew you wouldn't let us down. I just knew it," she said into his chest.

For a brief moment, he allowed himself the luxury of hugging her back. He thought he'd forgotten how to pray a long time ago. But in that moment, he found himself appealing to some higher power. *Please don't let me let her down. Please don't let any of them get hurt.*

Betsy let go of him and called softly over her shoulder. "Robin, he came back."

He heard light footsteps, and then she stood in the doorway. She was dressed in her male work clothes, and her face looked strained. He wasn't prepared for the deep, abiding joy it gave him simply to see her when he had thought he might never see her again. He read surprise and relief in her eyes when she looked his way, and some other emotion he couldn't quite read.

"They're coming," he told her quickly. "You need to blow out all the lamps. Where are Tommy and Jessie?"

"We put them to bed early in the boys' room," she replied. "Somehow I had a feeling it would be tonight. I was going to put Betsy upstairs where she could shoot from the front bedroom."

"All right. You can shoot from your father's study. You may want to break the glass yourself. If they shoot through the upper panes and it falls on you . . ."

"We've already removed the glass panes from both windows," she said coolly.

"That's good thinking." He almost smiled. Only females would go about preparing for a gunfight in a such a neat and orderly fashion. Robin had already turned away and begun blowing out the lamps, and Betsy was doing the same.

When the front of the house was dark, Nathaniel opened the front door and listened. The night was still quiet. The raiders from the Rafter S had probably stopped to light their torches. When she had finished with the lamps, Robin came to stand beside him. Even in the darkness, he could see her eyes were wide with worry.

He started out the door. Her voice stopped him. "I wish you wouldn't go out there," she said. "Surely you'd be safer staying in the house."

"I'll be of more help to you if I stay outside, and I can keep a closer eye on the twins."

She was silent for a long moment while she digested his words. "All right," she said quietly. "Thank you for coming back." She reached up and pressed a quick kiss on his cheek, and then she slipped away to take up her post in her father's study.

He stared after her, feeling foolishly pleased.

Then he turned to face the door again. A cold night wind sent small clouds scudding across the moon. He waited until one of those clouds briefly darkened the snowy ranch yard. He walked silently off the porch and took up his position behind the boulder that flanked the house. He was in the most forward and exposed position, but from here he also could cover the whole approach to the house.

He squatted down behind the boulder and pulled the collar of his coat up against the freezing wind. The cold would work in their favor. He doubted the Rafter S hands would wait long before they attacked.

After checking his guns one last time, he settled down to wait. The moonlit night was so pretty, he would have enjoyed sitting out here except that his toes were going numb, and he was desperately worried about each and every one of the Matthews clan.

He'd been waiting for less than a minute when he heard galloping horses in the distance, and he felt the pounding vibration from their hooves beneath his feet. The Rafter S hands were coming. He waved his hand to tell everyone to get ready.

The attackers came in a wild rush. There were a dozen all told. Carrying blazing torches, they yelled like wild Comanches and fired their pistols in the air. Nathaniel stood and fired his repeating Winchester as fast as he could. He didn't want to let those men close to the house or the barn. The girls opened fire at the same time. He picked off one cowboy, the girls hit another. Neighing frenziedly, a horse reared and threw its rider.

He heard the raiders' shouts of surprise and curses. Obviously, they had expected their raid would catch the Matthewses unaware. They snapped several shots his way, but he kept shooting. If their reception was fierce enough, he hoped they would break off the attack before any of the Rocking M defenders got hurt. Four raiders cleared the house. Jake and Luke opened up on them the moment they reached the barnyard.

The boys shot one rider out of the saddle, but two more got close enough to pitch their torches at the barn. One landed against the base of the building, the other on the low section of the roof. Unfortunately, it was a section the winter wind had scoured free of snow, and the dry shingles caught fire quickly.

Those two cowboys pounded back past him, and Nathaniel let them go. He'd already killed too many men in his time. The third paused long enough to give a hand up to the one left afoot, and then they galloped back the way they had come.

Nathaniel spotted two more men just as they were about to throw their torches up on the porch of the house. Trying to wound rather than kill, he shot one in the shoulder, and the other in the leg. He saw two others break off from the rest. They went galloping around the front, obviously hoping to find the far side of the house less defended. Moments later, Nathaniel heard the boom of Betsy's twelve-bore and more curses.

"To hell with this," one of the riders called out. "I'm getting out of here." He turned his horse and headed back out into the darkness, and all but one of the remaining men followed him.

"Goddamn it, you're all a bunch of lily-livered cowards," he heard Rick Dyer shout after them. He watched the foreman wrest a torch from one of the fleeing men. His face twisted with hate, Dyer rode right at the house. Nathaniel worked the lever on his Winchester, but the magazine was empty. Cursing fiercely, he dropped his rifle and grabbed for his pistol. By the time Nathaniel drew and got his first shot off, Dyer's torch had landed on the porch. Nathaniel ran forward and fired again, but Dyer was already galloping away into the night.

"Is everyone all right?" he called out to the girls in the house as he ran up on the porch and kicked the torch off it into the snow.

"We're fine. They broke one window and woke up Jessie."

The irritation in Betsy's voice would have made him smile, except he was too worried about trying to save the barn.

He leapt over the porch rail and raced for the back of the house. Jake was using a blanket to smother the one small fire started by the torch thrown against the base of the barn. But the fire up on the roof was gaining momentum. Luke had already clambered up a ladder and was doing his best to beat out the blaze with a blanket. Nathaniel grabbed a second blanket and climbed the ladder as fast as he could.

When he reached the roof, he knew they were in trouble. The wind was fanning the fire, sending embers to land higher up on the roof. Already the flames were swirling shoulder-high. Ignoring the searing heat from those flames, he stood next to Luke and slapped at the burning section.

Nathaniel glanced up a short time later. Robin was standing on the other side of the burning roof now, hitting at the edges of the flames. He yelled at her to be careful and not to stand too close in case the roof fell in. He doubted that she could hear him over the roar of the fire.

Despite their efforts, the fire spread rapidly. The arid Colorado climate and relentless sun had dried out both the shingles and rafters of the barn, making them as flammable as tinder.

When his blanket caught fire, Nathaniel swore and tossed it aside. "It's no use," he shouted at Luke. "There's nothing we can do. I'm going to go get your sister before she gets hurt." Luke nodded. Coughing from the smoke, the boy stumbled after him.

When Nathaniel reached the edge of the roof, he found the ladder was gone. Robin must have taken it. Rather than wait for Jake to bring the ladder back, Nathaniel jumped off the roof into a snowdrift.

He staggered to his feet and ran for the ladder. When he reached the top of it, he shouted at her, "Dammit, Robin, give it up," even though he knew she probably couldn't hear him over the crackling of the flames. When he scanned her section of the roof, his heart almost stopped. Robin was still hitting at the fire like a demon possessed, but the roof rafters supporting her had to be just about burned through. He crossed to her side in three great strides.

"Come on. This roof is going to go any moment."

"No! You don't understand. All of our feed and our best hay for the winter is in this barn . . ."

Rather than argue with her, he simply picked her up and carried her away from the fire. At first she fought him, but then she must have finally understood the futility of the situation, for she went limp in his arms. He set her down before the ladder.

After one long, bleak look at the fire blazing just feet away, she climbed down the ladder. Nathaniel started after her. His shoulders were even with the roofline when he saw the section where they had been standing just moments ago collapse with a shower of sparks and smoke. When he reached the ground, his legs felt shaky.

They all gathered in a forlorn half circle and stood watching the barn burn. Heat from the blaze became so intense they had to step back from it.

"It took Pa a whole year to build that barn," Jake said bitterly.

"Folks said it was the best built barn in Grand Valley," Luke added his own simple eulogy.

Betsy didn't say anything, but tears streamed down her cheeks. Robin didn't cry. Looking angry and bitter, she stood with a comforting arm around Betsy's shoulders.

The wind shifted. Burning embers sailed through the air and landed on the roof of the house. The northern side was covered with two feet of snow, but the southern side was just as dry as the barn roof had been. To cope with this new danger, they split up and began take turns snuffing out embers on the roof. Betsy kept checking carefully to make sure her precious hen-house didn't catch fire, either. At one point, Nathaniel found himself standing next to Robin near the barn.

"I'm sorry," he said simply as they watched the last standing section collapse in a whoosh of flame, smoke, and sparks.

"It could have been worse. I don't know what we would do if we lost the house."

He decided now wasn't the time to point out Dyer and his men could easily return another time and try for the house.

"They expected to surprise you. Instead they were the ones who were surprised. You all put up a heck of fight."

"Your coming back made all the difference. We were going to fight them, but we didn't think we could win. When you came back, we knew we had a good chance."

He didn't want to tell her how misplaced that confidence was. He didn't want to tell her how determined he'd been to keep riding on.

Her tone changed. "I'm surprised you're still in one piece, though, the way you stood up out there in the midst of all that shooting. I've said it before. You'd think a man who used to be in your line of work would have more sense."

"I reckon you're right about that," he said mildly. He leaned over and pressed a quick kiss on her lips, just because he was so relieved that she was all right. Then he went off to make another tour around the outside of the house. They were all bone-weary by the time the barn fire had subsided to glowing coals. Nathaniel trudged into the kitchen to thaw out and drink some hot coffee.

He was startled when Robin came striding into the room, her expression worried. "Have you seen Betsy?"

"Not for an hour or so, I guess. I just assumed she went inside to check on the little ones."

"So did I. But she's not upstairs, downstairs, or in the cellar. I've checked everywhere."

Nathaniel set his coffee down on the table. "Don't you go getting all worried. She's probably just outside talking to those precious cluckies of hers. I'll go find her."

He went outside and checked the henhouse. Betsy wasn't there, nor was she in the corral where she'd spent a good part of the night trying to calm the frightened horses. He enlisted the twins' help. After ten minutes of frantic calling and searching, they reached a frightening conclusion—Betsy was gone.

As he and the boys approached the house, Nathaniel knew they were all thinking the same thing. She never would have willingly left her family in the midst of a crisis like this one. Someone must have taken her.

Chapter Twenty-five

Robin was waiting for Nathaniel and her brothers by the back door. She could tell by their worried expressions that their search had been futile.

"You didn't find her," she said flatly. She stepped aside so that they could all make a beeline for the stove.

"I'm going to saddle up and take a quick look around," Nathaniel offered. "It's gotten pretty cloudy out there now. It's always possible she lost her bearings in the dark."

"That's possible, but it's hardly likely. Dyer took her. I know he did."

"We don't know anything of the sort yet," Nathaniel said firmly.

"This is all my fault." She wanted to scream her frustration. She wanted to ride out into the black night and shoot Rick Dyer down like a dog. Instead, she could only stand helplessly in the midst of the kitchen that her sweet sister loved and pray Betsy was going to be all right. "I never should have pushed so hard to stay on here."

"Betsy voted right along with the rest of us," Luke pointed out.

"She didn't know what a loathsome cur Dyer can be. I should have warned her." Instinctively, Robin looked at Nathaniel because he was the only one who knew how desperately she feared for her sister now.

Nathaniel crossed the room and took her into his arms. For a long moment, Robin allowed herself the luxury of leaning her head against his shoulder. His sheepskin jacket was still cold from outside, and he smelled like smoke. Thank heavens he was here. Even after receiving this, almost the worst blow she could imagine, she could find a way to bear it because she could draw on Nathaniel's strength.

"I promise, I'll find her, and I'll do whatever it takes to get her back."

She tilted her head and gazed up into his eyes. She saw the grim resolution there. In that moment, she realized he meant what he said. He would risk his life to get her sister back, partly for her sake, and partly for Betsy's. She knew what a soft spot he had in his heart for her little sister.

As she stared up into his hard, handsome face, she realized that she couldn't let him take that risk. He had become too dear for her to let him ride off to the Rafter S and challenge the ruthless riders Dyer had working for him. The odds were too high. Sutherland had over thirty cowboys on his payroll. Nathaniel couldn't take them all on by himself, and Dyer would be after his blood.

"All right," she said, her mind working swiftly. "I agree. You should check and make sure she isn't lost here on the ranch. Then we'll plan what to do next."

She stepped away from him. Before her face could give her away, she busied herself slicing some bread, cheese, and ham for everyone to eat.

Wordlessly Nathaniel went back outside.

She forced herself to eat a slice of bread even though her stomach was tied in knots. She'd need her strength for the long, cold ride ahead of her. When she was certain Nathaniel had ridden off into the dark, she went to her room to dress in her warmest clothing.

When she returned to the kitchen, the twins were still sitting at the table, both of them looking exhausted. Jake sat up a little straighter when he saw the way she was dressed. "Where the heck do you think you're going? Nathaniel's not even back yet."

"That's why I have to leave now. He can search all he wants around the ranch, but I know Dyer's men must have Betsy. I'm riding to the Rafter S right now. I'm going to tell Vance Sutherland that I'll sell him the Rocking M as long as we get Betsy back safe and sound."

"I think you should wait and tell Nathaniel what you're plannin' to do. He's not going to like this," Luke declared.

"I don't care whether he likes it or not. This is the way it's going to be." She relented when she saw how worried the twins looked. "When he doesn't find Betsy, he's going to go after her, and Dyer and his boys are going to be waiting for him. I know Nathaniel's a legend, but the Rafter S is too big an outfit for him to tackle on his own. Dyer is going to try to kill him after that beating Nathaniel gave him in town. I know losing the ranch is going to be hard for all of us, but I don't want Nathaniel to die, and I want to get Betsy back."

Just then, a sharp knock came on the door. Robin's breath caught. Could someone be bringing them news about Betsy? Without a word, Luke and Jake rose and picked up their rifles. With her brothers at her heels, Robin picked up a lamp and went to open the door.

Shorty Wilcox stood in the doorway, an ugly grin twisting his face. "Evening, Miss Matthews. Looks like you lost your barn tonight. We sure are sorry about that."

"What do you want?" Robin replied in a cool, even tone.

"Dyer sent me to tell you he's got your pretty little sister. If you want her back in one piece, you're to come with me now and sign over your ranch to the old man."

She'd guessed this would be their play. She'd meant to ride out to the Rafter S anyway, but going with Shorty Wilcox made it ten times harder. Just one look at his leering expression brought back with visceral, frightening clarity that afternoon that Rick Dyer had tried to rape her.

Robin stifled her rising panic. She had to make certain nothing like that happened to Betsy. She made her decision on the spot.

"All right. I'll come with you. Luke, saddle up Rusty for me." She could see the protest forming on his lips. "Please, there's no time for us to argue about this. I have to go now for Betsy's sake."

After a long moment, he nodded. He looked over at Jake, some silent message passing between the two of them she couldn't quite read. Then he headed down the hall toward the back of the house.

"I want some coffee while he's saddling up your horse."

Robin sent Shorty a disdainful glance. She'd much sooner feed him arsenic. Silently she led him back to the kitchen and poured him a cup. He helped himself to the bread and cheese she'd put out for the twins earlier.

It was agony, waiting while Shorty swilled his coffee and ate in her kitchen. All she could think about was Betsy and how frightened and alone she must feel right now. Robin tried to draw some comfort from the fact that she doubted Betsy had even reached the Rafter S yet. The big house on the Sutherland's spread was a good ten-mile ride from the Rocking M—if they were taking Betsy to the big house.

To distract herself from her worrying, she spoke to Jake instead. "You two look after the little ones. They're going to be upset when they realize Betsy and I are both gone—and finding out the barn burned may shake them, too. Hopefully, we'll all be back by tomorrow afternoon." How false those optimistic words sounded, even to her ears.

Luke poked his head inside the door. "Rusty's all saddled up for you."

Robin swallowed hard and looked at both of her brothers. "Tell Nathaniel there's absolutely no reason to come after me. I'd decided to sell out after the barn burned anyway. He mustn't come."

In the meantime, Shorty finished his coffee, belched, and wiped his lips with the back of his hand. "Boys," he said in his gravelly voice, "you can tell the big, famous marshal a message from me, too. If he sets foot on the Rafter S, Rick Dyer is going to be gunning for him. If Rick don't fetch him, the rest of us will." With a cruel laugh, Shorty spun about on his heels and headed for the front door. Her heart pounding in her chest, Robin followed him into the dark winter night.

Nathaniel was tired, cold, and sick with worry by the time he returned to the ranch house. Betsy was nowhere to be found. He was certain now that someone from the Rafter S must have abducted her. Logically, he knew that he had to check the area surrounding the ranch house to make certain she hadn't been hurt or lost in the snow, but he chaffed at the time he had just lost.

"Where's Robin?" he asked Jake the moment he stepped inside the kitchen. The boy was dozing in the rocking chair, his rifle laying across his knees. Jake came awake with a jerk and rubbed his face with his hand.

"She left about an hour ago with Shorty Wilcox. Dyer's got Betsy, but he said they'd let her go if Robin agreed to sell the ranch to Sutherland."

Fury and fear boiled through Nathaniel's veins at the notion of Robin riding off into the night with scum like Wilcox. "You let her go? Do you have any idea what Dyer would like to do to her?" As soon as he said the words, he wished he could catch them back.

Jake paled and stared at the floor. Nathaniel crossed the room and laid a hand on his shoulder.

"I'm sorry. I know there was nothing you could do. There's

no stopping your sister when she gets a notion in her head.'' Nathaniel withdrew his hand and went to stand close to the stove. He was chilled to the marrow of his bones after being outside so much tonight.

"Luke's trailing them. We talked it over before he left, and we think there's a good chance they're not holding Betsy at the main house. I mean, if a law officer beside Sheriff Campbell did find out about it, surely Mr. Sutherland wouldn't want to get into trouble for abducting someone.''

"I tend to agree with you. Dyer may have overplayed his hand on this one. Betsy is mighty popular in town. If we tell a few folks what happened, the news will travel fast, and they're going to be hopping mad.''

"Luke was going to follow Shorty and Robin until he's sure where they're headed. Then he's going to hightail it back to town, and meet you at Mrs. Beacham's house. That is, if you want to go after them.''

"I'm going after them all right. Did you think I wouldn't want to?''

Jake met his gaze levelly. "When you rode away from here yesterday afternoon, Luke and I didn't think you were going to come back. Betsy swore you would, but we didn't expect we'd ever see you again. It might have been better for Robin if you hadn't come back.''

Nathaniel found his cheeks flushing under the boy's steady gaze. "You could be right about that. I'm the first one to admit I'm wrong for your sister in a hundred different ways, but I swear I'll do anything I can to get her away from Rick Dyer. I don't believe he's going to let her ride away after he's forced her to sign a deed.''

"Then you best get moving,'' came Jake's simple rejoinder. He rose to his feet. "I'm going to load up Tommy and Jessie in the buckboard and leave them at Mrs. Beacham's. I'll be along as soon as I can.''

Nathaniel considered trying to talk him into staying on the ranch, and then decided against it. Jake and Luke's actions of the last twenty-four hours proved they were truly young men now. They had a right to try to help their sisters. *You've got to find a way to get all the Matthewses out of this sorry mess without any of them getting hurt.*

Even though he longed to start for town at once, he forced himself to hold his cold hands out to the stove for a minute longer. *You won't do anyone any good if you freeze your fingers on the ride to town.* When his hands were warm again, he wrapped his muffler tighter about his neck.

He'd just headed for the door when Jake spoke up behind him.

"Mr. Hollister, I don't think you'd be so wrong for Robin if you made up your mind to stick around."

"That's a kind thing for you to say," Nathaniel said, staring at the door in front of him. He didn't point out that the boy was dead wrong, nor did he point out how irrelevant that issue was right now. All he cared about was fetching Robin and Betsy safely back home to the Rocking M. He knew the kind of men he was up against, and he understood the odds were against him.

"You be careful traveling with the little ones. I think it's going to snow hard this morning," he added, and then he picked up a lantern and stepped outside. The cloudy skies were just starting to lighten in the east. It was already snowing lightly. Old Blue whickered at him when he strode to the horse corral.

Refusing to give in to his weariness, he made quick work of saddling up Old Blue. Before he mounted, Nathaniel made certain his pistol and Winchester were fully loaded. He pulled a second revolver from his saddlebag, checked its load, and shoved it in his belt.

He swung into the saddle and sent Old Blue jogging past the black, smoldering remains of Robin's barn. When they reached the lane leading to the road, he urged the steeldust into a lope.

He knew he'd drive himself crazy if he thought too much about the girls. Every time he started to picture Robin or Betsy with Dyer and his rough friends, terrible fear combined with hot red anger rose inside him. Letting that fear guide his actions wasn't going to save the girls. Instead, he coolly weighed and considered his options. He was going after Dyer, because Dyer posed the biggest threat to Robin. He began to plan his hunt, much the way he'd plan to take in any wanted killer.

The Rafter S hands had the advantage of numbers, and they knew the terrain far better than he did. He would have to find some way to sneak onto the Rafter S. It looked like the weather just might oblige him. It was starting to snow more heavily, reducing visibility. If only Luke had managed to stay with them. Knowing exactly where Robin and Betsy were being held would make all the difference.

Please, he found himself praying to a god he'd lost faith in long ago. *Please, let them be safe.*

Chapter Twenty-six

It was six o'clock in the morning when Nathaniel reached town. He'd just raised his hand to knock when Mrs. Beacham opened her door, still clad in a mobcap and a voluminous flannel dressing gown. The old lady looked mad enough to spit nails.

"Luke just rode in and told me everything. Vance Sutherland has gone too far this time. That Rick Dyer is the lowest form of scum. I'm going to get dressed, and then we're going to go haul our worthless sheriff out of bed. The townsfolk have been looking the other way for years while Vance played his dirty tricks, but abducting Betsy is the last straw."

"You do that, ma'am, but I don't think I can wait to find out if Sheriff Campbell is finally going to do his job. I'm heading straight out to the Rafter S."

"Those boys will be laying for you," the old lady pointed out worriedly.

"I don't want to leave Betsy or Robin alone with Rick Dyer a minute longer than I have to."

The worry and concern she saw in his face must have convinced her. "All right, then. I promise we'll have a posse heading out to the Rafter S within an hour, if I have to lead it myself." She led the way back to her kitchen where Luke was drinking coffee and thawing himself out next to her stove.

"You find them?" Nathaniel asked while Mrs. Beacham poured him his own cup and thrust it into his cold hands.

"I trailed them to the old Parson place," Luke replied. "That's a homestead with a house and a barn that the Rafter S swallowed up two years ago. It's about four miles south of town. I saw them take Robin inside the house, and then I hightailed it back here. I'm pretty sure they didn't see me."

"You did a good job." Nathaniel crossed to the window. It was snowing heavily now. "You think you're up for showing me where this place is?"

Luke put down his cup and stood in reply.

Nathaniel turned to Mrs. Beacham. "Jake's coming in with the little ones."

"I'll keep an eye out for them," she promised. Luke went out the back door to fetch his horse from the shed. Nathaniel took one wonderfully hot swallow of coffee and set his own cup down on the table. Mrs. Beacham followed him to the front door.

"Oh my heavens," she said suddenly. "I almost forgot. I've got a telegram for you. Mr. Peabody brought it by here three days ago. He knows I pick up mail for Robin and bring it out to the ranch for her frequently."

Hell, the last thing he needed to do right now was read a telegram. Then the thought occurred to him. What if it was from Joshua? "I better take a look at it," he said grimly.

The old lady hurried away to fetch it. It took him less than a minute to scan its contents. Joshua had hit pay dirt. He had managed to track down both the Jeffersons and the Schmidts. Nathaniel tucked the telegram carefully into his shirt pocket. If it came to a confrontation with Sutherland, Joshua might have just given him some valuable leverage.

"I take it that was good news," Mrs. Beacham guessed
shrewdly.

"It could help us today." He didn't want to take the time
to explain now, not while Robin and Betsy sat in that abandoned
farmhouse with Rick Dyer and his henchmen. If Dyer had laid
a hand on Robin, this time nothing would stop Nathaniel from
killing him.

Mrs. Beacham must have guessed the general tenor of his
thoughts.

"If he wasn't a such a skunk, I could almost feel sorry for
Dyer right about now," she said quietly. "You go bring those
girls back, safe and sound."

"I'll surely do my best."

By the time he'd reached his horse, Nathaniel had forgotten
all about Mrs. Beacham. Right now he had a job to do. As he
swung into the saddle, he considered what he'd observed about
Rick Dyer's character. Dyer considered himself a gunfighter,
but he was also smart enough to stack the odds in his favor.
He'd have several men with him, men who were good with
guns in their own right.

Luke rode up beside him. They kicked their horses into a
gallop, the freezing wind and the snow making for a miserable
ride. Nathaniel didn't mind the snow. He needed it if he was
going to have a prayer of reaching that farmhouse before Dyer's
men shot him full of holes.

After two miles, they pulled the horses back to a walk to
rest them briefly. Nathaniel asked Luke to tell him everything
he could remember about the layout and the number of men
he'd seen. Luke was fairly sure there were at least eight men
there including Dyer.

"Can you think of any way we can get close to that house
without Dyer's men seeing us?"

Luke frowned while he considered the question. "There's
an old streambed that runs behind the house. We played hide-
and-seek there when we visited the Parsons one summer. That

bed is pretty deep. We might be able to get close to the house if we followed it in.''

"Let's give it a try.''

"If we leave the road here and head east, we should hit that stream bed in a quarter mile or so.''

Nathaniel nodded in agreement and lifted his muffler higher against the wind. Luke's prediction soon proved accurate. They did find the streambed, and it was just as deep as the boy had remembered. They walked their horses slowly along the watercourse, the high banks on either side giving them some shelter from the biting wind and driving snow.

Luke pulled up a short time later. "There's the house,'' he said quietly and pointed to his right.

Nathaniel peered through the slanting snow. He could just make out the dim outlines of a log house approximately an eighth of a mile away. Robin and Betsy were there, so close now. A wild part of him was tempted to go galloping straight up to the house, guns blazing, but he knew he wouldn't do the girls a bit of good if he got himself killed before he took Rick Dyer out of the game.

"All right. We'll leave the horses here. Bring your rifle and cartridge belt,'' he told Luke.

They both dismounted and left their weary mounts ground-tied. He gave Old Blue a farewell pat in gratitude. Hopefully they'd back for them within the next hour. In the meantime, the streambed was the best shelter for the animals.

The going was treacherous, for the round stream rocks were covered with ice and snow. They both slipped and fell several times, banging their knees and shins painfully. As they drew closer to the house, they crouched lower to keep out of sight. At last they came to the place where the stream ran nearest to the house. From here, the back wall of the log dwelling was only a hundred feet away. Thanks to Luke, they'd gotten much closer than Nathaniel had dared hope without Dyer's men spotting them.

A lone lookout stood near the corner of the house, watching

both the side and the back of the dwelling. From the way the cowboy stood huddled in his coat, Nathaniel guessed Dyer's man was thinking more about how cold he was than the job he was supposed to be doing.

While he watched the house and the lookout, Nathaniel snatched off his gloves and put his chilled hands under his armpits inside his coat. For what was coming next, he would need every bit of coordination he possessed.

"All right. This is a good place for you to cover me. You stand right here, and steady your rifle on the ground," Nathaniel whispered to Luke. "Don't leave this spot unless you absolutely have to. You're firing from a good, safe position here. I'm going to be counting on you to take two or three of them out of it if you can."

He paused and studied the boy carefully. "You ready for this?"

Luke nodded. His face was pale, but his gaze was steady.

Nathaniel looked back at the house. Was *he* ready? A lifetime of fighting and hunting the most violent of men had come down to this moment. He'd faced a dozen fights almost as tough as this one. Why then did his mouth feel so dry? Why had his belly been tied into a cold, hard knot for hours now?

Because in this fight, Robin's life was on the line. He'd meant what he'd said to Jake back at the ranch. Dyer wouldn't be satisfied with forcing Robin to give up the ranch. Nathaniel knew his type only too well. Dyer was a cold-blooded killer, with little regard for anyone but himself. For a man like Rick Dyer, life was all about power and prestige. Robin had thwarted him and made him lose face, and therefore she was in terrible danger now.

The very thought of what she might have already endured made him ache. He didn't love her. He couldn't. He was too hard and cold a man to love anyone, but he surely cared for game, plucky Robin and her sweet little sister. The two of them had taught him there were still some things in life worth fighting for. He was willing to give his life in a heartbeat to save them both.

Nathaniel took one last look at the house. Chances were he might have to pay that price. He'd just make damn sure he took Dyer and the worst of them with him.

He stretched his fingers and hands. He slipped them back into his gloves and checked his guns a final time. When he glanced over the streambank again, the lookout was staring the other way, huddled deep in his coat.

Nathaniel drew his pistol from its holster and nodded to Luke. It was time.

The boy settled himself against the rocky bank, his rifle trained on the lookout. Nathaniel climbed up the frozen bank and ran as quickly as he could toward him. The new fallen snow muffled the sound of Nathaniel's approach. Some breath of sound must have warned Dyer's man at the last moment, but when he started to turn, it was already too late. Nathaniel slammed the butt of his pistol against the man's temple. His eyes rolled up in his head, and his knees sagged. Nathaniel grabbed him as he fell and dragged him behind the house.

He took the cowboy's pistol and shoved it into his own pocket. He took his rifle and tossed it into a snowbank. Maybe the Sutherland hand would come to before he froze to death, and maybe he wouldn't. Right now, Nathaniel didn't much care. Any man party to abducting a thirteen-year-old girl was lower than a snake.

There was one window on the back of the house. Nathaniel peered through the glass. Robin and Betsy were sitting side by side on a wooden bench. Robin had an arm around her sister, and she was glaring at someone out of Nathaniel's line of sight. That glare almost made Nathaniel smile. At least his Robin hadn't been cowed by the ordeals she'd been through during the last twenty-four hours.

He shifted his position, trying to get a count of how many men were in the room. There was one man standing behind the bench, holding a rifle in his hands. It was the burly cowboy with the ten-gallon hat who'd wanted his blood back at the Rocking M. He couldn't see Dyer, Johnson, or Wilcox. Damn. He didn't want to go crashing into that room until he knew exactly where everyone was.

Just then, the hair on the back of his neck began to prickle. Because he'd been so preoccupied with the girls, he was a second late listening to that sixth sense that usually warned him of danger. He spun about and lifted his pistol.

Shorty Wilcox stood by the corner of the house, his rifle pointed at Nathaniel's belly. Nathaniel saw the gleam of triumph in Shorty's eyes, and he knew his own shot would come too late to save him. A rifle cracked. Nathaniel tensed, expecting to be hit. Reflexes made him step sideways and snap off a shot with his pistol anyway.

A strange, stunned expression crossed Shorty's face. "I had you, you son of a bitch. I know I had you," the stocky cowboy said in a choked voice. Then he pitched forward into the snow and lay still.

Nathaniel lifted a hand to Luke. The boy's fine shooting had just saved his life. Nathaniel raised his pistol and waited for company. Those shots were sure to draw some attention.

Sure enough, moments later two men charged around the back of the house, their guns leveled. They both shot at him, but their bullets went wild. Standing still and ready, Nathaniel was able to drop them both before they had a chance to fire again.

Four down, four to go. After swiftly loading more bullets into the cylinder on his pistol, Nathaniel ran to the corner of the house and peered carefully around it. He couldn't see anyone. Were the rest of them inside?

Suddenly, Luke's rifle cracked again and a man shouted hoarsely from the far side of the house.

"I got him," Luke called quietly. "He's not moving."

That meant five were down. Assuming there were only seven men with Dyer and that others hadn't arrived later, there should be only two left beside the Rafter S foreman. Knowing he'd been damned lucky so far, Nathaniel eased along the side of the house, keeping his pistol cocked and a wary lookout for any sign of trouble. When he reached the front corner, he risked a quick look around it to take in the layout. The barn stood off to the left, the lower doors and the doors to the hayloft all wide open. He couldn't see anyone in the barn or yard, but he knew there had to be more men waiting for him.

He ducked back against the side of the house to do some quick thinking. If he'd been setting up the defense of this place, the first thing he'd do was put a shooter up in the loft of that barn where he could cover all the front approaches to the house. Deciding to test his theory, he took off his hat and placed it over the stock of his rifle. He inched the hat halfway around the corner and held it there. Moments later, a bullet tore through his hat, grazed the corner of the house, and sprayed his face with splinters.

Nathaniel swore under his breath and caught his hat back. That rifleman had him buffaloed. They could trade shots all day before he might manage to nail him. There was no way he could reach the front door. He'd simply have to find another way into the cabin.

"Don't shoot me," Luke said quietly behind him. "I just wanted you to know I'm here."

"I told you to stay put," Nathaniel growled at him.

"I thought maybe you could use a hand."

The fact was, he could use some help. It was almost impossible for one man to take on several in a gunfight when his enemies had had time to get entrenched in a place. If he wanted to get Robin out of that house in one piece, he was going to have to make use of the resources available to him—and that meant using Luke.

"All right. Here's the way we're going to play this. I'm hoping Dyer and the rest are thinking I'm alone out here. If you fire off a shot from time to time, folks inside the house will think it's me trying to get that fellow in the loft. They won't be watching that back window too carefully, and that's the way I mean to get to the girls. I don't want you poking your head around that corner, though. Just pretend like you're trying to get him.''

"If you'd let me try, I might fetch him.''

"He's too fine a shot. There's a good chance he might put a bullet in you, and then your sisters are going to be furious with both of us.''

"I think you're more scared of Robin and Betsy than you are of this whole Rafter S outfit.''

"You're probably right about that,'' Nathaniel said, proud of the boy for being able to joke at a time like this. "All right, fire off a few rounds so they get used to the sound of your rifle. When I whistle, I want you to fire four bullets off as fast as you can and yell like crazy. While they're wondering what you're up to, I'll make my play.''

"Good luck,'' Luke said simply, and then he fired his rifle.

Nathaniel ran to the back of the house. He found an old splitting log and rolled it beneath the window. He shook his head as he eyed the window frame. It was going to be a tight fit. He reloaded his pistols and then whistled quietly.

Moments, later, the boy did exactly as he was told. He fired his rifle four times and then started yelling like a banshee. Nathaniel raised the collar of his jacket to protect his face, took a firmer grip on his pistol, and dove headfirst through the window.

He rolled when he hit the cabin floor and came up on his knees with his pistol cocked. He saw Robin take one look at him. She grabbed Betsy and shoved her to the floor. The cowpoke who had been standing behind the bench reacted first. Nathaniel shot him in the chest just as he was raising his rifle.

Lunging to his feet, Nathaniel spotted another one of Dyer's men on the far side of the room. Just as Nathaniel fanned his pistol, he felt the bullet slam into his left shoulder. Grimly, he steadied himself and shot the Rafter S hand twice. The man fell back against the outer wall of the house and slumped to the floor. Nathaniel peered through the smoke from their guns.

Where the hell was Dyer? His left shoulder felt numb, and he could hardly lift his left hand. Awkwardly, he slipped more bullets into the chambers on his pistol.

"Dyer went outside just before you came crashing through the window," Robin called to him, answering the question he was just about to ask her.

Hell, Luke was outside!

"You two okay?" he asked Robin quickly.

"We're fine. Your timing was excellent. Things were about to get—"

"Put down your pistol." Dyer's voice, taut and high with excitement, slashed through Robin's words. "Put it on the floor, or I swear I'll blow this boy's brains to kingdom come." The Rafter S foreman stood in the doorway, his pistol held to Luke's head. Behind him stood Pete Johnson, still holding a rifle in his hands. Most likely he was the shooter from the barn loft.

"I'm sorry, Mr. Hollister," Luke said, his blue eyes full of remorse. "I'm so sorry."

"That's all right, Luke," Nathaniel said quietly. "You did just fine today. My own men couldn't have done any better." He leaned down and placed his pistol on the floor. He felt the blood soaking his shirt. When he stood up again, small dots danced before his eyes. He fought off the first wave of dizziness. He'd been in some tight corners before, but this was about the tightest he'd ever seen. He just wished like hell that Robin, Betsy, and Luke weren't trapped in it with him.

Damn it, Hollister, you've got to stay conscious long enough to find some way to take Dyer and that tall cowboy out. Your own number is just about up, amigo, but you've got to find some way to let Robin live.

Dyer shoved Luke into the room. "Sit down next to your sisters. If he so much as twitches, shoot his little sister first," he told Pete. The tall cowboy set his rifle against the wall and drew a pistol from his belt.

"All right, boss." After looking into Pete Johnson's cold,

vacant eyes, Nathaniel knew there was no use hoping that he might help the youngsters.

Luke stumbled forward into the room and did as he was told. The three Matthewses sat side by side on the bench, watching him out of white, set faces.

"Well, well, it looks like one of my men managed to put a hole in you, Marshal. I hope it hurts like hell," Dyer said with a sneer.

Nathaniel heard Robin give a small sound of distress, but he didn't dare look at her. Dyer walked up to him, careful not to get in Johnson's line of fire.

"This is for dumpin' me in a garden full of shit," Dyer said in a light, conversational tone. He raised his right hand and backhanded Nathaniel full across the mouth. Nathaniel's head twisted from the force of the blow, and he tasted blood in his mouth.

"This is for all the trouble and effort you've cost me." Dyer raised his pistol and brought it slashing down on the side of Nathaniel's head. He fell to his knees as the pain lanced through his skull. He fought off the blackness pulling him down toward oblivion.

"And this is for breaking my nose." This time the barrel came down on Nathaniel's wounded shoulder. He gasped as the waves of agony swept over him. Stubbornly, he fought to stay conscious. They all needed him. Robin needed him. Innocent lives were at stake. This time he couldn't mess it up. This time he couldn't let them down. Somehow he managed to stagger back to his feet.

"You are one sorry, used-up excuse for a lawman. I should just shoot you and get this over with," Dyer said with a disgusted voice. "But I've always heard you were one of the fastest draws in the West, and I want everyone to know I beat you fair and square. I'm going to give you back your pistol, and we'll face off right here in this house."

"How could it possibly be fair for him to fight you after you just pistol-whipped him?" Robin broke in angrily.

"One more word out of you, you little bitch, and Pete here will shoot your sister between her eyes."

Robin subsided, her green eyes glittering with rage and frustration. Nathaniel longed to comfort her. He wanted to tell her Dyer had just given them a way out of this corner. Instead, he stood still and silent while he concentrated on keeping the walls and the room from spinning away from him.

Dyer leaned over and picked up his pistol. He shoved it into Nathaniel's holster and then backed away toward the door. Nathaniel shifted three steps to the right to put the Matthewses farther out of his line of fire.

It doesn't matter if he beats you to the draw. You just stay on your feet and keep shooting until they both go down. He watched Dyer's eyes. He saw the moment Dyer decided to go for his gun. The Rafter S foreman's hand blurred, and then his pistol spat fire.

Nathaniel felt the first slug catch him someplace low. His own draw was slower, but he still managed to drill Dyer in the chest. He fanned his pistol, catching Dyer again above his third shirt button, and then he shot Pete Johnson just as the man was bringing his own gun to bear. Before Nathaniel could fire again, the cowboy lunged out the door.

"Don't shoot," Pete cried. "I'm getting the hell out of here."

Moments later, they heard hoofbeats as he went galloping off.

Suddenly, Nathaniel's legs couldn't hold him upright any longer. He slumped down against the log wall of the house. Within moments, Robin was kneeling beside him, her eyes bright with unshed tears. Vaguely he was aware of Betsy and Luke looking at him too, but he only had eyes for Robin. He raised his right hand and cupped her cheek.

"I fetched them for you," he said. "You can take Betsy home now." His hand felt so heavy, he had to let it fall.

"You sure did," she said, her voice husky.

He felt so weary, he just wanted to sleep forever, but there was something important he had to tell her first. She still might be in danger here, on the Rafter S. Then he remembered the telegram Mrs. Beacham had given him.

"Help is on the way. Mrs. Beacham was going to get a posse together. If Sutherland gets here first, you tell him my brother's found two families to testify against him. If he keeps after your ranch, tell him he can kiss his senate seat goodbye."

He let his heavy eyes fall shut.

"I'm taking you home, too, just as soon as help comes," she told him fiercely, "so you dang well better hang on for me, Nathaniel Hollister."

He wanted to tell her not to waste her effort. He'd rather she just let him be. It might be easier to slip away now than live with the pain of not having her any longer. He was so tired, he couldn't find the energy to speak. He couldn't even manage to open his eyes again. He felt her start pulling at his coat and muffler, and then he let the darkness claim him.

Chapter Twenty-seven

Dear Lord, please, please don't let him be terribly hurt.
Robin breathed this prayer like a litany as her clumsy fingers
fumbled at Nathaniel's jacket. She had to discover how badly
he'd been injured. With shaking fingers she managed to open
his jacket at last. She couldn't help moaning. There was so
much blood.

She swallowed hard and forced herself to find the sources
of that blood. The first bullet had grazed the top of his left
shoulder. The second had passed clear through his side, just
above his pelvic bone. She was hardly a medical expert, but
she didn't think either injury was life-threatening. The greatest
danger right now was blood loss. Both wounds were bleeding,
along with a cut Dyer had opened up with his pistol barrel
along the side of Nathaniel's head. That gash was bleeding
worse than the other two.

For once in her life, she wished she had thought to wear
petticoats. "Betsy, we need bandages."

"I know," her sister replied breathlessly. Robin looked up

to see Betsy was already in the process of shedding her under-garments.

"I'm going to check around outside," Luke said quietly. Robin knew he was right to be concerned. They were hardly safe here, yet all she could think about was Nathaniel. She was so afraid he was going to bleed to death right before her eyes.

They'd just managed to bandage the wounds on Nathaniel's head and shoulder when Luke returned, carrying an armful of rifles and pistols he deposited carefully in the corner of the house.

"How is he?" he asked, coming to look over Robin's shoulder.

"I don't know. I don't think any of these wounds taken separately is that serious, but he's losing an awful lot of blood."

"He's a strong man," Luke told her comfortingly.

Just then the door opened. Luke whirled about, reaching for the pistol he'd placed in his belt, but it was too late. Vance Sutherland stood in the doorway, a cocked pistol in his hand. "You set that gun down, boy, nice and easy."

Luke looked at Robin. She nodded after a long moment. Luke placed the gun on the floor in front of him.

"Buck, I want you to go pick up that gun for me." Vance stepped inside the doorway, and Buck followed him inside.

Buck's face lit up when he saw her. "Hello, Miss Robin. Hi, Miss Betsy."

"Hello, Buck," Robin replied, doing her best to smile at him.

"Go pick up that pistol, boy. Now." Vance said.

Buck lumbered over and picked up the gun carefully. "Say, Miss Betsy, Pa gave me some new marbles. Maybe you can play marbles with me later, but no keepsies. I don't want to lose any of those new marbles he gave me."

"No keepsies," Betsy said, a quaver in her voice.

In the meantime, Vance prowled around the cabin, obviously taking in the situation. He also took the pistol from Buck and placed it on a nearby table. Robin turned back to Nathaniel, intending to bandage his injured hip next.

"Miss Matthews, you can put that bandage down," Vance said in a cold, hard voice. "I think we'll just let the marshal bleed to death."

Robin whirled around. "You can't be serious."

"Oh, but I am, Miss Matthews. Originally, I was furious with Rick for abducting your sister, but I see how this situation could work out quite nicely for me. You see, my bastard son wasn't quite balanced, and he was so desperate to win my approval, he went off and did something truly shocking. He abducted your sister and possibly yourself as well to force you into selling your ranch to me. Marshal Hollister came to your rescue, and there was a bloody shootout. Unfortunately, all three of you youngsters were caught in the crossfire. You died of your injuries or froze to death before anyone found you here. Of course, I knew nothing of Rick's plans, and I'll be appalled by this outcome."

Robin stared at him, horrified that he could relate such a terrible scenario in such a cool voice. "Jake will still be alive."

"I'll send the poor boy my condolences and offer to buy the Rocking M from him for a better price than I offered you. I expect he'll see reason eventually. If you all die here, the Rocking M will be mine. This whole valley was meant to be mine from the start. This is the beginning of a Sutherland empire. I'll be a U.S. senator, and some day Alan will be the President of this whole great nation."

For the first time, she saw the light of madness in his eyes. The obsession he had with building his ranch must have pushed him over the edge. How did one deal with a madman? Reasoning with him wasn't going to make any difference, but she had to try.

"Who is going to rule this empire after you die?" Robin asked him. "You drove Alan away, Rick is dead, and Buck doesn't care."

"Alan left, and it was all your fault. You came between us. He'll come home again once you're gone."

Robin shivered. The unnatural light in his eyes frightened her. Vance Sutherland was definitely losing his grip on sanity. She had to try again, and then she remembered the weapon Nathaniel had given her.

"Nathaniel's brother, Joshua Hollister, has found two families willing to make sworn statements that you pushed them off their land. If the newspaper people find that out, you won't ever win your senate seat."

For a long moment, she thought maybe that threat had reached him. He frowned while he considered her words. "Who's going to believe a bunch of squatters over the word of Vance Sutherland?" he dismissed her claim with an airy wave of his hand. "Now, leave the marshal." He gestured toward the bench with his pistol and then pointed the weapon at her once more.

"Pa, don't point your gun at Robin," Buck spoke up in his slow, quiet way. "You told me it wasn't safe to point guns at folks. They can hurt people."

"I know, son, but this time I'm afraid I am going to have to hurt Miss Matthews. You know I'm your father and I'm always right. Maybe you should go outside so you don't have to watch."

"You can't hurt Robin. She's my friend." Buck stared at his father, his shock and confusion evident.

Sutherland seemed to realize his mistake. "All right, boy. I'm not going to hurt them. You go outside now and make sure our horses are all right."

"Buck, he's going to kill us." Robin hated to use Buck this way, but she was desperate. "Please don't leave. Maybe he won't be able to kill us if you stay here."

Buck pulled at his hair the way he did when he was upset. He looked back and forth between them.

"I'm not going to hurt anyone," Sutherland said harshly. "I want you to go outside right now, Buck."

"If he's not planning to hurt us, then he shouldn't point his gun at us," Robin said quickly.

"Robin's right, Pa. You aren't supposed to point guns at people." Buck always clung to the simple rules he'd been taught, especially when a situation grew too confusing for him.

"You do as you're told, boy."

Buck advanced on his father. "Don't point that gun at Robin. She's my friend. You're not supposed to point guns at people."

"Dammit, boy, if you don't do as I tell you, I'll take the strap to you," Sutherland threatened him, but Buck didn't stop. Moving with a quickness that belied his usual clumsy movements, he reached for his father's pistol. Vance made the mistake of trying to wrestle with him. He must have forgotten Buck's phenomenal strength. Moments later, the pistol went off, and Buck jerked. His hands loosened on the gun, and he stared down at his chest with disbelief.

"Pa?" he asked in a little boy voice. His knees buckled, and he sagged to the floor. Betsy flew across the room to him. Vance Sutherland fell to his knees beside his son, his face stricken.

Robin looked at Luke. Together, they advanced on Sutherland. Luke leaned over and firmly took the gun from Vance's unresisting hand. The older man didn't seem to notice. With trembling fingers, he reached out and stroked Buck's face.

"Boy, I'm so sorry. I never meant for this to happen." The rancher glanced about him wildly, his face ashen. "Jenna, please, you must forgive me."

Buck looked away from his father. His gaze fastened on Betsy, and he smiled that hopeful smile of his. Robin's throat went tight. "Miss Betsy, we gonna play marbles soon, aren't we?"

"We'll play marbles all afternoon if you want to," Betsy said, tears in her voice.

"Pa, you shouldn't point guns at people," Buck said the words like a sigh, and then his eyes drifted shut. Betsy reached out and felt for a pulse.

"I'm sorry, Mr. Sutherland. He's dead."

Vance looked up at them, his gray eyes gone strange and distant. "Jenna will never forgive me for this. It was my fault the horse kicked him. She was always telling me I should be more careful when the boys were around the horses, but I didn't listen to her. She always said I should take more care with guns, too. She turned so cold after the accident, and her babies dying one after the other. Now she'll never speak to me again."

Robin stared at the rancher, torn between horror and pity. Jenna Sutherland had died over fifteen years ago. Obviously, his mind was wandering. Robin nodded to Luke. He rubbed his eyes with his sleeve and went to stand between Sutherland and the stash of guns he'd brought in earlier. He kept his gun pointed at Vance, a fiercely determined look on his young face. Clearly, he wouldn't let the rancher menace his sisters again.

Robin took a final look at Buck. Sorrow and guilt over her part in his death threatened to overwhelm her, but she couldn't afford to feel it now. Her first job was to do what she could to save Nathaniel. She turned away from the tragic tableau of Vance Sutherland and his dead son and hurried to Nathaniel's side.

He looked so pale and still. For one endless, terrible moment she thought she'd already lost him. Finally, she saw him inhale. *Dear Lord, thank you. Please, let him live. Please, let him live.*

She was relieved to see the bandages they had fashioned for his head and shoulder had stopped the bleeding from those two wounds. The bullet hole above his pelvic bone was seeping just a little. Resolutely, she set about fashioning a bandage for that injury as well.

"You stay with me—you hear me, Nathaniel Hollister?" She talked to him constantly as she finished bandaging him, and then went to build up the fire. She knew she had to keep him warm until help came. He just had to hang on until Doc Peterson arrived.

Mrs. Agnes Beacham came storming into the cabin a half hour later, a martial light in her brown eyes. At her back was Zachary Tuckett, Lionel Brigham, Doc Peterson, Horace Peabody, and a half-dozen other men from town. Robin had never been so glad to see anyone in her life. Formidable Mrs. Beacham simply wouldn't allow Nathaniel to die.

For three days, they kept Nathaniel at the old Parson place, for Doc Peterson was afraid to move him. Robin and Mrs. Beacham took turns nursing him around the clock. Doc Peterson rode out and checked on him every day. A fastidious man, Doc insisted they change Nathaniel's dressings frequently with only the cleanest of linen.

Nathaniel spent most of those days sleeping. He woke only to eat and drink and would soon doze off again. Robin tried to use the time he slept to finish making her Christmas gifts for her family, but her heart wasn't in the presents she made. She was too worried about Nathaniel. Doc Peterson told her it was good news that none of his wounds had turned septic, but she knew there was still a chance he could catch wound fever.

Vaguely she registered the news Doc brought them. Something had snapped inside Vance Sutherland the day he shot his eldest son. The rancher hardly spoke to anyone anymore. He spent hours in a rocking chair, staring into space. There was going to be an inquest into Buck's death. Robin dreaded having to testify, but Sheriff Campbell told her the proceedings wouldn't take place until after Christmas. In the meantime, Alan had been sent for, and he was coming home to run the Rafter S.

Robin knew she should feel relieved that the threat to her ranch seemed gone at last, but she couldn't feel anything but a terrible, relentless fear that she was going to lose Nathaniel.

She was well of aware of the irony of the situation. She was going to lose him anyway when the snow melted and he started off on those travels that meant so much to him. Yet she couldn't bear the thought he might die because of the wounds he had received rescuing her and Betsy.

One night she crept to his bedside while Mrs. Beacham dozed in the rocking chair nearby. Robin gazed at Nathaniel, drinking in his dear, familiar features. He still was pale from losing blood, and his face looked gaunt. When he slept like this, the frown he wore too often was smoothed away. The stubble on his cheeks and the bandage about his head made him look like a rakish pirate. They were going to try shaving him tomorrow if he stayed awake long enough.

How she missed the old, vital Nathaniel who teased and argued with her constantly. What if he didn't get well? What if he did and left her to live out the rest of her life without him?

Robin buried her face in the blankets and let the tears come. Perhaps she let an audible sob escape, or perhaps Mrs. Beacham was a light sleeper. Suddenly, the old lady was kneeling at her side, stroking her hair gently.

"You mustn't go on like this. The good doctor says Nathaniel is doing just fine."

"He hasn't said he's out of danger yet. You know he hasn't."

"There's no use borrowing trouble. There's already plenty of it in this world as it is. Your Nathaniel is a big, strong man, and he's survived far worse hurts than these."

"He's not my Nathaniel," Robin said, her voice catching. *You know that's why you're really crying tonight. No matter what happens, he will never truly be your Nathaniel.*

"Oh, but he is. He just doesn't know it yet. He loves you, child. It's as plain as the nose on your face. You should see the way he looks at you when he thinks no one is watching him."

"If he loves me, why doesn't he say something?"

"He believes he isn't good enough for you, and he thinks he could never make you happy. I believe you should know more about his mother to understand the man he is today. You ask him, when he's better, just why it is that he thinks he would make such an awful husband for you."

Robin dried her tears and blew her nose. "I'll do that, but

I don't see how it could make any difference. He's the most stubborn man I've ever known. If he's decided he's wrong for me, I don't know how I could ever change his mind.''

Mrs. Beacham sent her a knowing smile. ''Your mother was the most stubborn woman I've ever known, next to myself, and you are definitely your mother's daughter. Now tell me, who would you wager your money on in the end—a stubborn man or a stubborn woman?''

Robin had to smile at that. ''Nine times out of ten, I'd bet my money on the woman.''

''That's my girl. Now, off you go to get your rest, and I don't want see you setting foot outside your bed until tomorrow morning. I'm jealous of my time with this handsome young man lying here, and you're infringing on it.''

''Yes, ma'am,'' Robin replied smartly. After she put more wood in the stove, she slipped away to the curtained alcove off the kitchen where she and Mrs. Beacham took turns sleeping.

Although she meant to obey the old woman's advice, she still had difficulty falling asleep that night. How many women had had their hearts broken over Nathaniel Hollister? She had a feeling there had been plenty before her. A man couldn't look the way he did, and be what he was, without attracting more than his fair share of ladies and their affection. The knowledge that she had company in her current miserable state was hardly any comfort.

She soaked her pillow with several new waves of tears before sleep finally claimed her.

On the fourth morning after the shootout at the old Parson place, Doc Peterson decreed they could move Nathaniel to Mrs. Beacham's house. It would be easier to care for him there and more convenient for Robin traveling back and forth to the Rocking M. With Mr. Tuckett's and Lionel Brigham's help, they carefully loaded Nathaniel into the back of a sledge and covered him up with a heap of blankets and buffalo robes.

"You pile any more of those on me, you're liable to crush me," Nathaniel said wryly to Robin when she tucked yet another woolen blanket about his feet. "I promise I won't freeze in the next hour."

"We aren't worried about you freezing. We're quite a bit more worried about your coming down with pneumonia," Robin informed him with a toss of her head.

"I don't reckon I'll catch that in the next hour, either. I'm just too plain ornery to die."

"That very thought has given me considerable comfort during the last few days," she said tartly as she settled herself beside him in the sledge.

He reached out and covered her mittened hand with his own. "I'm sorry you've been so worried about me."

"I'm sorry you got so badly hurt rescuing Betsy and me."

"I don't count that burn across the top of my shoulder, or that hole in my side as being badly hurt. Now, if one of those Sutherland riders had managed to plug me in my belly, that would be a *whole* different matter."

She knew he was trying to make her smile with his awful pun, but somehow it was hard for her to make light of his being wounded. "Seriously, I'm so grateful for what you did. At the time, I really didn't want you to come after us, but when I saw Rick again, I realized he wasn't going to just let me deed the ranch over to Vance and walk away."

"No, I didn't suppose he would," he said gently.

She knew she would just make him feel uncomfortable if she thanked him further, but she still marveled at what he and Luke had done. It must have taken such tremendous courage to ride onto Sutherland range, having no idea how many men they were going up against. She had a feeling that Nathaniel had understood, with much greater clarity than Luke had, what impossible odds they had faced. The fact that Nathaniel had been willing to die for her that day was a notion that humbled her completely.

She glanced at him surreptitiously. He was staring up at the sky right now, obviously happy to be outside again. His color was a little better, but he still seemed pale compared to his former robust self.

"After just three days indoors, I think I'd forgotten just how blue a Colorado sky can be," he said, sending her a smile that made her heart twist. It occurred to her that his eyes were just as blue as that sky, and she could lose her entire soul if she spent too much time looking into them.

"That kind of sky is part of the reason why I can't live anyplace else," she forced herself to say lightly. "I used to dream you could see to forever if you looked into a sky like that long enough."

They shared a companionable silence after that. Eventually, Nathaniel dozed off again. She was very aware that he still held her hand. *He truly does care for you, in his own way. He just doesn't care enough to give up his own dreams and goals.*

How that hurt. She wished she could simply enjoy whatever time she had left with him, but somehow she found it hard to live in the present when the future without him haunted her so. At least he would spend Christmas with them. She hoped she could make some of his Christmas wishes come true. She hoped she could give him a Christmas to remember.

Her eyes began to water, but she told herself it was the cold winter wind. She wasn't going to shed any more tears over this man—not a single one. It was a good resolution, but somehow she doubted she would be able to hold to it.

Chapter Twenty-eight

After they settled Nathaniel in Mrs. Beacham's spare bedroom, Robin began dividing her days between nursing Nathaniel and doing her chores at the ranch. Christmas was only eight days away now, and she felt duty-bound to help Betsy with holiday preparations.

Usually Christmas was Robin's favorite time of year. She loved making presents for everyone and anticipating the morning when they opened each other's gifts. It was hard to find the spirit of the holiday, though, when she continued to worry about Nathaniel and she grieved so for Buck. She knew it would be a long time before she forgave herself for her part in his death. More practical concerns weighed on her as well. How on earth was she going feed her team and her saddlestock, much less Hercules, for the rest of the winter now her whole store of grain was gone?

At least Nathaniel's health continued to improve steadily. By his fourth day in Mrs. Beacham's home, Nathaniel was looking much more alert and energetic. He specifically asked Robin to bring Luke into town with certain secret Christmas projects. She was happy to oblige Nathaniel. She'd been worrying about her brother, for Luke had been even more quiet than usual. The two men he'd shot out at the old Parson place were going to live, but she knew memories of that violent day troubled him. She hoped Nathaniel might say something to Luke to make him feel better.

The next morning Luke drove in with Robin. After giving Nathaniel a variety of intriguing bundles, Luke stayed and talked with him for almost an hour. When he emerged again from Nathaniel's room, Robin was relieved to see Luke looked a good deal happier.

When Luke went off to visit friends, Robin ventured into the guest room to see if Nathaniel needed anything. She found him gazing out the window, his expression pensive.

"It was good to see Luke. I miss him and the rest."

"They miss you, too."

He looked down at the lovely double wedding ring quilt covering Mrs. Beacham's guest bed. "You know, Doc Peterson thinks I'll be fit to drive out to your place by Christmas Eve, that is, if you'd want me at your place for the holidays."

"Of course we want you to come. We can't open these presents you've been working on unless you're there."

"Well, then, I'll come out to the Rocking M on Christmas Eve." He looked up and sent her one of those sudden smiles that made her feel breathless. "You still haven't told me what your own Christmas wish is."

It was her turn to look at her lap. She was afraid if she met his gaze, he'd read the truth in her eyes. More fervently than any Christmas wish she'd ever made before, she wanted him to stay, and love her as much as she loved him. "I wanted to keep my ranch, and it looks like that wish is going to come true," she managed to say.

"I think I had something a little more tangible in mind."

"I can't tell you outright what I'd like. That's against the whole spirit of the game."

"You Matthewses sure don't make things easy for a gent."

"No, I don't suppose we do," she said with a sigh. He'd meant the comment in jest, but somehow she couldn't help taking it seriously. Life itself just didn't seem easy these days. Instead, it seemed stark, hard, and cruel.

"You've been looking pretty blue this past week. You've been brooding about Buck Sutherland, haven't you?"

"I have been thinking about those last few minutes before he died," she admitted. "I wish with all my heart that I hadn't asked him to help us."

"What happened that afternoon was entirely Sutherland and Dyer's fault, not your own," he said sternly. "You take responsibility for too much already. Buck's death isn't a burden you should carry."

"I suppose you know something about that kind of burden," she said softly, thinking of that poor woman who had died in Kansas.

"More than I care to," he said shortly.

She rose to her feet and chose her next words with great care. "I'm sad now, and angry at what I did, but I know I'll forgive myself someday. We all make mistakes, and sadly, the very worst of them can lead to horrible, tragic consequences. You, however, don't want to forgive yourself for Mary McAllister's death. For some reason, you're determined to cling to your anger and guilt, and it's poisoning your life."

The fury in his eyes scorched her. She received the strong impression he was trying very hard not to yell a string of profanities at her. "You don't know a thing about what happened in Cameron." He crossed his arms and stared out the window. His message couldn't have been clearer. Obviously the subject was closed as far as he was concerned.

She drew in a deep breath and strode from the room. Why had she even bothered to try to help him? That stubborn man's ears were so full of mud, he probably couldn't hear if Jehovah Himself shouted at him.

* * *

Robin stayed at the ranch for the next two days. She had neglected all sorts of work to help Mrs. Beacham nurse Nathaniel. Knowing the old woman had her hands full caring for their patient, she sent Betsy into town in her stead. Like Luke, Betsy had been deeply shaken by the shootings she had witnessed at the old Parson place. She'd been quiet and withdrawn, and nightmares had been troubling her sleep. Robin hoped a few days in town would do her good.

Two days before Christmas, Betsy returned to the ranch in high spirits. Robin came out to greet her as she and Luke climbed down from the sleigh. Betsy's cheeks were flushed from the sleigh ride, and her eyes were bright. She started talking the moment she saw Robin and didn't pause for five minutes straight. Robin could only smile and feel relieved. Betsy's boundless energy and enthusiasm had obviously returned.

The moment they stepped inside the ranch house, Tommy and Jessie mobbed her. "How is Nathaniel?" Robin couldn't help asking her when she finally distracted the little ones with candy Betsy had brought.

"He got out of bed yesterday and spent all morning on the couch in the parlor. Today, he insisted on getting dressed and actually ate dinner with us. Doc Peterson says Nathaniel's got one of the strongest constitutions he's ever seen. He thinks Nathaniel is completely out of danger now. He's going to be tired and weak because of all that blood he lost, but Doc claims he should be right as rain in no time."

"That's wonderful news," Robin said, meaning it with all her heart.

"I hope you'll go see him tomorrow. I think he's missing you. Every time I knocked on the door, I could tell he was disappointed that I wasn't you. What happened? Did you two fight again?"

"If we did, that'd be our business," Robin said shortly.

"You two have more ups and downs than the Rocky Mountains." Looking sad, Betsy shook her head and retreated to her room.

"I know," Robin said softly after Betsy left, "and how I wish we didn't."

That night after the little ones were in bed, Robin realized she still hadn't finished her present for Nathaniel. She went to her room and fetched the little golden heart and key she was braiding from strands of her own hair.

Her mother had taught her this craft. She had loved to make elaborate, intricately knotted wreaths made from hair she saved from her brush. Robin wanted to give Nathaniel something to remember her by when he left the Rocking M. She had thought of this particular gift when she remembered how fascinated he seemed by her hair. A braided keepsake would be small and light, something he could easily keep with him in his saddlebags. It was a sentimental present and not in the least bit practical, but she hoped he would like it just the same.

She stayed up late finishing the little heart and the key. She was pleased with the way they turned out, but she still had to finish Betsy's and Luke's presents as well. The next morning she sent Jake in to help Mrs. Beacham with her chores. That day flew by as Robin and Betsy bustled about, cleaning the house from top to bottom and waxing their mother's finest pieces of furniture. They decorated the mantle with fresh-cut pine boughs and set out special scented candles. They finished making their presents and did plenty of holiday baking.

The next morning the whole family rose early and took baths. Afterward, they dressed in their Sunday best and drove into town for church. Robin spent the morning feeling all fluttery. She was going to see Nathaniel again. How she hoped he wouldn't still be angry with her. She'd only spent three days away from him all told, and yet she had missed him sorely. *If you miss him this much after three days, how on earth are you going to cope when he leaves?*

Stop thinking like that, she told herself firmly. *It's Christmas, and for these two days, you are going to pretend that you have Nathaniel forever.*

Nathaniel had elected to stay at Mrs. Beacham's house to rest up for the drive to the ranch, but they met Mrs. Beacham at church. Reverend Case performed a lovely service. His sermon on appreciating the miracles in every day of life made Robin resolve once again to enjoy this Christmas as best she could. She did have much to be thankful for. She had good friends in the valley who cared about her. She and her family had survived a terrible time of violence. She would be able to keep her ranch and her family together, and that was the greatest miracle of all—a miracle brought about in large part by a certain stubborn, courageous ex-marshal.

Her stomach tightened as they walked from church to Mrs. Beacham's house. When Robin walked into the parlor, he was sitting on the horsehair sofa waiting for them. He was looking very alert and dapper, dressed in his own fine suit. The pale cast to his features and the careful way he moved when Tommy threw himself at him were the only signs of how badly he'd been injured. Nathaniel looked at her, and then he smiled, and she knew it was going to be all right.

They all piled into the sleigh, including Mrs. Beacham who had gladly accepted their invitation to spend Christmas at the Rocking M. The bells on their harness ringing merrily, Ned and Nod pulled the sleigh briskly through the bright winter afternoon. Betsy led everyone in singing a series of Christmas carols. Mrs. Beacham sang along gaily in her piping soprano, and Nathaniel even joined with a less-than-tuneful bass on the choruses. Robin found her spirits lifting at last as she gazed at the people she cared about most in the world.

If only her life could go on like this forever. *Don't be greedy, Robin Matthews. Do as the good reverend suggested. Enjoy this moment now, and make some fine memories to last you a lifetime.*

When they returned to the ranch house, she helped Betsy

build up the stove and heat a warm supper. With Tommy at
their heels, the twins raced to fetch the tree they'd cut down
yesterday up in the forest. Robin and Betsy met the twins on
the back porch and launched into a spirited rendition of "O
Christmas Tree." Tommy danced with impatience and excitement, and Jessie's eyes grew wide as the boys hefted the big
blue spruce inside. Soon the tree stood upright in a pail in a
corner of the parlor, the clean, fresh smell of evergreen filling
the house.

After a hearty supper of stew, biscuits, strawberry jam, apple
cider, and pumpkin pie, they set about trimming the tree. Their
ornaments were simple—and mostly homemade. They had pine
cones painted gold and silver, and brightly colored chains cut
from paper. With great care, they wired twelve white tapers
Betsy had made for just this purpose to several strong branches.
Their best ornaments were eggs Betsy had blown the yokes
out of and cut open to hold small Christmas scenes.

Nathaniel helped trim some of the tallest branches, but for
the most part he sat on the sofa and helped keep Jessie distracted
from trying to climb the tree and pulling off the ornaments.
He watched the proceedings with an expression Robin couldn't
quite read. She couldn't tell if he was feeling amused or
bemused to find himself in the midst of such holiday preparations. The final touch came when Betsy lit the candles. They
all stepped back to admire their efforts.

"Golly, Robin, it's the most beautifullest tree I've ever
seen," Tommy said with such rapture that Robin had to lean
over and give him a hug.

Mrs. Beacham, who was skeptical of the whole notion of
Christmas trees because of the fire danger they posed, was
impressed despite herself. "It does look lovely, dears," she
declared.

They sang "Silent Night," and then with great ceremony
helped Tommy and Jessie hang their stockings up before the
fireplace. Overtired from the long, exciting day, Tommy dis-
solved into tears at the prospect of going to bed.

Everyone tried to calm him, but in the end, it was Nathaniel who succeeded. "I'll tell you what, partner. If you manage to stop leaking those tears all over the parlor, I'll come tell you a story when you're ready for bed."

That promise made Tommy's tears magically disappear. Robin sent Nathaniel a heartfelt smile. "Thank you for coming to our rescue, again," she told him as she herded the little ones from the room.

"You're welcome," he replied. "Take your time getting him settled, though. Taking on the Rafter S was easier for me than this job. I'm not sure I know any yarns fitting for a boy his age."

In the end, Nathaniel ended up telling Tommy the story of the Nativity, and he did it with such rough eloquence and poetry that he brought tears to Robin's eyes. Of course, Nathaniel didn't know that, for she was listening outside the door where he couldn't see her.

They stayed up for an hour more, loading Tommy and Jessie's stockings and quietly slipping the presents they had made for each other under the tree. Betsy hung mittens she had knitted for everyone on the upper branches while Robin tied a half-dozen small candy canes to the lower ones where Tommy and Jessie could reach them. When the girls finished, they held hands and sang "Silent Night" softly once again.

After that, the twins wandered off to bed, and Betsy and Mrs. Beacham followed them shortly. Because the house was so full, Nathaniel had insisted on returning to the bunkhouse. Mrs. Beacham was ensconced in solitary splendor in Robin's room, and Robin was going to sleep with Betsy.

When everyone had gone off to sleep, Robin and Nathaniel were left sitting alone in the kitchen. Robin brewed herself a cup of tea while Nathaniel drank his coffee. "Seems like old times," she said as she settled herself across the table from him. "It's wonderful to have you back."

He didn't return her smile. Instead, his expression was somber, his eyes dark and serious. "I'd be lying if I said I didn't like being back, but I don't want you to get too used to having me around. I'll be riding on after the New Year.''

She stared at him, unable to hide her pain and surprise. Why did he have to tell her this now? Why couldn't he have waited until tomorrow?

Because he's trying to be kind and he doesn't really understand how important Christmas is to you. Because he's an honest man, and he doesn't want you building dreams based on wishful thinking alone.

''I really stayed on this long because I was so worried about your fight with the Rafter S,'' he filled the silence when it became too awkward between them. ''Now that Alan's running the show, I know his riders won't be troubling you anymore. There are places I've been wanting to see, and a number of good reasons why I don't think I should stay on at the Rocking M any longer.''

She couldn't accept that. She wouldn't accept that. Before he rode off, she wanted to know where she stood with Nathaniel—she needed to know what she meant to him. ''Why, exactly, don't you think it would be wise for you to stay on?''

''There's one reason more pressing than all the rest.'' He looked up from the table, and that hungry look that did such strange things to her pulse was back in his eyes again. ''If I stay the winter here, I won't be able to keep my hands off you. We'll end up in my bed again, and there's a damn good chance I'd put a baby in your belly. If you got pregnant, I'd shame you in the eyes of your community, and make your job of looking after your family that much harder. Your bearing a bastard would also kill any chance you had of a nice, decent young man marrying you some day.''

The thought of marrying her hadn't even crossed his mind. Inside, she felt so hurt and angry she wanted to scream at him. She was too proud to cry, though. Instead, she concentrated on the reasons why she was furious with him.

''You've thought all this through pretty carefully, haven't

you?" She knew her voice sounded tight and sarcastic, but she couldn't help herself.

"One thing I've had during the last few weeks is time to think."

"I might have had some say in this interesting little future you imagined for us. I might have had the sense to say no to you."

"I don't think so," he said, shaking his head slowly. "You want me to kiss you now, and I damn well want to kiss you back. I want to take you out to that bunkhouse and make love to you a dozen different ways. I've thought about that time we were together until I'm almost crazy. I've never felt this way about a woman, and I know I'm not strong enough to resist temptation for a whole winter shut up with you on this ranch."

She started to protest, but he cut her off, his eyes full of torment. "For God's sake, don't be so bullheaded. Try to listen to what I'm saying. You're an honest young woman, Robin Matthews. That quality is one of the things I admire most in you. Tell me honestly—if I kissed and touched you the way I did before, would you really be able to say no to me?"

Of course, you wouldn't. He doesn't even need to touch you. You want to lie with him so desperately your body is trembling for him right now.

She looked down at the table, her sullen silence the only answer she was willing to give him.

"So, it's best for both of us if I go."

"All right," she said, her voice suddenly gone husky and tight. Even as she agreed, she couldn't imagine his words could possibly be true. He seemed so happy at the Rocking M. The twins looked up to him, Betsy loved him, and the little ones adored him.

And she loved him, loved him so much she couldn't imagine what it would be like living on the Rocking M without him. She was too proud to say those words aloud when it was only too clear they wouldn't make any difference. Nathaniel didn't love her in return, and he was too principled to stay and take advantage of what she would undoubtedly offer him again. She supposed she ought to love him for that, too, but right now she felt too wounded to do anything but hurt.

Tears were starting to well in her eyes. Desperately she willed them back. She didn't want him to see that he could make her cry. She stared at the table, afraid he would see the suspicious moisture filling her eyes.

After a long moment, he rose to his feet. "I guess I'll turn in."

"Do me a favor," she said, relieved that her voice barely quavered. "Don't tell the rest tomorrow that you're going."

"All right." He walked toward the back hall where he'd hung his coat. He paused in the doorway.

"I'm sorry it couldn't have been different for us. I'm sorry I couldn't have been different for you."

I'm sorry, too, she said the words in her mind, but she didn't dare say them aloud, because she was certain now they would come out in a sob. Instead of saying anything, she simply nodded. After a moment that stretched like infinity, he finally turned away. She listened to him shrug into his coat and close the back door quietly behind him.

When she was certain Nathaniel was gone, she lay her head on her arms, and wept.

Chapter Twenty-nine

After her first storm of weeping passed, Robin went to the parlor to blow out the candles. As she gazed up at the Christmas tree, she realized sadly that her first Christmas wish had been a foolish one. Nathaniel wouldn't stay. Whatever it took to make a worldly, experienced man like him fall in love and settle down, she didn't have it. She'd guessed that truth from the start, but her reckless heart had decided to love him anyway.

If only they could be together one last time before he went. It was so hard to simply let him ride away.

As she stared up at the lovely tree, the idea occurred to her. There was a second Christmas wish he could give her, one that would mean more than anything.

The last time she had decided to go to him, she had wanted him to take away her fear and show her she could love a man. He'd shown her that, only too well. He had roused her body to a passion she had never dreamed she could experience. He had said she could feel that way about another man, but somehow she doubted the truth of that statement. Nathaniel would always be her first and greatest love.

She wanted to be loved by him like that again before he left. Perhaps it was sinful, perhaps it was immoral. Somehow she didn't care. If he could just hold her in his arms one more time, somewhere within her she could find the strength to let him go.

She stared up at the tree and made her second Christmas wish. "Please, let him love me tonight."

Then she carefully snuffed the candles one by one until the parlor was dark. She went back to the kitchen and picked up the lantern on the table. In the back hall, she put on her jacket.

Once again, she made the trip through the cold dark night to the bunkhouse, her heart in her throat. This time she wouldn't resort to pulling his gun to persuade him. She could only ask. If he told her no, she would walk away and try not to show him that her heart was shattering into a thousand pieces.

As she drew closer to the bunkhouse, she was relieved to see the glimmer of lamplight shining through the front window. Nathaniel was still up.

She stood before the door for a long moment and drew in a deep breath. She was barely aware of the deep cold, or the fact her toes were already going numb in her boots. All she could think about was the man in the bunkhouse and what she wanted to say to him in the next few minutes.

Resolutely, she tugged on the latch string and stepped inside. He was lying on his bunk, the lamp still turned up beside his bed. Other than removing his collar, he was still completely dressed. He didn't seem to have been reading or doing much of anything. Now he was looking at her, his face closed and unreadable. She shut the door behind her and struggled to find the right words.

In the end it was simple.

"I want us to be together again," she said, and leaned back against the door, for her knees felt weak. Nervously, she moistened her lips with her tongue. She was heartened to see his gaze go to her mouth and linger there. When he didn't speak, she rushed to fill the silence.

"The first Christmas wish I made two weeks ago was a wild and impossible dream—I see now I had no right to reach for it. I made a second wish tonight, and it means the world to me. I want to be with you again, one more time before you leave us."

"You have the right to reach for any dream you want," he said roughly. "I just wish you could see that dreams involving me will only bring you pain in the long run." He swung his legs over the side of the bed and stood. After all her resolution-making, she found she wasn't bold enough to go to him. Instead, she stayed leaning against the door while he paced across the room to her. Again she was struck by how gracefully and quietly he moved for a man of his size. He stopped right in front of her, his face set in forbidding lines.

"Sweet Robin-girl, why couldn't you have had more sense? I've been sitting here just hoping and a-praying you'd come."

His tone was so grim and harsh, it took her several moments to absorb the meaning of his words. "Then, you won't send me away?"

"I don't think I could let you walk out that door right now for anything. A better man would be able to turn down what you're offering, but I don't have the strength."

He reached out and cupped her cheek. Although his tone was hard, his touch was gentle. He smiled that dry, self-deprecating smile of his, and she had to smile back.

"How could I possibly turn away my own Christmas wish?" he said in a softer voice. Then he bent his head and kissed her. She met him halfway, her body already alive and tingling. His arms went around her. It felt good and right to be held by him again. He was so big and solid and safe. The cold knot of fear around her heart eased.

There would be pain when he left, but for now, for this night, he was hers. She found herself smiling into his kiss. She put her arms around his neck and nestled closer. She wanted him to kiss her that exciting way he'd taught her, but he seemed in no hurry to deepen his kiss. Instead, he smoothed his lips across hers, savoring her, sampling her and driving her mad with impatience all at the same time.

Slowly he undid the fastenings on her jacket. He slipped his hands inside it and cupped her waist. Intensely aware of his touch, she felt little shivers radiate up her ribcage. She nipped at his lip impatiently and invited him inside her mouth.

At last he deepened the kiss. They leaned into each other, their tongues dueling and mating in a seductive imitation of the act of love until they were both panting. Nathaniel broke off the kiss at last.

"We've got to slow down, little gal," he declared ruefully. "If I'm only to have this last night with you, I want to relish every moment of it." He turned away and filled the stove with wood until he had built up a roaring fire within it.

"Stand near this. I don't want you to be chilled while I undress you." Obediently, she let him lead her beside the stove where waves of warmth were heating the whole snugly built bunkhouse.

"Take your hair down for me first, the way you did that night in the kitchen."

Her gaze never leaving his own, she did as he asked. Somehow the simple act took on a whole new kind of sensuality with him watching her every movement, the heat kindling in his gaze. When she had finished, he stepped forward and buried his hands in her hair. He lifted one lock of it and kissed it. He took his time, pulling her hair forward and arranging it the way he had before. In the process, his fingers trailed along the sides of her breasts. She felt herself pucker and harden. How she wanted him to touch her there, and everywhere, and all at once, but he seemed infuriatingly determined to go slowly.

He walked around behind her. After a long, tantalizing moment, he kissed the side of her neck and quickly undid the fastenings to her dress. The silk whispered down her arms, the bodice and skirt collapsing in a pool of shimmering green fabric at her feet.

As soon as she stepped out of the dress, Nathaniel drew

closer and gripped her hips. He pulled her back against him until she could feel his hardness thrusting against her petticoats. Wordlessly, he slipped his arms under hers and skimmed his hands up her rib cage, gently circling and touching the tips of her breasts through the fine fabric of her chemise. Her head fell back against his shoulder, and she heard herself gasp. He kissed the side of her neck and her hairline, creating wonderful, delicious shivers that made her nerves dance.

His skillful hands went to work on the buttons to her corset cover. Soon he had divested her of the cover and the corset both. She tried not to think about how familiar and comfortable he seemed at removing women's clothing. He shifted to stand before her before he raised the bottom of her chemise. When she saw the smoldering look in his eyes, she swallowed hard.

"Raise your arms."

She did as he ordered. He pulled the soft chemise over her head and tossed it on the bunk beside them. It took every iota of self-control she possessed not to cover herself, even though he'd seen her twice before.

His gaze darkened as he looked at her. Suddenly, he gave a very masculine sound of annoyance, but his expression was sympathetic. She looked down at herself and saw the red lines left by the whalebone stays. He reached out and traced one gently with his finger tip.

"You shouldn't wear those damn contraptions," he growled. "You don't need them."

"I don't wear them," she admitted, "not often anyway."

"Good."

She drew in a deep breath when he knelt before her and began to kiss the line he had just traced with his finger. He started low on her belly and worked his way up, his hair a soft, silky tickle on the underside of her breast. *Please, let him keep going.*

Moments later, he did exactly that, and she gasped again as his clever lips claimed her breast. She reached out and placed both hands on his shoulders. She wasn't sure her legs would keep holding her up. He laved and suckled her, teasing her peaks and sending shimmering waves of pleasure through her, waves that found a resonant pulse deep in her belly.

Just when she thought she couldn't bear any more, she felt him undo the ties to her petticoats. He slipped them off her and went to work on the buttons to her drawers. She tightened her grip on his shoulders as he eased the drawers down her, touching and smoothing the backs of her legs.

Next, he took his time rolling her stockings down. She guessed it was hardly accidental, the way his fingers lingered on the sensitive insides of her thighs and knees. By the time he had finished removing her stockings, her entire body throbbed. At last she stood completely naked before him, and he had aroused her so fiercely, she hardly cared for modesty.

"Now it's your turn," she said, determined to make him want her as much as she wanted him right now.

She was more clumsy than he, but fortunately he had fewer layers for her to deal with. Remembering how he'd set her nerves afire by his simple touches, she did her best to do the same to him. As she undid the buttons to his dress shirt, she paused and pressed her lips to the supple skin at the base of his throat. She was rewarded by his quick intake of breath. She trailed her fingers against his skin as she pushed the sleeves of his shirt down his arms. Purposely she brushed her hips against his arousal as she turned to place his shirt across the upper bunk.

By the time she reached for the buttons on his black woolen trousers, a muscle ticked in his cheek. Still, he managed to stand completely still as she undid the four black buttons with trembling hands. As much as she longed to be bold, she couldn't quite look down at that moment. Instead, she stared at his chest while she tugged his trousers down over his hips, careful of the bandage he still wore to protect his right side.

When his trousers fell down about his ankles, he stepped out of them. He leaned over and slipped out of his socks as well. She watched the play of muscles over his lean ribcage.

Their first time together, she'd never had a chance to study him like this. The thoroughly male beauty of his body left her speechless. He was long and lean, his broad shoulders and chest tapering down to a slim waist. He stood upright again, and she couldn't help admiring the planes and lines of his strong chest. It was covered with a dark mat of curling hair shot through with strands of silver. His arms were corded with muscle. His skin had an even copper cast to it, perhaps from that Cherokee grandmother of whom he was so proud.

She winced when she saw the freshly healed scar from his shoulder wound.

"I'm so sorry this happened to you trying to help me," she said, lightly tracing the outline of the scar on his shoulder.

"I expect a few more holes in this old hide didn't matter that much."

She looked at him curiously. With a wry twist to his lips, he pointed out scars she hadn't seen before below his right collarbone. Both looked like they'd come from bullet wounds.

"I gather being a U.S. marshal for fifteen years isn't the safest occupation a man could have."

"You could say that," he replied dryly.

Her gaze moved lower. Clearly he was very much aroused, and a great deal bigger than she had imagined.

"I just can't believe we fit together," she blurted, and then she felt a wave of heat burn her cheeks.

He raised one eyebrow, and she received the strong impression he was doing his best not to laugh aloud. "I reckon we managed pretty well before."

Determined to make him pay for teasing her, she summoned all her courage and reached out and stroked him. He went completely still at her first touch, and his eyes closed. He was velvety soft, and smooth, and so very hot and hard beneath her fingers. She wanted to keep exploring the intriguing new textures she was discovering, but his expression worried her.

"Am I hurting you?"

"Not . . . exactly," he said in a strange, taut voice. "What you're doing feels better than fine."

"Well, then," she said. Reassured, she reached out with her other hand as well. All too soon, he caught both of her hands gently and drew them away.

"In fact, what you're doing feels so fine that if I let you keep on, there'd be a real danger that this show'd be over before it ever got started." It took her a few moments to understand what he was saying. When she did, her cheeks heated again. Fortunately, he didn't notice, for he had linked his fingers with hers and was drawing her toward the bunk bed.

He flipped the covers aside and lay down, scooting toward the edge so there was room for her, too. She lay beside him, and he pulled the covers up around them both. Once again she was struck by how quickly his big body warmed a bed.

How wonderful it would be to go to sleep every night in his arms and wake up cuddled against him every morning. She pushed the treacherous thought away. Tonight wasn't a time for painful thoughts. She meant to make the most of her Christmas wish and enjoy every fleeting moment of her time with Nathaniel.

He leaned over and began to kiss her deeply. His big hands ranged across her, fanning the flames he had kindled earlier back to burning life. She lay back and let him touch her as he wished. He worshipped her breasts, kissing and caressing them until she felt a rush of warmth between her legs. His other hand slipped lower across her belly.

She drew in a breath when he began to touch her there, the source of so much of the tension and tightening pleasure inside her. He played with her curls, tracing her entrance delicately with his fingertips until she moaned aloud. She shifted restlessly. She wanted him to come inside her now, but he continued to massage and stroke her.

She even thrust her hips up from the bed in mute invitation, but still he took his maddening time. He began to kiss a trail down from her breast across her belly, following the trail his dexterous hands had taken. He slipped lower, still kissing her, his hands sketching magical patterns on the insides of her legs.

Slowly, it dawned on her that he actually meant to kiss her there. "You're not going to, I mean, people don't really . . ."

"Oh, but they do."

She couldn't hold a coherent thought in her head when he raised his head and smiled at her like that, all arrogant, irresistibly charming male. "If you don't like it, you tell me, and I'll stop."

He lowered his head and did such wonderful things with his mouth, the last thing on earth she wanted was for him to stop. She held on to the rough sheets and stared blindly at the bunk slats above her. Somehow, even in the midst of the powerful pleasure building inside her, she felt humbled and touched that he wanted to give her this.

All too soon, she felt her body starting to crest. "Nathaniel," she forced herself to speak from the midst of her passion, for she didn't want to go without him to that exquisite place he had taken her before.

"Shhh," he said. "Just let it happen, sweet Robin-girl."

He caressed her a final time with his mouth and his hands, and it did. Her body tightened in a glorious burst of sensation that went on and on. When it was over, she was panting and limp, completely enervated and deliciously happy.

When she finally summoned the energy to open her eyes again, she looked up to see he was staring at her with an intense hunger that made her shiver. Yet he was waiting patiently for her to catch her breath and float down to earth again. She decided right then, she was going to make sure he lost control and gave into his own desire.

She reached up and tugged his head down to hers. She kissed him deeply, the way he had taught her. He nudged her knees wide with his own and rubbed and probed at her center. At once, that wonderful tightness began to build inside her again. He drew back, and entered her with deliberate slowness, both of them enjoying the exquisite friction of being joined like this.

Before he sheathed himself fully, he pulled back and penetrated her again. She raised her hips and met his thrust, ensuring that this time she took all of him inside her.

Drawing in deep, shuddering breaths, they both stilled for a long moment to savor the feeling of their bodies being joined so intimately. He began to move, loving her with deep, deliberate thrusts, stroking that urgent pleasure ever tighter inside her. He quickened the pace, and she began to shift restlessly beneath him.

She wanted him even deeper inside her. Instinctively, she reached up and locked her legs around his middle. Too late, she remembered the wound still healing in his side. She opened her eyes in time to see his flinch of pain.

"I'm so sorry," she said, and lowered her legs immediately. "Maybe we shouldn't do this."

"We're going to do this, all right. I think I'd just about die if we didn't, but I know what might work better."

Puzzled but game, she let him guide and shift her. Moments later, she found herself sitting astride him.

"People do this, too?" She couldn't help asking the question, even though she knew she must seem hopelessly naïve to him.

"Some women like this way better," he answered her question with only a hint of a smile in his eyes. "Seems to me a strong-willed female like yourself might like taking the reins and setting the pace." Tenderly he tucked a lock of her hair beneath her ear.

She found he was exactly right. At first she felt awkward and unsure, but once he helped her lower herself upon him, he stretched and filled her once more, and somehow her body knew exactly how to move. Slowly, she began to raise and lower herself, experimenting with the different sensations that movement gave them both.

At the start, he reached up and toyed with the tips of her breasts, deepening her enjoyment, but as she grew more skillful, his body tensed beneath her. He stopped caressing her breasts and held tight to her shoulders, that intent, concentrated expression back on his face. She gloried in the knowledge that she was finally pleasuring him the way he had pleasured her. Yet the further she drove him toward the top, the tighter the need within herself coiled.

Just when she thought she couldn't bear the wonderful torment a moment longer, he clasped her hips hard and bucked beneath her. He thrust upward again and again, the repeated shifts in pressure sending her over the top in a dizzying spiral of sensation. Dimly, she was aware of his calling out her name and his body shuddering beneath her own.

When the waves finally ebbed, she collapsed in a nerveless puddle on his chest. For the moment, she was beyond thought or speech. Gently he reached up and stroked her hair.

His voice, when he finally spoke, was a deep rumble beneath her ear.

"Lord Almighty, Miss Matthews, you are one fast learner."

It was an effort, but she forced herself to prop her chin on her hand where she could look into his eyes.

"I've always been told that." She sent him a saucy smile.

"If you picked up this particular pursuit any faster, I'd probably be dead right now. But then again, I'd have died a happy man."

She started to shift off him, worried that her weight might be hurting his injured side.

"Where are you going?"

"I'm afraid it can't be real comfortable for you, having me lay on you like this."

"You feel mighty fine right where you are. I don't want you catching pneumonia, though." He reached up and pulled the covers up about her shoulders. She lay down again, her upper body resting on top of his.

She looked down and idly circled the two bullet scars on his right shoulder. "Did these happen in Cameron?"

"No, I got those hauling in a mean old sourdough named Crapper Jim early on in my career. He'd jumped four or five claims in various mining towns, and he had a bad habit of killing their owners first. He looked like such a gentle old duffer, I got a little careless with him, and he nailed me with my own Winchester. That taught me the danger of judging a book by its cover.''

''I bet you brought him in, anyway.''

''That I did. They hanged him two weeks later,'' he said with obvious satisfaction.

Robin tried not to shiver. Sometimes she forgot that ruthless, black-and-white side to Nathaniel.

He must have sensed her dismay, for he went on to explain, ''The second fellow Crapper Jim killed left five kids and a widow back in Chicago. Believe me, that mean old son of a gun had it coming.''

''It's sad to think how many folk have died chasing their dreams out here in the West.''

Nathaniel made a vague sound of agreement. A moment later he said soberly, ''I reckon Mary McAllister's kids and her husband are missing her something fierce tonight.''

How she wished she had never brought up the subject of Cameron. His eyes looked so bleak now. ''I suppose they are,'' she said softly. She slipped off him and came to lay on her side so that she could see him better.

He sighed and rubbed his face with his hands. ''There's something else I didn't tell you about Mary McAllister.''

She started to say he didn't have to talk about Cameron if he didn't want to, but he was already speaking.

''When she got shot that day, she was pregnant—seven months along with her third child.'' Robin drew in a breath in surprise.

''I'll never forget the look on her husband's face when he knelt by her side in the street and realized she was gone. Her two children were there, too, a little boy and a little girl. They both started pulling and tugging at her, crying because they didn't understand what had happened to their mama.''

He paused and cleared his throat. "That's part of why I can't stay. It's going to be a long time before I can forgive myself for what happened in Cameron. You were right when you said we all make mistakes, but mine tore a hole in that family. I was so set on catching that Carson gang and adding another feather in my cap that Mary McAllister and her unborn child ended up dying there in the street."

Perhaps it was time they had all this out. "Mrs. Beacham thought there might be another reason you were so dead set on leaving us. She said I should ask you more about your mother."

Nathaniel's expression tightened. "There're times I wish that sweet, interfering old lady would mind her own business."

"There are times I feel that way, too, but she's a mighty wise old woman. She wouldn't have said something like that to me unless she thought it was important. You really haven't ever told me anything about your mother or what your life was like growing up."

He was silent for so long, she thought he was going to ignore her request. At last he turned over on his side and propped his head on his hand.

"When I knew her, my mother was a sad, bitter woman. Supposedly she was a striking, lively girl before she married my father. She came from a fine but poor Maryland family. She met my father at a dance while she was visiting friends in Charleston, West Virginia. Passionate and heedless, they fell head over heels for each other the way only young folk can."

Robin decided this probably wasn't a good time to remind Nathaniel that she had yet to turn twenty.

"My mother's people," he continued, "overlooked the taint of Indian blood in my father because he was a promising and prosperous young lawyer, and because she was already carrying me in her belly. She had a fine future all planned out for my father. She wanted him to go into politics and take her to Washington someday. It wasn't until after their wedding that she realized he was dead set on staying in his hometown, Buford, West Virginia and continuing to build his practice there.

"I don't think she ever got over the shock that she'd doomed herself to living in a small West Virginia town for the rest of her days. I expect they probably fought a great deal in their early years together, but by the time I was old enough to wonder about their relationship, they had settled into a cold, polite, detached kind of marriage.

"My mother poured all her considerable energy and her love into her three boys and her social functions. Both avenues proved to be tremendous disappointments to her. She was the queen of Buford society. Because she believed that society to be so far below her, though, that position brought her little pleasure. About the time Joshua, Ethan, and I outgrew the nursery, we much preferred spending time outside with our father, hunting, rambling about the countryside, and tending the farm animals we kept. She would give us elaborate presents, lavished her attention on us, and tried to turn us into perfect little gentlemen."

He paused, his expression rueful. "Her plan backfired, and we turned into three of the worst terrors in town. Only fear of our father's wrath kept us from running completely wild.

"As we grew older, we began to treat our mother the same cool way we saw our father treat her, and that distance drove her to distraction. She grew more weepy and demanding as the years wore on. Joshua, Ethan, and I all left home early to escape her."

He met Robin's gaze then, his blue eyes troubled. "That's why I don't think I could ever be a fit mate. I take after my father. I'm too cold and distant to be a good husband for a loving, warm woman like you."

Robin was quiet for a time while she digested his story. "I don't think it was a coldness in his nature that made your father treat your mother that way. I think just the opposite is true. Because he was a loving man, he was deeply hurt that she couldn't be happy with him and the quiet, country life he wanted. If he spent that much time hunting and rambling with you, he must have loved his sons very much.''

''In his own stern way, I suppose he cared about us, but no one ever would have called him loving or approachable. As the years go on, I see more of him in myself. If you were foolish enough to tie the knot with me, you might grow as bitter and angry as my mother did. That whole notion just about tears me apart.''

''I will say this just once, Nathaniel Hollister,'' she poked a finger into his shoulder. ''I think you are completely wrong about yourself. There's a world of love inside you. You just don't realize it. You couldn't be so sweet and funny with Betsy, handle the twins just right, and give so much to Tommy if you weren't a caring man. I understand I'm not the right woman to make you settle down and give up your dreams, but I hope someday you will find the right woman.''

''This has nothing to do with your being the wrong woman,'' he said so angrily she blinked. ''This is all about what you need that I can't offer. You're wrong to go on thinking there's something inside me which isn't there. The kind of life I've lived hardens a man. I've spent so much time in rough company, I'm not fit to spend time with civilized folks. I'm not much better than the owlhoots I brought to justice for all those years. I've paid women down on the row a hundred times for their services. I should be horsewhipped for daring to touch you, much less make love to you.''

He looked so upset, she decided that she had to find a way to diffuse his anger, and diffuse it quickly. ''Well, if you learned half of what you showed me just now down on the row, I'm mighty grateful to those ladies,'' she said with a sly smile.

That comment brought him up short, just as she hoped it would. His eyes widened, and then he let go a gust of laughter. He fell back against his pillow, shaking his head. ''Robin Matthews, the things you say. I don't know whether I should try to shake some sense into you or take a paddle to you.''

''If it's all the same to you, I'd much prefer it if you made love to me again.''

The exasperated look gradually vanished from his gaze to be replaced by a kind of knowing, heated glance that made her toes curl.

''Now you mention it, that option sounds best of all.''

Chapter Thirty

Nathaniel began to kiss her, in that wonderful, slow, thorough way he had. He started with her face and lips. By the time he reached the base of her throat, her breath was coming faster. He worked his way methodically down her, lavishing attention on her breasts, trailing damp kisses across her belly. He brushed her with the lightest, most titillating of caresses in that place between her legs that was already on fire.

"Turn over," he said quietly. She did as he asked, and he started all over again, caressing her spine, her buttocks, the backs of her knees with his lips and hands. She had no idea she was so sensitive in these places, but his touch soon began to build that amazing tension inside her. The way he kissed and lingered over her made her feel beautiful and cherished and unbearably aroused.

He came to lie over her and slipped a hand beneath her hips. He cupped her and began a magical massage that drew a sob from her lips. She pressed herself against him even as she welcomed the feel of his hot, heavy arousal pushing between her legs. He murmured a masculine sound of approval when she quickly became damp from his touch. His breath was coming hard and fast—she could feel it warm on her neck.

When she thought she couldn't take any more, he helped her shift until she was lying on her back once more. He knelt, his knees between her own. She drew in a breath when she felt him probe at her entrance. She wanted him inside her more than anything, but she didn't want to hurt him.

"What about your side?"

"Sh, now. This way won't hurt it." He lifted her knees high and pulled them wide. When he slowly entered her, she realized this position made the exquisite pressure of him inside her that much more intense. He entered her with one slow, sure thrust.

When he was buried inside her, she looked up into his eyes. Beyond the heat of his passion, she thought she saw a sadness in his gaze that matched the sorrow in her own heart. For all she wanted to pretend that only this night mattered, it was hard to hold onto that illusion when their making love together like this was so natural and right and wonderful. Yet tonight would be their last time together. He'd made that more than clear.

He began to move inside her, and she gladly fled from reality and gave up all conscious thought. She simply felt as he drove her toward the peak. The pleasure pulled tighter and tighter within her with each thrust. When she hovered on the edge, he paused long enough for her body to relax a little, and then he began to drive her toward an even higher peak. Gasping and helpless, all she could do was hold tight to his shoulders.

Just when she thought she couldn't bear the intense sensations building inside her a moment longer, he paused again. "Come with me now," he said hoarsely. He reached down and stroked her as he pushed deep into her very center. She convulsed around him. His big body tightened, and they dove from the peak together.

She lay in his arms for a long time after. She felt so warm and relaxed, she was tempted to sleep, but she didn't want to miss a moment of being with him. His eyes fluttered shut, and soon his steady breathing told her he was asleep. She propped herself up on one elbow so that she could look her fill.

He looked so much younger in his sleep with his features relaxed. She loved the way his long black eyelashes made delicate fans on his cheeks. A day's growth of beard shadowed his cheek and jaw. The lamplight shone off the strands of silver in his thick hair. Gently she traced his black brows. She longed to press a kiss on that beautiful mouth that had given her so much pleasure, but she didn't want to risk waking him.

She caught back a sob. She wouldn't mourn his leaving before he left. There would be time enough later for that. Today was Christmas. Today she was going to wring as much happiness as she could from sharing the holiday with him, and from giving her family the best celebration she could.

Afraid Betsy might miss her, she slipped from the bed and dressed swiftly. By the time she stepped out of the bunkhouse, Nathaniel still hadn't stirred. Despite the deep chill of the night, she stopped halfway to the house to admire the starry heavens. It was one of those clear, cold mountain nights when the sky was ablaze with silver stars.

As she gazed up at them, she felt the magic of Christmas touch her at last. She wasn't sorry for what she'd just done. She was sorry she hadn't been able to change Nathaniel's mind, but now she could face his leaving with some equanimity. She had shown with her body how much she loved him, even though she didn't want to burden him by saying the words aloud.

If she couldn't have her first Christmas wish, at least she had memories from her second, memories that would have to last a lifetime.

Nathaniel roused the moment he heard the door close softly behind Robin. She'd left him. He stared at the door for a long time. At last he forced himself to dress in his warm union suit and stoke up the wood stove for what was left of the night.

When he climbed back into his bed, he found the scent of roses and lavender lingered on his pillow.

Trying to ignore that scent, he stared up at the dark slats of the bunk above him and willed himself to fall asleep. He didn't want to think, yet remorseless, pitiless thoughts ambushed him anyway.

Damn it, he was trying so hard to do what was best for Robin, and yet the pain he'd seen in her misty green eyes tonight haunted him. She'd never said the words aloud, but he was positive she'd convinced herself that she was in love with him. Why couldn't she see that she could do so much better than a burnt out ex-marshal fifteen years her senior? Why did she insist on seeing something in him that wasn't there?

Goddamn it, Hollister, you're going to hurt her when you leave, and that's the last thing in the world you want to do. If you are selfish and foolish enough to stay, though, you'll end up hurting her worse in the long run. You don't have enough love inside you to make a sweet, caring young woman like her happy.

The hardest truth of all stared him in the face. When he rode away from the Rocking M, he was assigning himself to a lifelong purgatory without her. Her joy and optimism had become as vital to him as breathing.

At last the weariness of his body gave Nathaniel relief from his despair and pulled him down into sound slumber.

He awoke the next morning to the sounds of young people trying to be quiet.

"Sh, I told you he was still asleep," he heard Betsy say softly.

"How can he sleep so late?" came Tommy's question in a loud, piping voice. "It's Christmas."

Nathaniel had to smile at the righteous indignation in the boy's tone. Suddenly, he remembered how wild he, Joshua, and Ethan had been in their younger years to race downstairs on Christmas morning. "That's all right, partner. I'm awake now. Merry Christmas."

Tommy raced from the door and flung himself on Nathaniel's bed. "You gotta come see. Father Christmas came last night. There are presents on the tree, and under the tree, and there's a bunch of presents in my stocking."

"What did he give you?"

"I dunno. I haven't opened them yet because I wanted you to see what he brung me."

Nathaniel stared at Tommy's excited face. Now that was devotion on a boy's part. He couldn't imagine waiting to open the presents in his stocking when he'd been five years old. "I tell you what, partner. Why don't you head on back to the house. I'll get myself up and dressed in a jiffy, and then we'll all find out what's under that tree."

Tommy leapt back off the bed and headed for the door. Betsy met Nathaniel's gaze, her expression apologetic. "I'm sorry. We tried to keep him away from the bunkhouse as long as we could. He's been up since six."

Nathaniel glanced at the pocket watch on the bed beside his bunk. It was eight. Two hours must have seemed like a lifetime to poor Tommy. "That's all right. I'll come along in a few minutes."

After Betsy and Tommy left, Nathaniel dressed quickly. When he stepped outside the bunkhouse, he discovered it was a beautiful, sunny morning. He paused halfway to the main house to admire the Sangre de Cristos. They were so dazzlingly white today, they almost hurt his eyes to look at them.

He sighed as he looked at Robin's home. From the beginning, he'd enjoyed entering this house. He knew that when he stepped inside, young faces would light at the sight of him, and he could always prowl over to the stove to steal a bite of whatever tasty concoction the girls were cooking.

Instead, of his own free will, he was going to start on those travels he'd put off for too long. He was going to see those wild places he'd always wanted to see, and travel through dozens of small towns where no one would have a claim on him, but no one would know him, either. Unutterably depressed by that thought, he plodded on toward the house.

Despite his dark mood, he found his spirits lifting the moment he stepped inside. The house was warm and smelled of pine boughs and baking.

"Merry Christmas," Mrs. Beacham greeted him cheerfully from the stove. Robin stood beside her, flipping flapjacks. She looked up from her skillet and met his gaze levelly.

She looked tired today, he saw with a wince. There were shadows under her eyes, but she managed to give him a real Robin smile just the same.

"Merry Christmas, Nathaniel."

Suddenly, his throat grew too tight to speak. He nodded instead and looked away from her. His gaze fell on a stack of freshly baked doughnuts sitting in the middle of the kitchen table.

"Who made the bearsign?" he asked, grateful for the distraction. He headed straight for the stack and reached to take one from the top. Mrs. Beacham smacked him lightly across the knuckles with her wooden spoon.

"I made them, you handsome scoundrel," the old lady informed him with a smile. "If we could wait for you to wake up, you can wait until we all sit down at the table like civilized folk."

Nursing his sore knuckles, Nathaniel took his usual place at the foot of the table. Soon all the grownups sat down to breakfast while Tommy and Jessie gleefully emptied the contents of their stockings on the kitchen floor. Nathaniel had to admire every simple gift Tommy found tucked in his stocking, including a miniature bow and arrow set Nathaniel had carved. Jessie, determined to do everything her big brother did, likewise brought him all her presents to inspect.

Despite the frequent interruptions, Nathaniel happily devoured a fine Christmas breakfast of bacon, scrambled eggs, flapjacks, and bearsign. He'd just downed his third cup of coffee when Mrs. Beacham, who had been hovering inexplicably by the front windows of the house for ten minutes now, suddenly called out, "Why, Robin, I believe you have some company coming. It looks like a parade."

Nathaniel studied the old lady as she made this announcement. He had a strong feeling she knew exactly why a parade was to arrive on Robin's doorstep.

Clearly mystified, Robin rose to her feet. Her excited family followed on her heels as she headed for the front porch. Over a dozen sledges and sleighs were coming up the road from town. As the conveyances drew closer, Nathaniel spotted a considerable amount of lumber tied to the sledges. All at once, he realized why they had come, and he smiled, deeply pleased for Robin's sake.

"Merry Christmas," Robin greeted Doc Peterson and Zachary Tuckett in the lead sledge cheerfully, even though Nathaniel could tell the reason for their visit puzzled her. Several sleighs pulled up before the ranch house.

"We've brought you a Christmas present from most of the folks in Grand Valley, Miss Matthews," Mr. Tuckett declared. "Today, we mean to build you a barn. It won't be as big as the one your pa built, but it should do to shelter your stock and hold your feed for the winter."

Robin's hand went to her chest. Her eyes widened as she looked at the beaming group of men, women, and children sitting in their sleighs and sledges.

"I can't believe you're going to give us both a barn and your precious Christmas Day. My land, I don't know what to say, except thank you."

"We all feel sorry for the trouble you had with Vance Sutherland," Doc Peterson said soberly. "You were the only one who stood up to him while he rode roughshod over the rest of us. This is the town's way of saying thank you."

Betsy burst into tears, and Robin looked like she was hovering on the edge.

"Well, you all come right in and get warmed up." Mrs.

Beacham stepped into the breach in her usual practical, brisk fashion. "Then we'll set to work."

Soon the ranch house filled with people. After a quick round of hot drinks, the menfolk went outside and set to work framing the walls for the Matthewses' new barn. The twins had been busy during the time Nathaniel had been laid up clearing away the burnt timbers and debris from the fire. The warm winter sun had dried the foundation out, so the barn site was ready for its volunteer builders.

Most of the women stayed inside, readying a Christmas feast big enough to feed the small army of volunteers who had converged on the Rocking M. Occasionally they took cider and coffee out to the men. Throughout the morning, more folks arrived, the women bringing baskets of food, the menfolk going straight to work outside.

The weather proved perfect for a barn raising. It had turned into one of those bright Colorado winter days, the sun shining so warmly that the men could work in their shirtsleeves.

Nathaniel pitched in wherever he could. He found his side was too sore for much of the heavy work, but he could pound nails easily enough. At one point in the morning, Doc Peterson wandered over to stand beside him.

"Thought you ought to know we up and fired Ben Campbell yesterday," the older man said in a conversational tone. "He's been the most worthless sheriff this town has ever seen. When he refused to go after Betsy, it was the last straw. Folks asked me to let you know the job's open, and we're all hoping you'd consider it if you decide to stay on in Grand Valley. I know being sheriff of a small town like ours probably seems like kind of a comedown after being a U.S. marshal and all, but I still hope you'll think about it."

After dropping that mortar shell in Nathaniel's lap, Doc Peterson went back to helping the others. Nathaniel gazed after him, trying to get over his surprise.

Of course he couldn't fill the sheriff's position. He wasn't going to stay around Grand Valley long enough to take any sort of job. Still, he couldn't help feeling pleased and flattered that the townsfolk of Grand Valley wanted him to be their sheriff. Throughout the day, other men approached him and said in their gruff, friendly way that they hoped he'd stay on and take the job Ben Campbell had just vacated. After the folks of Cameron had almost spit on him, this offer of the sheriff's job and the trust that accompanied it was like balm on a festering wound.

Around one o'clock, the ladies called a halt to the men's labor, for it was time to enjoy Christmas dinner. Reverend Case said grace, then the menfolk served themselves plates of food from the heavily laden tables in the kitchen and the dining room. The womenfolk of Grand Valley had packed up their Christmas dinners and brought every course, from relishes to desserts. Thus, Nathaniel had a difficult time making up his mind whether he wanted ham or beef, venison, or elk. Reflecting the international origins of Grand Valley's residents, there were scores of fascinating Christmas dishes, breads, puddings, and pies from a dozen different countries. In the end, like many others, Nathaniel took a little bit of everything and happily planned on going back for more.

People sat in every room of the house, the porch, and the barn foundation itself. Betsy and Robin wrung their hands over the fact they didn't have nearly enough chairs for everyone, but no one minded. It was definitely a festive and interdenominational affair—Presbyterians and Lutherans, Baptists and Catholics all sharing their Christmas dinner with one another. Tommy and Jessie were so excited to have little ones to play with, they ran until they couldn't run anymore, stuffed themselves with Christmas goodies, and fell sound sleep in Betsy's lap.

Refreshed and reenergized from the enormous meal, the men set to work again. Because dusk came early in December, those who had the farthest to drive slipped away in the late afternoon after receiving the Matthewses' fervent thanks. Those who lived closer continued on by lamplight until the basic structure of the barn was finished.

Zachary Tuckett and Lionel Brigham stayed until the very end, making sure the big barn doors were hung properly. Both men turned down Robin's invitation to stay for supper, for they were eager to return to their own homes.

"Alan Sutherland plans on sending you all the feed and hay you need to last the winter," Mr. Tuckett assured Robin before he drove off in his sledge. "He'll be over here tomorrow with some of his boys."

At this news, Nathaniel clenched his hands and strode off to the bunkhouse. He knew he was being ridiculous, but he couldn't seem to help himself. Now that Vance Sutherland was mentally incapacitated, most of the problems keeping Alan and Robin apart were gone. If the young man developed a little backbone, he could be a fine husband for Robin.

If that simpering little worm goes near her, I'll stove his face in.

He's just what you wanted for her, you idiot. He's an upstanding young man who happens to own one of the finest ranches in Colorado. She could hardly do better for herself.

That doesn't mean you have to stick around and watch him start courting her.

Nathaniel decided right then that he would leave first thing in the morning. He had most of his gear packed up by the time Betsy came to fetch him for supper. He was glad he'd thought to stuff his saddlebags under the bed before she opened the door. She looked so merry and happy that he didn't want to dampen her mood. She linked arms with him while they walked back to the main house.

He glanced down at her profile in the lamplight as she talked a blue streak about their day. Leaving Robin was going to tear a hole in his gut, but he'd miss Betsy, too. She was like the little sister he'd never had.

They were a weary bunch when they sat down at the kitchen table. The leftovers from the midday feast tasted plenty good.

Tommy and Jessie were still up. They both had taken long naps this afternoon, worn out from the morning's excitement, and Robin wanted them to see the adults open their presents.

Tommy was almost dancing with excitement by the time they finished their meal. "Come on, Nathn'l. You gotta see what Jake and Luke made you."

As glum as he was feeling, Nathaniel found himself looking forward to the moment each of the Matthewses opened the presents he had fashioned for them. They moved to the parlor and watched Luke and Jake light the candles on the tree. Robin presided over the handing out of parcels. She had a way of drawing out the suspense that made Nathaniel grin.

"Hm, could this be the new saddle blanket which Jake's been wanting?" she wondered aloud as she held up a small box wrapped in brown paper with a bright bit of ribbon. "No, I think it's too small. Could it be his very own shaving brush?" And so she teased them all as she doled out their presents, with proud Tommy's help.

Just as Robin had predicted, everyone in her family had made Nathaniel gifts. He had a pile of presents stacked in front of his chair by the time Tommy had finished delivering all of the parcels from beneath the tree. As he stared down at his gifts, it occurred to him that it had been years since someone had given him a Christmas present.

As he went to work on his pile, he was impressed and touched by every gift. Jake and Luke had pooled their talents and made him a handsome wooden box with a leather lid stamped with his initials. Betsy had knit him a maroon muffler from a wool much softer than his old one. Mrs. Beacham flummoxed him completely by giving him her husband's gold cufflinks.

When he started to protest her gift, she interrupted him mid-sentence. "Can't see that they're doing me much good," the old woman said in her no-nonsense way. "It would please me to know you were getting some use out of them. I thought they'd look pretty good with that dress shirt of yours."

He stopped in his present-opening to give Mrs. Beacham a big buss on the cheek. She chuckled and waved him away.

"If I'm not mistaken, Tommy's about to bust his shirt waiting for you to open his present."

Nathaniel looked at the last present in his pile. Tommy was standing beside it, almost dancing in impatience. "Well, what do we have here?"

"It's my present. You gotta open it right now. Robin and Betsy helped me wrap it."

He opened up the bright fabric and saw Tommy's prized iron pyrite glittering in the lamplight. His first reaction was to ask the boy if he really wanted to give up something that mattered so much to him, but when he looked into Tommy's eager face, he realized he couldn't hurt the boy's feelings by asking that question.

"Thank you, Tommy. This is a mighty fine present you gave me. I'm going to keep it in my saddlebags for good luck."

In return, the Matthewses were satisfyingly pleased with the presents he had made them. Jake was obviously tickled by the stock whip he'd braided for him. Luke kept stroking the soft leather of his new knife sheath. Nathaniel had wanted to give Betsy something pretty and feminine, which meant he had to bend the Matthewses' Christmas rules and buy her something store-bought. The reverent look on her face when she lifted her new lace shawl out of its wrappings made the garment worth every cent of the five dollars he'd spent on it. Mrs. Beacham professed to be thrilled by a similar shawl he had purchased for her.

Tommy was ecstatic about the leather bag Nathaniel had made him and the five marbles he found inside it. Jessie started playing with a soft leather ball Nathaniel had sewn for her, and she proceeded to kick and toss it around the room at once.

As much as he enjoyed their reactions, he was dying to see Robin's face when she opened his present. She was so busy watching the others open their gifts, he had to remind her to keep working on her own pile. At last she came to the simple brown parcel from him.

She opened the paper and her eyes widened when she saw the plaited reata he had made for her. "My heavens, you didn't really make this, did you?"

"He sure did," Tommy informed her importantly, "and I helped him."

Nathaniel cleared his throat. "You've shown me a woman can run a ranch as well as any man. I thought I ought to make you something you could use most everyday doing ranch work."

Robin was silent for a long moment as she stroked the intricately braided lariat in her lap. The workmanship was beautiful. She'd seen reatas before, but never one this finely crafted. More importantly, she valued the meaning and the message in his gift. It meant so much to her that he accepted what she was.

"There's a smaller package you need to open, too," he urged her.

She found it beside the coils of the reata. Inside the package lay the lovely inlaid combs he had tried to give her months ago.

"Don't you dare give them back to me again," he growled at her. "I think they'd look pretty in your hair when you're all done up in that green dress. I want you to have them, and that's that."

As she stared down at the two presents he had given her, she realized he might be the only man who would ever understand and appreciate the two sides to her. She loved the rough, outdoor ranching life, and yet there was a secret part of her that hankered after feminine things. He'd helped her overcome her fear and shown her how to take joy in her womanhood again. It probably wouldn't change anything between them, but before he rode away, she had to tell Nathaniel how she truly felt about him.

"You haven't opened my present yet." She reached under

the tree and found the small package that had been overlooked in the first rush.

Her heart pounded in her chest as she handed him the little packet.

He opened it quickly, with a kind of boyish excitement that made her smile despite her nervousness.

"I made them from my hair. I meant them as a keepsake for you." She swallowed and forced herself to go kneel beside him. She was aware that her whole family was watching her, somehow aware of the importance of this moment.

He was staring down at the small golden heart and key, a wondering expression on his face.

"You will hold the key to my heart always," she told him softly, "and you will always have all the love that lies inside it. I had to tell you the truth before you left us. You are capable of loving and giving. The fact that my whole family has come to love you in such a short time must tell you something. They wouldn't give their affection and trust to the cold, hard man you believe yourself to be.

"Mrs. Beacham wouldn't have given you the cufflinks that belonged to the man she cared for more than anyone in the world if she didn't love you. The people of Grand Valley offered you that sheriff's job today because they saw you as a man worthy of their respect and trust. Could we all be so blind, or could it be that you are blind about yourself? I have to ask you one last time—do you really have to go?"

Nathaniel stared down into her earnest green eyes, and the world seemed to shift around him. If he tried, if he worked at it, maybe he could be a fit husband for her and a decent father for the little ones. Bit by bit he'd lost faith in himself over the years. The violence and the killing had stolen away a part of his soul, and then Mary McAllister and her unborn child had died because of his ambition and carelessness, and suddenly he didn't know who he was anymore. Robin was offering him back his soul, and if he didn't take it now, he knew he'd wander through the rest of his life an angry and bitter man.

As he stared into her sweet, pretty face, a wave of longing washed through him so intense that it was painful. *Lord, I want her. Lord, I want to be with her the rest of my life. I want to wake up with her in the morning and see us both grow into stubborn old people together. I want to see her awkward and pregnant with our children. I want to see her nursing our baby at her breast.* The secret wishes he had barely allowed himself to imagine slammed into him one after the other in dizzying succession.

More than anything he wanted for himself, though, he wanted her to be happy. He didn't mind taking a gamble with his own future, but marrying up with him would be a huge risk for her.

His throat was so tight, his voice came out strained and gruff. "Do you truly want to saddle yourself with me for the rest of your days?"

"You were my first and only Christmas wish," she replied simply.

He tore his gaze away from her to look at the others. "Do the rest of you honestly want me to stay on?"

"If you mean to marry her, I reckon we'd like your staying on with us just fine," Jake said after a long look at his twin.

"We'd like it more than fine," Betsy said, tears in her eyes. "You'll make a wonderful husband, Nathaniel, and you'll be a fine papa for Tommy and Jessie."

Tommy had been listening intently to this whole conversation, and his eyes had been getting bigger and bigger. When he heard the word "papa," he headed straight for Nathaniel.

"Are you gonna be my papa now?"

"We're trying to figure that out right now, partner." Nathaniel looked from Tommy's excited blue eyes into Robin's green ones.

The serene acceptance he saw there decided him. Robin might be young, but she was wise for her years, and he did have a good feeling she knew the best and the worst of him, and loved him anyway. He'd do his damnedest from now on to be the best man he could be for her and for her family. He didn't deserve her, but he'd do all he could to protect and love her for the rest of his days.

He drew in a deep breath. He was startled to realize his heart was beating faster than it did during a full-blown gunfight. "Miss Matthews, would you do me the honor of becoming my wife?"

"Yes, for now, for always, forever and completely—that's so you know there's absolutely no doubt in my mind," she said with one of her blinding smiles and laid her head on his shoulder.

The twins let out war whoops. Mrs. Beacham sniffed and reached for her handkerchief, and Betsy cried and laughed at the same time.

It took Nathaniel a moment to realize Tommy was still standing in front of him, his blue eyes pleading and desperate. The little boy reached out and shook his sleeve impatiently. "Does this mean you'll be my papa now?" he asked again.

"I'm going to be Robin's husband." Saying the words aloud almost took Nathaniel's breath away. After a few moments, he decided it was a good kind of breathlessness. "Robin's not exactly your mama, but she loves you just as if she were, and I'll do the same."

"So you'll be just as good as a real papa?"

"I'll surely try, partner," Nathaniel promised, and Tommy's face lit up.

"For Christmas, I wished you'd be my papa, and it came true after all. Robin said it would."

Nathaniel sent Robin an ironic look.

"I thought he was asking whether or not his wish for a toy bow and arrow would come true," Robin said with a chuckle. "I never dreamed his real wish was so ambitious."

"I'm glad we could oblige him. I hope I don't disappoint him in the long run, though. I don't have much practice being a father."

"So far, I think your instincts for being a papa are right on," Robin told him soothingly and patted him on the knee.

Jessie climbed down from Mrs. Beacham's lap and headed straight for Nathaniel. "Papa!" she shouted, obviously pleased to have a new word.

Nathaniel felt his cheeks warm. Damn, she had to be the smartest, quickest, cutest little gal West of the Mississippi. To cover his pleased embarrassment, he scooped her up into his arms and blew kisses into her neck.

"Looks to me like the vote's unanimous," Mrs. Beacham said, looking pleased as punch. "Congratulations, Nathaniel Hollister, and thank you for making my own, dearest Christmas wish come true. I'd so hoped you two would come to your senses and see that you were made for each other. Merry Christmas to us all."

That evening after the rest had finally gone to bed, Robin slipped out to the bunkhouse. This time she felt no trepidation or worry—only joy. Nathaniel met her at the door.

Before she had a chance to say a word, he started to kiss her. He didn't stop kissing her until they both had shed their clothes, made love in his bunk, and lay breathless and content in each other's arms.

"This is so much fun." Robin stretched happily, enjoying the wonderful, warm lassitude induced by Nathaniel's lovemaking. "I'm surprised married couples ever get out of bed."

"It's fun all right, but I'm sure looking forward to making love to you in a real, full-size bed for a change," Nathaniel said, shifting his shoulders to a more comfortable spot on the narrow bunk.

"I think your bed is cozy," she said with a smile and kissed his shoulder.

"Whether it's cozy or cramped doesn't matter much anyway. We won't be doing any more of this until we're married up proper, Miss Matthews," he said, wagging a finger at her.

Robin sighed. "Even though I know you're right, it's going to be so hard to wait. I wish we could get married tomorrow, but I want to send for your brothers, and we have to let Mrs. Beacham and Betsy have their chance to plan a wedding with all the fuss and trimmings.''

"I think you might enjoy a wedding with all the fuss and the trimmings more than you let on," he teased her in his deep voice while he played with a lock of her hair. She loved that warm, humorous light in his beautiful blue eyes. She was going to work hard to make sure she rarely saw that angry, bitter look in his gaze again.

"I might at that," she had to admit.

"I thought you might like our wedding trip even better. How would you like to go to Colorado Springs and stay in one of those fancy hotels for a week or two?"

Robin propped her chin on her hands so that she could look down at him. "That's the sweetest idea, but I'd be happy if you just took me to lunch there. I don't want you spending all your hard-earned savings on my wedding trip."

"I think it might take more than a week or two to spend what I've got tucked away. My grandfather and my father were both pretty fair hands at making money, you know, and I never spent much of the money I made working as a marshal. I can't say I'm a rich man, but I have a good bit stashed away in a bank in Denver and back in Maryland."

"How much might a good bit be, exactly?"

"Around eighty thousand dollars, give or take a few thousand. I haven't checked on it recently."

"Eighty thousand dollars the man says—give or take a few thousand?" Robin collapsed back on the pillows and shook her head. "Well, aren't you one for surprises. I guess this means we can afford to keep Hercules now. We've all grown so attached to the sweet old fellow—I hated the notion of having to give him away."

She was silent for a moment, and then she laughed aloud. She raised herself up on one elbow. "I think we should tell Mr. Peabody that you're actually a millionaire and he'll tell everyone else, and then folks won't be saying you married me for my ranch.''

''Hell, that's not why they're going to think I married you. They're much more apt to guess we've been doing exactly what we just did a few minutes ago and that I decided to make an honest woman out of you. Obviously, I couldn't keep my hands to myself around a pretty little gal like you.''

''Nathaniel Hollister, you say the nicest things to me.''

''Hmm. Remember that the next time you're mad at me.''

''Why, now we're engaged, I don't think we'll ever fight anymore,'' she said sweetly.

''And snakes wear shoes,'' he sent her one of his lazy, heart-stopping grins. ''Still, I think I'm looking forward to a lifetime of quarreling with you.''

''I'm looking forward to making up, anyway. Seems like we see eye to eye on ranch business most of the time, at any rate.''

''Speaking of ranch business, I wondered what you would think if I spent some of my money on starting up a horse breeding operation here on the Rocking M. We both like working with horses a hell of a lot more than cattle, and with my contacts around and about, I think I could find us a good, steady market for them.''

She gave him a long, enthusiastic kiss in reply.

''I take it that's a yes,'' he said when she finally let him come up for air.

''You better believe that's a yes. I'd love to ship every darn cow off this place next fall.''

''Well, maybe we better make sure the horse operation is making some money before we go that far.''

''I hope horses aren't all that we'll be breeding.''

He smoothed a hand over her belly reverently. The idea of her growing their baby inside her terrified and thrilled him all at once. ''At the rate we've started out, we should be filling up a nursery full of babies for Betsy and Mrs. Beacham to fuss over.''

''Wouldn't it be lovely if we conceived a child on Christmas night,'' she said dreamily.

''I wouldn't be the least bit surprised. Seems like just about anything you wish for somehow happens.''

''If I wish for us to live happily ever after, you believe that will happen, too?'' she asked with a smile that went straight to his heart.

''I know I will love you, for now, for always, forever and completely.'' Solemnly he echoed the words she had used to accept his proposal. Courageous, sweet, generous Robin Matthews was his own miracle now, and he was going to do his best to keep her safe and happy. ''And just to show you there's absolutely no doubt in my mind ...'' With a wicked smile, he proceeded to show her exactly how he felt.